T0161824

THE WITCH OF STALINGRAD

Acclaim for Justine Saracen's Novels

"*Mephisto Aria* could well stand as a classic among gay and lesbian readers."—*ForeWord Reviews*

"Justine Saracen's *Sistine Heresy* is a well-written and surprisingly poignant romp through Renaissance Rome in the age of Michelangelo. …The novel entertains and titillates while it challenges, warning of the mortal dangers of trespass in any theocracy (past or present) that polices same-sex desire."—Professor Frederick Roden, University of Connecticut, Author, *Same-Sex Desire in Victorian Religious Culture*

"Saracen's wonderfully descriptive writing is a joy to the eye and the ear, as scenes play out on the page, and almost audibly as well. The characters are extremely well drawn, with suave villains, and lovely heroines. There are also wonderful romances, a heart-stopping plot, and wonderful love scenes. *Mephisto Aria* is a great read."—*Just About Write*

"*Sarah, Son of God* can lightly be described as the 'The Lesbian's *Da Vinci Code*' because of the somewhat common themes. At its roots, it's part mystery and part thriller. *Sarah, Son of God* is an engaging and exciting story about searching for the truth within each of us. Ms. Saracen considers the sacrifices of those who came before us, challenges us to open ourselves to a different reality than what we've been told we can have, and reminds us to be true to ourselves. Her prose and pacing rhythmically rise and fall like the tides in Venice; and her reimagined life and death of Jesus allows thoughtful readers to consider 'what if?'"—*Rainbow Reader*

Waiting for the Violins "…was a thrilling, charming, and heartrending trip back in time to the early years of World War II and the active resistance enclaves. …Stunning and eye-opening!"—*Rainbow Book Reviews*

"I can't think of anything more incongruous than ancient Biblical texts, scuba diving, Hollywood lesbians, and international art installations but I do know that there's only one author talented and savvy enough to make it all work. That's just what the incomparable Justine Saracen does in her latest, *Beloved Gomorrah*."—Jerry Wheeler, *Out In Print*

"Saracen blends historical and fictional characters seamlessly and brings authenticity to the story, focusing on the impacts of this time on "regular, normal people"…*Tyger Tyger* [is]a brilliantly written historical novel that has elements of romance, suspense, horror, pathos and it gives the reader quite a bit to think about…fast-paced…difficult to put down…an excellent book that easily blurs the line between lesfic and mainstream."—*C-Spot Reviews*

Visit us at www.boldstrokesbooks.com

By the Author

THE WITCH OF STALINGRAD

by

Justine Saracen

2015

THE WITCH OF STALINGRAD

© 2015 By Justine Saracen. All Rights Reserved.

ISBN 13: 978-1-62639-330-1

This Trade Paperback Original Is Published By
Bold Strokes Books, Inc.
P.O. Box 249
Valley Falls, NY 12185

First Edition: March 2015

THIS IS A WORK OF FICTION. NAMES, CHARACTERS, PLACES, AND INCIDENTS ARE THE PRODUCT OF THE AUTHOR'S IMAGINATION OR ARE USED FICTITIOUSLY. ANY RESEMBLANCE TO ACTUAL PERSONS, LIVING OR DEAD, BUSINESS ESTABLISHMENTS, EVENTS, OR LOCALES IS ENTIRELY COINCIDENTAL.

THIS BOOK, OR PARTS THEREOF, MAY NOT BE REPRODUCED IN ANY FORM WITHOUT PERMISSION.

CREDITS
Editor: Shelley Thrasher
Production Design: Susan Ramundo
Cover Design By Sheri (graphicartist2020@hotmail.com)
Cover Model: Celine Bissen

Acknowledgments

I must first thank Colonel Julie Tizard, U.S. Air Force Reserve, for educating me about the Night Witches in the first place, and then for giving me information on how to fly a plane. Lt. Col. Barbara L. Sawyer, USAF, Ret., also kindly helped by providing a diagram of the Yak cockpit. Galina, a valuable friend of Lesbian Literature in Moscow, assisted with the Russian expressions, so I wouldn't embarrass myself. While it would be tedious to list a bibliography, I wish to credit my main source regarding Soviet women pilots, *Wings, Women, & War*, by Reina Pennington, which I strongly recommend to anyone wanting more historical details.

For this novel, and for all its predecessors, I owe profound gratitude to my editor Shelley Thrasher for her sharp eye, open mind, and general wisdom. Recognition is due to Sheri for a great cover design, and to Celine Bissen for agreeing to pose for it. And above all, thanks to our Alpha, Radclyffe, without whom this would all just be lesbian fantasizing.

Dedication

For Lilya Litviak, Katia Budanova,
Marina Raskova, and the other women of the
Soviet Air Force who died fighting fascism.

PROLOGUE

August 1943
Airspace over the Ukraine

Lilya Drachenko was ferocious when the demon burned in her. Now, clear-eyed and murderous, it focused her eye on the German Junkers 88 and let fire. The bomber belched a spray of smoke and fire and spiraled downward. She careened away, indifferent to the scream of its descent and the detonation of its crash, and made a tight loop back. Another Junkers came into view, and within seconds she had locked onto it. She sensed no sky, no earth, no world, had not a single thought but the yellow spot at the center of her cannon sight that trembled along the enemy fuselage. She fired. Tracer bullets showed her aim was true, and the incandescent burst confirmed it. She banked to scan for other craft, and then she saw them.

Messerschmitts. A cloud of them.

She dove precipitously, but she was a second too late and her Yak-1 jerked with a hit. Smoke filled the cockpit and she struggled for control as another hit took off her wingtip. She tried to pull up, to use her momentum to curve back eastward, toward friendly territory.

She was over woodland now, and the trees rushed up with terrifying speed. She banked, but one wing struck a branch, and the force of the blow ripped her out of the cockpit. As she tumbled between the branches, she felt the agonizing pains that told her bones were breaking, and when she crashed to the ground, she lost consciousness.

Moments later, she came to with a pounding head and blurred vision. Every breath was excruciating, and moving her left arm caused a jolt of agony. She smelled smoke and panicked; she was going to burn alive.

But as she peered upward she could make out patches of green overhead and realized she'd been thrown from the plane. Before she had time to be grateful, the hazy forms of German soldiers gathered around her, rifles pointed at her head. In the last moments of her fading consciousness, the faces of those she'd failed passed before her: her mother, Katia, Major Raskova, and, most cruelly, the one she loved. *Oh, Alex*, she thought. Then merciful darkness closed in again.

CHAPTER ONE

October 12, 1941 (two and a half years earlier)

Cold, filthy, and exhausted, Lilya Drachenko hefted another shovelful of dirt onto the bulwark that would form Moscow's outermost ring of defense.

The Germans had overrun their borders and their airfields, virtually wiped out their air force, bombed and slaughtered all the way to the outskirts of Moscow.

They were close now, terrifyingly close. When the wind was right, you could hear the faint sound of artillery in the distance, and the air raids had been battering the city for weeks. The foreign embassies, many government offices, and some of the factories had evacuated toward the east, and the hospitals were filled to bursting with wounded streaming in from the outlying areas to the west.

And here she was, a young pilot full of aspirations, grounded and laboring with the old men and the women of Moscow.

The crunch of her blade slicing into the gritty subsoil was broken by the harsh voice of a neighbor, a bitter, broken-toothed old party member who shared their apartment block.

"What a comedown, eh, Lilya? No more flying around like a big shot. Now you're stuck in the dirt with the rest of us." She cackled and forced her shovel again into the resistant ground.

Lilya said nothing, for the accusation had an element of truth. She simply recalled the last time she flew in the flying club's old U-2 biplane. The June day had been bright and clear, and the land below heartbreakingly beautiful with patches of cultivated land broken by woodlands. She'd flown low, following the deep *S* curve of the Moscow river, with the Kremlin jutting from the top of the lower curve like a bauble on a swan's breast. *Rodina*, the Motherland, she'd murmured, and could have wept.

The next day, Germany had invaded and all flights were grounded. All the male pilots had been pressed into military service and the women assigned to fortifications. And by fortifications, they meant dirt.

A whistle sounded. "All stop, comrades," the foreman said. "Come on, there's tea in the workers' hall."

Gratefully, she laid her shovel next to the others and climbed from the pit, brushing the damp soil from her overalls. How futile it seemed, like the anti-tank obstacles on the main streets, pathetic blockage to the invasion.

A central stove warmed the hall, and two enormous and slightly battered samovars fueled by charcoal stood at opposite ends of the room. She lined up with the others, receiving a speck of rationed sugar and a shot of syrupy black tea, then filled her tin cup from the samovar with hot water to dilute it. At the end of the table she helped herself to one of the slices of larded black bread.

The murmur in the room became subdued as the foreman switched on the radio to the All Union First Programme. Patriotic songs floated over their heads for a while, until an announcer spoke and the murmur died down.

The war news was brief, all of it bad. Many references to courage but no mention of the word *retreat*, though that was all the Red Army could do. Lilya paid little attention until the announcer said the magic name, and Marina Raskova began to speak.

Marina Raskova, heroine of the Russian skies. Everyone in the hall knew her from her magnificent achievement in 1938 of flying the width of the Soviet Union, breaking all records. Lilya stood up and approached the speaker box, watching it as if it contained the woman herself.

Comrades, I speak to you all, bravely struggling for our Motherland. You know of the heroic men who are fighting at the front every hour of every day. We women struggle, too. Soviet women, the hundreds of thousands of drivers, tractor operators, and munitions workers, who are ready at any moment to sit down in a combat machine and plunge into battle. Today, on the initiative of Comrade Stalin, the State Committee for Defense has authorized me to form air regiments, of women who know how to fly, navigate, or service airplanes, and those who want to learn. And so we call upon you, our sisters and our daughters, to take up this

task and to enter the battle directly with our men. Dear sisters, the hour has come for harsh retribution. Send your name and qualifications to the Ministry of Defense attention Marina Raskova, and I promise you that I shall read every one of your messages personally.
Thank you.

A minute of crackling followed and the grim news report resumed.

Lilya continued staring at the speaker in a silent dialogue with herself. Did she qualify? As a flight instructor she surely must. Were there enough aircraft for training all the new recruits? German bombers had, after all, destroyed squadron after squadron on the western airfields. But if Comrade Stalin had suggested the regiments, perhaps they would build new ones. Would her mother allow it? Probably not, but she'd find ways around that. She set her doubts aside and concentrated on the details.

Good writing paper. Yes, she could get some from the flight school. Scarcely looking where she walked, she stumbled back to her post. As she took up her shovel, she formulated what she would write, and by the end of the duty shift, she had composed the entire letter.

CHAPTER TWO

December 7, 1941
New York, Office of Century Magazine

Alex Preston hated working on a Sunday, but she had a deadline, and she hadn't been able to develop her photos of the steel factories until that morning. Arriving at two in the afternoon, she passed her editor, George Mankowitz, leaning back in his desk chair and listening to the baseball game. Through the open door, she could hear the hissing of the crowd and the high-pitched sing-song voice of the sportscaster. Giants vs. Dodgers, she recalled, but she didn't give a damn who won.

She reached her desk and had barely opened her briefcase and taken out the folder of photographs when someone at the tickertape machine called out, "Holy Christ!"

"What? What is it?" She was less annoyed at the profanity than by the interruption of her train of thought.

"The Japs. They're bombing our base in Hawaii. It's going on right now." He held up the tickertape as if she could decipher it from across the room.

"What?" She rushed to his side to read it herself. At that moment, Mankowitz appeared in the doorway of his office. "Listen to this!" He waved them all toward him, and Alex filed with the others into his office.

This is WOR radio reporting. We repeat, Washington has confirmed that the naval base at Pearl Harbor, Hawaii is under assault by the Japanese. The attack, which began at 7:55 local time, includes Pearl Harbor, as well as the Hickam, Wheeler, Ford Island, Ewa Field, and Kaneohe air stations, and reports are coming in that it is still in progress.

The staff stood quietly throughout the broadcast. Someone said, "This means war, of course." Another grumbled, "The Japs are gonna regret that."

When the report was finished and the others filed out, Alex stayed, deep in thought. What a horror, to have to listen helplessly as American ships were sunk and American men were dying.

"George, let me go and take pictures," she said. "I can fly out tomorrow morning. You know I can get you great shots."

He shook his head. "You're the best photographer we've got. You have the prizes to show for it, but this is out of the question. For starters, they're not going to let civilians fly there." He drew a pack of Pall Malls from inside his jacket and tapped the open end against his fingers to extract one of the cigarettes.

"How do you know that?"

He fumbled in his jacket pocket until he came up with a sleek black cigarette filter and pressed the cigarette into one end of it. From yet another pocket he brought out a lighter and ignited the tip, sucking in a lungful of smoke. "I'm no expert in national security," he said, the words coming out of his mouth embedded in smoke. "But I'm betting the navy won't want the world to know how much damage there was, or to what ships. That's all strategic information now. The military's going to scrutinize every photo—down to specific weapons that appear and soldiers' ranks and insignias—so enemy intelligence can't use the data."

She ran a hand through her hair, flattened by her hat. "I'm sure you're right. It's the start of the war. But damn. I'll be stuck here photographing steel factories, unless they're making war material, and that'll be off limits, too. Crap." She dropped down, sullen, onto one of his office chairs.

"What do you think of going to Russia?" He puffed again on his cigarette, gripping the ebony filter in his clenched teeth like FDR.

"Russia? Whatever for? I know the Germans are crawling all over Russia, and Stalin has his back against the wall. But what do we care about the Reds?"

"When we enter the war, which is inevitable now, the Russkies are going to be our allies. We're already sending them tons of munitions and supplies."

Alex grimaced. "Allies. With Communists. What a mess, eh?"

"Not a mess, an opportunity. You know as well as I do how much the Russians depend on Roosevelt's Lend-Lease program. They lost most of their rolling stock in the Blitz, and they wouldn't have any railroad at all if the US wasn't shipping them locomotives and railcars. A lot of their planes and trucks are coming from us now, too. There's a great story there, one that begs for photos, and no one has any yet."

"I suppose so, but damn. I don't *want* to go to Russia. My parents fled the Communists in 1918 and would turn over in their graves if they knew I was headed back there."

"Your Russian background's exactly the reason I'm sending you. You're the only person on the staff who speaks Russian. Don't worry about Pearl Harbor. Everyone and his brother's going to be fighting with the censors to get the story. Meanwhile, you'll be getting us a scoop on Stalin and the Eastern Front. Consider it the chance of a lifetime."

Alex let out a long breath of surrender. "Stalin. Eastern Front. Crap. So when do I leave?"

"We'll need a few weeks to get you a visa and press pass, and to set up travel. You have plenty of time to collect the things you'll need and enjoy the holidays. When the time comes, I'll have Sally book you a flight to Hvalfjord, Iceland."

"Iceland? How does Iceland come into it?"

"That's where the arctic convoys start. From Hvalfjord you'll go to Murmansk or Archangelsk and then train to Moscow."

She protested weakly. "You said they had no trains."

"I said they stopped building them. They have *our* trains now, with at least one line running to Moscow. You'll do fine."

"Jesus, George. You had this all planned, didn't you?"

He shrugged. "That's how you get ahead of the game." He edged her toward the door.

She stood in the open doorway for a moment. "Just how long is this little jaunt going to take?"

"Couple of months. Depends on how long the war lasts. You'll be home in time to enjoy a New York summer."

In a daze, Alex took the elevator down to the lobby of the Manhattan skyscraper. Stepping through the revolving door, she pulled up the collar of her coat and bent into the wind blowing up Broadway. She thought first about Pearl Harbor, the men who were dying, and the many more who were going to die when the United States entered the conflict. Would things change at home, with rationing or an accelerated draft? Well, that needn't concern her much longer; she wouldn't be here. She'd be in bloody Russia.

She headed downtown on Broadway, gazing at the streets lit and ornamented for Christmas. On two corners of Broadway and 42nd Street, little red Salvation Army buckets hung from tripods tended by men in shabby Santa Claus costumes. Obviously word of Pearl Harbor hadn't reached the street yet.

Winter in Russia—that would require some planning. She'd definitely need to buy a thick wool parka. A fur hat and heavy wool scarf, too, and she'd charge them to *Century* magazine. She also fancied the blue polka-dot scarf in silk on display in Macy's window.

With a vigorous tug, she yanked open the department-store door, and a wall of warm air enveloped her.

❖

How pathetic Terry's penis looked as he snored next to her. Come to think of it, that part of Terry left her cold at the best of times. Fortunately, his extraordinary talent in the oral department had kept their relationship going. He played her "little place" well, while she closed her eyes and imagined Esther Williams, Ava Gardner, Rita Hayworth, or Marlene Dietrich, naked and rubbing deliciously against her. Poor guy. If it weren't for that penis and the conspicuous lack of breasts, he'd have made a great lesbian.

He snorted once and then jerked to wakefulness. "Oh, sorry. Must've dozed off." He slid himself up to lean against the bedstead and scratched a hirsute chest. "A shame this is going to be our last time for a while." He grabbed his pack of Chesterfields and lit one, blowing smoke out of the side of his mouth, looking like Errol Flynn in a cigarette ad.

"I'm sure you'll find lots of girls while I'm gone."

"In my business, it's not so easy to meet girls." He took another drag on his cigarette. "Strategic Services is in such a tizzy about spies, they want to know everything about my contacts." He pinched her shoulder playfully. "You have no idea the ruckus you caused when my boss found out your real name was Aleksandra Vasil'evna Petrovna."

"Terry, you know that's ancient history, and that they changed my name at Ellis Island. I was just a kid. I'm as loyal an American as you are. Russia may be our ally now, but I hate the Communists."

"No one's questioning your loyalty, Alex. But we were talking about me meeting other women, and if I hope to rise in the ranks, I have to keep my face clean. So to speak." He scratched his upper lip.

"So what exactly will you be doing while you're keeping your face away from ladies' wet places?"

"Protecting America's shores. Moving secret people in and out of dangerous places. Catching bad guys. Secretly." He took another puff and tilted his head to exhale smoke upward like a chimney.

"Good man. Try to catch a few of them on my route to Russia so I make it to Moscow alive."

"Roger, will do." He stubbed his cigarette out in the glass ashtray and looked at his watch. "Someone's supposed to pick me up right about now, but I think I can squeeze in another fifteen minutes. What do you say?" He leaned sideways and slid his hand over her breast.

She gently nudged him away. "Sorry, old boy. It's late and I have to go to work early tomorrow. Put your pants on now, and go save America. Secretly."

He obeyed, grumbling, drawing on his boxers and trousers, tucking in his shirt while she rose and pulled on a bathrobe to walk him to the living room.

At the door to the corridor, he took his trench coat from the coat rack, popped his fedora on his head, and gave her a peck on the cheek. "Bye, sweetheart. Promise me not to go to bed with any Russian men. I hear they're brutes."

"Promise," she said with sincerity, and closed the door behind him.

Bored, and not yet sleepy, she wandered over to the window. The morning's snow had turned to slush, as it always did in Manhattan, and 112th Street at night looked positively dreary. Idly, she peered down at the sidewalk as Terry exited the building. A woman, gray-haired and portly in a heavy winter coat, stood by a car and returned to the driver's side as he climbed in. Then they pulled away from her building.

Hell of a secretary, to pick up her boss at midnight from his girlfriend's house. Obviously the Office of Strategic Services had a larger budget than *Century* magazine.

She showered and returned to her bed to read another chapter in her detective novel. Then she flicked off the light and fell asleep within minutes. She dreamt, bizarrely, of Russian soldiers sitting around a fire, and one of them was her father in a Tsarist uniform.

CHAPTER THREE

October 15, 1941

Lilya shifted her pack higher on her shoulders and tried to avoid stumbling on the blacked-out Moscow street. She had passed the tests and interviews for the women volunteers and had thought the final transport to the training school would be more joyful. But the dark forms of Muscovites all around her fleeing the city produced an atmosphere of mute terror. An air raid had struck just that evening, leaving a shell hole on Red Square, as if to underline the mortal danger that menaced them. Everyone was rushing to escape, in near panic.

Next to her and several inches taller, Ekaterina Budanova cursed as she tripped and then caught herself. "It's this damned uniform they've issued me. The pants drag on the ground."

"I know. Mine's just as bad. We'll just have to cut them down to fit. Don't you know how to sew?"

"No. I only know how to fly. Besides…Ooof—" A bulky black form stumbled against her. "Oh, sorry," a young woman said. "I'm not used to the crowds, and I don't know where I'm going. Is this the way to the Belorussia Railway Station?"

"Oh, yes," Lilya said. "That's where half of Moscow has been running since the air raids started. Are you trying to evacuate to the east like all the rest?"

"No, not in that sense. I'm going to flight school with Marina Raskova. If I can find the right train."

"Well, we're going, too. I'm Lilya Drachenko and this is my friend Ekaterina, um, Katia." She held out a hand, realizing a moment later that the gesture was invisible in the darkness. It brushed against the woman's coat and she took hold of it, shaking it vigorously.

"Inna Portnikova, pleased to meet you. You're right. The crowd's getting dense and obviously moving in one direction. Let's try to stick together." She linked arms with Lilya, and the three of them plowed forward shoulder to shoulder.

Near the station, she could make out the outline of its two towers, black against the lighter cloud-filled sky. With the station in sight, the crowd was more aggressive. The stream of evacuees shoved and jostled them through the great archway into the main station. In the sudden light, she could now see families with enormous bundles dragging along toddlers, schoolchildren, old people. Was this what the death of a city looked like?

They stopped as they reached the overhead departure panel. It listed tracks and train destinations but no departure times. All three stood, momentarily at a loss.

At that moment, Lilya caught sight of a woman in an air force uniform facing away from them. She approached her and tapped timidly on her arm.

"Excuse me, please, Comrade Colonel," she said, and the woman turned to face her. Shocked, Lilya took a step back. It was Marina Raskova, Heroine of the Soviet Union, whose face was known to every person who flew, and to millions who didn't.

Raskova chuckled. "Not a colonel, my dear, just a major. I suppose you're looking for our train. It's over there on track eight. We have the last five railcars." With a pat on Lilya's shoulder, Raskova turned away and directed her attention to the entryway, apparently on the watch for more of her charges.

Lilya, Katia, and Inna elbowed their way through the murmuring crowd toward track eight, where a long freight train waited. Uniformed men stood guard at the entry doors.

Lilya held out her identification papers. "We're new recruits. Major Raskova sent us over here."

"Very good, move along." The guard seized her by the upper arm, shoving her up a gangplank into the last car. She stood for a minute, to get her bearings, until Katia and Inna nudged her from behind.

The car was fairly full, with some twenty other women sitting with their knees drawn up on bedrolls or straw mattresses. Wire had been strung along the entire wall of the freight car, and naked bulbs hung at intervals. They were unlit, but presumably would illuminate once the train was underway. A stove, currently cold, had been anchored to the floor on a metal plate at the center of the car. Next to it, a bucket held a supply of coal.

Scattered amid the women were some still-unoccupied bedrolls, and they claimed three that were together. Another scan of the murky interior revealed the corner partitioned by a curtain. Lilya assumed it covered the hole over the tracks that would function as their toilet. She hoped people wouldn't use it too frequently while they were stopped in the station.

It was a relief to be part of something purposeful, rather than flailing about like the people in the train station, struggling for space on one of the trains. Inside the women's car, the roar of the anxious and aggressive crowd was muted.

Once settled in, Lilya glanced around at the other recruits, many of whom she'd met during the interview days. Some of the women near the door had removed their military shirts or trousers and, wrapped in a blanket, had begun to sew on them by the light of the station. Others were simply curled up on their pallets, talking. She chatted with the others, getting to know them, then dozed lightly in the close warm air of the car. Finally, in the third hour, a figure appeared in the entryway.

"Good evening, comrades," Marina Raskova said in a voice that was at once authoritative and congenial. "You'll be glad to know that we have clearance to leave so I can tell you that our destination is Engels airfield and training school. It's not far south of us on the Volga, but the whole country is mobilized, and we have very low priority. We'll have to stand aside and surrender the tracks to trains moving west with troops and supplies and those moving east with factory equipment and workers. I suggest you occupy yourselves learning military regulations and the mechanics of your planes. If you brought sewing materials, it might also be a good time to cut your uniforms down to size so they'll fit when you arrive."

"What about our boots?" someone asked. "They're gigantic."

"I'm sorry, we can't do much about those. You could try doubling your foot cloths. That will keep you warmer, too."

"What will we do about food?" Inna ventured.

"I've arranged for a few crates of herring and some bread to be distributed. And there should be enough tea. We're hoping the trip won't last longer than three or four days. You were all issued long wool underwear, and I suggest you get into them. You have a stove, but the coal ration is limited so you'd best save it for nighttime."

Raising a hand, she said, "Welcome to the air force," and turned back out of the train car onto the platform.

❖

"Unngh, what day is this?" Katia mumbled as she awoke, her contralto voice even lower than usual. She sat up and ran a hand through her hair. "I can't remember. Five? Six? Twenty-seven? Days and nights are all the same." She rubbed her face. "Uff! Is there any bread left?"

Inna already knelt by the stove, shoveling in the last of the coal, though the heat scarcely reached the far ends of the railcar. "No, nothing left. But we've got hot water and a little bit of tea. I'll make us some. If only we had some sugar."

"Sugar? What's sugar?" One of the women close by groused. "I've forgotten what it tastes like."

"Anyone know where we are?" Lilya looked around at the other faces, puffy and unwashed.

"On another siding someplace," Inna said. "I went outside to pee instead of using the privy, but no one was about."

At that moment, the steel door slid open with a dull metallic screech and Marina Raskova appeared again. She looked weary herself, with dark rings around her eyes, though her hair was still immaculately parted in the middle and held in a tight knot at her neck.

"How's everyone doing?" she asked. Her cheerfulness seemed strained, but Lilya appreciated the effort.

Katia spoke up in her distinctive low voice. "We're all fine, I think, but we're out of food. We're hoping—"

"Of course you are. I understand. Unfortunately, we have no provisions left. But take heart, comrades. We're close to Engels, and with any luck, we'll arrive tonight."

❖

The promise of "tonight" was fulfilled, though they arrived at three in the morning at the Engels station. Tying their bedrolls over their rucksacks, they clambered out into the shock of cold and fog. Like Moscow, the town of Engels was in blackout, so, exhausted, they marched with their ponderous packs behind their leader like shades in the underworld.

Men from the school met them carrying blue-tinted flashlights and guided them to a massive hall. "It's the barracks' gymnasium," the guide informed them. "The men gave it up so you could have it as a dormitory."

Lilya glanced around at the sea of bunk beds, in rows along the walls and down the center. Bare bulbs hung on long cords from the ceiling, giving the entire space the look of a warehouse. She marched in line to her assigned bunk and hefted her pack and bedroll onto one end before dropping down on it with a long exhalation. Katia and Inna, she noted, had bunks close by.

Forcing wakefulness, she sat up and rummaged through her rucksack for a few personal items. She would arrange her field kit and extra clothing in the morning and stow them in the wooden lockers beneath the bunk beds.

She peered toward the far end of the hall where signs indicated the toilets. But a long line of women was already waiting. She had relieved herself in the train only two hours before, and her teeth could go a night without cleaning, she decided. Grainy eyed, she undressed and drew on her woolen shirt and trousers, then slipped under the blanket. In spite of the buzz of the multitude of other women, she fell asleep in minutes.

An overhead buzzer roused her from sleep, and she rose automatically from the bunk to stand before it, like everyone else. Rubbing her face, she turned her attention toward the platform at the end of the hall. On the gymnasium wall hung an enormous red banner with the hammer and sickle, and next to it, a portrait of Josef Stalin looking powerful and avuncular. Marina Raskova stood in front of it with a microphone.

"Good morning, comrades. We have allowed you to sleep a bit past the usual hour since we arrived so late. But this is the last time you'll have this luxury. Starting now, you have half an hour to stow your belongings in the lockers below your beds and dress for morning report. At nine o'clock you will fall in at the parade ground for roll call. Your first duty will be to receive your metal identification tags, instruction manuals, training equipment, and a haircut."

Lilya heard an audible gasp at the last word.

"Then, and only then, will you march to the mess hall for breakfast. That will be all." With that, the commander stepped off the platform and exited the hall.

"So it begins," Lilya said to no one in particular and then emptied her rucksack of its contents onto her bunk.

She set the military items on one side: mess kit, flashlight, thick *ushanka* cap, first-aid kit, regulation underwear and footcloths. The smaller pile consisted of her personal items: a hairbrush, tin of tooth powder, block of prized pine soap, tiny mirror, photo of her mother, and her precious bottle of peroxide.

She took her place in line for the toilet, and then, standing at the long trough that served as a communal sink, she did a cursory wash of body and teeth. When the buzzer sounded at nine exactly, she and all the other women lined up in the yard outside the gymnasium in the same order as they had marched in from the station.

The October air was frigid. The wind reddened their faces and turned their breath to steam. Off in the distance Lilya could see the airfield laid out on a bare, windswept plain. Not a single tree in sight, and no hill to block the wind.

After roll call, they filed into the regimental barbershop where long rows of chairs had been set up. A man stood behind each one with a pair of scissors. While Lilya waited her turn, women passed her anxiously feeling their bare necks. A few were sniveling at the loss of their girlish curls, which she found a bit foolish.

To her surprise they had all suddenly turned into beautiful boys, with soft eyes and girlish lips, and she felt a strange, disorienting attraction to them. It seemed wise to keep it to herself.

CHAPTER FOUR

January 8, 1942

As Alex stepped off the military transport plane in Hvalfjord, Iceland, she couldn't help but swagger just a little. The Soviet government had granted her a visa, and George had arranged with the US Air Force to accredit her as a war correspondent with the rank of lieutenant. The photo on her press pass was atrocious, but she quite liked her uniform of a green wool blouse and slacks. Even the weight of the heavy winter parka she wore didn't detract from her élan as she strode into the terminal.

She collected her luggage and then realized she had no idea how to get to her ship or even how to find it. All she knew was the name *Larranga*. Fortunately, a man in a white uniform approached her and touched the bill of his hat.

"Good afternoon, Miss Preston." He shook her hand. "I'm Charles Murdaugh, radio operator of the *Larranga*. The crew calls me Sparks. The captain asked me to meet you and escort you aboard."

Pale and lanky, with rather sparse hair, he didn't fit any of her images of sea-faring men, but she was happy to find someone who knew where to go.

"She's no beauty, but she'll get us there," he said. Taking up her suitcases, he guided her outside the terminal to an open jeep and loaded her luggage into the back. The mud-covered vehicle was no beauty either, she noted as she climbed in next to him.

"It's one of eight merchant ships in the convoy, the only American one. We'll also be escorted by various armed vessels." He started the motor and headed out from the terminal onto a road busy with trucks. In less than twenty minutes they were at the dock and she studied the vessel that would be her home for about two weeks. It was not an uplifting sight. A long, low freighter, with a superstructure at the center, it had obviously seen better days.

He unloaded her two suitcases and they started up the gangplank. On board, rough-looking seamen were loading crates and what appeared to be engines into the hold. She glanced toward the bow where others were just securing a fighter plane with a tarp and cables and made a note to photograph it once she'd settled in.

"I'll take you to your quarters, but then I'm afraid I have to go to work," Murdaugh said. He led her along the passageway and down a narrow ladder to the first level below decks. "This is deck number one. You're on the port side," He walked ahead of her tapping on each hatchway.

"The compartments are numbered fore to aft, and yours is number three. The head is at the end of the passageway, and the mess deck is below decks on number two." He set down her luggage and opened the hatchway into a tiny compartment with two steel-framed berths, one above the other. Thank God the porthole was above the water line.

"We're scheduled to embark at sixteen hundred, but I have to be at my post an hour before. If you need anything, you can ask one of the seamen."

"Thank you, Mr. Murdaugh. Uh, sixteen hundred, that's four p.m., isn't it?"

"Sparks will do fine. And yes, ma'am. Four p.m."

After he left, she studied the steel bulkheads that would be her home for ten to fourteen days, and they were anything but cozy. Well, she wasn't on vacation, and the important thing was to arrive safe in Archangelsk. She wondered if it was as nice as its name.

Damn. She'd forgotten about the twenty-hour nights. To avoid being seen by enemy aircraft, the ships traveled in total darkness, navigating by compass and asdic alone. But imagining the entire convoy creeping like blind phantoms through the pitch-black waters gave her the creeps.

Once or twice during the very short days she ventured outside the quarterdeck thinking to snap a few photos and was astonished. Away from the harbor, the full arctic cold struck them, and every surface touched by the ocean spray turned to ice. She anchored herself near the hatchway to her compartment and stared, hypnotized, at the spectacle of the nearby ships. Covered, like the *Larranga*, in sparkling frost they caught the sunlight and dazzled like fairy vessels. It was impossible to associate the majestic scene with warfare.

At night, and it was almost always night, the sight was more ominous, as they sailed like ghosts over the heaving black water. Already on the third day the wind and spray became too violent, and she retreated to her compartment. She filled the time with cleaning and preparing her cameras, two small Rolleiflexes and a large 5 x 7 Corona View with accordion bellows.

She'd resigned herself to a week of boredom, but on the fourth day, an alarming increase in the pitch and roll of the ship awakened her. She dressed, climbed the ladder to the open deck, and regretted it immediately. With each mountainous wave the bow of the ship shot up high out of the water, hovered for an instant, and then slammed down again into the trough. The impact caused water to shoot up on both sides and wash over the bow, which seemed to strain upward once again out of the froth to repeat the violent cycle. The passageway was awash, and the seamen on deck duty had to grip the railing to avoid being swept overboard.

She could hear nothing but the shrieking wind that rendered speech impossible. The sound was reduced but not eliminated when she pulled the hatch shut again and retreated below. She huddled, anxious, in her compartment, wondering which was worse, to be washed off the deck into the frigid water or to drown trapped in her compartment.

By the next day, the gale had subsided, and she went topside to take a few photographs. When she opened the hatchway to the quarterdeck, she was stunned. Every surface was covered in a thick layer of ice. At the ship's prow, the fighter plane was also encased, as if in glass, and glittered with the reflected light of the rising sun just in front of them. With its nose pointed forward, it was like a ship's figurehead in crystal, and it made the rusty old merchant ship seem noble, their mission heroic.

"Be careful, miss," someone said behind her. "It's slippery, and if you fall overboard, we can't stop and fish you out." She turned at the touch on her elbow.

"Oh, Mr. Murdaugh, uh…Sparks. I was just enjoying this…vision. Is that what we're carrying? Airplane parts?"

"Yes, parts, and fuel, and several dismantled planes. The Russian Air Force is apparently desperately in need of aircraft."

He blew into his hands. "The ice happens on every trip. During the night, the spray collects on the metal and freezes. It makes us top-heavy so the men have to break it up, and unfortunately, you're in the way."

She edged back toward the hatch as four seamen brushed past her with axes and bats and began to smash the slippery crust around the railings and stanchions. Ice broke off into shards and chips, and the men shoveled them over the side, where they floated alongside the countless other ice chunks of the Arctic Ocean.

Murdaugh guided her back down the ladder to the lower deck. It was difficult to manage the frozen metal steps while being thrown about by the pitching vessel, but she'd learned to anchor herself at every point.

She arrived gratefully at the door of her berth, when she heard a deafening roar, and a shuddering of the ship threw her to the deck of the passageway. A second later an alarm bell rang through the intercom, followed by "General Quarters. General Quarters. This is not a drill. This is not a drill. Man all battle stations!"

Had a bomb or torpedo struck them? She lurched into her compartment and cowered on her berth. A tiny voice in her head lamented not being able to photograph whatever it was, but the louder voice begged for it to go away.

When she peered through the tiny porthole on her outer bulkhead, all she saw was smoke. But no further detonation occurred, and her compartment didn't flood. The roar of distant guns told her the battle was elsewhere.

After what seemed like an hour, the call came. "Stand down from General Quarters. All Clear. Stand down." Curiosity overcame her fear of the unknown outside, and, grabbing her smallest camera, she climbed the ladder to the quarterdeck.

The two men were still at the deck guns peering at the sky, and two others stood on the stern over the unused depth charges, but most of the crew stood at the port side railing staring somberly out at the sea.

Some thousand yards away, one of the other merchant ships was sinking. Its prow bobbed at the surface for several minutes as if taking a last breath and then disappeared under the icy water. Lifeboats were already dispatched to pick up the survivors, but they came back empty. The hundreds of men floating in the frigid water were all dead, and no one bothered to collect them. Nauseous, she snapped a few photographs, though she was pretty sure the War Department wouldn't let the magazine run them.

When the lifeboats were drawn up and stowed in their davits, the announcement came, "Full speed ahead," as if nothing had happened.

"Come back inside, miss." It was Sparks. She shook her head and gripped the railing, stunned by what she had seen and the apparent callousness of the crew. "Does that happen on every convoy?" she asked.

"Sometimes not, sometimes it's worse. I've only been on four."

"It's…it's awful." It seemed a very banal word for what she felt. "How can you stand it?"

He stared with her at the churning water where the ship had gone down. "You don't, really. You just get a little more dead inside each time. Every man here is glad it wasn't him, but nobody says so. Even if we win the war, no one who signed up for this job is going to have a happy ending. No sailing into the sunset for any of us." He turned away, leaving her at the railing.

The two fatalities of war, she brooded. The death of human beings and the death of the spirit. Would the war break her that way, too?

Finally, the *Larranga* docked. A team of Russian stevedores came on board, and while the American seamen continued to chip a pathway through the layer of ice around the vehicles on deck, the Russians brought lines into place to lift out the cargo from the holds.

The radio operator helped her carry her luggage down the gangplank to the dock and tapped one finger to the brim of his cap as a sort of salute. "Good luck, Miss Preston. I hope things go better for you than they did on the trip."

"Thanks for the thought, Sparks. Have a safe trip back." She turned away and stood for a moment, getting her bearings, smelling the disagreeable harbor odor of soot and diesel oil, then hefted her suitcases and staggered toward the reception terminal. After displaying the relevant documents and receiving a stamp on her visa, she staggered with all her luggage outside the terminal and considered how to proceed.

When she grasped the obvious solution, she all but slapped herself on the forehead. On the snow and ice-covered ground in front of her, everyone carried their loads on runners. She approached an elderly man who was just unloading bundles of wool onto a truck from a child's sled. When he'd finished, she offered him a sum that would have presumably paid for several such objects.

He wrinkled his face in surprise at the offer, then appeared to grasp the extent of her need and doubled the amount. She agreed and took the sled rope with one hand while pressing the ruble notes onto his glove with the other, then pivoted around before he could change his mind.

The sled proved its worth once she'd loaded her bags onto it, and it slid smoothly along until she located a horse-drawn cart and driver and negotiated a ride to the train station on the eastern edge of town.

On the long ride, she gazed around at Archangelsk and found it disappointing. The name had always evoked images of a shimmering sunlit city, somehow touched by angelic forces. Perhaps in peacetime its fields, wide streets, and low wooden houses had seemed blessed by the nearby forests and the fresh air of the White Sea. But war had made it shabby; the ongoing traffic of trucks, tanks, and assorted combat vehicles moving from the harbor inland had both clogged and pitted its streets.

At the buzzing of their engines, she glanced up to see two planes passing overhead toward the harbor. They swooped low and dropped their loads, though she couldn't see if they struck their targets. Then she heard the metallic scream and detonation as they were shot down by flak. Had the *Larranga* been hit? She thought again of the ship she'd watched sink in the arctic waters and of the white bodies floating toward them. Her first sight of death. Sparks's words came back to her, that every horror you saw or heard made you a little more dead inside. She shook off the thought and moved on, as the convoy had done.

At the Yaroslavl-Moskowsky railway station, she climbed from the wagon, loaded her luggage once again onto the sled, and towed it to the entryway. Inside, she elbowed her way into the crowd and studied the posted departure schedule.

To her relief, one more train was leaving for Moscow that day, in two hours. She purchased a ticket and directed her attention to food. Fortunately, bread was available from a state-owned shop inside the station. It was gritty and tasted of sawdust, but she made herself eat it and wondered if it was a preview of her new diet.

She boarded the train at four in the afternoon, though the winter sky was already pitch-black. The train was packed, and she managed to move forward only by shoving the heavy suitcases in front of her. She held the child's sled under her arm, and when the crowd ahead of her would move no farther, she found she had at least achieved a space by a window. She made herself comfortable sitting on her suitcase and placed the sled in front of her knees.

The chatter of the people around her and the *clackety clack* of the train wheels blended into a soothing white noise, and in the warmth of the train corridor, she became drowsy. She pulled her woolen air-force cap down over her forehead and leaned her head against the window. She dozed, woke, and dozed again, repeatedly.

Twenty-eight hours, and four agonizing trips to the filthy train toilet later, she watched as the train pulled into Yaroslavsky Station, Moscow.

Dull-witted, hungry, and stiff she stepped down from the car with all her luggage. She hoped living in Moscow would be easier than getting there.

❖

The Hotel Metropole was within sight of the Kremlin, so all she had to do was find a tram that she could struggle onto with her sled and luggage. She accomplished that too, and finally, there it was. Red Square.

She knew from news reports that the German advance had stopped just short of Moscow and that the Russians had even mounted a counter-offense, but when she stepped off the tram, it wasn't at all what she'd imagined.

All the famous buildings were camouflaged. The walls of the Kremlin were painted to resemble a row of low houses, while Lenin's tomb had been made up to look like a village cottage. A strange zigzag pattern was painted the length of the main street, and it took her a moment to realize it was supposed to look like housetops when seen from above.

The golden domes of the Kremlin churches, which would otherwise have been highly visible, were encased in dark timber boxes, and the bright green of the other buildings' roofs was darkened to brown. How effective could it be when the snaking curves of the Moscow River were so distinctive from the air, and any map would reveal the location of the Kremlin atop the highest bend? Not to mention the forest of barrage balloons that cried out "target here."

Red Square itself had anti-aircraft artillery emplacements at both ends, though the snow-covered outline of a small crater revealed that at least one bomber had gotten through.

Only the Hotel Metropole, across from the Bolshoi theater, was not camouflaged, and she trudged toward it across the icy square amid lethargic Muscovites.

The double doors of the entryway opened to the cavernous lobby where the air, though still cold, was a relief from the deadly outdoor temperature. Her sled seemed out of keeping with the hotel elegance, so she left her luggage by the entryway and proceeded to the desk.

"I believe I have a reservation that was made by the US War Department."

"Yes, madam," the elderly clerk said with exaggerated deference. "And your name is…"

"Oh, sorry. Preston. Alexandra Preston."

"Ah yes. Here it is. Welcome to Moscow." He took her passport and wrote out a lengthy registration, then handed her a large brass key. "Room 315. I'm afraid you'll have to carry up your own bags."

She nodded, concealing consternation, but as she turned away a figure stepped into her field of vision. Tall, unhealthily thin, he wore a pinstriped business suit and tailored coat. His face was long and pale, and his hair, when he removed his hat, was thin.

"Miss Preston. So glad you could make it," he said, to her surprise, in English. At her befuddled expression, he added, "Harry Hopkins, at your service." He offered a long, smooth hand and she shook it. "President Roosevelt's envoy," Hopkins added, sensing her uncertainty.

"Ah, yes. My editor, George Mankowitz, said it was you who arranged for the Russian visa. Thank you very much, but you're the administrator for the Lend-Lease program, aren't you? Shouldn't you be back in Washington?"

"Lord knows, in the dead of winter, I'd certainly prefer to be, but alas, I have matters to discuss with Mr. Stalin, and some things are best addressed in person."

"Lend-Lease, yes. I came here on one of your convoys." She snorted. "It was the worst two weeks of my life. Not just the storms, but I also saw a merchant vessel sink, all hands lost."

"Yes, I heard. War casualties, like our men at Pearl Harbor. I'm afraid there will be many more. I'm sorry Mr. Mankowitz didn't forewarn you, of that and of the hardships here in Moscow."

She tried to lighten the mood. "Hardships, indeed. I've just learned I have got to carry my own bags upstairs."

Hopkins smiled slightly. "Yes, everyone who isn't fighting at the front has been pressed into labor service, digging trenches, dismantling industry for transport, camouflaging the city, manufacturing armaments. No able-bodied men left to wait on us, I'm afraid."

Alex pressed her glove palm to the tip of her nose, to warm it. "The lobby's not exactly toasty either. Is this also what I have to look forward to?"

"I'm afraid so." Oil and coal are scarce. Did you notice the wood piled up in Red Square? It's cut in the woods and brought by barge or train into Moscow, where it's distributed. And of course there's never enough."

"Does that mean I'll have to...?" The high whine of a siren interrupted her question and she looked around, puzzled.

"Air raid," Hopkins said. "They come almost every day at this hour." The hotel clerk stepped out from behind the counter and signaled them to follow him down a flight of stairs.

They sat side by side on a bench with the guests who had been in the lobby and others who had filed down the stairs from their rooms. Concussions muffled by the thick walls told her that planes were dropping bombs, but thankfully not many. The other, louder sound of the flak guns on both ends of Red Square seemed to scare the attackers away. After less than an hour, the hotel clerk waved them back up the stairs.

Once again at the desk where she'd left her luggage, Hopkins took up one of her suitcases. "Come on, I'll help you with these. What floor are you on?"

She took hold of the other one and walked alongside him to the stairs. "Third. Could be worse. But do I have to actually worry about air raids every day?"

"They come most days, but the worrying part is up to you. The flak cannons keep them from doing too much damage, but it's not very pleasant. Do you plan to stay in the city? What's your program, anyhow?"

She stopped at the landing after the first flight of stairs and paused for breath. "As you know, *Century* is a photo magazine, so I'm here for pictures. Of the Soviet leaders, of the action, of the war. And that reminds me, can you arrange to get me into the Kremlin? My boss is hoping for a portrait of Mr. Stalin. The press has been using the same old photograph of him, and it's time we had an up-to-date one."

Hopkins's wince told her he thought the idea was daft. "I seriously doubt that in the midst of the battle for the survival of Moscow, Josef Stalin will want to sit for a portrait. You might be better off asking to photograph the new female aviation regiments he's ordered. That's something he seems rather proud of."

"Female soldiers." She chuckled, imagining broad-shouldered, brutish women. "How very Russian. In any case, I would be most grateful if you could inquire about photographing Stalin. My editor will be much happier with that." She resumed climbing.

"Um…well…We might be able to convince him that the American public, which is, after all, paying for all his war material, would like to see what he looks like. But please do not be disappointed if he doesn't reply. He's got a war breaking over his head and…you understand. He's not the most congenial of men."

She thought of the bloody purges, of thousands of political opponents, sentenced to labor in the Gulag, if they were lucky—to execution, if they were not. News of them had reached the United States even before the war began. "So I've heard."

❖

In the course of the next day, Alex set up her darkroom in her bathroom and made a point of learning the layout of the vast hotel. She hadn't questioned George's booking her at the Hotel Metropole, and now she understood the reason. The vast complex held what amounted to the Moscow foreign-press community, and correspondents from major British, American, and French journals wandered its corridors.

They also filled its dining room, where they presented their foreign ration tickets and received their dinners. On her first evening, there were no vacant tables, so she sat down at one whose only occupant was a plump, amiable-looking man with heavy eyebrows and a wide mustache.

"Do you mind?" she asked in English, indicating the empty chair.

"Oh, not at all." He held out his hand. "Henry Shapiro, United Press Bureau manager."

She reciprocated. "Alex Preston. *Century* magazine. Been in Moscow long?"

"Since 1934."

"Ah, an old hand. Then maybe you can tell me how to get into the Kremlin. I'd like to photograph Stalin."

Shapiro's expression of disbelief was a near duplicate of the one she'd seen on Harry Hopkins the day before.

"Oh, my dear. Every man, woman, and dog here wants to get into the Kremlin and interview Stalin. We've all written letters, which are never answered. On rare occasions, someone gets a personal invitation from the Kremlin Press Department, but we've yet to figure out what the criterion is."

The waiter approached their table and set down bowls of beet soup and a platter of black bread in exchange for their ration tickets. She ate for several minutes, then wiped her mouth with the linen napkin. "Is this what our meals are going to be?" she asked.

"By and large, yes. But you learn to enjoy them when you realize that the Muscovites have to stand in long lines every day to get anything like this. This is a privilege we have simply because we can pay for it."

Chastised, she changed the subject. "So how do you get your information about the war?"

He dabbed at his mustache. "Mostly through the Soviet Press Department. For the moment, we're stuck with summarizing information given to us by the *Sovinformburo*."

"Ah, the Soviet Information Bureau. Of course."

"It holds regular press conferences where it hands out official communiqués in Russian describing the military action. I can read Russian, but most of the others need a translator. Then we write our reports and submit them to the censors. When they get finished blacking out what they don't like, they stamp their approval and we're allowed to rush down to Central Telegraph to transmit them."

"That's it? *That's* the war reporting?"

"Well, we can also quote articles from Red Star, the official army newspaper. But that's propaganda, too. The best is to just talk to people, assuming you speak Russian. Even then, you'll need luck, persistence, and guile. Did I mention luck?"

"Hmm," she said, returning to her soup to conceal her shock.

This was going to be more complicated than she'd expected.

CHAPTER FIVE

January 14, 1942

Lilya Drachenko banked sharply to the left, executed a barrel roll, and leveled out in the Polikarpov U-2. The biplane was so basic, so utterly simple in design, that flying it was much like riding a bike. It was slow; its cruising speed was below the stalling point of most of the high-powered German fighters, but it could skim along only a few hundred meters from the ground and felt, as no other plane felt, like an extension of her own limbs.

The sight of the aircraft slightly above her at eleven o'clock yanked her from her reverie. Two of them, flying in tandem, and she recognized their shape. Heinkels, she was pretty sure.

She banked right and returned to the airfield, then marched to the office of the commander.

Through the crack in the half-open door, she could see her hunched over her desk poring over flight schedules. Lilya watched her for a moment in quiet awe. Marina Raskova held a nearly divine status among her students but was never aloof. Lilya, and most of the women at Engels, would have flown into hell for her.

She glanced up as Lilya knocked on the doorjamb.

"I'm sorry to interrupt you, Comrade Major." She took a breath. "While I was making a practice flight today, I spotted two Heinkels. That means their base is close by."

Major Raskova rubbed the side of her face, and Lilya could see the fatigue in her eyes. "We are aware of them. Our reconnaissance knows the exact location of the base, in fact. The Air Ministry has ordered us not to engage them. We don't have enough fighter planes to take the risk. In a month, perhaps, after the American deliveries."

"A month? Couldn't we simply bomb them? We could use the U-2s that we train in. A surprise attack by a squadron, each one carrying, say, two bombs, would do real damage, don't you think? We could at least keep them awake all night."

"The U-2s?" Major Raskova frowned slightly. "The enemy flak could shoot you down the minute they see you."

"Yes, but I have an idea about how to deal with that, Comrade Major. May I explain?"

❖

"Lilya, I can't believe you convinced her to go through with this." Inna Portnikova trudged alongside Lilya and the other three volunteers on the airstrip. In the sub-zero January air, they walked fast to keep from freezing, and on her short legs Inna had to almost run to keep up. "And that you…" She jabbed Katia Budanova in the side. "You fell for this lunacy, too."

"It's not lunacy. It's a good plan. Just make sure our engines are oiled and warmed up. We'll do the rest."

Inna snorted. "Don't worry. You two may be big show-off pilots, but I'm still the best engine mechanic on the airfield. The engines are oiled, and the armorers have loaded both your planes with bombs."

Lilya slapped her on the back. "I never doubted you for a minute. Now, help us turn the propellers and then please stick around. There's almost no moon, and with the blackout, we can't land without your light to guide us."

"Don't worry. I'll be there. I'll always be there."

Lilya stepped up onto the wing of the biplane and into the cockpit. As promised, it was warmed up and started immediately, in spite of the freezing air temperature.

Behind her, in the navigator's seat, Tatyana plotted their course with her map and a stopwatch.

In the air, half an hour later Tatyana announced, "We're one minute away from target."

"All right. Time to dance." Lilya cut the motor and shoved the stick forward, bringing the U-2 into a steep, soundless dive. At an altitude of only 300 meters, she glided to where the target should be, then yanked both drop wires to release the bombs. At almost the same moment, she started the engine again and accelerated on a steep curve upward. She'd barely climbed another 50 meters when the bombs detonated and the force threw them sideways. She regained control and a moment later heard the second two bombs from Katia's plane detonate. And never a peep from the anti-aircraft guns.

"Wahoo!" Without radio contact, either with the ground or with the other pilot, Lilya could share her glee only with her navigator, but that was enough. They'd shown that even in their flimsy all-but-toy airplanes, the women could bomb German positions. The men back at the airfield wouldn't be snickering now.

❖

Morning came, and Lilya and Katia filed in with all the others to stand before the newly posted lists. Katia scratched her forehead. "Damn."

Lilya's heart sank. "I didn't make it to the fighter-pilot list. You didn't either. That doesn't seem fair," she added bitterly.

"Stop complaining, you two," a stocky woman standing next to them said. "I don't get to fly at all. I'm listed with the armorers. I'll be dragging bombs out to the field every night for you to go out and play heroes with."

"Shameful talk. Stop it now!" It was Major Raskova, and the women parted on both sides of her, dropping their glances. "Listen to yourselves, all this talk of '*I* deserve this' and 'Look where they put *me*.' Do you think we can fly missions without navigators, without technicians and armorers? Individual ambitions are unworthy of a Soviet woman."

Her voice softened, and she laid a hand on the shoulder of the woman who'd complained about being an armorer. "Don't worry. You'll all have your chance to prove yourselves, and you'll all be heroes in your own way."

She pointed with her thumb. "As you can see by the lists, we've divided you into three regiments. The 588th Night Bombers, the 587th Regular Bombers, and the 586th Fighter Force." Each regiment has its own pilots, navigators, armorers, technicians, and office staff."

"Excuse me, Comrade Major." Katia spoke up, her somber contralto always giving her a sort of authority. "Who'll command the night bombers?"

"That will be Major Bershanskaya. I'll command the day bombers, and no one has yet been chosen as commander of the fighters. So, are there any other complaints? If not, return to your quarters."

The women drifted away grumbling. Only Inna seemed content. She linked her arm into Lilya's as they walked. "I'm so glad we'll be serving together, the three of us. I love being in the air force, but I never for a moment wanted to fly a plane."

❖

Lilya lay in her dormitory bed brooding at the injustice. "We have to get into the fighter regiment," she whispered to Katia, who sat on the bunk next to her brushing her thick, short hair.

"Don't be in such a hurry. They don't even have any planes yet. They're waiting for some to arrive on the convoys from America."

"Nice of them to give us planes and weapons." Inna's voice came from the other side. "But I don't think they're such good soldiers themselves. They're all a bit pampered, and I hear the women dress like tarts."

Lilya rose on one elbow. "Really? I saw the American ambassador's wife once in Moscow, and she looked nice. Just because we all look like boys now, we shouldn't make fun of attractive women."

"That's easy for you to say, Lilya, with your little blond curls," Katia said. "No matter what they do to you, you look adorable. The Americans will have nothing on you."

"Don't be silly," Lilya said, but she smiled to herself. Amazing what a few drops of peroxide would do.

The evening buzzer sounded lights out, and the entire dormitory went dark. Lilya lay in the darkness, random thoughts trailing through her drowsy mind in no particular order.

Her assignment to the night bombers. Aerial battle against the Germans for the Motherland. A good first step, and not at all bad for the daughter of an enemy of the people. She rarely worried about that stain any longer, not since she'd made her rite of passage through the Komsomol and regained her honor as a good Communist. But now she could even allow herself a bit of pride and work toward flying bigger and faster planes. God, how she loved being up there.

American fighter planes. Could she learn to fly one? She was sure she could.

American women. Where they really all that attractive? Would they find *her* attractive?

The thoughts swam together in her sleep-befuddled brain, the women and the planes—foreign, powerful, alluring.

CHAPTER SIX

After her sixth air raid spent in the roomy and well-lit cellar, Alex appreciated the advantages of living at the Hotel Metropole. She'd even grown used to the ever-repeating meals of soup or rice with chunks of meat or fish, which she appreciated was far above what the Muscovites were getting.

This morning she sat idle over her powdered eggs and dipped her dry bread into her tea. The same pudgy man with a small bald spot and in a slightly rumpled brown suit sat again at a table within sight of her. He wasn't a hotel guest because she'd asked at the desk about him. That, and his sleekness when most Russians were undernourished, convinced her he was NKVD.

It didn't much worry her. True, she'd snapped a few photos from the windows of the embassy of the women digging trenches and painting camouflage. She'd shipped them, uncensored, to the *Century* office via diplomatic pouch to be published without her name. But she could photograph only so much from embassy windows, and if she wanted to expand her range of subjects, she needed to work within the system.

She sipped her tea, which now had bread crumbs in it, and wondered how she could spend the day. She regretted taking so few photos on the *Larranga*, with a fighter plane like a figurehead on its bow, but then remembered the weather.

The familiar figure appearing in the doorway of the dining room improved her mood significantly. She waved him over. "Mr. Hopkins, how nice to see you."

He pulled out a chair and sat down in front of her, smiling. "I've just had a rather productive meeting with Foreign Minister Molotov. We discussed increasing the monthly tonnage of Lend-Lease materials, in exchange for greater cooperation with our journalists. I thought you'd be pleased. Dozens of other foreign journalists are in Moscow, but only you had the audacity to ask for photographs of Stalin. Molotov agreed."

"Oh, that's wonderful news. Did he say when I'd be allowed in?"

Hopkins shrugged amiably. "I couldn't get him to commit to a date or time, of course, but he hinted that if you appeared at the palace and were willing to wait, Stalin might try to find a few minutes' time for you. I would suggest you go today, while the iron's hot, so to speak."

She leapt to her feet. "All right then. Just let me get my cameras."

"Don't take too much equipment. I doubt he'll want to pose for very long," he called after her.

She met him at the hotel entrance in fifteen minutes, in parka and boots, with her Corona View camera and a dozen flashbulbs in a sack slung over her shoulder.

In the icy winter air, it was difficult to speak through several layers of scarf, so they marched silently together along the Theatralny Street onto the expanse that was Red Square. The air raids never came in the morning, so the soldiers manning the anti-aircraft guns in the square were idle, and the atmosphere was almost serene.

They reached the entrance to the Kremlin, and Alex explained who they were to the soldiers on guard. Stone-faced, they telephoned someone inside and obviously obtained approval.

With Hopkins at her side, Alex followed the Soviet guard along the path, paying close attention to the slippery ice underfoot. Glancing up briefly, she caught sight of the white plaster walls of several boxy churches. The Assumption, Annunciation, and Archangels cathedrals she knew from her earliest St. Petersburg school days, but she couldn't recall which one was which. Farther toward her right, the Ivan the Great Bell Tower rose up over the entire Kremlin, and she was certain that no camouflage could conceal it from above.

They entered the Grand Kremlin Palace, where another set of guards again telephoned ahead to advise of their arrival, and the original guard saluted and retreated. The two new guards led them just as stiffly down a corridor to a tiny gilt and red-carpeted elevator, which barely had room for the four of them.

It labored creaking to the second floor, where they continued along a winding hall with countless doors and corridors on each side. Twice an intermediary guard telephoned ahead and changed places with the previous one, who then departed. Clearly, Premier Stalin was well protected.

The final set of guards admitted them to a sparsely furnished salon obviously intended as a waiting room.

She recalled why she'd been granted the audience. "The Russians really depend on Lend-Lease, don't they? Enough so you could leverage this meeting."

"Yes, they do. They've moved many of their armament factories east of the Urals and are still rebuilding them. That's why they're way behind their pre-war production. And did you know they lost almost their entire air force in the German invasion?"

"I hadn't heard that."

"Yes, they obviously had far too much trust in their non-aggression pact with Hitler and left hundreds of their planes lined up on airfields near the western frontier. The Luftwaffe just swept down and obliterated them." He made a swooping gesture with a long, pale-white hand. "Now they're having to rebuild almost the entire force except for their old World War 1 biplanes."

"And this time I hear they're adding women." She chuckled. "That should be—"

An officer with a row of medals across both sides of his chest entered abruptly. He nodded in greeting and then beckoned them into an adjacent room. Though larger, it was as sparsely furnished as the previous one except for a desk, and next to it stood the most powerful man in the Soviet Union.

Josef Stalin was a disappointment. Shorter than she was, with little musculature in his chest, the great dictator looked like a street sweeper. His eyes were slightly Asiatic, his skin terribly pockmarked. Only his thick hair and mustache bespoke a certain virility. His dull khaki tunic, devoid of any medals, impressed with its simplicity and made the over-decorated officer standing at his side look slightly foolish. Two other men stood some distance behind him, and the word "lurked" seemed appropriate. Her memory of newspaper photos told her they were Molotov and Beria.

"Good morning, Premier Stalin. Thank you for receiving us."

"Ah," he said, still unsmiling. "An American who speaks Russian. I understand you want to take my picture." He turned to the gaudy-chested officer who had escorted them into the room. "General Osipenko, what do you think? Should I allow it?"

The general bent slightly at the waist, an officer's way of expressing agreement. "It might be very nice for the Americans to see what the Father of All the Soviets looks like."

"I think so too, but you must do it quickly. I have a meeting soon."

"Yes, of course." Alex cursed inwardly for not bringing her tripod and thus guaranteeing a good formal portrait. But she could make do with the Corona. She snapped one of the peanut-sized flash bulbs into the reflector and took a quick shot, then popped in a second one and shot another one from a different angle. She was about to insert a third one when the sound of someone entering drew his attention away from her, and Alex turned to see what had distracted him.

A woman had just come in—young yet somehow matronly, with hair parted severely in the middle and drawn back into a tight bun. "I'm sorry to interrupt, Comrade Stalin, but our meeting was scheduled fifteen minutes ago, and I have an air-force regiment awaiting my command."

Alex stepped back, astonished that anyone would use such a tone with Josef Stalin. But he simply laughed as she strode toward him.

"Major Raskova, you know General Osipenko, but allow me to introduce Mr. Hopkins, from the White House, and Miss…"

"Preston."

"Preston," he repeated, pronouncing the P like a B. "Miss Preston, this is Marina Raskova, organizer of our women's aviation regiments."

She smiled at Alex for a tenth of a second, then returned her attention to Stalin. "Yes, and now that they are organized, they need planes. Bad enough that our night bombers have to use the old U-2s from the training schools. I'm sure we can do better with the day bombers and the fighters. I understand the Americans have sent a new shipment of aircraft, and I'd like to put a claim in for my women."

General Osipenko raised a hand in warning. "Major Raskova, you should not bother our leader with personal demands. You will have your aircraft in good time, after the men."

The general was apparently annoyed by the demand, but Stalin, in contrast, appeared amused. The smile that had been missing in her two photos now appeared.

"Who shall get our new planes?" Stalin asked rhetorically, weighing his empty palms against each other. Why don't we ask our American allies? What do you think, Mr. Hopkins?"

In the absence of a formal interpreter, Alex translated and then repeated Hopkins's answer in Russian.

"I can't really say, Premier Stalin. It's a purely strategic decision, though I would assume they should be given to the best pilots."

Alex saw the desperation on the woman commander's face and felt a sudden solidarity with her. "I understand that Commander Raskova has trained this regiment at your behest. Since the public will see them as more or less belonging to Premier Stalin, I should think people will expect them to have the best aircraft."

Osipenko's face darkened. "Those are tactical decisions and not worthy of Comrade Stalin's time. The Air Defense Force committee, over which I preside, will tend to such matters."

"Calm down, Aleksandr Andreevich." Stalin used the affectionate patronymic. Obviously they were friends. He clapped a hand on the general's shoulder board. "How about we give some of the new planes from our factories to the women, the American planes to your men."

If Osipenko was only partially appeased, Marina Raskova was obviously delighted. A smile spread over her wide maternal face, and she executed the same officer's half-bow as Osipenko had. "Thank you for your decision, and once again, I apologize for taking up your valuable time." With that, she saluted and let herself out of the chamber, leaving the air behind her to resonate with her absence.

Stalin chortled. "Are the women in your country as determined as that, Mr. Hopkins?" Alex translated again.

"Some are. I believe the wife of our president is, though she doesn't fly airplanes. If your women do, you have reason to be proud of them."

Alex could see now why Harry Hopkins had been chosen as the man to go between the White House and the Kremlin. He had a soft-spoken, middle-American charm and a sharp diplomatic mind that managed to overcome language and cultural differences.

Sensing that the audience was about to end, she seized the moment. "Premier Stalin. The American public will no doubt admire the portrait of the leader of the Soviet Union, but I think they would also be greatly impressed to know about your innovation, these female combat aviators. The Soviet Union is more advanced, in this respect, than the United States. Might I be allowed to photograph them, too? It goes without saying I will submit all photos to your Press Department for censorship."

Stalin reflected for a moment, and to fill the silence, she added, "It would be the best sort of war propaganda, both for your people and for mine."

The word propaganda seemed to be the clincher. "Yes, yes. Go ahead. But you will report to General Osipenko and the Aviation Force Committee. And now I must end this meeting." He urged them with his hands toward the door. "I have work to do before the next air raid."

As they stepped into the corridor and followed the guard back to the elevator, she spontaneously took Hopkins's arm. "We *are* good, aren't we?"

CHAPTER SEVEN

January 1942

When the Soviet counter-offensive began, the bombing raids let up slightly and so did the terror. Trains were still moving machinery and workers eastward, and fighting troops westward, but the panic had abated, and with the addition of several Lend-Lease locomotives, the railroad was beginning to master the heavy traffic. Alex managed to reach the town of Engels in three days rather than nine.

The Engels airfield and school stood near the town of Engels and across the Volga from Saratov. It was larger than she expected, with dormitories, classroom buildings, mess hall, and hangars. With German forces close enough to threaten Saratov, an air of urgency hung over the entire complex.

"Come in." Marina Raskova invited Alex into her spare utilitarian office and gestured toward a chair. Raskova herself took a seat and carefully moved aside the maps and papers on her desk. She had the same schoolmarm look she'd shown in the Kremlin, though her manner revealed an openness and gentility that belied the severe hairstyle. Her mustard-colored uniform was well tailored, and though Alex couldn't read Soviet rank from military shoulder boards, she knew she was speaking to a major.

"I'm honored to meet the 'mother superior' of Russia's women pilots."

"Is that what people call me? I suppose we do have a touch of the convent about us. My 'novices' are mostly young and innocent." She chuckled. "If you can call girls hungry to kill Germans innocent."

"I passed by some of them coming in. In uniform they all look more like young boys."

"Yes. I made them cut their hair when they arrived, and some of them were very upset. At that age, young women are very sensitive to men's attentions."

"They're all unmarried?"

"No. A few are married, and some are already widows. Many of them come from places already overrun by Germans, and three of them, I believe, have families trapped in Leningrad. As you can imagine, they're all very keen to fight."

Alex glanced past the major's shoulder and saw a photograph of an older woman holding a young girl in her arms. "You have children?"

Raskova turned toward the photo. "Yes, a daughter. Eight. She lives with her grandmother." A look of tender affection slipped quickly over her face and then disappeared. "But I think you are here to talk about military things."

"Yes, of course. Can you tell me more about the training? Maybe some personal details or anecdotes the reading public might enjoy."

"Well, they're my charges and I value every one of them, but I'm not the person to have pretty stories about them. Why don't I just take you around a bit and you can decide what you want to tell." She stood up.

"Can I take pictures?"

"I should think so, as long as they're not of the planes or military equipment. And you know you must submit them for review before you send them off."

"Yes, of course."

Raskova led her across a freezing-cold square into an adjacent classroom building and allowed Alex to peer briefly inside at students wearing padded jackets sitting in rows. "They're learning geography, Morse code, plane mechanics, the nature of their weapons, and so forth. Later on they'll specialize, so that the navigators learn navigation, technicians learn airplane engines, and armorers learn about explosives."

"How long is the training period?" They continued along the corridor.

"In peacetime, the school produced good pilots after two years. But now that we're at war, the women must learn the same amount in six months."

Alex recalled the discussion about aircraft. "Will I be able to see the planes they're training with?"

"The U-2s? Yes, I'm taking you there now."

Outside, they bent into the blustery February air and Raskova guided her toward a row of planes. At the last plane, they halted, and Alex got her first close-up view of the U-2s. She was appalled.

The open-cockpit biplane was nothing but wood and canvas-like fabric. Thin struts held its double wings together, and it stood on equally flimsy legs that ended in wheels.

At the nose of the plane, a woman stood on a ladder with her head and shoulders in the open engine compartment. A canvas canopy was all that protected both woman and engine from the frigid wind.

"Sergeant Portnikova, I hope I don't disturb you," Raskova called up to the mechanic, who uncurled herself out of the engine compartment.

"Not at all, Comrade Major. I was finished anyhow." She wiped her bare hands on a rag, saluted, and inserted them into the gloves that hung at her waist.

"Miss Preston, this is Inna Portnikova, one of our mechanics. She can answer your questions about the planes. When you've learned enough, you can join me back in my office." She gave an informal return salute to the sergeant on the ladder and then turned back in the direction they'd just come.

The young mechanic climbed down and gave Alex her full attention. Her soft round face was cheerful, almost cherubic, and it was hard to imagine a single violent thought passing through it.

"Cold work." Alex said the obvious. "Why don't they let you work in the hangar?"

Inna pulled down the side flaps of her wool cap to cover her ears. "Because when we're deployed, there won't be any hangars. We fly from auxiliary fields in the open and always at night. For oiling and between flight maintenance like this, we have to do it on the field."

Alex nodded, trying to imagine how maintenance was possible in the prickling snow. "The planes look so..." She tried to find a less insulting word than flimsy. "So lightweight. It's hard to see how you can use them as bombers."

"Yeah, these U-2 trainers are light. We can even push them by hand across the runway. But they're easy to fly and they're tough. These have been refitted to carry bombs up to 100 kilos under the wings."

Alex squinted upward at the cockpit. "There's no cover. And how does the pilot hear her radio?"

"Yes, it's deadly cold. That's for sure. And they don't have radios. The pilots have to plot their way by compass and by visuals. If they have a problem, they have to solve it themselves. It's hard, but the pilots get used to it." She patted the fuselage, as if to forgive the aircraft its deficiencies. "Oh, there's my pilot."

Alex pivoted a quarter of the way around to see her first female Soviet pilot.

She was of average height, and her gait was neither that of a male nor a female but merely purposeful. The blond curls that poked out from under her leather pilot's cap at the forehead and temples were the first suggestion of femininity.

As she neared, Alex could make out pale-blue eyes. The slender nose started high and dropped in a soft curve over full lips and a well-defined mouth.

Her finely cut features suggested a slender, even delicate woman inside her bulky flight outfit, and the effect was strangely alluring. Alex couldn't have said what attracted her, only that the still-nameless woman had a strange combination of feminine beauty and masculine authority.

As she approached, she glanced up quizzically at Alex.

"Lilya," Inna said. "We have a visitor. An American journalist. She wants to write about us."

"Alex Preston." She offered her hand.

"Lilya Drachenko." The pilot returned the handshake, though with both their hands gloved, it felt superficial. Lilya's inquisitive look remained. "An American? To write about us. What an honor."

Alex suddenly could think of nothing to say that didn't sound stupid. "May I take a photo?" she blurted out.

"Of Inna and me? Of course." Lilya went to stand next to her mechanic.

Alex fumbled with her camera case, then took off her gloves. The metal of the camera was painfully cold, but she felt foolish now and had to get the shot. She stepped back, focused the little Rolleiflex, and snapped two frames before her subjects moved apart.

"Nice to meet you, but I'm sorry, I have to test-fly this plane." Lilya edged toward the wing.

No, don't leave. Not yet. Alex searched for a way to hold her. "Uh... do you have any idea when you will be deployed?"

"Well, that's up to Major Raskova and the Air Defense Force. But we'll train at least until May."

Alex tried to think of other questions, but Lilya had already climbed up the wing into the cockpit. Inna gave a forceful yank to the propeller blade and stepped away as it began to spin and the low-power motor began a sewing-machine-like clatter.

The flimsy craft bumped along the runway for a few meters, then lifted off into the air. When it was about 100 meters overhead, the plane circled back and the wings wobbled back and forth in a sort of salutation. Inna laughed and waved back, but Alex felt a curious titillation imagining the wing-wave was for her as well.

They walked together off the airfield, Inna carrying her short wooden ladder on her shoulder. "We're very lucky to have Major Raskova. The male instructors don't think we're up to the job, but she doesn't let them belittle us. I was in her office the other day when one of the generals was complaining to her that the women were wasting everyone's time and that men should fill their places at the school. Just then the secretary came in and announced she had a telephone call from Stalin. Can you imagine the general's face? Stalin himself calling her. That shut him up pretty fast."

"I take it the women really like her."

"Oh, yes. They'd do anything for her. Our group has been broken into three regiments, with different officers, but everyone who won't be under her command is disappointed."

They passed other women, some rolling oil drums, others hurrying out to their aircraft in padded flying outfits and goggles. Inna stopped them and asked them to pose for photographs "for the Americans." They posed happily in pairs and threes, linking arms like school chums.

At the door of the administration building, Alex offered her hand. "Thanks for the information, Inna. I hope we'll see each other again." She meant what she said. She liked the pudgy little mechanic and had no trouble imagining her on a farm some place chopping wood.

Major Raskova opened the door to her again, though she halted momentarily in the doorway as another female officer stood up from her chair. Tall, muscular, somber. Were it not for the ample breasts delineated under her tunic, she might have passed for a man. *Finally, the true Soviet woman soldier, just as I imagined.*

"Allow me to introduce my colleague, Major Bershanskaya," Raskova said.

"Pleased to meet you," Alex replied. Bershanskaya nodded and remained silent. All three sat down.

"Did you find out what you needed to know?" Raskova asked.

"I don't think I know yet what questions to ask. Mostly I'm trying to listen and take pictures. I did just talk to one of your pilots."

"Lilya Drachenko," Raskova said. "She's one of our best. Likes to break the rules, though."

"Really? She was on an assignment and didn't have much time for me. Perhaps I can meet again with her later."

Raskova ignored the suggestion. "She'll be with the night bombers, though we may move her. We're also training dive-bomber pilots, which I will command, and a third regiment of fighter pilots, for which a commander has not yet been chosen."

Women dive-bombers and fighter pilots. The phrases sounded almost cartoonish. "Women pilots in the United States are only allowed to test-fly and ferry planes to the airfields."

"Our leaders were also reluctant to let women fight on the front," Raskova said. "But having an enemy sweeping across your land and destroying your cities does change minds."

"Do the women have the same duties as the men?" Alex thought of the cherubic mechanic Inna and the delicately formed Lilya.

Eva Bershanskaya spoke up for the first time. "They do the same work for the same number of hours as the men, and if two women have to lift a 100-kilo bomb rather than one, so be it. They carry their weight. Don't ever doubt it."

Sensing she'd offended her hosts, Alex changed the subject. "I was a pilot myself in my youth. I loved it."

"Why did you stop?" Major Raskova asked.

Alex shrugged. "The demands of life, I suppose. Finishing university, beginning a career as a photojournalist. Which reminds me, may a take photos of you both?" She drew her camera from its case and held it up. "You'll certainly have admirers in the US."

Raskova shrugged. "I suppose if Stalin allowed you to photograph him, I shouldn't refuse."

She leaned back in her chair and looked into the lens of the camera and, unlike Josef Stalin, she smiled.

Alex snapped the photo. "And you, Major Bershanskaya?"

"If it's really necessary," she said, then stood up from her chair and clasped her hands awkwardly in front of her. Turning her head to three-quarters, she squinted as if about to reprimand one of her cadets and waited. Alex rolled the film and snapped the second photo.

"Oh, the vanity of women," someone said acidly, drawing their attention.

A bulky male figure stood in the doorway.

"Come in, General Osipenko," Raskova said, seeming unperturbed by the insult.

The officer took several more steps into the room, and Alex remembered him now. The head of the Aviation Force Committee. She didn't like him, but she couldn't remember why.

A woman came in directly behind him—slender with small sharp features that hinted at beauty. But her dark hair was cut shorter than any of the other women's, and she held her mouth in a tight, almost hostile masculinity. Her expression was somehow more menacing than the softer manliness of Eva Bershanskaya, who towered over her.

"Major Tamara Kazar," he said, introducing her. Then he pointed to them in turn. "You already know Majors Raskova and Bershanskaya, and this is an American photographer, Aleksandra Preston."

Kazar bent stiffly from the waist, like a Prussian officer, and said nothing.

"Please, everyone sit down," Osipenko said, taking a seat along with his tight-lipped companion.

The five of them made up an awkward circle, and Alex wondered if they would ask her to leave while they discussed military matters. But Marina Raskova directed the conversation. "We were just describing the three regiments and their commanders to Miss Preston."

"Their commanders. What have you decided?" Osipenko crossed his arms over his chest in a faintly condescending way.

"Major Bershanskaya will command the night bombers, and I will lead the daylight dive-bombers. For the fighter pilots, I thought perhaps Katia Budanova."

"No." Osipenko raised a hand. "Budanova does not have the discipline. In fact the Aviation Committee has assigned Major Kazar to take command of that regiment. That's why I've brought her to meet you."

Raskova's eyebrows rose faintly. "You decided this without consulting me?"

"Major Raskova, the Aviation Committee is not obliged to consult you on anything. You have already been given extreme liberty to choose two commanders, although we could have appointed those as well."

Raskova's voice was cold. "I will see to it that the women are informed. The public, as well." She gave a quick sideward glance toward Alex.

It did not escape his notice, and, in the mild tone of a man who rarely encountered disagreement, he replied. "Given that these are strategic military decisions, I think it wise for our little journalist to return to Moscow and obtain her information from Sovinformburo."

Little journalist? The condescending bastard.

Raskova's expression remained neutral. "Will that be all, General Osipenko?"

"For the moment, yes. Thank you for your time. I look forward to the reports of your progress." He stood up and Tamara Kazar shot up next to him, as rigid as he was relaxed.

Majors Raskova and Bershanskaya got to their feet as well, and a round of salutes followed as an adjutant opened the door. Osipenko strode through with the confident step of a victor, but his companion, Alex noted, had a limp.

What was going on there? What was Osipenko's interest in promoting her? And Kazar herself was a puzzle. Was it a turf war?

"I'm sorry, Miss Preston." Major Raskova's voice called her back to the present. I have no objection to your presence, but it appears that it must come to an end. Perhaps the circumstances will change."

"I'm sorry, too, since I've barely arrived." Alex tried not to sound bitter as she gathered her camera and parka. "Can you have one of the men drive me back to the train station?"

"Yes, of course. I hope you got enough information to do your story. I'd like the world to know about my pilots."

"I assure you, it will."

❖

Interesting woman, the American, Lilya thought, taking the U-2 up to 2,000 meters, where the icy wind whistled through the struts. She was well padded and gloved, and the only place the wind chilled her was around her throat. In the future, she'd have to wear a larger scarf.

God, how she loved flying. High above the earth with its mud and stink, she sensed a connection she couldn't express in words. The lightweight craft let her feel the air as a substance, a fluid that could lift her, oppose her, or send her into a spin. But if she gave herself to it and heeded its laws, it would embrace her and let her slip deliciously along its surface, kissing her with its icy breath.

She practiced evasive maneuvers, doing somersaults and barrel rolls, testing the power and agility of the little crop-duster. The simple structure could take a lot of damage and still stay aloft, and it had the capacity to fly low and slow, well under the stall-speed of both the

Messerschmitt 109 and the Focke-Wulf. Like a mouse pursued by an eagle, it could turn sharply and repeatedly, while the high-speed predator plane continually overshot it.

Over the Volga, she thrust the stick forward and dove precipitously a thousand meters, then another five hundred, then another three hundred, hearing the wind shriek. At the last minute, she pulled up sharply and cut off the engine, to coast quietly along the river.

Her fuel was getting low, so she ascended again and circled leisurely, making figure eights over the airfield in a last dance before landing. Could the American woman see her? Alex, she was called. Aleksandra.

The first American woman she'd ever met. Did they all look like that?

She tried to imagine life for Americans under capitalism. Surely they needed a people's party to hold them all together and direct their productivity for the general good. She'd learned in school and in her district Komsomol that social equality was impossible without Communism. So why were the Americans so cheerful?

She was a good Communist and had spent years living down the shame of having a father who was an enemy of the people. Did the capitalist Americans have such internal enemies, and if so, what made them so? Communism? The thought gave her a headache.

Under her flight suit, the too-large male underwear they'd all been issued began to itch, but her padded leggings were so thick she had to endure the discomfort. What did American women wear for underpants? The thought of the elegant journalist wearing something scant and silky under her uniform was slightly titillating. Did she have a husband? Someone who bought her nice underpants?

CHAPTER EIGHT

I've brought you something." Terry Sheridan sat down at the table in the Hotel Metropole dining room and laid a small package in front of Alex. "It's nylons. From Macy's. I thought you'd have a hard time getting them here."

"Thanks, Terry, though in the Russian winter, I wear slacks most of the time."

"Well, keep them till spring. They're meant to cheer you up."

"I could use cheering. Here I am back again from Engels airfield, tossed off the premises, as it were. Really depressing." She stirred the remnants in her teacup.

"What happened? I thought Stalin had approved your being there."

"He did. But it wasn't as if he'd issued an order. It was just a 'Sure, go ahead. I don't care' kind of thing. The Aviation Committee and, more precisely, this General Osipenko apparently have more direct authority. He seems to not even like the whole idea of the female regiments. I don't know how to get around him. Even Major Raskova, who convinced Stalin to set up the regiments in the first place, has to obey him."

Terry fished his cigarettes out of his shirt pocket and tapped one out. "That's the way this regime works. The Supreme Leader makes a casual decision, but the political and military functionaries around him get to do the fine-tuning. And most of the time, they're all in competition with each other." He ignited the cigarette with a Zippo lighter and clicked it shut.

"How do you know so much about the workings of this regime?" she asked. "I'm the one living here."

"It's the business of the Office of Strategic Services to know. We have to understand these guys to be able to negotiate with them." He inhaled deeply and blew the smoke from the corner of his mouth.

"Isn't that what the State Department's for?"

He laughed softly. "The State Department's just the pretty face of the government. We do the real work, sneaking in spies, sneaking out information and informants, and State acts on the basis of the intelligence we provide." He poured out another glass of the black-market champagne he'd brought into the dining room. "So, tell me about the School for Women Pilots. Were they all the big hairy brutes you expected them to be?"

"No, not at all. Some of them were rather attractive. I only got a few shots, mostly of the women posing together, so the censors passed them and I sent them back to the magazine. Otherwise, I spend all my time here in Moscow photographing people getting on trains—the soldiers going westward and the factory workers going eastward."

"Well, you may end up photographing the fall of the Soviet Union."

"Really?" Her voice grew somber. "The war news is that bad?"

"Yes, it is. Stalin and the winter weather have kept the Germans from taking Moscow so far, but the Soviet offensive has pretty much halted. The Germans have Leningrad encircled and are battering their way toward Stalingrad."

"Does the War Department think Russia might lose?"

"Chances seem about fifty-fifty now, and we're keeping an eye on what the Red Army's doing. And if they win, we're just as concerned with Stalin's plans *after* the war. That's another reason I want to talk to you."

"You want me to tell you what Stalin's planning?" She laughed. "You're joking."

"No, I'm not. Stalin needs the Allies to save Russia, and so he more or less cooperates. We give him millions of dollars of materials too, so we do have his attention."

"But…?"

"But we don't trust the man an inch, or his international aspirations. Communism is…well, you know, 'Workers of the world unite,' and all that nonsense. We need to keep an eye on that."

"What do you want me to do?"

"You speak excellent Russian, and other than Harry Hopkins and the ambassador, you're the only American who's been inside the Kremlin. We want you to go back in there and win their trust. Then talk to people, keep an eye on things, *notice* things. It wouldn't hurt if you got a little extra friendly with someone in the Kremlin hierarchy, if you know what I mean."

"You want me to be a spy. And sleep with Communists."

"In so many words, yes." His smile bordered on the unctuous, and he fingered the package he'd brought. Were nylons a symbol for sexual trade-offs?

"My answer, in so many words, is no. I'm as patriotic as you are, but I'm already being watched. You see that plump man with the bald spot sitting behind me a few tables away? He's not a guest, but he shows up in one corner or another of the dining room every day watching all the foreign journalists. He's almost certainly NKVD, and right now he's watching you and me. I'm the last person you want to spy for you."

"You've got a good eye. Yes, he is NKVD. My office already knows him. But the fact that you spotted him so fast tells me you'd make a good agent."

"Or that he's a really bad one. Anyhow, it's still not my milieu. I'm a journalist. I expose secrets, not keep them."

He crushed his cigarette stub into the ashtray and shrugged. "All right. Forget I asked. I have a few other leads, so I'll be in Moscow a few more days.

"Only a few days? It takes two weeks to get here, and you stay for only a few days?"

"It takes two weeks if you're hitching a ride with a convoy. Those of us with more important business fly in from the other direction, through China. It's still a haul but takes three days instead of two weeks."

"Bastard! I had to go through hell for two weeks to get here when there was an alternative?"

"George Mankowitz arranged your trip, and it had to be by convoy. I'd have had to pull a lot more strings to get you that kind of diplomatic transportation and couldn't do it just for a journalist."

"But you would for, say, spies, moles, informants."

He took out his Chesterfields again and fingered one out. "Don't be naive, Alex. You know how governments and their agencies work. In any power hierarchy, you have only so much capital and you want to spend it judiciously."

"Well, maybe you might some day find it judicious to spend some of that on me."

"That depends on how nicely you treat me." He poked her shoulder playfully. "So, how about our getting together? It's been awhile."

Alex thought for a moment about a young blue-eyed pilot with blond ringlets under her flight helmet and bombs under her wings. Did anyone ever blackmail her into sex?

"Sure. Why not? I'm in room 307. Come by this evening after dinner. And bring more champagne."

CHAPTER NINE

May 1942

All things come to those who wait, Alex thought. For three months, while the male journalists staying at the hotel came and went and filed their battle stories based on printouts from Sovinformburo, she had obediently photographed acceptable subjects: the faces of women and children, soldiers on leave, factory machinery being loaded onto railcars, the anti-aircraft emplacements throughout the city, the *aerostat* women raising and lowering the barrage balloons.

But she found fewer and fewer scenes to photograph in Moscow, where the wretched populace worked fourteen-hour days on strict rations, where the available food for which they had coupons still had to be obtained by standing in endless lines in all weathers, and where they went home to unheated apartments and slept in their coats under whatever covers they had. In winter they all looked the same: round bundles of wool, under fur ushankas or thick scarves, they scuttled by with their sleds of firewood or coal for their pathetic cooking stoves. When the warm weather came, they froze less, but the lack of coat and ushanka revealed how gaunt they'd all become. She photographed them discreetly, for her own records, but the pictures were of no use to the magazine.

The Press Department censors passed only the most robust and smiling faces, of citizens cheerfully laboring for the Motherland. And in the second year of the war, she didn't see any of those.

Yet finally, after the hundredth photograph of smiling soldiers boarding troop trains, the Press Department and the Aviation Committee approved her application to rejoin the women's regiments.

On the second of May, Alex caught the train back to Engels.

❖

Marina Raskova was still immaculately uniformed and combed, but her face was thinner.

"I'm afraid you've come too late," she said, admitting Alex into her office. "Two of our three regiments have been deployed to their respective airfields. My own regiment is still in training, learning to fly the new aircraft, and frankly, I'd rather not have the Pe-2 appear in photos. They're new and their design is still classified. I can't let you anywhere near them with a camera."

Alex stood awkwardly, her cameras dangling from her shoulder, and absorbed the bad news. "Would I be able to photograph the women who've been deployed, then? I think the Kremlin might approve the image of Soviet women in action."

Raskova frowned. "You mean the fighter pilots? I can't imagine that Major Kazar would permit you to invade her territory."

Alex's heart sank. She searched her memory for arguments. If the promise of propaganda wasn't enough, she had nothing. Unconsciously, she took a step back.

"She can visit the 588th," someone said. Alex turned to see the figure who'd just come in behind her. Damn, what was her name again? Borodin? Bezinsky? B…

"Major…Bershanskaya," she exclaimed. Shaking hands with the sullen and virile woman, she summoned all the warmth and sincerity she could manage.

"The 588th? That's the night bombers, isn't it? Oh, yes, that would be wonderful. When, and…uh…where can I join you?" Alex made a conscious effort not to show too much exuberance.

"If you're prepared to travel right now to the south of Russia, wait in hangar B across the field. The 588th airfield is near Stavropol. I'll check the duty roster and see who's still at Engels who can give you a ride."

"Oh, thank you, Major. I promise—" But the major had already walked away.

Alex turned to Major Raskova, who was finally smiling. "I'm happy we could find a solution for you," she said, and offered her hand. Her grip was firm, her fingers long and graceful, and Alex remembered hearing that she played classical piano. So much for her earlier notion of coarse women pilots.

She began the trek across the airfield, gazing up at the spring sky. Good weather for flying, she noted, and tried to remember where the hell Stavropol was.

When she reached the hangar, the men working ignored her, so she stood patiently, staring out at the bare horizon. After some fifteen minutes, a figure approached from the distance. Small, female. She wondered if it was one of the pilots she'd met three months before. The figure came closer and took on a face.

A lovely face, with blond ringlets at her forehead and behind her ears. Alex felt the grin spread across her face. "Lilya Drachenko, is that you?"

"You remembered my name?"

"Of course I do. And your mechanic was Inna, wasn't she?" Alex fell into step with her as they walked onto the field.

"Inna Portnikova. Yes. She'll be flattered you remembered her. By the way, how is it that an American speaks such good Russian?"

"A long story. But basically, my parents were Russian immigrants. From St. Petersburg. Oh, sorry. Leningrad."

"When did they leave?"

"Around 1918."

"Anti-Bolsheviks, then. Were you born here?"

The conversation was heading in a dangerous direction. It was certainly not helpful for her Communist host to know she'd been raised anti-Communist, but she was unwilling to lie. "Yes. As I said, in Saint Petersburg. Why they left, I don't know, really. I was a small child and only remember growing up in New York. Can we talk about you and your plane?"

They stopped at one of the biplanes. "Yes, of course we can. Have you flown in this kind of craft before?" Lilya looked directly at her, and Alex felt the same confusion she'd experienced at their first meeting. Why was that?

"Nothing as…um…exposed as that. I piloted something called the Grumman Goose. A long time ago."

"Grumman Goose." Lilya repeated the name in English. "How did it fly?" She stepped up on the wing.

"It was sort of a flying boat, with wings over the cockpit and two engines. Amphibious. Roomy interior, too. Lots of fun to fly."

"Why did you stop and become a journalist?" Lilya stared at her again, throwing her off her train of thought.

"Studies took over. I had to make a living. But I never forgot the thrill."

"No. One never does. So, up we go." Lilya lifted her up by the elbow and helped her into the rear cockpit. Alex stowed her pack and camera carriers under her legs and strapped on the safety harness. Anticipating the icy wind, she pulled her silk polka-dot scarf out from under her uniform and rewrapped it high on her neck.

"Pretty scarf," Lilya said.

"Thank you. It's turned out to be useful."

"You'll need cover on your head, too." Lilya handed her a leather flight helmet and she slipped it on. It fit nicely and brought back pleasant memories.

"This is the navigator's cockpit and also has a set of controls, but it's best if you leave that to me."

Alex laughed. "What if we have a difference of opinion on where to fly? Say, you want to bank one way and I want to bank the other."

Lilya laughed back. "Oh, that won't be a problem. I'm the one with the gun."

"Good point. But seriously, how do we talk during the flight? Is there an internal radio?"

Lilya swung a leg over the side and dropped down into the pilot's seat. Looking back over her shoulder, she said, "Sorry, no radio. No ground communication either."

"That's a little scary. How do you navigate at night?"

"It's not hard when there's a moon. The Volga reflects the moonlight, but otherwise, we measure the distances on a map and calculate flight time to the target and back. Then it's just compass and stopwatch."

"Unbelievable. And how does the navigator talk to you? She just shouts at you from behind?"

"No, she talks into the hose hanging by your shoulder. If you want to say something to me, tap me on the shoulder and speak into the tube."

The engine began a throaty clattering and they taxied some distance to the runway. They picked up speed quickly, and in just a few minutes they were airborne and over the Volga.

The bite of the wind on her face was unpleasant, so she pulled her collar and scarf as high as possible, then concentrated on the landscape below.

The plane rocked slightly in the wind, and Alex remembered the sensation of piloting a light craft. She wondered how similar the old U-2 was to the Grumman and how quickly she could learn to fly it.

She lifted the communication hose from its hook and spoke into it. "It's a bit windy. Could you shut the window?" It was an old joke but would break the ice.

Lilya laughed. "This little breeze is nothing. You should feel it at higher altitudes at night, on your sixth and seventh trip. Even with a thick flight suit, you shiver."

"You have to fly seven times in one night?"

"We fly all night long, one after another, and rest only as long as it takes to re-arm the plane. In winter, the sorties are endless."

"My God. I just can't imagine it. No defensive weapons."

"The plane can take a lot of bullet holes and still fly, that's the good thing. But it's also flammable, and tracer bullets can set it afire. It's not a nice way to die."

Alex shuddered. "Can you bail out? Oh, wait. You don't have a parachute." Her hand went spontaneously to her chest. "Um, neither do I. That's unnerving."

"The plane itself is supposed to be the parachute, since you can land it almost anywhere. If it doesn't burn up, that is."

"How long did it take you to learn to fly this thing?"

Lilya turned back for a moment, revealing a handsome profile. "Not long at all. I learned when I was quite young at the government flying club. After that, the U-2 seemed quite simple. Why do you ask? Do you want to learn?"

"That could be fun. Who could teach me, and where?"

"*I'll* teach you. Right now? You've got controls in front of you. If you could fly your Grumman, you can fly this old crate."

"If you're sure...I don't want to kill us."

"We're high enough now that you probably can't. Look at the instrument panel. The four dials at the top are the important ones: heading, airspeed, altimeter, attitude."

"Yes, I recognize all of them." Alex took hold of the control column. "I'm guessing the stick moves the ailerons and governs the roll and pitch, right?" She moved it slightly and the plane banked to the left. "Ah, yes."

She glanced down at her feet. "The rudder pedals control the yaw..." She touched it lightly and the plane changed its heading by a few degrees. "This, of course, is the throttle." A faint tug caused the plane to lift slightly. "Well, I guess I *can* fly this thing." She banked again to the left, then to the right, increased and decreased speed, and, when she had sufficient confidence, she made a small swoop and dive. "This is fun. I could do this till the cows come home."

"The cows? Do you have cows?"

"Sorry. I was translating an English expression. I must remember not to do that."

"I'd like to learn English," Lilya said brightly, as she took over the controls. "I could talk to the Americans when we meet them."

"What would you talk about?"

"Oh, everything. Clothes, food, films. Your culture fascinates me. The cowboys, the automobiles, the Coca-Cola."

"Is that what you think we are? I wish I had the time to tell you more about us. We have as many cultures as the Soviet Union."

"Well, Stavropol is another three hours, with a refueling at Stalingrad. We've plenty of time to talk."

"What would you like to discuss? Capitalism? Cowboys?"

"Can we talk about love?"

"Love?" Alex laughed nervously. "What do you mean?"

"I mean how you do that in America. How old are you when you get married?"

Alex thought for a moment. "All ages, really. But young men usually marry when they have a job. Of course, right now most of them are in the military, just like here."

"What about the girls?"

"That depends. Some girls marry around eighteen or nineteen. Others stay in school and marry around twenty or twenty-one."

"How old are you?"

"Thirty-four." The plane banked slightly, shifting the stream of wind on her face.

"And are you married? Do you have someone that you love?"

An intimate question coming, disembodied, out of a rubber hose. If Alex's brow hadn't been frozen by the wind, she would have furrowed it. "Why aren't *you* married?"

"Oh." Lilya was silent for a moment. "I never met anyone I loved. And then the war came."

Alex thought of Terry, his cajoling or extorting her for sex, and realized she didn't miss him a bit. "The same for me. I don't love anyone that much."

"Well, I love Inna and Katia, of course, but—OH!"

A stream of projectiles struck diagonally through the left wings and passed under the fuselage. Alex ducked instinctively.

"Messerschmitt." Lilya sent the plane into a steep dive, and the rapid change in air pressure caused Alex's ears and sinuses to ache. She held her nose and blew, equalizing the pressure, then gripped the sides of the cockpit as they lurched and banked, trying to evade the attacker.

They reversed direction, a maneuver that bought them a little time, as the high-speed Messerschmitt overshot them and had to swing back. They dropped farther and the altimeter in front of her swung to seven hundred meters, then five, two, then one. The wind whistling through the struts of the shuddering plane and the screaming of the engine were deafening. The sparsely wooded ground below rushed up to meet them, and she gripped the sides of the cockpit, certain they would crash.

The altimeter needle trembled just under 20 meters as they wove between the trees along the curves of a winding creek bed, the only avenue where their wings wouldn't be ripped off. Alex stared, unblinking, at the banks and bushes she could almost touch, terrified their wheels would catch on them.

She didn't dare make a sound, for fear of distracting Lilya from the delicate maneuvers, and stifled a scream each time a wingtip came within inches of some obstacle.

Finally, mercifully, the streambed widened, an opening appeared, and Lilya took them into a steep curve upward. Alex scanned the sky, and it was empty. The Messerschmitt had given up the chase.

She dropped back against her seat and lifted the talking tube to her mouth. "Jesus H. Christ," she breathed.

In the front cockpit, Lilya reached for her tube. "No." She laughed. "Lilya Grigorevna Drachenko."

Alex giggled, a nervous, over-excited, relieved-to-be-alive sound. "You are…amazing."

CHAPTER TEN

May 1942
Air Base near Stavropol

"Here we are," Lilya announced as they touched down in the semi-darkness and bumped along uneven ground.

Alex peered over the side of her cockpit, puzzled and slightly alarmed. The light that remained from the sun hovering on the horizon revealed the dark forms of planes lined up some distance away, but otherwise she could make out nothing to suggest an airport. No buildings, no tower, no runway. The whole dusky landscape was grim and desolate.

She was sorry the six-hour flight was over. They'd told each other their stories, as much as one would tell a stranger, and she felt a closeness to her new comrade. She chuckled inwardly at the word.

Lilya stood up in her cockpit and faced toward the back, kneeling on the pilot's narrow seat. "It's been nice talking to you."

"For me, too." Impulsively, Alex undid the silk at her throat. "You admired my scarf and I'd like to give it to you. It's from a store in New York." She pressed it awkwardly into Lilya's hand.

"Really? Oh, I couldn't…I mean…thank you. I'd love to have it. It's not military issue, so I'll have to wear it under my uniform, but when I'm in the air, I can let it show." She brushed it against her cheek.

"Here, take mine in exchange. It's a crude thing, made out of parachute silk, so you can consider it a gift from the 588th regiment." She untied the scarf and handed it to Alex, just as another woman arrived beside the plane.

"What's keeping you?" she called up to them.

"Oh, sorry. Am I on the duty roster tonight, or should I take it off the field?"

"Of course you're on duty tonight. Right after me. We're four and five. But Inna has to move you."

Lilya signaled agreement, then added, "Katia, we have a guest. An American journalist who wants to write about us."

Katia seem unimpressed. "You can show her around later, after the mission. Please get out of the plane so Inna can check the engine and move it to the refueling station."

"All right. All right." Lilya threw her leg over the side of the cockpit and jumped lightly off the wing. Alex first handed down her cameras and rucksack and, dropping to the ground, realized how muddy the field was. Each footfall sank into the soggy ground, and the wheels of the aircraft would have sunk too, were it not for the ingenious track they'd laid out.

It looked as if they'd taken apart a fence and laid the slats side by side in the field, creating a hard surface. The track was only twice the width of the plane, so the pilot would have to aim with precision to land on it by torchlight. A second fence-track ran parallel to it, presumably so planes could take off and land simultaneously. Other similar tracks spread out on both sides to enable the planes to leave the main runway.

"Welcome," Katia finally said. "Do you speak Russian?" she asked slowly, as if talking to a child.

"Yes, I do. You can speak normally." She studied the one-woman welcoming committee. Katia was tall and imposing, her hair shorter than Lilya's and combed back like a man's. Alex had known a few women in New York who affected that style and it had become fashionable to call them "butch," but in a military regiment, where women had to assume men's roles and dress, she wasn't sure if the term was useful. For the moment, she found the woman intimidating.

"Come on. We'll take you to the bunker while the mechanics get the planes ready." The two pilots started toward what looked like a hillock at the edge of the field, and Alex trudged after them, each foot making a sucking sound as she lifted it from the mud.

When they arrived at the hillock, the tarp hanging over one end of it indicated it was a shelter. Katia pulled it aside, revealing the interior where kerosene lanterns presented a soft and pungent glow. It wasn't what she'd expected.

Something between a bunker and a dugout, it was about five feet wide and twenty feet long. A row of planks on each side made up beds for perhaps sixteen women. Wooden panels laid against the sod walls didn't disguise the fact that the shelter had been dug out of the raw ground. The roof was a rough *V* of cut bows covered with sod, penetrated at the center by the ventilating pipe from a primitive stove. The interior held the odors of wood smoke, damp earth, and human bodies.

Lilya stepped in behind her. "Girls, we have a visitor who'll be sharing your quarters. This is Alex, an American journalist. Can we find a bunk for her?"

A short, cherubic woman stepped forward from the semi-darkness. "I remember you from Engels. I'm so glad you're staying with us."

"Inna, hello." Alex embraced her lightly, then glanced around at the others and smiled.

"There's an empty place over here, and a bedroll," Inna said. "No pillow though. You'll have to use your rucksack."

Alex marched to her assigned plank, unrolled the thin mattress and blanket, and laid her rucksack at the head. Feeling all eyes on her, she sat down and patted the spot next to her. "Very cozy," she said, eliciting a chuckle from Inna. "What do you do for a latrine?"

"Outside." Katia jabbed her thumb over her shoulder.

"I see. Um…is this the bunker where *you* stay?" Alex asked, trying to engage the gruff woman in conversation.

"No," she answered, and stepped out of the bunker.

As if to make up for her comrade's cold manner, Lilya explained. "The pilots and navigators are just off the air base, in a cowshed. We've got a little more light, so we can read our maps, but the place stinks like cows."

"It's time to report." Someone stood in the doorway, holding back the tarp. "The major wants a briefing, and by then, your planes will be armed."

Lilya turned back toward Alex. "All right then. I'll see you at breakfast," she said, and disappeared.

Alex warmed her hands over the stove, noting that the bunker had no floor. "What do you do when it rains?"

"We get wet," Inna answered.

Alex lifted a foot and noted the mud caked on her boot sole. "I see."

"You'll get used to the smell after a while, too," Inna said, as if reading her mind. "No running water, so we wash with a rag in canteen water. They promised us a bathing truck once a month, but we'll see how *that* works out."

"Can we go outside and watch the planes take off? I can't photograph them, but I'd like to see them."

"Sure. They'll be starting in about fifteen minutes. The target area isn't far, so they should return in less than an hour."

Leaving behind cameras and rucksack, Alex filed out behind Inna onto the field. A cluster of women, the armorers and mechanics, Alex supposed, already stood at the end of the runway, and they joined them at the periphery. "Do you have any men here? For the heavy work?" she asked.

"No, not a single one," Inna said with evident pride. "We shoveled our own dugouts and built our own bunkers. We cut our own wood for the stoves, too. You should see us swing an ax."

After some fifteen minutes, Alex stood amid the ground crew watching the sortie begin. It was a curious, otherworldly experience, seeing them rumble along in single file, great awkward insects in the darkness, each one guided only by the form in front of it. They lifted off, like condemned souls, yearning upward and disappearing.

When the last one had taken off, Inna began to pace and Alex paced with her, to keep warm. "If you're real quiet, you can hear the sounds of the bombs. They're about ten kilometers in that direction. You can see the enemy's searchlights, too."

Alex squinted in the direction she pointed and could just make out a whitish flickering on the horizon. That glimmer and a soft, dull thudding announced the battle going on. "How do they do it without being shot down?"

"I'll tell you, but you can't write about it in your magazine."

"No, of course not. I never write anything tactical."

"Well, the first plane has the hardest job because everything's dark. She has to drop flares to see the target, and when she does that, the enemy searchlights come on. But while the lights target her, the second plane bombs from a dark position. When the light columns move to search for the second plane, the first plane swings back to drop *her* explosives."

"Assuming she hasn't been shot down."

"Yes. And assuming they survive, they have to return by compass in the dark. The whole airfield is in blackout, and we uncover the kerosene lanterns only when we hear the first plane."

"It sounds nightmarish."

"You could say so."

"Listen, I hear something," someone said. Alex peered into the night sky and saw nothing, but could make out the familiar clattering of the U-2 engine. Then a shadow appeared overhead, black against the cobalt sky.

"It's mine," another woman said. "I'd recognize that noise anywhere." In a few moments, the craft had landed and taxied to the new start position. The armorers ran toward her dragging their carts.

Number-two plane came in, then three and four. Number five, Alex remembered, was Lilya, and Inna seemed nervous. They waited the scheduled three minutes, then four, then five. "I hear another one coming in," Inna said. "But I don't recognize the motor. It's not Lilya."

A plane rumbled to a halt on the field and swung around to the takeoff runway, where it was surrounded by its service team. The figure that climbed out and lumbered toward them was Katia, her face smeared with soot.

"What happened?" Inna asked. "Where's Lilya?"

"I don't know. They caught us in the searchlights and I couldn't see anything. We were choking on the gunpowder, from the anti-aircraft shells exploding all around us. We had to scatter."

Long minutes went by while Inna stood hunched and grimacing into the night breeze, her arms across her chest.

Finally she lifted her head. "Ah, there it is, thank God." She turned up the flame in her lantern and held it out in front of her.

Lilya's U-2 swooped down out of the darkness onto the runway. She swung around behind her predecessor and Inna ran to meet her. Alex exhaled relief.

Lilya joined the other pilots waiting to be refueled, and someone handed her a tin mug of tea. She took a long drink and wiped her mouth with the back of her hand. "The flak was heavy, and by the time I got there, the searchlights were everywhere. So I went off course and came from the other side. I had to drop my load a little off target, but close enough, I think."

"So that's it, then? The job's done?" Alex spoke to the figure in the dark.

"Not at all. We have to go back and bomb them again from a different direction. And then again after that. And after that." Lilya handed back her mug.

"My God," Alex murmured. She watched the pilots and ground crews as they came and went in an order that obviously made sense to them. But to Alex, they were shades in the underworld, condemned, like

Sisyphus, to repeat the same labor over and over again, in the darkness, for eternity.

Inna appeared again. "You're oiled and armed. Ready to go."

Lilya took a deep breath and blew on her hands. "All right. Keep me in your thoughts."

"I will," Inna and Alex replied simultaneously. *Ah, that was meant for Inna.* Alex felt her face warm and was glad it wasn't visible. Inna said nothing.

They stood together for the next round, like family members, while their common hero went forth into the night. And forty minutes later, she returned, only to take off again twenty minutes after that. Alex stayed by Inna, proving her mettle, but by daybreak, when the planes returned from the last circuit, she could hardly stand up.

The sky was orange when Lilya's plane touched the ground and clattered to the end of the runway. As she clambered out of the cockpit, finally visible in the morning light, Lilya took off her gloves and flight helmet. Her blond hair was matted with perspiration, and she squinted with fatigue as she embraced Inna. "It was a good night."

She laid her arm across Alex's shoulder as well. "Thank you for waiting for me. It's good to have someone to come back to." Then she followed Katia and the other pilots and navigators off the field toward the officers' quarters, which they'd nicknamed the Flying Cowshed.

"Bedtime," Inna announced, taking hold of Alex's arm. "Better enjoy it while you can. We have to be up by eight."

"Eight?" Alex looked at her watch. "That's only two hours from now."

"You can sleep longer if you want. The pilots and navigators are allowed to sleep longer. Only the mechanics have to report."

"I…I'll try to get up with the others. It's only fair."

Inna chuckled as they entered the bunker and dropped onto her bunk. "Thanks for your loyalty. Let's see how tough American women are." She chuckled again, then tugged off her boots and struggled out of her overalls.

Alex tried to be discreet but couldn't help but notice that Inna and some of the other women were wearing men's boxer drawers far too large for them and held together at the waist by string.

Inna caught her glance. "They look ridiculous, don't they?" She held the material out at the sides. "This is all we were issued. Three of them to each of us. I cut two of them down to fit, but when you run out of clean ones, you have to fall back on the originals."

"At least no one sees them when you're dressed."

"No, but they do see these." A woman feeding wood into the oil-drum stove held up one of her boots. "Also men's issue. We can walk in them only when we wrap double footcloths around our feet. And they expect us to work wearing these."

"How awful," Alex said, undressing near the stove for the warmth, slightly self-conscious in her perfectly tailored uniform. Her sleepwear, at least, was basic flannel and looked much like that worn by the other women.

She fell wearily onto her bunk, the hardest bed she'd ever lain on in her life, and her rucksack the worst pillow. *I'm never going to fall asleep on this*, she thought, as she dropped off into unconsciousness.

The sound of the other women moving around dragged her up from deepest sleep. Aching in every muscle, she forced herself to stand. The women were preparing for the morning duty, and out of solidarity she dressed as well. At least she'd get some good photos, she reminded herself as she laid her camera strap over her shoulder.

The mess hall was another dugout, though in place of an oil-drum heater, it had a rolling field-kitchen stove with openings at the top that could hold wide steel pots. To the side, an industrial-size samovar held boiling water for the tea. The same sort of planks that had been used to make up the bunks were carpentered into a narrow table and benches.

Having had no dinner, she was ravenous and was sure the other women who'd been doing hard physical labor were even more so. But breakfast, she learned, was a slice of hard black bread and sugarless tea. The bread was covered with a slice of meat of undeterminable origin. She studied it.

"Spam," her neighbor said. "A gift from your government. How do you like it?"

Alex took a cautious bite. "It's not bad. Considering."

"We love it and don't get it every day. It's better than the horsemeat they're eating in Moscow."

"Or the sawdust they're eating in Leningrad," one of the others added.

The conversation broke off suddenly, and all heads turned toward the entrance as Major Bershanskaya strode in.

"All right, ladies, finish up. The planes are waiting to be serviced and wood needs cutting. I'm sure someone has noticed that we had runway damage last night, and a team has to repair it before tonight. We don't want to shame ourselves in front of our journalist, do we? So fall in."

Alex glanced at her watch. The women had spent scarcely half an hour at breakfast before returning to duty. Was it the war, or was Bershanskaya a sadist?

"Miss Preston, would you care to join me on my inspection? You may bring your camera."

"Oh, yes. Of course." Alex caught up with the major, who'd started off toward the incoming runway. She could see now the section that had broken and sunk into the mud. Two of the mechanics were examining it, and two others were arriving with more fence posts. She marveled at their speed, all the more since she knew, by the pain in her own back, how dog-tired they were.

"The mechanics seem to work night and day. I have to say I'm in awe of them." She reflected for a moment. "What about the pilots and navigators?"

"They're allowed to sleep an hour longer simply because their lives depend on their being alert. Ah, but here some of them come now."

Alex glanced to the side where eight women were approaching the mess bunker. In their midst, though she could have spotted her anywhere, Lilya was in lively conversation with Katia and her navigator. Embarrassed by the inexplicable joy she felt, she turned away and photographed the women repairing the damage.

The major led her farther along the corduroy runway. "Do you have family, Miss Preston?"

"No. I'm on my own. Having a family would make doing what I do impossible. And you?"

"I have a son. Some of the other women have children, too. But all of them volunteered freely and competed for the right to serve."

"I don't doubt it for a moment. Last night on the field, I heard no complaints at all, except about the men's clothing that makes them look clownish."

"I can imagine. They're at the age when they care a lot about appearance. And they should. These women are in the flower of their lives, and many of them will perish. It would cheer them to think the world is watching them. As long as you don't interfere with their work or photograph anything strategic, you may take their personal pictures as much as you—and they—wish."

"I'll be happy to do that. They're all so photogenic anyhow."

Alex glanced back at the group of late sleepers who were arriving at the mess bunker. Lilya had fallen back to the rear of the group. At the last moment, before entering, she turned around and waved.

Alex's heart leapt.

CHAPTER ELEVEN

June 1942

The spring rains had finally stopped, and the ground had hardened enough to support heavy vehicles. Alex stood by one of the empty trucks as the armorers began rolling bombs and oil barrels from the storage depot.

"An advance-aerodrome? What's that?"

Inna lowered the panel of the truck bed and leaned a wooden ramp against it. "Since the range of our planes is limited, we need to take off from a spot as close to the target as possible, but the target keeps shifting. So, as the troops advance, we scout out fields near the front line and truck in bombs and fuel. Then, just before nightfall, we fly the planes there, arm and refuel, and make the attacks. That way, we increase our range."

"Logical." Alex snapped a single shot of Inna rolling one of the 100 kilo bombs up the ramp, then joined the woman behind her in hauling up the second one. "Don't you have to lay a runway first?"

"Not in this weather. As long as the ground is dry, the U-2 can land and take off almost anywhere, even a city street."

"So what's the plan?" Alex grunted as they reached the top of the ramp and nudged the bomb into its place. Behind them, a line of women rolled another twenty bomb cartridges along a wooden track.

"We'll ready the planes just before sundown, do the sorties for the next seven hours, and then return here to the main airfield. Then, in a couple of days, the strategists pick a new target, and we look for another new field."

"And this is ongoing?" Alex asked breathlessly as she dragged a can of machine-gun cartridges up the ramp.

"More or less. But we do have days when we don't fly. On Tuesday, for example, Red Army Rear is sending the bath truck along with the post and the food requisitions."

"Bath truck, oh, thank God." Alex's uniform had never been intended for battlefront use, so Major Bershanskaya had provided her with Russian overalls. After a week in the mud, she looked like all the others. And smelled like them, too.

The thought of a bath put a spring in her muscles as she hoisted the ammunition can onto the truck bed.

By peacetime standards the bath left much to be desired. The curtained-off tin tub on the back of the truck, fed by a coal-burning boiler on the side, was warm enough, and she didn't even mind that she had to bathe along with three other women. But the water wasn't drained, only recycled through the burner to refill the basin after each contingent passed through.

As a lieutenant and a foreign guest, Alex was allowed to bathe with the officers, so her group of four was the second to occupy the tub. After them came the pilots and navigators and, last of all, the ground crews, who needed it most.

Each woman had been issued a small disk of gritty military soap for the month, not nearly enough for a thorough scrub. Consequently she and most of the other women had scraped off the worst of their grime in buckets of water in their quarters before marching out in blankets to the common tub. Each group enjoyed only ten minutes submersed in the hot water, but those ten minutes were exquisite.

Then they had to climb out, retrieve the blanket they'd adapted as a towel, and descend from the truck to make way for the next bathers. Wrapped in a real towel pilfered from the Hotel Metropole, Alex rushed with the other freshly washed women back to the bunker to dress. For convenience, the pilots, too, used the mechanics' bunker as a changing station.

Alex rubbed herself dry, drew on fresh underwear and not-too-fresh trousers, and finished toweling her hair. At that moment, the next group of bathers arrived, of pilots and navigators. And Lilya.

With their widely separated quarters and conflicting schedules, Alex had caught sight of Lilya only at meal times, usually with Katia. They always smiled at each other and exchanged pleasantries, but nothing more. Now, here she was, dripping wet.

She stepped to the back of the bunker to make room for the others behind her and stood directly across from Alex, clutching an old blanket around her.

Alex smiled weakly, looked away, and drew on her shirt. She began to button it slowly, looking everywhere but at Lilya. Yet something drew her glance back.

The other women chatted among themselves, and as if they were in a sort of private, silent space, Lilya let the blanket drop to her waist. For what seemed an eternity, though it was probably only a few seconds, her blue eyes burned into Alex, and she exposed her pale, youthful breasts like a gift. Was it girlish innocence or deliberate provocation? No way to know. But, oh how lovely they were. Small and full with hard pink nipples that pointed upward.

Aroused and confused, Alex fled the bunker hoping the sun on her face concealed her blush. Had anyone seen the highly charged moment between them? Or had there even been one?

She paced for a moment, wondering what to do with herself while the others finished dressing. It was ridiculous, the whole thing. The other women didn't mind undressing together. What kind of idiot was she, behaving like a fourteen-year-old boy in front of Lilya's breasts?

A footstep caused her to turn around just as Katia Budanova emerged from the bunker freshly dressed. She nodded cordially, ran fingers through her short, still-damp hair, then sat down on one of the ammunition cases. Without speaking, she drew a small sack of machorka tobacco and a fragment of paper from the pocket of her tunic and began to roll out a cigarette.

Alex watched, intrigued. Katia was one of the few women in the regiment who smoked, and the habit seemed to fit her character. "Nice day for a scrub, isn't it?" She looked up at the early summer sky, making conversation.

"Uh-huh," Katia replied, striking a match on the wooden case and lighting the tightly rolled cigarette. It smelled sooty.

"Sort of too bad we have to go back to work tonight and get dirty again." Alex persisted.

Katia took a short puff and spit some speck of something to the side. "We're off duty tonight."

"Really?" That was good news, but now she was going to have to pry the reason out of this taciturn woman. "Why's that?"

"Red Army Rear's called off tonight's bombing. Because of the new assignments."

"New assignments? What does that mean?"

"Katia took another puff and finally looked directly at her. "It means that some of the pilots are being moved to the 586th fighter's regiment."

"Some of the pilots? Who?" Alex could already guess, and her heart sank.

"Well, me. Raisa Beliaeva, Lilya Drachenko. Couple of others." She leaned forward, elbows on her knees, twirling her cigarette.

"Oh." Alex tried to conceal her dismay. That's what you all wanted, right?"

"Yep. Come to the Flying Cowshed this evening and bring your mess kit. We'll have a little food—to celebrate."

Still reeling from Lilya's breasts, and now from the announcement that she was leaving, Alex stammered acceptance.

Alex stepped into the Flying Cowshed, and her first impression was that it didn't smell nearly as bad as the pilots had complained it did. It was less damp and better ventilated than the mechanics' bunker and so seemed to hold less of the cumulative female body odor.

The dozen pilots and navigators were sitting on their bunks or on the wooden floor next to an ammunition crate that served as a table. At the far end, Lilya sat on her bunk with her knees drawn up, talking to one of the navigators. She glanced up as Alex came in but didn't smile.

"Oh, looks like someone got packages from home." Alex pointed with her chin toward a basket at the center of the table that held potatoes, onions, and small green apples.

"Yes, my mother has a garden," a wide-faced woman said. Alex seemed to remember she was called Klavdia. "We also traded with some of the peasants for pickled beets, red sauerkraut, pickled herring, and… pickles."

"I sense a theme here," Alex said, and found a place on the floor. After several weeks on the sparse regimental diet, she was as hungry as all the other women. With the black bread that was also on the table, it really was a feast. "What did you trade from this side? I hope you didn't give away any of our bombs."

Klavdia laughed. "A pity we couldn't get rid of a few of them that way. No, just some of those stupid men's underpants. We all hate them, but the peasants always ask for them."

"Don't forget, we also have this." Tatyana, one of the navigators, reached up to a shelf over their heads and brought down a bottle. "The vodka we're supposed to be issued but never get. Since no one's flying tonight, Major Bershanskaya let us have it. Everyone, hold up your cups."

Alex unhooked hers from her mess kit and held it out, receiving a generous portion.

"To the bravest women in the Soviet Air Force." Katia raised her cup.

"So tell us the real reason for the party, Katia," Klavdia said. "Why am I sacrificing my mother's vegetables?"

"Because tomorrow, Lilya, Raisa, and I are transferring to the 586th fighter regiment."

"Oh, you lucky beasts!" Tatyana slapped Katia on the back. "We're so jealous. There's not a pilot here who doesn't dream of being a fighter."

"Guess so," Katia said, fishing out her machorka for another cigarette roll.

"Just make us proud while you're there." Major Bershanskaya came through the door. "It'll be a different game, you know, shooting down enemy planes. I know you have courage, but this will test your aviation skills. And you'll be flying alone." She raised her cup. "To you! And to the witches."

"Witches? You're calling us witches?" Lilya said.

Bershanskaya laughed. "I didn't give you that name. The Germans did. Our intelligence picked it up on their radio. Apparently we're keeping them awake all night and they're sick of it. They've named us *Nachthexen*. Night Witches. I think we should wear the name with distinction."

"Lilya the witch. Hmm. I like it. It has a certain menace to it."

"It sure does. They could have called us the night milkmaids."

Bershanskaya raised an authoritative hand. "My point is that the Germans have noticed us. We blow up their ammunition depots and vehicle pools, and we make it impossible for them to sleep. All in a night's work. Now someone pass me the bread."

Alex handed over the loaf and watched while the women consumed the various pickles, remembering the office parties at *Century* magazine. Layer cake, cheese blocks, platters of assorted cold cuts. Her stomach growled at the recollection, but only of the food. She wouldn't have traded a single boring, champagne-soaked evening with reporters for this battlefront picnic with the Night Witches.

She stayed for an hour, until she was slightly dizzy from her second cup of vodka. Lilya had remained curled up on her bunk the entire time, and when it seemed that nothing would budge her out of it, Alex decided it was time to leave. She struggled to her feet.

"Thank you so much for inviting me," she said, and groped along the wall to the door. It was pitch-black outside, and they weren't allowed to use torches except in emergencies. "Oh, crap," she muttered.

Someone touched her arm. "Come on. I'll walk back with you to your bunker."

"Lilya. Oh, yes, thanks." She was suddenly more lucid, if not exactly sober. "Guess I'm not much for vodka."

"It's all right. I know the layout of the field. I've landed in the dark often enough." Lilya took her by the arm, and the touch of her shoulder was thrilling. They took a few steps together, until Alex's eyes adapted to the dark.

The crescent moon shed a faint light on the field, and now she could see the shapes of the planes lined up like huge insects. The field was mysterious and silent, and she could still hear the distant laughter of the other women. She leaned against Lilya, smelling the soap she'd obviously used to wash her hair that morning.

"I'm sorry you're leaving. You have a lot of friends here."

"I know, but Katia will be with me, and I've requested that Inna be transferred so she can be my mechanic. She's awfully good, and Major Raskova knows she can learn the new engine fast."

Alex slowed her pace, to prolong the conversation. It didn't matter what they talked about. "Are the planes much different?"

"Oh yes. The Yak has ten times the speed and power of the U-2. And it's for fighting. They've got machine guns on the wings and a cannon in the propeller shaft. The firing button is on the control stick, and when all the guns fire at the same time, the whole plane shudders."

"You've flown one before?"

"Only once, on a test flight, and it was a thrill."

"I'll miss you. I think I'll be leaving shortly, too. I have to develop and send my pictures. It's what my boss is paying me for."

Lilya halted. "You're going back to Moscow?"

"Yes. I stay at the Hotel Metropole, where most of the correspondents live."

"Moscow. That's wonderful. Would you...could you take a note to my mother? Her name is Anna Svetlanova Drachenko, and she lives on the Smolenskaya Square, Number 22. She works in the factory making machine guns, but she's on the evening shift so you can find her at home in the middle of the day. She also works one day a week in the hotel laundry, but I don't know which day."

"I'll be happy to, of course, if you think it won't endanger her to talk to an American. But can't you also send letters through military post?"

"I do send letters through military post. But all our field letters are censored, and if you carried my note, I could say more. Please be discreet, though. Our family is already under suspicion, and talking to a foreigner would just be another black mark."

"I'd love to meet your mother. Give me the note at breakfast tomorrow before you leave."

They were standing face-to-face now. Lilya laid a hand on her shoulder. "Thank you. And I'm sorry we had so little time together. It seems all I did was fly and sleep."

Alex wished she could make out Lilya's expression. But her face was just a vague image in the dark with a thin halo of hair that caught a bit of moonlight. "I understand. As for you, please be careful."

Lilya chortled. "I'm not sure what a careful aerial dogfight would look like."

"No, I suppose there isn't any such thing. But will you at least wear your New York scarf to keep warm?"

"I'll wear it every day. I promise." Then, suddenly, she bent forward and pressed a quick light kiss on Alex's lips. "Keep me in your thoughts."

"I will. I do. All the time."

❖

Pure inebriation enabled Alex to sleep the rest of that night, but when she awakened late in the morning to an empty bunker, it was to a sense of deep loss. She'd missed breakfast, the last opportunity to see Lilya and take possession of the precious letter. She felt an overwhelming sense of guilt and fecklessness. Some beacon of liberty she was.

She dragged herself to the mess dugout, hoping some food was left, and found Inna. They sat together over their tasteless kasha and bitter tea. But they had nothing to say, and when Inna left to join the ground crews, Alex didn't go with her.

Instead, she returned to the bunker, where a few of the armorers had come off duty and were writing letters or embroidering. The needlework, she supposed, was a way to leave off being a soldier for a little while and do the quiet girlish things their mothers had taught them. Most, she noted, didn't even have embroidery thread but used fibers from their blue underwear or from any fabric they could unravel without incurring penalties for damaging military property.

She watched them for a few moments until one of them glanced up and smiled. "This would make a good picture, don't you think? To show America that we're not all brutes."

Alex agreed and opened her camera case for her Rolleiflex. Her finger brushed against something paperlike, and she drew it out.

Lilya's letter with a Moscow address in rounded girlish letters. She must have slipped it in while Alex slept off her vodka. Her lethargy evaporated.

She hid it again, took a few photos, and left the bunker.

It didn't take her long to spot the tall, broad-shouldered Major Bershanskaya out on the field. She was in the process of reprimanding one of the mechanics for taking off her boots while she worked on the plane, but it seemed less a berating than a discussion.

Alex liked that about her, that when she exerted her authority, it was always with an eye to finding a solution rather than exercising power. Even here, she finished her reprimand by saying, "There's a shoemaker in the village. Maybe you can get those boots cut down."

The moment she stepped away, Alex approached her. "I'm sorry to bother you, Major."

"Yes, what is it, Miss Preston?"

"I appreciate your letting me photograph the women, but I've run out of film. It's time for me to return to Moscow. And I was wondering…"

"How you'll get there."

"Yes, of course. Lilya Drachenko flew me here as you'll recall, but I don't suppose anyone is flying in the direction of Moscow in the next days."

"Unfortunately not. But you're in luck. The bath truck will be returning to the railroad station, and from there you can take one of the troop trains to Moscow."

Alex cringed inwardly at the agonizing trip ahead of her, most likely under strafing fire, but the women around her were enduring worse. "Thank you. I'll be ready to leave when the truck does."

As she strode back to her bunker, she fingered the letter in her side pocket. A letter that tied her to Lilya Drachenko.

CHAPTER TWELVE

It was the afternoon of the Fourth of July, but Alex begged off the vodka-fueled celebration by the Americans in the hotel dining room.

Instead, she developed her film in her tiny toilet darkroom. Roll after roll of the Night Witches, doing everything but flying their U-2s. No doubt it would have been embarrassing, even dangerous, to reveal the flimsy antiquated craft the Soviet Air Force flew.

But she smiled at the half-dozen photos of Inna, dwarfed in her overalls, of Commander Bershanskaya looking stern, and of the virile Katia Budanova in flying gear studying a map.

The long-distance takeoff and landing shots by the partial light of dawn or dusk wouldn't pass the censor, but she liked them and would keep them for herself, unpublished. The censors would certainly approve photos of the women hauling the 100-kilo bombs, chopping wood, digging trenches, and laying fence boards over the mud. And George would love the human-interest shots of the off-duty women sitting on the ground and mending or writing home.

The most precious ones still hung on the drying line, and now she regretted taking so few. Just those two, snapped as Lilya crossed the field and the original and unpermitted photo of her and Inna in front of Lilya's U-2, would be her personal treasures.

She'd had it all wrong about Soviet women soldiers. They were personable and warm, and she felt enormous affection for them. Inna, Katia, Raisa, and even the two commanders Raskova and Bershanskaya. She felt real pleasure talking to them, laughing with them, watching them work.

And then there was Lilya. Who'd kissed her. What was it that attracted her so?

She wasn't ashamed of her desire for women and hadn't actually slept with one simply because no woman she cared for had ever sought her out. But *had* Lilya sought her out? Or was the kiss merely a bit of reckless play, like flying somersaults in her plane?

Alex brooded. Some new emotion she hadn't experienced before was nibbling at the back of her mind, and she finally recognized it. Longing.

She shook it off and snatched up her jacket. She had a letter to deliver.

The rumpled NKVD man was on duty, as always, and she didn't want him following her. Fraternizing with Russians wasn't illegal, but discouraged. Part of Stalin's paranoia, she supposed, that all foreigners were suspect and might pry information out of innocent Muscovites. She suspected also that the Kremlin didn't like their tightly controlled citizens learning too much about foreign prosperity.

She'd studied her map of Moscow in the privacy of her room and found Smolenskaya Square near a metro station. The trick was to ditch her minder.

In the end, it was ridiculously easy, since the poor fellow apparently had several charges to keep an eye on at once and was slow to react. Or perhaps he simply hadn't seen enough espionage movies, for all she had to do was descend to the hotel kitchen and leave through one of its service doors.

Smolenskaya Square was shabby but no worse than much of the rest of residential Moscow. She walked quickly until she found a large apartment building with four entryways, and Number 22 was the third one. Lilya had been right. It was midday, and no one seemed to be home.

At the entrance she faced a staircase. She followed it up to the second floor, where it opened to a narrow corridor, and she continued down to the door marked Number 9. Now, if only Anna Svetlanova Drachenko was home.

She tapped gently on the door.

"Who is it?" someone inside asked.

"Aleksandra Preston," she said, hoping there were no neighbors to overhear. "A friend of Lilya. May I come in?"

The door opened a crack and a woman peered out at her.

Alex leaned in close and dropped her voice. "She asked me to deliver a letter to you."

Wordlessly, Anna Drachenko stepped back to admit her.

Alex stopped directly inside and glanced around as Anna shut the door behind her. They stood in a sort of entranceway from which she could see a kitchen, presumably shared, and a short interior corridor with two doors on each side. The entryway smelled of boiled cabbage and unwashed laundry.

Anna led her to the second door on the left and drew her into what was obviously her allotted portion of the apartment. A narrow single room with a painted cabinet near the door and a minute table across from it. Above the table a set of shelves held dishes, folded cloths, books, and a row of small photographs.

At the far end of the room was a bed, and at its foot, the only window. It looked out onto the wall of another apartment building. Close by, against the wall, a cushioned bench held several elaborately embroidered pillows. Had this served as Lilya's bed?

There was no bathroom in sight, and Alex assumed that this too was shared with the co-residents of the collective apartment. She cringed inwardly at the overwhelming sense of confinement.

"Please, have a seat," Anna said, gesturing toward the covered bench, and Alex sat down.

While Anna drew up a chair from the table for herself, Alex studied her face and movements. She greatly resembled her daughter, though her hair was white rather than blond. The same bright blue eyes shone from eyelids sagging with age and fatigue, and she had the same full musculature around the mouth. But her face was gaunt, due, no doubt, to the scant rations allowed the Muscovites.

"Please, tell me about my daughter." Anna clasped long, callused hands. "Is she all right?"

"She's doing very well," Alex was happy to say. How dreadful it would have been to bring bad news to this woman. "She's been promoted to another regiment and is flying better planes."

"Yes, she sent me a field post to say that."

"Good. So you know that already. But she also gave me a letter, a much longer one. It's sealed, and I came here discreetly, so no one knows about it but us." She slid it from her side pocket and laid it on the table.

Anna held the envelope for a moment in her hand, her face brightening at the sudden gift, then tore it open. She read the full page of text, nodding faintly and pressing her lips together, then folded it again.

"Thank you, Aleksandra Preston, for bringing me this. My daughter tells me here that you are a trusted friend. She also writes of looking forward to flying the new planes but worries about the commander. Do you know her?"

"The commander? That's Tamara Kazar, I believe."

Anna skimmed the letter again. "Yes, that's what she writes. But that woman doesn't fly herself and has no knowledge of flying strategies. Lilya's sure she was appointed by someone for political reasons."

General Osipenko. Alex remembered his appearance at Engels.

"I'm sorry to hear it. Nothing damages morale more than knowing one's leaders are corrupt. On the other hand, I did meet Major Raskova at Engels, and she seemed to have fully earned the loyalty all the women give her. Major Bershanskaya, too."

"My daughter spoke highly of them as well. But..." She dropped her voice. "Sad to say, this government has much corruption and injustice. I know from bitter experience."

Alex leaned forward, muting her voice as well. "Do you mean Stalin's purges? We heard about them in the United States, though not in much detail."

"Yes, exactly. Lilya's own father was denounced as an enemy of the people just for complaining about Stalin's policies. Though I'm sure she never told you."

"No, she didn't. But that makes her own patriotism all the more courageous."

Anna shrugged faintly. "I suppose you could look at it that way. But it was a cruel thing to make her reject her father, who loved her. She was only seven when he was arrested, and she never knew how close she came to losing both of us. There's a special work camp for wives of enemies of the people, and she would have been put into one of those horrible state orphanages."

"What happened to your husband? Was he sent to the Gulag?" Alex knew little more than the word itself and that it referred to the system of forced labor camps in inhospitable terrains.

"No. He was executed in Lubyanka prison. And I couldn't even let his daughter mourn him. She had to survive among the other children, you see, and she could only do that if she accepted the condemnation. She was terribly confused for a while, because she loved him, but she was young, and in time she came to accept the lie."

"That must have been terrible for you."

"Yes, but Lilya was the most important thing in my life, and I had to help her succeed. I encouraged her to enter the Komsomol as a way to remove the stain of being the daughter of a traitor. It was the only way to have a decent life."

Anna stood up to fetch something from her shelf and returned with a framed photo. "This is from the time she was at Engels. She finally got a tunic that fit properly and had her official photo taken." Anna held out the picture. "My angel, all in uniform."

It was a frontal, upper-body image of Lilya, apparently sitting down. She wore her new uniform, with shoulder bars and three metal buttons on the high tunic collar. Wavy short blond hair fell back from a round face that stared, unsmiling, into the lens. Alex handed it back. "I suppose your letter doesn't say where she's stationed."

"No, they're not allowed to tell us that. I'd give a lot to know and to be sure she's safe."

Anna brushed dust off the frame and set the photo back on its shelf. When she returned to the table, she said softly, "I love Russia, but the great ideals of Lenin were never fulfilled. Of course we keep repeating them, in the face of the most outrageous cruelties. I lost all faith in Stalin after they killed my husband. A good, honest man." She stared off into space for a moment, as if gathering her thoughts.

"Do you know Pushkin?"

Alex blinked at the non sequitur. "No, I'm afraid not. My brief schooling in Saint Petersburg didn't include Romantic poetry."

Anna nodded. "He was our greatest poet. I always thought he was too cynical, but now I understand him. He wrote once, 'Dearer to me than a host of base truths is the illusion that exalts.'"

"Yes?" Alex didn't see the connection.

"What I mean to say is, the ideals of Communism are the illusion, while the base truths are what our government has actually done to us."

"I see. But I suppose now that the Soviet Union is at war, it's more important than ever to keep the illusion." She also thought for a moment. "I wonder if that's true of all forms of nationalism."

Anna shrugged. "Now there you have surpassed my powers of analysis. And I'm weary of analysis, anyhow. All I care about now is my child. Do you understand? Even if she were to flee Russia, as long as I knew she was safe, I'd be content."

"Yes, I do understand. If I had a loved one, she would be more important to me than any doctrine." Alex stood up. "I should probably leave before your neighbors come home, don't you think?"

"You're right." Anna got up as well and led her through the apartment to the front door. "Thank you for bringing me this lovely gift. If you see my daughter, please tell her I think of her every hour." Anna embraced her lightly and planted a quick kiss on her cheek.

"Of course I will," Alex responded mechanically, though she had no idea how she could manage to see Lilya again. But suddenly she wanted to, urgently.

CHAPTER THIRTEEN

July, August 1942

Alex strode into the Hotel Metropole just as dinner was being served. Without bothering to return to her room, she swept her gaze around the dining room, hoping to see a table where she could sit by herself. But Henry Shapiro happened to catch sight of her, and he waved her over.

Of all the foreign correspondents living or working at the hotel, Henry was one she got along with best. He could be abrasive, but he was one of the very few who also spoke Russian, and he was knowledgeable about Russian history and politics. He was sitting with Eddy Gilmore, whom she liked less, but he was a decent fellow. They both seemed unusually cheerful as she pulled up a chair.

"What are you two smirking about? It can't be the vodka. They haven't served it yet."

"Nope. It's the good news we just got," Henry explained. "You know, up until now it was hard as hell to get near the battlefield. Most of the time they just took us on little tours with military guides who explained what the troops had done or were going to do."

The waiter interrupted their conversation with the evening meal, boiled potatoes and something brown that had probably once been beef. She thought of Anna Drachenko and what she was probably eating that evening and refrained from comment.

"So, what's changed?" she asked, then began chewing a chunk of meat.

Henry surveyed his plate and added quantities of salt. "The war's changed. For the first time since Moscow, the Germans have been held up, this time around Voronezh, and the Russians are mounting a counteroffensive. For some reason, the Press Department has decided they want us to see for ourselves how great they are. Approval came through today." He took the first bite.

"Voronezh." She stared into the air recalling the geography of southern Russia. "That's almost directly south of Moscow, near the Don, right? When are you leaving?"

"They didn't say, exactly. In three or four days, probably," Eddy said.

"That's great. You guys need a photographer?"

Eddy speared a piece of potato. "Not up to us. If you want to come along, contact the Press Department. Voronezh is the front line, though. You may have to sleep rough."

She thought for a moment. She could hang around a Moscow hotel snapping more and more photos of air raids and refugees, or get a little dirty again and see the actual war. "I'll apply tomorrow."

Alex tossed her rucksack up first, and then one of the men helped her climb onto the back of the truck. Wooden crates of ammunition, fuel, and food took up most of the space, and five of them crouched in what was left.

As the truck took off, she glanced around at the men she'd be spending the next months with. Besides Henry and Eddy, she recognized Ralph Parker of *The London Times* and Larry LeSueur of CBS.

She shook hands with the four of them. "So, do we have any idea what we're getting into?"

"More of the Russians getting their asses kicked," Gilmore said. "They've attempted a counteroffensive against the German 4th Panzer Army, but it goes back and forth. So far, it's a stalemate."

He flicked a cigarette butt out of the truck onto the road. "I don't expect much. The Reds only keep fighting because we keep feeding them, but they stink at it."

"Don't mind Eddy," Henry said. "He hates everything Communist. Me, I have a bit more hope. It does look grim, though. The Germans have taken the west side of the Voronezh River, and it looks like their opening move to get to Baku and then Stalingrad."

Parker spoke up. "They want Baku for the oilfields, but why Stalingrad? It has no strategic value."

"Prestige," Alex said. "A morale booster. They couldn't take Moscow, so the next best thing is to take down the city with Stalin's name."

"Pretty interesting theory from someone who hasn't seen battle," Eddy remarked.

"Oh, but I have. I spent a few weeks with the women's regiment."

"Women's regiment? Never heard of that." She heard derision in Parker's voice. "What do *they* do? Try to seduce the enemy?"

She bristled. "It's always sex with you guys, isn't it? In fact, they're night bombers. And they fly without radio or parachutes. What does it say about the West when the Communists have more respect for women than you do?"

"Hey, take it easy." Parker raised a conciliatory hand. "It was just a wisecrack. I appreciate that Russian women are tough. I've known a few of them, if you get my drift."

Alex turned away and studied the war-torn landscape. Were these guys going to be her only support for the next weeks? Suddenly she longed for quiet and unpretentious conversation with Eva Bershanskaya and Marina Raskova. How much more would she have learned about the war and the Russian people from them?

CHAPTER FOURTEEN

September 1942

Katia Budanova landed her Pe-2 on the airfield, relieved to be on the ground. The three aircraft had successfully engaged the enemy planes and downed two of them. But in view of the worsening weather conditions, Commander Raskova had ordered them to halt pursuit and return to base.

Grumbling at the missed opportunity, Katia obeyed. She had been assigned to the 586th regiment on another airfield, but then Stalin's "Not a step backward" order had arrived. Suddenly, pilots were switched around like chess pieces, and she'd been thrilled to learn that she was to fly with Marina Raskova and her dive-bombers.

With the skies around the Stalingrad quadrant full of Luftwaffe, they had made four runs, broken only by brief refueling and rearmament stops, and the last one had left her head buzzing with hunger and fatigue. Still, it would have been nice to take out that last enemy plane.

Marina Raskova walked just ahead of her, but her labored gait and round shoulders told Katia she was just as exhausted. Of course she was. She demanded nothing of her pilots that she didn't do herself. She had a strange combination of womanly warmth and unflagging determination, and Katia would have followed her anywhere.

Katia was well aware that she loved the commander more than she could ever love a man. It had shocked her at first, but then she came to accept it wasn't a bad thing. She could admire and emulate her commander's courage without shame, and in a sort of chivalrous loyalty, she imagined that every enemy plane she shot down was a gift to her.

And she'd done quite well in that department, too. Her only scoring competition was from the slightly more reckless Lilya Drachenko, who was momentarily out of action. But sweet Lilya was more like a younger sister, who always seemed a bit dreamy and lately had talked about nothing but the American journalist.

She'd let her thoughts drift to supper and a smoke when she was brought up short. Just ahead of her, Major Gridniev, commander of the airfield, had come out to meet Major Raskova, and the conversation seemed serious. Katia drew close enough to hear.

It was what they all dreaded. One of their planes that had set out earlier was down. The crew had survived their crash landing but sustained serious injury and had radioed in their coordinates.

Raskova turned to the pilots who stood at her shoulders. "You're dismissed, but I'm going back."

"I don't think so, Major," Gridniev said, laying a hand on her arm. "We'll send another crew. You've been up four times already."

She shook her head. "Out of the question. They're my women and I'll take care of them. Have the mechanics refuel my plane so I can leave immediately."

"I'm going too, Comrade Major," Katia said, falling into step with her as they headed toward the mess bunker. I'll ask Inna to refuel my plane."

"Thank you, Katia. I knew you'd volunteer. Come have some hot tea before we take off again." She glanced over her shoulder, and Katia was shocked to see her eyes, bloodshot and with dark circles around them. Even her hair, always held so tightly in a bun, was coming apart, and strands hung loose on both sides of her face.

"I know I'm out of place to say so, Comrade Major, but you look exhausted. Commander Gridniev was right. Why don't you rest for a change and let Klavdia and me take care of this?"

"Impossible. I know those women personally. Many of them joined the regiment because of me, and I couldn't rest for a moment knowing they were injured and waiting in the cold for help." She laid a hand on Katia's shoulder, something she'd never done before. "No. We'll bring them back and then *all* of us will rest."

In less than twenty minutes, the two Pe-2s took off again into the fog. The same fog that had prevented their earlier pursuit of an enemy plane less than an hour before.

They ascended to 1,900 meters and cruised westward, though the cloud mass they flew in gradually became so dense Katia lost any sense of moving forward. "Visibility is almost zero, Comrade Major. Please advise, over," she said into her radio mouthpiece.

From her earphones she heard, "Descend five hundred meters and see if we can get under this cloud cover. Over."

They dropped to 1,400, then to a thousand, and flew in a wide circle over the crash-site coordinates according to the compass, but still had no visibility in any direction. "We're losing daylight," Katia said. "Even if the clouds open up, we won't be able to see them on the ground. Over."

"You're right, Lieutenant. We'll have to try to land before we run out of fuel. Over." Exhaustion and disappointment at their failure was evident in her voice.

"I've lost visual of you, Comrade Major. I'm flying blind. My altitude is currently 500 meters. Should I try to land as well? Over."

"Stay at that altitude until I advise. I'm going in low to look for landing space. At some point I should be able to get beneath the cloud cover. Circle until I've landed safely and I'll guide you in by radio. Over."

"Yes, Comrade Major. Standing by. Over."

A few minutes went by with radio silence and only the roar of the airplane engine in her ears as she watched the compass. Suddenly, soundlessly, the gray mist all around her flashed pink and orange, and a second later she heard the dull sound of the explosion.

"Comrade Major, what happened? Major Raskova, please reply. Repeat, what happened? Reply! Reply!"

CHAPTER FIFTEEN

September 1942

Alex's "tour" lasted longer than any of them had expected. Voronezh, Rostov, Stavropol, Krasnodor. They'd just been names on a map, but now their images were marked in her memory, filled with blood and smoke. Some towns they'd reached before the onslaught, others were already ruined, and occasionally the battle still raged. She photographed men hunched behind their exploding cannons or silhouetted against flames, their long bayonets like spears.

As they edged south- and westward, more fighter planes began to appear overhead, and Henry taught her how to identify them by their outlines as German or Russian. When she could spot the Russian Yaks and Sturmoviks, she wondered if the pilots were women, if one of them might have blond hair curling out from under a flight helmet.

She traveled back with the others to Moscow twice, submitted her photographs to the Press Department censors, and sent the approved ones off to *Century* by way of diplomatic pouch. The four men submitted their dispatches as well, grousing at every deletion by the same censor, then dutifully cabling their sanitized stories at Central Telegraph. Each trip back she wired George Mankowitz that she was alive and well and photos were forthcoming. Then she went back to the hotel to hand wash her laundry.

On her third trip back to the front, as she cleaned her lenses in preparation for another patrol, Parker came into the press dugout.

"Hey, this should interest you. I was just at division headquarters trying to get an interview when the news came in. One of their big women aviators just crashed."

"Who? Which one?" *Please let it be someone I don't know.*

"I don't remember the name, exactly. Roskov, Kosova, something like that."

"Marina Raskova?" Her heart sank.

"Yes, that's it. That's the one. Here, I can't read Russian, but you can. Take a look yourself." He held out a copy of the military newspaper *Red Star.* "The Russians seem to think it's a big deal."

Alex recalled a brilliant, dedicated woman who, in peacetime, she might have sought as a friend. The mother superior to hundreds of women pilots, navigators, and ground teams. They must be shattered.

She skimmed the article, hoping Parker had misunderstood, but the text confirmed the tragedy. Even Stalin had paid homage, signing his name to the list expressing condolences.

"She'll have a state funeral," she said. "On Sunday."

Parker brightened. "You think there's a story there?"

Annoyed at his ignorance of Marina Raskova, she brushed him off. "Couldn't say. Anyhow, I knew her. I'm going back to pay my respects. When can I get a ride?"

"Talk to the division commander. He'll know if anyone's going to the Kremlin."

She was already out of the dugout.

It took two days for her to hitch a ride on a medical-evacuation flight returning to Moscow, but she need not have hurried. Marina Raskova's remains had to be transported to Moscow on a special train. Once there, they lay in state in a covered casket at the House of the Unions for three days while thousands of mourners passed by in a somber line.

Alex joined them on the day of the funeral. When she reached the coffin surrounded by red flags and Communist symbols, she stepped out of line and waited until the honor guard arrived. The six uniformed men lifted the coffin and carried it out to a gun carriage drawn by a jeep. Governmental figures as well as officers and soldiers carrying a wreath slow-marched into Red Square. One of them bore a small red cushion displaying her medals. Alex followed as the gun carriage moved across the square to the Kremlin Wall Necropolis and stopped for a brief funeral ritual. An old woman stood now beside the coffin holding the hand of a young girl. Marina Raskova's bereaved mother and daughter, she supposed.

General Osipenko, as well as a few others from the Kremlin whom she didn't know, addressed the crowd, and at the end, the color guard fired off a gun salute. The Soviet national anthem sounded through the public speakers on the wall as the gun carriage moved on into the necropolis. It was purely ceremonial, she knew, since Marina Raskova would not be buried, but cremated, and her ashes placed within the Kremlin wall.

Alex snapped her photos as discreetly as possible, for all around her people wept, and she shared their bereavement. She didn't believe in an afterlife and would have scoffed at the notion that the major's spirit knew she was present. But it seemed important to be there at the coffin to mark the passing of an extraordinary woman.

As the other Muscovites began to wander away, she started back toward the Metropole, wondering how she would get back to the Southern Front, though she was already weary at the thought.

Someone stepped out directly in front of her, bringing her to a halt.

"Anna Drachenko," Alex said softly.

"Hello, Miss Preston. I hoped I'd find you here taking your pictures. I was afraid to ask for you at the hotel."

"How did you know I was in Moscow?"

"I didn't, of course. But Lilya sent me to look for you. She thought you might be here photographing this tragic moment."

"Lilya?" Alex brightened suddenly, trying to make sense of the remark. "Lilya sent you? How?"

Anna took her by the arm and led her in the direction of the Metro. "She was shot down and wounded two weeks ago. The hospitals are so full, she requested to recover at home with me. She's there now and wants to see you."

"Wounded? How seriously?" A jumble of thoughts crowded in all at the same time. "Aren't you afraid of being spotted with me?"

Anna replied to the last question first. "Not today. Today we're just two people in the crowded Metro." She pulled her along faster. "She was wounded in the leg, but she can tell you about it herself."

Neighbors on the street and in the corridor witnessed Alex's arrival, but if any of her neighbors were denouncers, Anna had apparently decided to take the risk. She led them into the collective apartment, where several women stared dumbfounded at her. As if in defiance of them, she pointed to Alex in her air-force uniform and said, "This American lieutenant was a friend of Marina Raskova." That seemed sufficient to turn their expressions of suspicion to admiration.

Then Anna opened the door to her private space and drew her in.

Lilya Drachenko sat upright, supported by pillows on the bench that Alex had rightly guessed was her bed. Her face was radiant. "Come, sit down," Anna said, and Alex realized she hadn't budged.

Without taking her eyes from Lilya's face, she drifted over and kissed her on the forehead. "I'm…so happy to see you again."

Lilya brushed her fingertips along Alex's chin. "I didn't know if you were in Moscow. I just hoped."

"When I heard about Major Raskova's death, I returned as soon as I could, to say good-bye. If I'd known you were here I'd have come sooner, much sooner." Feeling the chair Anna shoved behind her knees, she sat down.

"I've been crying since I got the news. I loved her. We all loved her. Did you take pictures?"

"Yes, a few. I'll send them through the embassy and bypass the censor. I may get in trouble, but I don't care. I want the Americans to see them and learn the name Marina Raskova."

"Yes, I like that. I want them to know her, too. Where were you when you heard?"

"In Kamensk, with some other journalists. We go where the Kremlin lets us go."

Lilya offered a wan smile. "How ironic. I took off from Kamensk the day I was shot down."

Alex winced. "Shot down. Such terrible words."

"Yes, they are," Anna said, standing behind her. "I almost fainted when the air-force people contacted me."

Lilya's eyes shone at the change of subject to the air battle. "You should have seen us, Alex. We were six in our Yaks facing six Messerschmitts. An even fight, you'd think, but I got separated from my team and it seemed like all six Me-109s were after me. I couldn't escape them, so I dove toward them and knocked out one of them. His mate circled back, though, and got my plane and my leg."

"I can't bear to hear the story," Anna said. "While you two talk, I'll go dress for work." Anna took a towel from the shelf and left for the communal bathroom, closing the door behind her.

Lilya continued, still excited. "It didn't even hurt at first, it just felt wet. I bent down for a second to look at it, and just then, another shell crashed through the canopy, right where my head had been. I suppose the wounded leg saved my life."

"And you were able to land?" Alex was incredulous.

"Yes. I swung back to the airfield, which wasn't far, got the plane onto the runway, and rolled to a stop. Then I blacked out. When I came to, my comrades were dragging me like a sack of coal out of the cockpit. They got me to a hospital, where they said the bullet actually chipped my leg bone but didn't break it. They kept me for a few days, but when the doctors needed the bed for more serious cases, they let me come home."

Alex lifted the blanket to see the damaged leg, but it was splinted and bandaged to the knee. "How long have you been here?"

"Ten days already. As soon as I can walk normally, I'm going back. A lot more German planes need to be shot down."

"It sounds very different from being a Night Witch. I mean, you actually engage the enemy, face-to-face, in daylight."

"It is. And the planes are completely different, too. I love the Yak, though it was hell to learn. They're single-seat machines so the instructors couldn't fly with us. The first few trips were pretty hair-raising."

She was looking off into space now, obviously remembering. "It's incredible. You can do swoops and dives, all kinds of rolls and loops, zigzags and spins, with so much *power*! It's intoxicating." Alex could see the excitement in her eyes.

"When do you think you can walk again?"

"I can walk now, with crutches, and each day I get a little stronger."

Alex stifled the urge to caress her. "You look…wonderful."

Lilya's expression grew somber. "Do you have to go back? To the front, I mean? Can you stay a few days in Moscow? It's so quiet here when Momma's working. I go crazy."

Alex considered for moment. "It's a little complicated. Stalin has given certain journalists permission to travel with the troops, and I'd have to reapply with the Press Department for another occasion. But, yes. I'll do that."

Lilya stared with eyes that paralyzed her. "You're amazing," she whispered in admiration. "You've come from so far away, from the other side of the world. And when I'm around you, it's like a door opens up and I feel a little bit of that other world trickling in."

"There *is* a whole other world outside. I hope I can show it to you some day."

Lilya still held her hand. "You talk like my mother. About all the possibilities. She's a loyal Communist, of course, but doesn't like Stalin."

"She has good reason. She told me about your father's arrest. I'm sorry. It's a brutal regime, isn't it?"

"Lilya grimaced as if slapped. "I don't want to talk about my father. Besides, those of us who fight, we don't do it for Stalin. We fight for the Motherland, for each other."

Bringing up Lilya's father had obviously been a mistake, and Alex blushed at the faux pas. She touched Lilya's cheek with her fingertips. "I wish you didn't have to fight at all. You have a long life ahead of you, with children and grandchildren, and a dacha somewhere in the Ukraine."

Lilya grasped the hand and held it to her face. "I never dream about that, only about flying. Flying all over the world." Then abruptly, she said, "Tell me about New York."

Alex heard the door open behind her and turned. Anna came in wearing overalls.

"Momma, Alex was just about to tell me about New York."

"Oh, yes. I'd like to hear about it," Anna said, kicking off her slippers and pulling on a pair of battered work boots.

"Is it true that the rich capitalists live in the high buildings while the workers and the black people live in poverty?" Lilya asked.

Alex thought for a moment. "Yes, you see a lot of difference between the rich and the poor, and yes, the very rich live in penthouses at the top of the buildings. But it's possible to climb up from poverty, at least for some. My father arrived poor, but he knew horses and got a good job taking care of them for the police department."

"What about the black people?" Anna asked, though her tone revealed genuine interest, not sarcasm.

"That's a sore spot for Americans. Yes, most black people are poor and live in the worst parts of the cities. And many of them don't have jobs, or have very bad ones. I...I don't know why."

Anna tied up her boot. "Under Communism, at least everyone has a job."

"I was never much interested in politics," Alex admitted. "But I think it's a trade-off. In the hard capitalist world of the US, each person has a lot of freedom but no real protection. President Roosevelt brought in Social Security, but that's based on having a job in the first place. Each one has to struggle for himself, and if things go against him, he just falls to the bottom. Here, everyone has a job and food and healthcare, but each person has to do what the government tells him to, and no one can speak out against the party."

"Every nation has its dogma," Anna said. "Remember, 'Dearer to me than a host of base truths...'"

"'...is the illusion that exalts.'" Lilya finished her sentence. "That's my mother's favorite Puskin quote. Please don't think we're always so cynical."

"Maybe some day after the war you both can come visit me and see what it's like under *our* dogmas." She had said "both" but looked directly at Lilya.

"Oh, that would be fun. Is your Times Square anything like our Red Square?"

"I can assure you, it's not at all. It's full of private businesses and shops, and it's not even a square. More a crossing of two main streets. But if you come, I promise to take you there, and to Macy's and buy you all the scarves you want."

Anna stood up and glanced over at a small clock on the shelf. "I'm sorry, my shift starts in fifteen minutes. Please stay, Miss Preston. My daughter is lonely and I can see you're good for her." She gave them both quick kisses and let herself out.

The door clicked closed, and Alex realized she and Lilya were alone for the first time since the night on the airfield—when Lilya had kissed her.

She fidgeted for a moment, trying to recall what they'd just been talking about.

"I've missed you," Lilya said suddenly.

"Have you? I'd have thought you had your mind on other things."

"Did you miss me?" Blue eyes looked up at her with great earnestness.

"Yes. I did. And I always worried you'd be shot down."

"And then I was, so you can stop worrying now."

"Well, please don't do that anymore."

"I'll try, but the Germans, you know...they're very rude. We keep asking them to leave, but they refuse. Very annoying."

"I'm glad you can joke about it, but it was by the sheerest bit of luck that you survived."

"It was you who brought me luck. I was wearing your scarf. It still holds a bit of your smell."

"My smell? Oh, dear. That must not be very nice."

"But it is. It smells of, I don't know. Of warm potatoes, something welcoming like that. The same smell that night we said good-bye on the airfield. Do you remember? I kissed you."

Alex blushed. "Of course I remember. I just wasn't sure what it meant. I still don't know."

"Perhaps I should show you again, and then you'll know."

Alex's heart pounded. Lilya was playing with her, and she was at her mercy. She gazed for long moments into eyes as blue as the Russian sky.

"Perhaps."

"I can't get up. You'll have to come to me."

"Come to you," Alex repeated inanely. "Yes." She moved from her chair to perch at the edge of Lilya's slender bed. A smile opened slowly across Lilya's full lips as Alex bent over her.

Loud thudding came from the door, and Alex jumped away.

"Lilya Grigorevna." A voice came through the closed door. "Someone is here to see you. An official."

Lilya looked anxiously at Alex.

Official. That was never something good, Alex thought, cracking the door. To her shock, she recognized him. A short, plump man with a bald spot in a rumpled suit. The NKVD man.

"You will come with me, please," he said.

Fear, guilt, regret. As he led her down the grimy staircase, Alex could hardly focus her thoughts. Had she mortally endangered the Drachenko family? Was she in danger herself? God, what had she done?

He led her to a car parked around the corner. "Get in," he said, opening the door on the passenger side, which diminished her anxiety somewhat. In all the abduction movies she'd seen, the victim was always pressed into the backseat. Or the trunk. His hard expression fixed, he came around to the other side and started the car. Another kind of fear struck her.

"Who are you and where are you taking me?"

He spoke without looking at her, staring straight ahead. "Never mind who I am. More important is where I am *not* taking you. To NKVD headquarters."

The words NKVD headquarters nonetheless struck fear in her heart. "I'm with the US Air Force and they'll be looking for me." She was bluffing.

He ignored the threat. "You're causing trouble," he announced abruptly. "The Drachenko family is already suspect because of the father. Your presence does nothing but rekindle suspicion."

Alex was momentarily speechless. He wasn't arresting her. It was almost as if he was trying to reason with her. That simply did not compute.

Emboldened, she replied in a tone that bordered on truculent. "She's a Soviet hero, the pride of her regiment. Why isn't a journalist allowed to talk to her?"

"Don't be stupid," he snapped. "Your meeting was not journalism. It was a private visit to a politically suspect family by an American."

"So what are you saying? That I can't visit the Drachenkos?"

"Not if you want to protect them."

Alex stared through the sooty windscreen, noting that they had turned the same corner twice. "Why are you telling me this?"

"Because NKVD does not want to arrest a hero."

"The NKVD, or *you*? I've never heard about NKVD mercy before."

"You ask too many questions. Just believe me that you cannot go back. I am not the only one watching you." He pulled up to the sidewalk in front of the Hotel Metropole.

Leaning past her he lifted the handle and pushed open the car door. "Now you can get out."

CHAPTER SIXTEEN

Alex felt like a whipped dog as she dragged herself back into the hotel. The Metropole, for all its cavernous dimensions, was increasingly like a prison.

She stood for a moment in the hotel entranceway, then forced a smile and marched to the main desk. "Is there any mail for me?"

"Yes, Miss Preston. There is." The clerk drew a yellow envelope from some place under the counter and slid it toward her. "A cable from the United States."

"Thank you," she said, and opened it as she walked toward the stairs. No surprise and always a comfort, it was the weekly cable from George Mankowitz.

PHOTOS GREAT STOP DONT NEED ANY MORE BATTLE STOP CAN YOU GET MORE OF STALIN OR SOVIET WAR PRODUCTION STOP PUBLIC EATS THAT UP STOP END

It lifted her spirits to be reminded of her success at home. At least she was getting something right. Perhaps this was a wake-up call to get her back to work and away from her personal fixation on Lilya, which was dangerous to them both.

She phoned the Press Department. Could she get permission to return to the Southern Front? If not, could she photograph war production anywhere?

The answers were no to the former and yes to the latter. While the Soviets were beaten back and their inferior armaments blasted to pieces, they had no desire for that fact to be published. But now the factories in the East were manufacturing a new design of tank and powerful new aircraft, and these she could photograph. She accepted without hesitation.

❖

On November 2, the orders came permitting her to photograph the Saratov Aviation Works. It took her an hour to pack and a day to join a troop transport to Saratov. They came under fire, but only the tracks took damage, not the railcars. The train stopped, teams came to lay new tracks, and within half a day, they were moving again. She descended at Saratov, and the troop train rolled on to points south.

As she expected, the production line had many women, but she decided it was an equality they could have done without. The working conditions were appalling. The sound of steel upon steel was deafening, the factory meals weren't even as good as those provided on the front line, and, worst of all, the factory air was freezing. The workers' overalls were ragged and filthy, and their breath came out as steam.

She was able to talk with some of the women briefly on the way to their dormitories after their twelve-hour work shifts, and though they were plainly exhausted and gaunt, their patriotism appeared sincere, even when the factory commissar wasn't watching. She was impressed and tried to capture the industry and hardship in her photographs.

On the second day, the foreman guided her to the Yak production line, and she snapped photos of the welders, electricians, and gun mounters. When the foreman invited her to stand on the wing and gaze into the cockpit, Alex's face warmed with the memory of Lilya's enthusiasm for the craft.

"This one's already finished," he announced. "As soon as we paint the red star on the tail, it'll be tested and then go into action."

"Who flies them," she asked, expecting to hear that it was a state secret. He surprised her.

"This one will go directly over to the Saratov airfield to the women."

Had she heard right? "You mean the 586th Fighter Regiment?"

"Yes. Their commander just arrived to sign the papers for the handover. Would you like to meet her?"

"Major Tamara Kazar? Yes, of course I would."

The office adjacent to the hangar was already crowded when they arrived. The major stood at a table covered with papers, and four other aviators stood behind her.

Tamara Kazar had the same erect posture, extremely short hair, and the tight, almost hostile masculinity she'd displayed ten months before at Engels. Apparently she was signing the necessary receipts and releases, and when she finished, she caught sight of Alex.

"Miss Preston. You are photographing our new Yaks?" She stood up.

"Yes, I've just finished, in fact. They're quite impressive."

"I am sure you've made us all look good. What's your next project?"

Flattered by the commander's interest, Alex replied with some sincerity. "I don't know, frankly. I go wherever the Press Department allows me."

Kazar looked at her intently for a long moment, as if coming to a decision. "Why not photograph the 586th? Surely we're as photogenic as our planes." The burning stare continued.

"I...uh...well, I'd love to. I'll have to submit a request with the Press Department. She glanced around at the other pilots. You'll be flying back with the new planes?"

"Yes. We came here in a transport, but my pilots will have their own crafts to fly now," Kazar said. "Why don't you return with us to the Anisovka air base, and we'll contact the Press Department from there. They'll be less inclined to refuse you if you're already on site by personal invitation of the commander."

"What can I say? I accept."

❖

Alex collected her camera equipment and rucksack and rejoined the group in the hangar. Once everyone had saluted everyone else, the team of aviators left the hangar and each pilot laid claim to her respective Yak-1.

Alex had assumed Major Kazar would pilot one of the new planes, but to her surprise, she limped out to the transport plane and signaled Alex to follow her.

She obeyed, dropping down onto the narrow seat along the wall next to her host. During the noisy flight, they didn't speak, but Alex snatched an occasional glance at the strange woman beside her.

Tamara Kazar was not at all like the other female commanders. Marina Raskova had on occasion been almost nurturing, and even the stern Bershanskaya had sometimes let a bit of warmth show through. But Tamara Kazar was made of ice. What, then, was behind her sudden decision to allow her regiment to be photographed? And why did she not fly her own plane?

A frigid wind was blowing when they landed at the Anisovka air base, and Alex knew it was the precursor of another deadly Russian winter. The fighter pilots, she noted, were housed in better conditions than their night-bombing sisters. The women lived in wooden huts, camouflaged and built low against an earthwork to both conceal and protect them from bombardment.

Kazar led her to the nearest one. "Lieutenant Ratkevich, will you set up a bunk for our guest?" To Alex she said, "In the meantime I'll telephone the Press Office and explain your presence here. After you've settled in, please stop by. My quarters are over there." She pointed toward a wooden hut adjacent to the hangar. "Shall we say in an hour?" She bent slightly at the waist in the hint of a military bow and marched away, in a strange, stiff posture that exacerbated her limp.

"Well, come in and make yourself at home. You're the photographer, aren't you?" One of the women guided her by the arm to an empty bunk.

She dropped her rucksack and scanned her surroundings. A brick stove heated the room, but, like the oil barrels the night bombers used, its warmth extended only a meter or so. The wooden floors, however, were a significant improvement over dirt and mud.

Mosquitos seemed to be a problem. She slapped one on her forearm.

"The women from the night regiment told us about you. You're going to send pictures of us to America?"

"Yes, if they're approved. For a magazine." She held up her camera case. "I just have to take care of these." She unpacked her rucksack onto the bunk, noting that she'd gotten quite good at traveling light. All she really carried was clean underwear, sleepwear, a comb, and a toothbrush.

Someone had just brought more wood in and fed it into the stove, causing the fire to blaze up for a moment and send out a delicious wave of heat. "The latrine is the last shed on this side," the newcomer announced. "If you want to wash, you have to heat water here on the stove. As for bathing, well, once every ten days, they truck us in to Saratov to the baths." The young woman laughed. "You're lucky we were there just a couple of days ago."

Alex studied the faces of the young pilots. "I remember some of you from Engels. Forgive me if I've forgotten your names."

"That's all right. We'll remind you. I'm Raisa Beliaeva, and this is Klavdia Nechaeva. We remember you. Lilya talks about you a lot."

"Lilya talks about me?" Her face warmed. "Has she returned to the regiment since her accident?" *Since I abandoned her,* she thought.

"Yes, she's been back for a week now. She's already shot down two Junkers."

"Oh? Is she in this bunker?" Alex glanced around at the bedrolls, as if she could spot which one belonged to Lilya.

"No, she's in the other one, with Katia Budanova." Klavdia laughed. "The two of them are the best in the regiment. They make the rest of us look like amateurs."

"And Inna Portnikova? I know she wanted to be transferred."

"Yes, she's here, too. In the ground-crew bunker. She does all the work for Lilya and Katia. They refuse to fly until she's examined their engines."

"That sounds like Inna. I mean, she's the ace of mechanics, isn't she?" Alex glanced down at her watch. "Oh, excuse me. I believe the commander's waiting for me."

"She's in the shed next to the hangar," Raisa said in a faintly deprecating way. "But be careful to agree with everything she says."

"Really? Of course I'll be diplomatic. I'm a guest, after all." She shouldered her camera bag and started toward Commander Kazar's quarters.

Knocking, she heard an immediate "Come in." Tamara Kazar sat at a makeshift desk with an open map. Behind her was a bulletin board with other maps and what looked like duty lists. The tiny bunker had a single cot on one side and, on the other, a brick stove much like the one in the pilots' bunker. It heated the small space nicely.

"Are you all settled in?"

"Yes, though I don't have much to 'settle.' Will I be able to take meals with the women in the mess?"

"Of course. Though perhaps you will dine with me occasionally. You can even have your own vodka ration. Let's start with today's share, to celebrate your arrival."

"Well, I…uh." Alex stammered, but the major already had the bottle and two glasses in front of her. She poured intimidating quantities into the two glasses and handed one over. "Health!" she said, and drank hers in a swallow.

Alex followed, out of courtesy and a fear of offending, but the sudden assault of high-octane alcohol caused her to cough. "Sorry, American here. We mostly drink beer."

"Is that so? I seem to recall your cowboys drinking whiskey all the time."

Alex smiled. The vodka was already warming her and putting her at ease. "Only after they've rounded up all the cattle and shot all the cattle rustlers." She couldn't think of the Russian word for rustlers. Perhaps there wasn't one, so she substituted "cow bandits," and Kazar burst out laughing.

"What a wonderful image that is. Cows with masks and pistols." She laughed again and poured out two more glasses of vodka. "Drink up, Miss Preston. May I call you Aleksandra?"

"Alex will be fine." She sipped at the glass until the major tapped at it from the bottom, encouraging her to drink it down like water. Then she poured a third glass for them both.

Alex raised a hand. "Sorry, two's my limit. Beyond my limit, actually. I can't drink like a Russian."

"I understand. Drink that one up, and we'll put the bottle away." She downed her own third glass.

Alex acquiesced and tossed it back, though she was already becoming dizzy.

Kazar corked the bottle and set it aside. She tugged her tunic down into place and took a deep breath, as if to begin a speech. But all she said was "So, Miss Pres...Alex. How does an American speak such good Russian?"

Alex took extra care to pronounce all the consonants in her words. "Immigrant parents."

"I see. Anti-Bolsheviks, eh? Well, we all have dark family secrets, don't we?" She held a cold smile. "Nothing friends can't forgive. So how did you end up back in Russia in the middle of a war? Why aren't you home with your husband?"

She hated questions like that. "I could ask you the same thing? Why aren't you?"

"That should be obvious. My country was attacked."

"So was mine." The vodka was definitely going to her head now, and she hoped the conversation wouldn't get political.

"Come, come, Alex. Your country hasn't been invaded. You haven't been forced to put the rest of your life aside and fight for the very survival of your people."

"Yes, that's true. I'm here because I want to be where the great events are happening. I don't want to be tucked away some place safe and treated like a doll. I want the same freedom as men."

The major beamed. "I see we're kindred spirits. We both know that women are capable of the same achievements as men. But I've learned that a woman can't be soft, for if she is, men will take advantage of her."

"Do you think so?" Alex was beginning to find it hard to separate her words. "Surely it's possible to be both soft and strong-willed."

"No, women have to be hard on themselves and learn not to break under pressure. As commander, I am unyielding because I must be. If my women are to have the same privileges as men, they must endure the same rigors. Perhaps things are different under capitalism."

Alex was silent for a moment, trying to both order her thoughts and control her lips. "I...um...can't speak for all of capitalism, just like you probably can't speak for all of communism." She paused again. What did she mean to say? How could she say it succinctly? And politely.

"I think our people are basically the same." She licked her lips, to make them work better. "Women in both countries are under constant pressure to prove themselves as good as men, but they shouldn't try to act like men. I like women who are hard when they're flying planes but soft with their friends. With me." She stood up unsteadily.

The major came to her side. "In vodka *veritas*, eh? Aleksandra Preston, I like your ideas. We must do this more often." She laid her arm across Alex's back and guided her to the door. Was it Alex's drunken imagination, or did she feel an unusual pressure of the major's breast against her side?

She staggered from the bunker, and the ice-cold evening air sobered her a little. She buttoned her collar and pulled down her cap before glancing around the Anisovka air base.

It was clearly meant to be permanent, for it had a hangar and several solid bunkers. The runway too was more than wood laid over mud. She took a few unsteady steps toward the first airplane and studied the ground underneath it. Concrete octagons were laid out in an interlocking pattern, forming a hard, stable surface that resisted mud. Ingenious. Even in the event of bombardment, the shell holes could be quickly refilled and covered with the same segments to re-establish the runway.

Clever people, these Reds, she thought as she shuffled, trying not to stagger, toward her own bunker. She glanced back at the field behind her where the sun was just setting. The entire field had a cold solemnity about it. Empty and dead on the outside, but just a few meters away, crouching in their shelters around their stoves, dozens of women were very much alive. She'd missed being surrounded by women, and now she was among them again. Was that what "comrade" really meant?

❖

Damn. When she awoke the next morning, the other women had already left. How embarrassing. She recalled groping her way along the bunks the evening before and undressing to the friendly snickering of the women. She remembered struggling with the laces of her boots and finally yanking them off her tired feet. But nothing after that.

The fire in the stove had burned down to ashes, so she had to dress in icy cold air. Hurrying from the bunker, she asked the first woman she passed where the mess was.

"In that bunker over there, but you'd better hurry. Everyone's starting duty." Alex could see now that several clusters of women had gathered on the field. Lilya had to be in one of them, but there was no way to know which one. It seemed a kind of punishment.

"You're lucky. We still have tea and a little kasha left," the mess officer said. Sugarless tea and kasha, apparently the universal diet. The powdered eggs of the Metropole were delicious by comparison. She rewarded the mess officer by photographing her with her cooking equipment. Everyone, it seemed, liked to have her picture taken.

She turned to one of the other stragglers. "What are the pilots doing today?"

"Can't tell you exactly. "Some of them escort the bombers that come in from Saratov, and others fly defense of the positions our army holds. The best pilots go out on active missions."

"Does that include Lilya Drachenko?" It gave her a tiny thrill to say the name.

"Sure, it does. And Katia Budanova, Raisa Beliaeva, Klavdia Nechaeva. They make up the first squadron. They took off already at dawn to escort some bigwigs to Stalingrad."

"Ah, so Lieutenant Drachenko is fully recovered from her injury." She feigned casual interest. "I'm glad to hear it."

"Recovered or not, she's top-notch. Hasn't anyone told you the story of the barrage balloon?"

"Barrage balloon? No. What about it?"

"Well, the Germans had this balloon for their artillery spotters, see? They lowered it for the spotters to climb into a basket, and when they let it float again, the spotters could find our positions and direct their guns. The balloon was surrounded by flak cannons, so all our attempts to knock it out failed. But Lieutanant Drachenko found a better way." The young woman took a long drink of her tea, no doubt to increase the suspense.

"Only Lilya was brave enough, or maybe crazy enough, to fly along the front line before swinging back through enemy territory. She came at the balloon from the rear, where they had no cannons."

"Did she succeed?"

"On the first pass."

Alex smiled. "That sounds like her. I'll send the story to my magazine, if the censors let me."

Another of the mechanics appeared in the doorway. "First squadron's come back."

Alex hurried outside and watched the three fighters taxi to their respective places on the airfield. She waited by the hangar until a handful of figures approached from the field, obviously to make their report.

Inna Portikova was first, beside Katia, hands dancing in the air in some mechanical description. Raisa Beliaeva came next, and two women ran to greet her.

Lilya Drachenko was alone. As she approached the hangar, she slid her helmet back on her head, and blond hair erupted over her forehead. Alex let the others pass and walked out to meet her.

Lilya stopped and simply gazed at her for a moment. She seemed small inside her bulky flight clothing. The brown wool *gymnasterka* gathered under a wide black belt made her upper body look inflated. Her chest was a jumble of pockets, canvas parachute straps, and the small cord-cutting knife. Enormous padded jodhpurs and the parachute that dangled behind her gave her a slightly comical look. But around her throat, barely visible under her collar, was the thin line of a blue polka-dot scarf.

"Hello," she said simply.

"Thank God you're all right." Alex swallowed hard. "I thought about you every day."

"Why did you disappear? I waited for some word from you. Anything."

Alex winced at the reproach. "You can't imagine how much I wanted to come back. But that man who came to the door was NKVD. He said we were being watched and that I endangered you simply be being there. I had to stay away."

Lilya studied her, as if trying to decide whether to believe her, then glanced for the briefest instant to the side. "We can't keep standing here this way, with people watching us. I'll find you later, all right?" With a noncommittal nod, she strode away and followed the other three pilots of the first squadron into the hangar.

Alex watched from the hangar entrance while the women gave their report. She was too far away to hear anything, but Major Kazar seemed to be berating the group for some reason.

Afterward, Katia headed toward her quarters, but the others returned to the airfield. Lilya passed her once again but this time gave no sign of recognition. Alex watched, troubled, as she and Raisa climbed into their Yaks and took off once again.

She caught up with Katia, who seemed to be fuming.

"What's going on?"

Katia scowled. "Commander Kazar found something to complain about for all of us. Little nothings. But she really hates Lilya and Raisa, so she sent them out to escort some big-shot party boss. Double duty as punishment."

"Is she that rough on everyone?"

"Yeah, but she despises those of us who complain. And the stupid woman doesn't even fly."

Alex realized that Katia was talking to her in whole sentences, confiding in her. It was deeply flattering. "I noticed that when we came in from the Saratov Aviation Works. Does anyone know why?"

"Supposedly she has an old wound that never heals and so she can't use the pedals in a cramped cockpit. Maybe that's true, but then, she shouldn't have been appointed to lead an air regiment. No one knows what kind of pilot she was, so no one really respects her."

"How did she manage to be appointed, then? Oh, wait, I remember. That was General Osipenko's doing. I was actually there in the room with Major Raskova when he made the announcement."

"Major Raskova." Katia repeated the name softly and stared into space for a moment. "I joined the regiment for her, and each time I engaged the enemy, it was for her. I'd give my life, if only she could come back and lead the regiment."

Alex was moved, as much by the memory of the commander as by Katia's devotion to her. "Yes, she knew how to lead. What a difference between the two of them."

Katia's grimace returned. "Major Raskova confided in me that Kazar got the appointment because she had the Order of Lenin. But she shouldn't have even qualified for that, since she'd never done anything exceptional in aviation. We decided it must have been for denouncing people. The Kremlin rewards that."

Alex was speechless. That hadn't occurred to her.

Katia shrugged resignation. "Don't worry about it. Those are our quarrels, not yours," she said, and marched back toward her own hut.

Night fell, and Alex waited with Inna at the end of the airfield, stamping her feet and blowing into her hands to keep warm. "Do you wait this way every night?"

"Someone has to. The pilots don't have any light otherwise."

"You don't use any kind of landing lights?"

"Just a couple of us on each side of the landing strip so they can aim."

"Is she very late? *They*, I mean. Are *they* late?"

"Not so...ssssh. Listen. Two engines. They're back." Inna handed her one of her flashlights. "Go over there about twenty meters. Then flash on and off with me. That means it's all right to land."

Alex did as she was told. The sound of the engines grew louder, and in a few moments, both Yaks were on the ground taxiing toward them. When they pulled into their designated spots and the pilots climbed from the cockpits, Alex couldn't distinguish one from the other. Then one of them pulled her leather flight helmet back on her head, and a halo of pale hair became visible even in the dark.

Lilya and Raisa strode toward them with large, hurried steps to make their report. Lilya smiled at Alex in passing, then at her mechanic. "Thank you for waiting, Inna. Did they leave any supper for us?"

"I'm sure they did," Inna called after her. "We'll storm them together after you've reported."

The report was fortunately brief, and within ten minutes, the two pilots had returned. "Let's eat, comrades," Alex said. "I'm famished."

Comrades. Had she actually said that? What would Terry think?

Dinner had been borsht with potatoes and larded bread, but the cook reheated the soup for the latecomers, and the warmth alone did them all good. A few of the other pilots and navigators had lingered, on their own time now, and they gathered around them. Alex was content to be near Lilya again without fear of NKVD scrutiny, but for the moment Lilya's attention was focused on the simmering resentment she shared with the other pilots.

"Sending you both out again when we had a dozen other pilots that could have gone, that was vicious," Klavdia said under her breath. "How much longer are we going to put up with that?"

"Not much longer," Lilya said. "I'm going to send a complaint to the division commander. Will you all sign it with me?"

"I will, and I know at least eight others who have the courage to do it, too," Raisa said.

"Good. It's settled then." Katia wiped out her mess kit with the last of the bread and folded it up. "We have a journalist from an American magazine with us, and we don't want her to think we're all rebels and malcontents."

"Don't worry, none of that's my business. I'm just here to photograph the heroic deeds."

"Heroic. That's us, all right." Raisa poured the last of her tea into her mess dish and swirled it around before drinking it. "And right now, this hero's going to the latrine. Good night, all."

"Everybody out," the mess officer called. "I'm closing up." She rinsed the empty soup pot, set it upside down on a bench, and blew out the lanterns. Raisa and Katia drifted out of the mess and headed toward their huts. Alex stood in the doorway, wondering if she would ever get close to Lilya. How were they going to talk?

But Lilya brushed past her and murmured, "At my Yak. In half an hour. Say you're going to the latrine." Then she caught up with Katia.

CHAPTER SEVENTEEN

Alex lay in her bunk waiting for the time to pass. Was anything sweeter than this, the first invitation to intimacy? It made no difference that, in the frigid night air, "intimacy" could mean little more than brief conversation, perhaps an embrace, before the cold drove them back inside. It would mark the beginning of...of what? Nothing in her experience prepared her for this moment. The longing for someone so vastly different from herself, from a culture and politics she'd grown up hating, left her off balance.

She checked her watch. Half an hour had passed. Most of her hut-mates had used the latrine and climbed into their bunks. It was time.

She drew on her parka and ventured outside, where the temperature had dropped and she felt the chill on her face. She let her eyes acclimate to the darkness, and after a few minutes, she could make out the aircraft by ambient light. Whatever was pale gray was field or sky; whatever was black was a Yak.

She hurried to the second plane, still standing where it had taxied in an hour before. Passing the tail, Alex could see the number 44 painted in white on the fuselage.

Lilya leaned against one of the wings, and when she was close enough, they clasped gloved hands, like children about to circle dance. Lilya's eyes were black pits, but wisps of her pale hair flickered around her face in the night breeze.

Alex gripped the gloved hands more tightly and pressed them against her chest. "I was so worried about you, after I left your apartment. It broke my heart to not be able to look after you and bring you things. But the NKVD man said you might be arrested for...oh, I don't know... fraternizing with a capitalist. I had to go."

"But now you're back."

"Yes, but I don't want to put you in danger again."

"It doesn't seem fair. The Germans out to get me in the sky, the NKVD on the ground."

Alex chortled. "The NKVD, maybe, but not the people. They love you. I hear you've become a sort of aviation hero."

"Lilya brushed off the compliment with a shrug. "Do you want to see the inside of my Yak?"

"*My* Yak. I love it that you have your own plane."

"Yes, it's my second home. Come on, I'll let you sit in it." She pulled Alex up onto the wing, then slid back the canopy. "Go ahead. Get in. I'll explain everything to you."

Alex climbed into the cockpit, settling in on the narrow seat with the control stick jutting up between her knees. "It's all a black hole in here. I can't see a thing."

"You don't have to see it. You can just touch it." She leaned over the edge of the cockpit and took hold of Alex's hand, brushing it lightly over one of the tiny displays. "This is the fuel gauge. The other instruments are altimeter here and airspeed indicator here, heading and attitude indicators right below them, vertical-speed indicator and turn coordinator over there."

"Hmm, different from the planes I flew at home. But I bet I could learn it."

"I bet you could, too. Anyhow, the radio is right in the center, and the switch for the landing gear is on your right by your knee. As far as the guns are concerned, they're all controlled from the stick and you can fire them all at the same time."

"Oooh, major mayhem. But a great plane. It's only too bad the enemy planes have guns, too."

"Well, that's the way things are." Lilya was leaning over her now, her face only inches away, her breath warm.

Alex reached up with her gloved hand and touched her collar. "You still wear my scarf."

"Yes. Always. It brings me luck," she murmured, then brushed her lips against Alex's brow, in the narrow spot between her fur hat and eyebrow.

Alex grasped the fabric of Lilya's jacket and pulled her down. She sensed rather than saw the lovely young lips as she tilted her head back and placed an upward kiss on them.

Lilya made some soft sound and returned the pressure, sliding her left arm into the cockpit to cradle Alex's head.

How wonderful and strange to kiss in the ice-cold dark. Everything outside of them was freezing, hostile, hard. Only the spot that connected them was alive and warm. For a few precious moments, there was no war or winter—only Lilya's hot mouth.

Alex drew her in closer and the heat leapt to the place between her legs, though she knew she could do nothing about it. Lilya must have felt the same, for her breath came hard through her nose as she gave herself to the kiss.

Strange, too, the power of an embrace, when they had only that. In the frigid air and confines of the plane, with gloved hands and heavily padded bodies, no other touch was possible. But for a few moments, the kiss was a pledge, a surrender, the center of the world, the star around which both their lives orbited.

Too soon Lilya broke away. "We have to go back," she breathed. "The others will start to miss us soon."

"Yes, of course." Cold reality menaced them again. Alex clambered out of the cockpit and slid down the wing behind Lilya but reached out to grasp her hand again.

Wordlessly, she pulled her into her arms. Then, bending her back against the wing, she kissed her again. This time she could sense the outline of Lilya's body, the warmth of their interlocking thighs.

But this embrace too came to an end, as the cold invaded them both, and Alex pulled her upright. "I know. We have to go," she said. "And we can't go back holding hands."

"No. Nothing like that. Ever."

They both fell silent. Words were paltry now, though a shared euphoria seemed to hold them together. As they separated before the bunkers and each one continued on to her own, Alex thought she saw a shadow. Someone stepping out of sight behind a plane.

No. It must have been her imagination.

What a strange torment to have new love requited, yet no time or place to express it. Alex swam in a haze, where every glimpse of Lilya set her heart racing, every smile Lilya gave to others made her jealous, every mission Lilya flew filled her with fear.

Yet she grew proud of the whole regiment and every victory they achieved, as Lilya was proud of them. She found reasons to delay her return to Moscow, shooting fewer photos so as to conserve her film, caught up completely in their struggle.

Lilya was becoming a star, even among the other pilots. Scarcely a week later, she and Raisa landed after a mission and rushed with unusual haste to the hangar to report. Alex and half a dozen other women hurried behind them to listen.

"A swarm of them, Comrade Major," Raisa said. "Junkers 88s escorted by Me-109s. Headed southeast, toward Stalingrad."

"We engaged them." Lilya interrupted her. "Raisa knocked out one of them and I got another one. The remaining bombers dropped their load on empty territory and escaped."

"We shot down one of Messerschmitts, too, and I pursued the other one but ran out of ammunition. Then Comrade Drachenko followed him down."

"I winged him, but he managed to circle and came back at me, and got me in the tail. But then I climbed above him and dove. My last shots caught his fuel tank, but I'm pretty sure he bailed out before the explosion."

"We should look for him, Comrade Major. I'm pretty sure I can locate the spot. It was near a river bend, and we'll see traces of the fire on the ground." Raisa was obviously still excited and annoyed at missing the kill.

Kazar crossed her arms over her chest. "I'll notify the division commander and he'll send someone back to the site."

Lilya scowled. "Why can't we capture him ourselves?"

"Capture is not our job. Besides, if the pilot's still alive, the colonel will want to interrogate him. Refuel and await my orders." The cluster of pilots dispersed and the matter seemed settled.

Major Kazar contacted division command as promised, and late in the afternoon the men from the nearby airfield brought in the German pilot. Since he counted as one of the kills of the 586th, the interrogation would take place at their field. To Alex's surprise, the major asked her to be present and to take photos for headquarters.

The pilot had obviously parachuted safely, for he was unharmed. He sat, rigid and sullen between his guards, as Major Kazar, then the division commander and his interpreter entered.

Alex photographed discreetly from a corner and studied the German aviator. Though she knew little of German military decorations, she did recognize the iron cross at his throat, and the row of other awards on his tunic was impressive. Clearly, he was a top pilot.

"What's your name," the colonel said, and the interpreter repeated in German.

"I am Kurt Stengler. I hold the rank of Hauptmann. My serial number is 7566348."

"What field did you fly out from?".

"I am Kurt Stengler. I hold the rank of Hauptmann. My serial number is 7566348."

"Would you like a drink of water, Hauptmann Stengler? Tell us what airfield you're from."

"I am Kurt Stengler. I hold the rank of Hauptmann. My serial number is 7566348."

The colonel scratched his chin. "You seem an exemplary airman. All those medals and awards. I bet you're a real hero." He paused to allow his interpreter to repeat.

"Do you want to see who shot you down?"

The German reacted. "Yes, I want to meet the man who could outfly me."

When the interpreter repeated his response in Russian, everyone in the room snickered. The colonel turned to Major Kazar. "Would you summon our aviator?"

Kazar stepped out for a moment and returned with Lilya behind her. The German pilot's mouth twisted in a sneer. "Is this how you insult a fellow air-force officer, by ridiculing me with a stupid girl?"

"This 'stupid girl' is the aviator who shot you out of the sky," the colonel said.

"I don't believe you." He looked away in contempt.

Lilya glanced once at the colonel for permission, and when he nodded, she stepped before the captive. She still wore her flight suit, Alex noted, perhaps to taunt him.

"You were the second of two Me-109s and your number was 34. My comrade and I shot down the first one, and I followed you when you dove. At about 1500 meters, I winged you, but you managed to circle and come back at me, and got me in the tail. I had enough power to climb above you and then dive. You fired toward me, but you were looking into the sun, so you missed, while I had a good shot at you from overhead. My fire swept across you and finally caught your fuel tank. You must have seen that coming, because you bailed out seconds before it exploded."

The translator repeated the story in German, sentence by sentence.

"It *was* you, then." His voice was raw with bitterness and loathing. "Sheer luck. One of us will get you next time." He looked away.

"Maybe. Maybe not," Lilya said indifferently, and stepped away.

The colonel presumably had lost patience with the airman and signaled the guards to take him away. The next interrogation wouldn't be so friendly, Alex thought, but her job was over.

"Thank you, Major Kazar. And thank your pilots for their work. We will see that this capture is noted on their records." With a round of saluting, the men left with the prisoner in a troop truck.

❖

"Well done, first squadron. Well done, us!" Sitting in the mess hut, Klavdia Nechaeva play-punched Katia on the arm.

"Sorry we left you behind that way, you two, but we didn't see him," Katia said.

"It was nothing. Don't even mention it." Lilya waved a dismissive hand. "We cleaned up the stragglers, didn't we, Raisa?"

"Did we? I didn't notice. I was polishing my nails," Raisa wisecracked, and the others broke into laughter.

Alex sat at the end of the table watching their banter, grateful to be involved in it, if only peripherally. Lilya seemed radiant.

"Hey." Klavdia landed another soft punch. "I got another package from home in the last mail and was saving it for something special. I think this is it. But you have to promise not to devour *everything* in five minutes."

"Agreed." Lilya clapped her on the shoulder, and the six of them left the mess hut as a group and gathered in the First Squadron hut.

Raisa ignited the paraffin lanterns that served as their light, while one of the other women fed more wood into the stove and stirred up the ashes. When the chill was off the hut, they sat in a circle around an ammunition crate. Klavdia opened the cardboard box with great drama and drew the items out, one by one. First the inevitable package of hard black bread and the more welcome tin of herring. Then she passed around a cloth bag of sunflower seeds, as a sort of appetizer. A few small cakes of pine nuts baked with dried apples and berries provided a bit of the sugar they all hungered for.

While they nibbled on the food, all eating as slowly as possible, one of the women began to sing, and soon the others joined her. A song about snow falling, tragic and unbearably poignant. It was as if the women, scarcely more than girls, were anticipating their own deaths.

While they sang about flowers, young love, patriotism, Lilya circulated around the shed, leaning now on one comrade and then another.

Casually, inconspicuously, she ended up next to Alex, who perched on the edge of a cot next to Katia.

The touch of her hip and the occasional accidental brushing against her arm was exquisite.

"It's amazing, isn't it, how much we accomplish with an incompetent commander," Katia said suddenly.

"You know how she was chosen," Lilya reminded her. "She's one of Osipenko's cronies. Both of them are rotten to the core. They'd denounce their mother if they thought it would gain them something." She shook out a few sunflower seeds and handed the bag on to her neighbor.

Katia crossed her arms. "It's true. It's outrageous that we—the best female pilots in Russia—are under the command of a woman who can't fly. Of course we said all that in our letter to the division commander. Eight of his best pilots signed it, so he can't ignore it."

"It really breaks my heart that we lost Major Raskova." Across from them, Klavdia drew up her legs and rested her chin on her knees. "You knew she really cared about us. She was ten times better than that stick of wood we have as commander."

The sound of a hinge creaking caused them to all look toward the door. Major Kazar stood there, stone-faced.

"Lights out, all of you." She directed her attention toward Alex. "Miss Preston, I believe you are in the wrong hut. I will accompany you back to your quarters."

The women grumbled obedience, and Alex, puzzled by the infraction, followed the major out into the night.

"I'm sorry. I didn't realize the first squadron's hut was off-limits to me."

Kazar walked stiffly beside her. In contrast to their vodka-filled evening weeks before, the major laid no arm over her shoulder, or even looked at her, her demeanor as glacial as the air around them.

"I am disappointed in you, Miss Preston. I understood you to be an intelligent woman. I'd hoped we'd get to know one another. But it appears you've chosen to socialize instead with the lower ranks. These young women are inexperienced, naive. They have nothing to offer you but girlish cheerfulness."

"Under the circumstances, Major, cheerfulness seems welcome. What do you have against it?"

"Do not mock me, Miss Preston. I am charged with maintaining an efficient regiment of fighters, and I will remove anything that interferes with that."

They were at the door of the Squadron 3 hut now, and Alex replied. "I understand. Good night, Major Kazar."

The major marched away without replying.

❖

Late November 1942

The morning mission, Alex learned, was to escort three Tupolev bombers and their tethered gliders from Moscow to the Anisovka base. By the time she was awake, pilots from both squadrons had long been in the air. She knew, without asking, that Lilya would have been one of the women assigned.

Within three hours, they'd returned. Inna, in her padded jacket and breeches, and Alex, in a sweater and winter parka, crunched through the frost-covered snow of the airfield to meet them. In spite of the slippery surface of the field, the two bombers landed smoothly, towing the slender, motorless gliders. "Looks like they're using the G-11s," Inna remarked.

"Why are they stopping here?"

"They're picking up some fuel tanks, ammunition, antifreeze, food. It all comes by train from the factories south of here. But from what I hear, the trains haven't arrived in Saratov yet, so the gliders will have to wait."

"Where do they go from here? The supplies, I mean."

"To Stalingrad. The Tupolevs tow the gliders filled with supplies and bring them back filled with wounded."

Alex was about to reply when two more Yaks arrived. One of them buzzed low overhead, wobbled its wings, circled around, and made a smooth landing. Inna laughed. "Lilya, of course. It must have been a good morning. She only wobbles her wings like that when she's knocked out a plane. It irritates the hell out of Comrade Kazar."

The two Yaks landed, and Katia and Lilya reported in at the hangar. When they appeared again outside, Lilya yanked off her flight helmet. "I don't know about you," she said to Katia, "but I'm off duty now, and I need to wash my hair."

"Great. I'll get the buckets." Inna was suddenly enthusiastic.

"Be discreet." Lilya smiled conspiratorially. "I'll meet you in our hut."

Puzzled, Alex followed Inna, certain something was going on that wasn't allowed. How could they wash hair with no hot water and in the middle of winter?

Inna led her to the supply shed, where she hauled out a wrench and three buckets and handed one of them to Alex.

"Buckets, for a shampoo?"

"Yep. It takes too long to boil water on our lousy little stoves, and it uses a lot of wood. But we have another source of hot water."

By then they were in front of Lilya's Yak Number 44, and Inna handed her a bucket. "You hold this up while I unscrew the valve. Be careful not to let the water touch your hands. Even with gloves, you'll get scalded."

Inna reached up overhead and first unscrewed the engine cover, then the radiator valve. After the first turn, hot vapor spurted out, and after the second a thin stream of steaming water began to flow out in a curve. Alex lifted the bucket over her head and stepped under the stream. The superheated water hissed and sputtered as it struck the cold metal. She could feel the heat through her leather gloves, and when the weight of the bucket grew too great, she stepped aside and set it down at her feet, where it sent up a plume of mist.

"I think there's another half a bucket in there," Inna said, holding up the second bucket until the radiator flow became a trickle and then a drip. "In cold weather we empty the radiators anyhow, so they don't freeze up at night," Inna explained.

On the way back, they filled the third bucket with clean snow and joined the group of pilots gathered inside the hut. Both Lilya and Katia were kneeling on the floor over an empty bucket, with blankets around their shoulders.

Inna scooped snow into the half-filled hot water bucket and tested it with her hand. "Perfect," she announced. "Ready, girls?" she asked the two pilots and, at their signal, tipped the bucket over their bowed heads.

Katia held up her disc of military soap, and Inna rubbed it over her hair until a slight lather appeared. Lilya, meanwhile, held her soap toward Alex. "Would you be so kind?"

Amused, Alex imitated what Inna had done, scrubbing the curly blond hair until the gritty soap produced a foam. Together she and Inna massaged the two scalps, warm from the radiator water, until the bathers seemed satisfied.

Like a cartoon chemist, Inna concocted another pail full of snow and radiator water and did the rinsing. With steaming heads, both pilots stood up and rubbed their scalps dry with their blankets.

"What's going on here?" Tamara Kazar was suddenly at the entryway, righteousness itself.

"We're just washing our hair, Comrade Major," Katia answered, clutching her blanket around her shoulders.

The major swept her glance across them, as if she was measuring how far she could push them.

"Misuse of military equipment." She nudged one of the still-warm buckets with her boot and tugged at Katia's blanket. "You could get a penal battalion for that. As it is, I'm putting you in five days' detention, starting tomorrow."

"What? You mean the blankets?" Katia was indignant. "They'll be dry in an hour. The buckets aren't damaged either."

"Be careful, Lieutenant Budanova. I can also write you up for insubordination. Get this equipment back into its shed, and don't let me catch you at this nonsense again. The rest of you all have duty assignments. Get to them." With a final scathing look at Alex, she marched away.

"Five days' detention?" Alex was astonished. "How are you going to fly missions when your best pilots are on report?"

"She'll simply double the duty of the others," Inna muttered. "It's just a way to keep us afraid of her." She snatched up the handles of all three buckets and left the bunker for the supply shed. The other women, who had been watching from their bunks, filed out to their duty stations, and as Lilya passed, she murmured, "Tonight. Twenty-two hundred. At the third bomber."

Puzzled, Alex caught up to the major. "Why are you so hard on them? They're dedicated, top-notch soldiers, all of them. This kind of thing simply improves morale. How can that be against regulations?"

"It is unmilitary and inappropriate to a war zone. As is your fraternization with Lieutenant Drachenko. I invited you here to photograph the regiment, and since you have gone beyond that role, I suggest you now arrange your return to Moscow."

She marched away, leaving Alex stupefied. Did the major appreciate the resentment brewing in the squadron? Something was going to break, she feared, but would it happen at the top of the command or the bottom?

Damn. Wasn't it enough that the Germans were trying to kill them all?

CHAPTER EIGHTEEN

The winter day was short, and the night, which began already at sixteen hundred, was broken only by the two shifts in the mess shed, at eighteen and nineteen hundred. Alex made sure to eat in a different shift from Lilya and afterward retreated to the relative warmth of her hut.

Her bunkmates always wanted to chat about life in America, about women's dresses and what the men were like. She marveled at how women who knew how to fly and shoot down enemy planes could care about such girlish things as clothing, hairstyles, and courtship.

By twenty-one hundred, they were dozing off, as she knew they would, and she was glad she was sharing quarters with fighter-plane crews, who worked in the day and slept at night. An evening tryst, if that's what it was going to be, would be impossible among the night bombers.

But was a romantic meeting possible in subzero temperatures, anyhow?

She pretended to get ready for bed, too. But when the last lamp went out, she drew on her clothes and parka again, and crept out.

The night was clear and the much-too-bright moon was ominous. They were all too visible to the Luftwaffe, and they had only two anti-aircraft guns to protect them.

She strode past the familiar Yaks to the Tupolev bombers and their tethered gliders. They looked enormous in the dark and cast jagged shadows on the airfield surface. A figure stepped out from behind the third bomber.

"Lilya." She loved to pronounce the name, to feel the way her tongue moved around the *L* sound. She took her hand, drawing her closer, then pressed her back against the fuselage of the plane. Their padded clothing was bulky, but even sensing the vague outline of Lilya's body thrilled her.

She buried her face in Lilya's neck. Her hair smelled of military soap with a faint metallic taint of an airplane radiator, but under it all was the warm, sweet animal fragrance of a young body.

"Why tonight? At this temperature?"

Lilya kissed her ear. "I'm going to be in lockup tomorrow for five days, and who knows what happens after that?" She pulled away. "Come on, follow me."

She led her past the bomber to the attached glider and ducked under the wing. Shaded from the moonlight, the surface was uniformly dark, but Lilya felt her way along the side until she found the handle to the door. It opened with a creak of hinges.

"It's pitch-black in there," Alex whispered. "We'll crash into things."

"No, I checked earlier. They haven't loaded it yet. Come on, don't be afraid." She crawled inside the opening and tugged Alex after her.

Alex obeyed but, once inside, was completely blind. It made no difference whether she closed or opened her eyes. She groped around and, with her fingers, traced the outline of a bench along the wall of the fuselage.

She fumbled along the wooden floor until she felt Lilya's knee and giggled. "This is crazy, you know."

"I know. Come here."

"Here? Where's here?" She giggled again but crept farther in. Tapping her way blindly along the padded form, she lay down alongside it and fumbled for Lilya's head under her fur hat. She explored now with her lips instead of her gloved hands, sliding them toward the only part of Lilya that was exposed. Finally she tasted skin, fragrant but cold, and snickered.

"It's like embracing a pile of laundry. Somewhere, deep inside of all this, is you."

"Be brave. You'll find me. I'm in here, waiting for you." Thickly padded arms encircled her neck and pulled her forward.

How strange it was to kiss in total darkness without seeing the beloved. Smells and taste became intense—of wool, sheepskin, military soap, and the salty-sweet moisture of Lilya's mouth. Then something more basic than perception began inside her, something deep and animal urgent, the need to join, to couple, to melt into her.

Anchoring on one elbow, Alex pulled the glove off her other hand with her teeth. With her free hand she unbuttoned Lilya's winter coat, then her collar, exposing her warm throat. She kissed it and wet it with her tongue. Button by button, she worked her way down Lilya's chest in the narrow strip of exposed skin.

The Russian gymnasterka shirt defied her, for the buttons went only halfway down the chest. But she was excited now, and Lilya whispered, "Yes, touch me, please. I want you to do it."

She fumbled under the gymnasterka from below to the breeches and unbuttoned those as well. While desire heated her body, she couldn't help but be amused at herself, awkward as a teenage boy. A *blind* teenage boy.

But Lilya leaned toward her, murmuring encouragement, as Alex rested her hand on her hot belly. Alex caressed gently, cautiously, waiting for her hand to warm, then slid it down the last dangerous distance to the prickling place of Lilya's sex. She gripped and pressed gently with her palm, as if stroking the breast of a bird, until Lilya's soft sounds told her she could go on, then traced a line down the widening groove and slipped inside her.

"Ohh." Lilya moaned dully, covering the invading hand with her own. Still with thick layers of wool between their bodies, Alex kissed her again, more forcefully, joining with her only in the two small hot places she could reach.

Lilya kissed back with equal fervor, the short spurts of her exhalations warming Alex's cheek. She penetrated more deeply and encountered an obstacle that tore away with the next thrust, and she stopped for a second in shock. She'd just deflowered a virgin.

Whatever pain Lilya had felt at the tearing didn't diminish her ardor, for her kisses became bites, and Alex stroked now in a rhythm that seemed to excite her. She teased the innocent place as long as she dared, then reentered the hot, eager part of Lilya that rose to meet every stroke. Lilya thrashed, pounding against her in sightless coupling, a primordial motion, like waves surging toward a shore.

The swell of Lilya's desire crested and she convulsed, grasping Alex around the shoulders and breathing a long, soft groan onto her throat. They lay still, as if suspended.

A thud on the wall of the glider caused them both to jump. Someone was outside, inches away from them.

They froze, listening.

Male voices, unintelligible but for a few bawdy words. The pilots of the Tupolev. What the hell were they doing on this side of the airfield instead of in their own quarters? Their language suggested they were prowling around the women's huts up to no good. She would have happily confronted them if she herself weren't up to no good.

Finally the voices faded as the men apparently moved off, but Alex still sat, blind and motionless, in the dark. She felt Lilya next to her rearranging her clothing. "Are you all right?" she whispered.

"Of course I'm all right. I'm delirious," Lilya whispered back. "What did you do to me?"

Alex chortled very softly. "You never experienced that before? I'm so happy I could be the first to do that for you. It was new for me too, I mean with a woman."

"Whatever it was, I want to do it again. But maybe not now."

"Yes, let's get out of here before those men come back. I don't even think I can find the door."

"It's down by your feet. There's a row of benches folded up against the wall, and where they end, that's where the door is."

Alex got to her knees and reached forward into the darkness until she touched what felt like a bench bottom. "Yes, they're right here." Lilya came up beside her, and together they slid on their knees to the last bench. Alex groped along the wall above and below it and finally brushed against a handle. She turned it slowly, cracking the door.

The airfield, which had seemed so dark when they arrived, held a dull blue-gray light. Enough for them to see the men in the distance, leaning against the tail wing of one of the Tupolevs.

They had only to get to the other side of the closest bomber to be out of the men's line of sight. Rather than make a noise whispering, she simply took hold of Lilya's arm and ran.

It wasn't until they reached Lilya's hut and parted that Alex realized she'd left her glove in the glider.

CHAPTER NINETEEN

The morning roll call in front of the mess hut was always informal, although on this day the atmosphere was tense since everyone knew that three of the best pilots were incarcerated. Major Kazar stepped up onto the small platform and, without making mention of their absence, gave a rundown on the recent engagements, then read out the current assignments. Since the trucks from the railroad depot had arrived, and Stalingrad had priority, they wouldn't fly. Instead, the air and ground crews would assist the men in loading the gliders for immediate takeoff.

No one needed to be reminded that it was almost December and the brave men fighting in "the cauldron" were desperate for food and ammunition. By fourteen hundred hours, both bombers and their gliders were fully loaded. At fourteen thirty, Alex watched them take off from the airfield, escorted by four Yak-1s, piloted by the women of the 586th regiment. None of them, of course, was Katia or Lilya.

"I noticed you were working today with only one glove." Alex was startled by the voice behind her. "This must be yours, then." Major Kazar held out a fur-lined leather glove.

The gloves were unique, finer than those the pilots wore, so she had no choice but to brazen it out. "Thank you, Major. I was looking for that," she said, sliding it on.

"How do you suppose it ended up last night in an empty glider?"

"I couldn't say, Major." It was as defiant as Alex had ever been, but she could think of no possible excuse.

"I believe you have surpassed your usefulness here, Miss Preston, and we have a war to fight. The train that brought the Stalingrad supplies will go back tomorrow to Moscow. See to it that you are on it."

❖

Choking injustice was all Alex could think of. Two top pilots and their mechanic jailed for a shampoo, and an honest journalist expelled for…for what? A bit of jealousy? And she couldn't even say good-bye to Lilya.

Well, a lot of that occurred in wartime, she told herself, though it was no comfort. She packed her belongings, which took fifteen minutes, then moped. Was there *anything* she could do to dispel the major's wrath? Several scenarios crossed her mind, all of them appalling.

The sound of a large plane landing roused her from her funk, and she watched from the door to her bunker as another Tupolev taxied toward the hangar. An officer stepped out. A portly one.

General Osipenko marched with one of his lieutenants toward Major Kazar's headquarters and disappeared inside. What did it mean?

Alex glanced at the women standing nearby, but all of them seemed as surprised as she was. She returned to her bunk, restless and idle.

An hour later, the buzzer sounded for a surprise general roll call. When the regiment fell in and stood at attention, General Osipenko walked down the line of women, reviewing them like a field commander before battle. Apparently satisfied, he stepped up onto the platform.

"Comrades, I have some important announcements," he said. "First of all, the Air Defense Force has promoted your commander, Tamara Aleksandrovna Kazar, recipient of the Order of Lenin, to the Air Force General Staff, where she will assist me."

Alex glanced over toward Raisa, whose expression hinted faintly at amusement. Apparently, the aviators' complaints to division headquarters had finally borne fruit.

"In her place, Major Aleksandr Gridniev will assume command," he added.

Alex saw sudden consternation on many of the women's faces. They were to have a male commander. Was it a necessity of the war or punishment for making trouble?

"In addition," the general said, "seven of you have been selected to form a hunter's squadron that will join the men at Stalingrad." He drew a folded paper out from under his arm. "These are the names: Raisa Beliaeva, Valeria Khomiakova, Evgenia Prokhorova, Maria Kuznetsova, Klavdia Nechaeva, Ekaterina Budanova, Lilya Drachenko. The latter two will be released from punitive confinement immediately, and all will report for duty tomorrow at the usual time." He folded the paper again. "That will be all, Comrades. You may fall out."

The women broke ranks slowly, and the buzzing among them told Alex they were as stunned as she was. She joined Klavdia and Raisa as they strode toward the penalty bunker. "What do you suppose happened there?"

"I think we got the prize and the punishment at the same time," Klavdia said. "We got rid of the tyrant but have a man in her place."

The detention bunker was little more than a covered hole in the ground, with benches along two of the walls and a deeper hole in the corner for urination. The worst, of course, was the lack of heat, for which the blankets provided did little to compensate.

The three prisoners huddled together on a single bench under their blankets, and though they had been confined only about six hours, they were obviously elated at the arrival of the others.

"Katia glanced up first. "Please tell us you're not here just to commiserate."

"No. We're here to spring you," Raisa announced. "Osipenko just arrived. Kazar is out. Promoted 'up' and away. Come on, we'll tell you the rest outside."

"Justice! Finally." Lilya threw off her blanket and climbed out of the hole. "There's more?"

"Yeah, but it may not be so good. I don't know," Raisa said. "Some of us are being sent as free hunters to Stalingrad. Almost everyone on the transfer list is a woman who signed the complaint against Major Kazar. Looks like, with Osipenko's help, she's found a way to get rid of us."

"Stalingrad. Really?" Katia slowed her step.

"Yes, really. And since the Germans have taken over almost all of the city, that's more or less a suicide mission."

Katia's lips compressed. "Maybe. But it's also real fighting, not just this constant escort flying and defending train stations. I'm ready for it."

"She's right." Lilya nodded. "Though we have no choice anyhow. Suicide squadron or not, I'm ready to go, too."

Klavdia changed the subject. "I wonder where we'll be based. I thought the Fritzes held all the airfields from here to Stalingrad."

"I think we still hold Akhtuba, just east of the Volga. Within range," Alex offered, noting that she'd said "we." But dread was sinking like clay into her chest. It was hard enough to face death standing by people you loved, but the thought of Lilya sent off to fight and die in Stalingrad, the bloodiest battle of the war, was crushing. She turned away from the group and forced herself not to drag her feet like a child as she headed back to the hangar.

"Miss Preston," a familiar, harsh voice called to her.

"Major Kazar. Congratulations on your promotion," she forced out.

The major was expressionless, surely an indicator that she also understood she'd been dismissed, not promoted. And surely she knew that Alex knew.

"I'm happy to inform you that General Osipenko has room in his plane for a passenger. You don't have to wait until tomorrow for the train. He can take you directly back to Moscow." She paused, letting the announcement sink in, then added, "Perhaps you would also like to be assigned to the Stalingrad arena. Covering that battle would certainly be a journalistic coup."

The major stood with raised eyebrows, waiting for a reply. Alex knew it was a poison chalice, a vengeful gift to her, for having been part of the rebellious group. Foreign correspondents had so far been barred from Stalingrad, but Kazar and Osipenko could pull strings and send her, too, on a suicide mission. If she was willing to go.

She pondered for a moment, as Katia had, weighing the risks against the benefit of being near Lilya and perhaps getting great material. "Don't I have to first get permission from the Press Department?"

"General Osipenko can arrange that and even get you a place on one of the troop planes flying to Stalingrad."

"I see you've discussed it with him."

"I take that as a yes," the major said with a cold half smile and seemed to glide away.

"Very kind of you," Alex said to her back, then muttered, "like a cobra."

It appeared that even suicide missions involved red tape, and although the Press Department had given permission, it was another five days before a troop transport was scheduled.

Alex killed time at the hotel, playing cards with the other correspondents and listening to them grouse about being kept away from the big battles. She'd also gotten used to the hotel vodka and found it an effective way to ward off boredom as she watched the endless snow fall outside.

Finally the telephone call came and she found herself in a glider packed with terrified young recruits being flown to the cauldron, as they called it.

They had a fighter escort, but she wasn't sure how much that helped. You could survive enemy strafing in a train. In a glider, not so much.

Once she was seated on one of the side benches, she glanced around at the pale young faces and felt a wave of sympathy. They were so young, superficially trained, she knew, and some of them weren't even armed. She shuddered, imagining the unarmed ones being thrown into battle, waiting for their companions to die so they could pick up a fallen weapon. The baggy white camouflage that covered their winter uniforms made them seem ghostly, as if they were already in their burial shrouds.

But was she any better off? All she had was a camera case.

Mercifully, they did not come under fire on the way to Akhtuba. It was night, but the snow-covered landscape had a dull blue-white and slightly mysterious luminescence of its own, and the towing bombers landed their load of troops and supplies on the airfield without incident.

A sergeant stood at the open door of the glider and prodded the troops under shouts and threats toward four transport trucks covered only in canvas. Two other trucks waited while a team unloaded the supplies and ammunition from the second glider.

Shivering in the icy December air, she headed toward the low buildings at the edge of the field, her boots crunching on the snow.

Akhtuba Air Base 473 was the most primitive one she'd seen. Mere flattened dirt, hardened to stone by winter cold, formed the underlayer. The hangar was smaller, lower, and camouflaged, though now that, too, was covered with snow, which rendered it nearly invisible from above. A short distance away, pits had been dug into the ground, she guessed, for storage of fuel and ammunition. On both sides of the field, anti-aircraft guns pointed at the sky.

The planes were lined up for servicing, and she saw, to her shock, where the servicing mechanics emerged from. Their shelters couldn't even be called bunkers but were rather hastily dug trenches alongside the airfield. No trees or bushes protected them from the wind and blowing snow. She saw no sign of a mess hut or covered latrine.

The air, though icy, had a sooty odor, and in the distance, on the western side of the Volga, a dull-red glimmer beneath a layer of smoke told of a city on fire.

She reached the single large shed that she assumed was the headquarters and asked for the commander. In the corner, a senior officer studied a map, and she waited until he glanced up.

"I'm sorry to bother you, sir. General Osipenko sent me to take photographs, and I wonder if I can get a ride to the front."

He looked at his watch with apparent exasperation, and she was sorry to have brought him yet another problem to solve. "All right," he grumbled. "We'll try to get you out before dawn and put you down somewhere near headquarters." He turned to a soldier waiting nearby. "Would you summon Lieutenant Budanova?"

"Katia Budanova. I know her, and Lilya Drachenko, too. Is there any chance I could speak with her?"

"Lieutenant Drachenko is in the air," he said brusquely, ending the conversation.

Alex stepped back and waited silently, but in just a few moments, Katia appeared at the dugout door and saluted casually.

The officer glanced up. "Lieutenant Budanova. Please have one of the U-2s fueled up and take Miss Preston to General Chuikov's headquarters. Someone from the map room will show you the exact location."

"Yes, sir. Will that be all, sir?"

"That is all." He saluted in return and turned immediately back to the map he'd been studying.

As they passed through the doorway, Katia bumped elbows with her, a gesture that told Alex she'd passed some kind of friendship test. "So, what reckless impulse made you come to Stalingrad?"

It was a comfort to see Katia, who was a bit like an older sister—or brother—to Lilya, and she smiled. "Couldn't stay away. Moscow's gotten too quiet these days."

"Crazy like a Russian. Well, to the cauldron. Just give me a minute to get the coordinates of the headquarters."

Katia stepped into a blocked-off corner of the bunker, which obviously had been designated as their map room, and emerged a moment later with a map. She held it under a lamp, studying it, then folded it and slid it inside her flight jacket.

"Got your bags packed?"

"My bags," Alex said, holding up a single case that contained everything she required for a week. The rest of what she'd need in the Russian winter was already on her body.

Almost lighthearted, she strode alongside Katia and returned the elbow bump. "Hey, did you see *Pravda* last week? My photo of you and Lilya showed up on the second page. Apparently you're both heroes now."

"Yes, they showed it to us here. I'm sure both our mothers were happy to see we were still alive."

"So far, so good, eh? And where are the others? Raisa, Klavdia, Valeria...?"

Katia became solemn. "Raisa and Klavdia were shot down. Valeria Khomiakova went back to the 586th, and the others transferred to another male regiment. It's just us two now."

The announcement of the two deaths drained the cheer from their conversation, and they trudged through the snow to the U-2. It looked terrifyingly fragile. To dispel the gloom, Katia pointed below the plane. "Skis instead of wheels. They attached them at the end of November. A lot harder to stop on those things, though. Sometimes you land and just keep sliding."

"I'll drag my feet," Alex said, following Katia as she climbed the wing to her cockpit and set on a pair of headphones. "Hey, you've got communication now."

"Just between pilot and navigator. We still can't hear anything from the ground."

Katia started the motor and they taxied along the runway, skidding slightly and making a wavy line in the shallow snow with their pontoons. After a remarkably short trajectory, they lifted off the ground with a sideways lurch.

Alex had forgotten how cold the open cockpit of a U-2 could be. When she'd flown with Lilya back in May, the wind had been an annoyance, but now, in December, it assaulted her face like needles. Her goggles, fur ushanka, and high woolen collar protected most of her, but the skin below her goggles and around her mouth was exposed. At first her skin burned, then grew numb. Would she ever be able to move her lips again?

They flew over a stretch of snow-covered land, then what she judged to be the Volga River, though it was frozen and just as white as the surrounding landscape. Smoke wafted across it in several places, and in the predawn light she could just make out the movement of men crossing with sledges.

Katia flew up the Volga a few hundred meters and banked left.

"Right below is the Red October Factory. That's still heavily contested, though our men seem to have claimed more of it." Alex leaned over the cockpit edge and, without removing her goggles, snapped a series of photographs.

"And that black spot right ahead is Mamayev Hill. The Germans are on one side of it and the Russians on the other."

Alex snapped several more shots of the hill, ghostlike in the faint orangey light. In the east, the rising sun ignited the sky in reds and pinks, indifferent beauty over the slaughter below.

"Where's the Luftwaffe? Shouldn't they be attacking us?"

"They'll be out in a few minutes. They have fewer patrols these days, probably because we've managed to cut off some of their supply lines and they're low on fuel. They're still a menace, though."

Katia banked again, giving her a good view of the shore, then descended at a sharp angle. The landing skis bumped over the lumpy ice and they skidded to a stop. "All right, old girl. Here we are. Chuikov's headquarters is right over there, dug out of the Volga bank. You see it? Near the burnt-out truck."

"Yes, I see it." Alex climbed over the side of the cockpit. Just before she scrambled over the wing onto the ground, she leaned in and kissed Katia on the cheek. "That's for both you and Lilya. Take care of yourself, and her." Then she leapt onto the frozen river that gave back a dull sound under the hard sole of her boot.

"I'll be back tomorrow." Katia waved and, after a run of no more than two hundred feet, lifted into the air again.

Alex stood for a moment, suddenly anxious. Beyond the western riverbank the city smoldered. Clouds billowed here and there over a dirty orange glow, and after the popping of the U-2 had faded, she could hear the crackle of small-arms fire.

The smoky pink sky provided enough light for her to make her way over the wreckage along the bank. But she hadn't gotten far when two heavily padded figures ran toward her with rifles pointed at her chest. She stopped and raised both hands.

"Journalist," she shouted, holding up her pathetic little press pass, but at least they didn't shoot.

When they were face-to-face, one of them held out a mittened hand. Alex presented her papers, but the figure brushed them aside. "Zoia Kaloshin," a woman said, pumping her hand while her comrade, who now also appeared to be a woman, held her papers up to her nose.

"Can you take me to General Chuikov's headquarters? I'm supposed to report to him."

Just then a shell exploded behind them on the river, blasting a hole in the ice. Debris rained down on them.

"Watch out. The fighting starts as soon as it's light enough." They scrambled toward the wall of the embankment.

The soldier shouted over the noise of the explosions that followed. "Looks like there's been a mix-up. General Chuikov is not even here and certainly won't have time for journalists. We use the cave now as the medics' bunker. I can still take you there if you like."

Alex frowned, then decided medics made better photos than generals anyhow. "That's fine. Lead the way."

"It's right over there." She pointed toward the embankment just ahead of them.

"How's the battle going? Is it safe to cross the Volga in the day?" She stepped over rubble and shell holes and other debris.

"No, not yet. The artillery has tapered off and we think they're short of ammunition. They've got plenty of infantry, and we're still fighting everywhere in the city but gaining ground. I think the Fritzes are finished. It's only a matter of time."

She patted her well-padded chest. "We got a new issue of winter uniforms and *valenki*, and the Fritzes are still running around in rags. For every one of them we knock off, the cold knocks off two. So, here we are, the medics' quarters. We're heading out into the city soon, but we'll get you settled."

She hurried up the hillside toward a cave fronted by a wall of oil drums. A single plank on one side functioned as a door. She slid the board to one side and led Alex inside.

The cave wasn't unlike the dugouts she'd already slept in at Akhtuba. Here, too, planking appeared to serve as a sleeping space. Some five or six women were just preparing to go on duty. The brown and red stains on their padded jackets revealed the hardship, if not the horror, of their job, and their gaunt young faces attested to overwork and hunger.

"Please, sit down. You're going to take our pictures?"

"I sure am. The Kremlin thinks it's good propaganda to show how brave their women are, but bad propaganda to show the wounded. I'm not sure how to get around that."

"Hmm. Difficult. That's sort of what we do," Zoia said. "Well, maybe you can just photograph us with our first-aid packs and our guns in hand. Brave but without the gore."

"What else have you photographed?" one of the other women asked, buckling a belt over a padded jacket.

"Oh, factories, soldiers boarding trains, and a lot of pictures of the women's regiments. The night bombers and the fighter pilots."

"Major Raskova's regiments! How lucky you were to meet her. Did you get photos of the famous pilots—Budanova, Beliaeva, Drachenko?"

"Yes, I did, in fact. I didn't realize their fame had spread so far."

"Of course it has. We get *Red Star* every week with our mail, and we read about the heroes."

"Well, I think *you're* heroes, too. Tell me what you do." She asked the group in general, but again it was Zoia who replied.

"We run over to the west bank of the Volga in the morning and look for wounded. If they have a chance, we drag them back to the Volga bank. They stay there under blankets until a sled arrives to bring them across to the ambulances."

Another woman spoke up. "Before, so many wounded were on the bank they couldn't evacuate them fast enough, so they died just waiting. Now that the river's frozen, the sleds can bring them across pretty fast. But it's also winter, and if they lie there more than a few minutes, they die from the cold."

Zoia's wince showed she agreed. "But if they make it across the Volga, the ambulances take them to the field hospitals."

"How do you carry them?" Alex glanced around at the women who were no larger than she was.

"On our backs, usually. It's slow, and we make a big target. Sometimes the snipers shoot both the wounded man and the medic. But we also shoot back." She patted the pistol at her side. "Anyhow, we have to report now. Are you coming with us?"

Alex considered the dangers and cringed inwardly. But to refuse would be a grave insult to the young medics. "Yes, of course I am."

"You stay here," Zoia ordered her, pointing to a corner protected on three sides by broken concrete. "Don't move until I come to get you." The constant rattle of machine-gun fire all around them and the intermittent blast of a grenade ensured that Alex would obey.

The smell of smoke and brick powder from the blasted walls of the factory was overpowering, but Alex tried to ignore it. She drew out her camera and photographed the medic overseeing the carnage, like some Valkyrie about to descend to earth to lift up broken warriors.

Within minutes, someone cried out, "Medic! Help me! Medic!" Crouching low, Zoia clambered down to where a man lay writhing. She knelt over him and unbuttoned his field coat, shoving a wad of bandage inside. She whispered something to him, then stood up and ran back to cover next to Alex.

"Aren't you going to carry him out?"

"No. He has a big hole where his stomach used to be, and he won't last. I told him I'm sending some men to bring him out, but he'll die before he knows I was lying."

Alex scarcely had time to react to the remark when the call came again. "Medic! Medic here!" and Zoia scuttled away again in another direction. A moment later, she appeared again, dragging a man by his coat into some cover. He was obviously heavy, and Alex got to her feet, to run to her aid.

At that moment, she heard a crack, and a chip of concrete flew off the wall next to her head. Another crack, then another, each time dislodging concrete but missing her head by inches. Loose powder blew into her face. Sobbing with fear, she dropped down and made herself as small a target as possible, waiting for the barrage to stop. She dared not even raise her head to see if Zoia was still alive.

So this is what cowardice is, she thought, her heartbeat pounding in her ears. The assault continued, the cacophony of small-arms fire punctuated by grenades and the whoosh of the Soviet flame-throwers. Occasionally a portion of wall fell, adding to the dust in the air.

She couldn't tell how much time had passed as she crouched, trembling, in her corner, waiting for rescue. It came, finally, in the form of Zoia, breathless and sooty.

"Are you all right?" Zoia asked.

"Yes," she said, her voice tight and tremulous. "What happened to the man?"

"Another medic came and we carried him to the shore."

"I wanted to help you, but…I'm sorry. The gunfire was too heavy. How do you stand it, day after day?"

Zoia shrugged. "I ask myself the same thing. But you're still shaking. It looks like you're ready to get out of here."

"Yes, I think I am." She heard the tremor in her voice and was ashamed.

"Don't worry. I'll guide you down to the riverbank and you can go back with the sleds."

Alex followed dutifully, like a child, as Zoia led the way through the labyrinthine ruins to the river.

She was right. Horses were arriving, harnessed to sleds and protected by riflemen. She assuaged her guilt a little by assisting the medics to lift the wounded onto them. Hating herself for her timidity, she ran alongside the horses as they trotted across the ice. On the east bank, she helped lift the wounded onto the ambulances before returning, deeply chagrinned, to the cave shelter of the medics.

It was late afternoon now, nearly sunset, and she stood at the entrance of the empty shelter, watching the skies over Stalingrad. Messerschmitts appeared, but two Soviet fighters quickly engaged them. The four aircraft carried out their murderous ballet for some fifteen minutes before one of the German fighters was hit and went down. The other one disappeared into the distance.

Alex wondered who the fighter pilots were. Women from the 586th? Could one of them even have been Lilya? What would she think of her cringing journalist? Alex turned and retreated to the interior of the cave.

❖

When the exhausted medics returned from duty, no one reproached her. They simply shared their meager fare and repacked their first-aid bags, talking in low voices about everything but what they'd done all day while Alex photographed them, using her last flashbulbs.

Zoia threaded a needle and, leaning close to the lamp flame, began to mend a rip in the elbow of her jacket. "You know, just before I left, when it was dark and the shooting had stopped, I could hear the Germans singing. It was the strangest thing."

"Singing? Whatever for?" one of the others asked. "Are they demented?"

A light went on in Alex's memory. "What's the date today?"

"Um, let me think. The 24th, I believe," Zoia said.

Alex smiled, strangely touched. "It's Christmas Eve for them. In Germany, it's a big deal, you know."

"Really? How sad." Zoia went on sewing. "They must know by now they've lost. What a Christmas gift."

"They should have stayed home and celebrated it there," one of the others said, pitiless. "A million Russians are crying tonight for their destroyed homes and dead children, not for missing Christmas."

Alex nodded softly. She was right. So many dead, so many mourning, on the night that, more than any other, was supposed to celebrate peace. A pox on their piety, Alex thought, sullen, and wrapped herself in her blanket.

❖

The next morning, Alex and Zoia stood together in the dull predawn light, watching for the aircraft that would rescue Alex from the purgatory of Stalingrad. "There she is," Zoia said, pointing toward the U-2 that swung down onto the frozen river and bumped toward them. The medic hugged her in farewell. "I'm sorry you can't stay another day."

"Thank you for sharing your company," Alex said, and forced a bit of cheer. "Perhaps we'll meet one day in peacetime."

She scurried across the river and leapt onto the airplane wing, swung her leg over into the rear cockpit, and settled in, relieved.

"So, how was it?" Katia asked.

"Awful. Chuikov wasn't there. His headquarters had been taken over by medics so I photographed them instead. They were incredibly brave, and when we went to the west bank and came under attack, they just kept working. I'm afraid I did nothing but cower in fear."

"Don't worry about that. You're a journalist, not a soldier. You can't expect to be a hero."

"I know, but I didn't expect to be a coward either. I simply fell apart."

"Bravery's a funny thing. It doesn't have much to do with character."

They were high over the Volga now, and in the few moments between landing and takeoff, the sky had brightened. Below, she could already hear the sound of artillery. "Uh-oh," Katia said. "The fighting's starting up again. I should have come sooner."

As if to confirm her remark, tracer bullets zipped past them suddenly, like a line of Morse code. "Messerschmitt, at two o'clock," Katia said, and pulled up to gain altitude.

More bullets zipped past her head. The Messerschmitt was now pursuing them and hammering them with machine-gun fire. Alex gripped the sides of the cockpit, praying Katia could somehow miraculously get them away from it.

But no miracle occurred. Instead, Katia grunted suddenly and fell forward onto the control stick. The aircraft dove precipitously.

White terror blanked out Alex's mind. Then some survival instinct emerged, and she tried to pull back the navigator's control stick.

Nothing happened.

Christ! Alex cursed. Katia was lying over her control column, holding it down.

She snarled, then leaned forward in the cockpit and took hold of Katia's collar. Yanking the limp form upright with all her strength, she pulled back on the stick. The plane leveled out and began to curve upward again.

Something exploded in her right shoulder. She was hit. She cursed again, but while white-hot pain flashed down her arm and across her back, she managed to not pass out. Fighting to stay focused, she held the stick firmly, feeling the plane rise. She surveyed the dials. Which one displayed altitude? Oh, that one. She was at 500 meters, exposed to ground fire, but she was over the Volga now. Damn, the Messerschmitt was directly above her, and in a moment, he'd blast her out of the sky.

Miraculously, and at that moment she would have thanked any saint for it, a Yak came into sight. By diving-bombing, he managed to draw the German plane away from her and harassed it in a series of interlocking curves and swoops before finally shooting it down.

Okay. She exhaled through clenched teeth. They weren't dead yet, but now she had to fly the plane nearly blind. Katia's lolling head blocked her view of the airspace in front of them.

Panting heavily, the icy air freezing the inside of her mouth, she unsnapped her safety belt and stood up, still holding the stick against her belly. In such an awkward position, she overdid every adjustment, causing the plane to pitch and yaw.

She was on the opposite side of the Volga now and bent down to see her heading on the dial. South by southeast. That seemed right. They'd flown north by northwest on the way out. Would she recognize Akhtuba in the snow? And even if she did, could she land?

A small part of her agonized at the thought that Katia might be dead in her hands, but with the rest of her consciousness she focused on the instruments. She had to master them. Fast.

She tried to remember landing the Grumman, nearly ten years before. What was her glide speed? She checked the dial. Her speed seemed high, but she dared slow only a little, afraid to stall. She sat down to steady the plane and reduce her vertical speed, then, still gripping Katia by the collar, stood up again to look for the airfield. She saw nothing but white.

Her back was cramping from the awkward positions, the shoulder wound hurt like the bottom of hell, and warm blood was soaking the inside of her sleeve. How long before her arm would go numb or she'd lose consciousness? She let the plane drop another fifty meters and scanned the landscape. Now she was afraid she was lost and would run out of fuel and crash. She cursed the fact that the U-2 had no radio to ask for help.

Something off to the side caught her attention. Dear God. Another Messerschmitt. She sobbed out loud.

No, as it approached, she saw the red star, probably on the Yak that had shot down the German. He must have seen how badly she was handling the U-2 and come back to guide her in. Traveling at a much greater speed, he shot past her, but he raised his hand to signal that he'd seen her standing in the open cockpit. He knew now that she was flying the plane from the rear.

He flew ahead, then circled back, guiding her again, bringing her ever closer to the airfield. The circles grew smaller until she was right over it, and then she focused completely on manipulating the plane with one hand, peering over Katia's head to watch the ground rise toward her.

It was a bad landing, a terrible landing, and she careened and slid sideways for long minutes before she crashed into a snowbank. Women ran out onto the field and climbed onto the broken wing.

She was still sitting, one cramped hand clutching Katia's collar. Prying her clenched hand open, two of them lifted Katia out of the front cockpit. They laid her on a litter, draped a blanket over her, and carried her across the rough field to the commander's hut.

Two others remained and Alex tried to focus on them, but a ring of darkness was closing in. Someone lifted her under her armpits, and she groaned. "Sorry about the plane," she said and passed out.

She lingered in semi-consciousness for a few hours and felt herself lifted into an ambulance. The only thing she understood was a voice saying "Evacuation to 833" and the name Budanova.

CHAPTER TWENTY

A lex woke up to the touch of someone taking her hand, then recognized Lilya sitting on an ammunition crate at her bedside. She managed a weak smile. "I wondered where you were."

"I was on duty when you arrived. After I landed, they told me you were with the medics on the west bank, and I worried about you all night long. Then today, they brought you in unconscious and I was terrified of losing you. The doctors said it was loss of blood and they gave you a transfusion, so it looks like you're going to be all right." Her voice was strangely raw, her eyes swollen and red.

Alex glanced around. "I'm in a hospital?"

"Soviet military field hospital number 833. Do you remember what happened?"

"I was flying back with Katia when a Me-109 got us. Katia! Is she all right?"

Lilya pressed her lips together to stop their trembling. "She came to, in the hospital. This hospital. And we told her you'd flown the plane in. She said to thank you for bringing her home."

"Then she's all right?"

"No. She died right after that." Alex understood the swollen eyes now. "But she knew she was home, with us," Lilya added, and wiped her cheek with the back of her hand. "We buried her next to the airfield."

"Dear God," Alex whispered, choking up. "Katia gone. And it's my fault. She flew in to take me out of Stalingrad."

"Don't say that. She flew into the cauldron every day. We all did. That was just the day they finally got her. It has nothing to do with you."

"Yes, but—"

The voice of a doctor, a harried-looking gray-haired woman, interrupted her. The filthy smock she wore fit her badly, like the white camouflage the ground troops wore. Her red, half-closed eyes suggested she hadn't slept for a long time. Alex looked up quizzically.

"I asked how you felt," the doctor repeated.

"I'll live," Alex said.

"Good, because you have to leave. We need your bed for worse cases. Lucky for you, a GAZ-55 bus is outside the hospital about to return to Akhtuba. And since we have men here dying of typhoid, you'll be better off at your base."

"Typhoid." Lilya echoed the terrifying word. "Thank you for telling us, Doctor. Would you call someone to help me carry the litter?" She reached for Alex's parka at the foot of her bed.

She turned to Alex. "Can you sit up?"

"Umm, yes, I think so." She lifted her head while Lilya pulled her up. "Oh, dizzy, but give me a minute." She sat swaying for a moment, then, with difficulty and a groan of pain, she slid her injured arm into the sleeve of the parka. Her hand brushed the dried blood inside.

A moment later, a young medic arrived with a folded canvas stretcher. She laid it crosswise over the bed and opened it, revealing an ominous patchwork of dark stains.

"Don't try to stand up. Just slide over onto this," the medic ordered her, and Alex obeyed, lying down on her good side with a muffled moan. "My camera. Where's my camera?"

"It's here." Lilya lifted the battered case from the floor and laid the strap over her shoulder. She took the head end of the stretcher while the medic lifted the foot end, and they trotted together through the ward into the corridor. Alex saw immediately why she had to surrender her place. All along the corridor floor, hastily bandaged men lay on blankets. Some were unconscious, while others whimpered in pain.

The snow-filled air outside the hospital was a shock, but they needed to scuttle only some twenty feet to the ambulance. Once inside, Lilya thanked the medic and closed the rear door. The interior of the vehicle was plunged into darkness, but after a few moments, Alex's eyes adapted to the gray light coming through the ice-covered windows, and she could see the crates piled up all around them.

"Is anyone else in here?" she asked as the ambulance bumped and lurched over the road.

"It looks like we're the only passengers in this direction," Lilya said, squatting next to her on the floor. "How are you doing? Are you warm enough?"

"I'm all right. Besides, we're alone in the dark again. Remember the last time?" she asked, trying to cheer them both up.

Lilya chortled. "My sweetest memory."

"Good, because I want to say I love you. I want you to come back with me to New York."

"I love you too, but how can I leave? This is my land, my language, my people." Lilya gripped her hand, her voice betraying a new anxiety. "You're going back to New York now?"

"No, I don't mean now. I'll stay here as long as I can. But when the war's over, if we're both still alive. Please, think about it. I know the Russians are your people, but Stalin's a tyrant. He's killed so many—his kulaks, his own officers, men like your father."

Lilya pulled her hand away. "You don't understand about my father. Or about how important it is for Communism to succeed. It wasn't Stalin who killed him. He was an enemy of the state, of the people."

"Darling, do you really believe that? Do you really believe Stalin didn't order and approve the purges, the denunciations, the Gulags, the labor camps, the tortures in the NKVD prisons? Why do you have to send secret letters to your mother for fear of being arrested? Why do we have to whisper this entire conversation, if not that you could be executed for having it?"

"Stop, please. I don't want to hear this now. I don't want to talk about Stalin. I've just gotten you back from the dead, and all I want is for us to be together and safe."

Alex tried to reach out toward her in the dark, but the jolt of pain that shot through her shoulder stopped her. "Take my hand again, please."

"Yes, of course." Lilya clasped the closest hand between both of her own and kissed the cold fingertips. "We have so much to talk about, I know. But not now. Not when we're both fighting to stay alive."

"You're right. We barely know each other, and there's so much more I want to learn. I don't even know if you like dogs or what kind of music you prefer."

Lilya pressed Alex's hand to her chest. "I love dogs, big ones and little ones, though I never had one. I love folk songs and Mussorgsky."

"Did you ever have a boyfriend or fall in love?"

"In school once I kissed a boy named Dmitri. We were twelve. The first person I really adored was Marina Raskova, but everyone loved her. No, I've only been in love with you, your lips, the incredible things you can do to me with your hands."

With her good arm, Alex tugged Lilya down to her and kissed her gently. "I wish I could keep you from going up in your plane ever again."

"You can't. But you'll always be with me in the cockpit. I wear your polka-dot scarf all the time. But what about you? You lost so much blood, and you can't even lift your arm. I can't take care of you in a bunker. Where will you go to recover?"

"I'll be all right staying at the Hotel Metropole. The air raids have mostly stopped, and I can still afford to buy food. I'll be fine."

Lilya kissed the palm of her hand. "I'm so glad. You know the other journalists, too. Yes, that's a good solution. I'll always know where you are, at least for a few weeks."

Alex's sigh merged with a grunt of pain for her injured shoulder. "I wish I could say the same for you."

❖

The Metropole was nothing like a hospital, though in some respects, it was better. No one looked after her while she lay feverish and in pain, and no medicine was available other than the aspirin she'd brought with her from New York a year before. But, unlike thousands of injured Soviet soldiers, she had a real bed to lie on, and, by paying extra, she could have the hotel's food brought to her room. What she mostly suffered from was soul-killing boredom.

But some days later, while she lay shivering in the under-heated room, someone knocked at her door. "Come in," she called out. "It's not locked."

The door handle turned and a foot slipped into the opening. Slowly a black-clad figure slid into the room, awkwardly clutching a cooking pot wrapped in towels.

Anna Drachenko smiled timidly. "They told me in the kitchen that you were wounded, so I brought you some borscht. I made it myself."

Alex was momentarily speechless, then waved her closer to the bed. "It's dangerous for you to come here. I mean, fraternization—"

"I work in the laundry here on Saturdays, so it's a small risk. Anyhow, I knew you were alone." She stood now in the middle of the hotel room holding her pot. "Do you have any cups?"

"Yes, the hotel bowls and spoons are still here from breakfast." She pointed with her chin toward the night table. Anna set the pot down and carried the used bowls to the corner sink to wash them.

"You brought a pot of hot soup all the way from your house?"

Anna drew up a chair to Alex's bed and set the bowls next to the soup pot. "Of course not. I carried it in a jar, and they let me heat it in the hotel kitchen. It's not really allowed, but I have a few friends there." She poured out the crimson liquid, which was still hot enough to give off an aroma.

They ate together silently, and Alex was surprised at how good the borscht tasted. Anna had probably put a week's ration of vegetables and fat into it. The ache in her shoulder didn't stop, but the simple fact of being cared for did her good.

Anna finished her soup first and set down her bowl. "How do you feel?"

"I can't complain. It still hurts like hell, but the fever's gone, so it looks like I have no infection. I should be fine in a couple of weeks."

"Is anyone looking after you?"

"Not exactly, but if I really need someone, I can send for one of the other journalists."

"That's good." Awkward moments passed while Anna collected the empty bowls and took them again to the tiny sink. While she washed them a second time, she spoke over her shoulder.

"Please do not think I'm prying, but you said once you went to school in Leningrad. Is that where you were born?"

Alex saw no reason to be secretive. "Yes, and lived there until I was ten. My father worked in the Tsar's stables, so you can imagine that the Bolsheviks didn't love him. I don't remember the revolution, though. Only the horses."

"Interesting how children remember only what they need to. My father was a locomotive driver with the railroad. He drove the train that took the Romanov family to their deaths in Yekaterinburg. But of course I don't remember any of that either. Just the locomotives. Do you still have any relatives there?"

"None that I know of. That saves me from agonizing too much about the siege. It's bad enough to know how many Leningraders are starving to death. It would be worse if I had names for them."

"Yes, names make all the difference, don't they?"

"They do. Before I came here, the Russians were a faceless people, a culture that my parents had run away from. They even gave up their Russian name. How different everything looks now that I know you and the aviators, and Lilya."

"You care for her a lot, don't you?" Anna's glance seemed penetrating.

"Yes, I do. I want all the best things for her, just as you do, I'm sure. I don't mean fame—she has that already—but some kind of happiness after the war."

Anna clasped her long, callused hands. "I wish that for her too, but the NKVD will always watch her because of her father."

"If she could be safe living in another country, what would you think?" Alex asked tentatively.

"You mean…defection?" Anna looked alarmed.

"It's only hypothetical. Would you be disappointed in her?"

Anna thought for a moment, then shook her head. "Nothing she could do would disappoint me. I'd miss her horribly, but if I knew she was happy, I'd be content." She stood up and slipped into her coat again. "But we've never had this conversation, you understand?"

"I understand."

"I'll stop by again next week, before I go to work." She bent over and placed a quick kiss on Alex's head, and then, gathering up her pot and towels in one hand, she let herself out with the other.

Alex lay back and stared at the ceiling, drowsy from the warm soup. She quite liked this intelligent woman. Could Anna ever understand Alex's love for her daughter? She dozed off, thinking *probably not*. She scarcely understood it herself.

Another knock awakened her. Who was it this time? Too early for breakfast. And struggling to her feet was much too painful to do for anything other than the toilet.

"Who is it? The door's open."

Henry Shapiro poked his head through the opening. "An open door? Isn't that a little dangerous?"

"Better than having to rip out my shoulder to get up. Hi, Henry. What's new downstairs?"

He stepped into the room. "Oh, now look what you've done," he said, raising his hands in feigned lamentation. "You go off without us, and first thing you know, you get banged up. What happened?"

"A genuine war wound. Stalingrad, actually."

"Ah, a real Frontovik," he said. "Well done."

"It's a distinction I'd rather have missed. What kept you? I've been lying here for five days."

He pulled over the only chair in the room and sat at her bedside. "I was at the front myself. Leningrad."

"Ah, my father's city. Is it as bad as I've heard?"

"Whatever you've heard, it's worse. Bomb damage, of course, of the royal palaces and great houses. But the worst is the starvation. People died in the thousands last winter, huddling in their houses with no fuel, no light, no food. This year, more supplies are coming along the ice road across Lake Ladoga, and foreign journalists are allowed in now, too. I got a great story, if the censors let me file it."

"If it's about death and starvation, they definitely won't. Why don't you bypass the censors and send it through the embassy?"

"Too dangerous. Their Press Department reads all the journals we write for. They'd see the article under my byline and I'd be expelled."

"What a pain, eh? Sometimes, when I miss my luxury existence in New York, I think expulsion wouldn't be such a bad thing."

"It'd be a disaster for me. I have a Russian wife and two children."

"What? A family? Then why do you live at the Metropole?"

"Convenience. Our house is outside Moscow. Safe from bombardment, but too far to come and go every day. I go home on the weekend."

"I thought Russians were forbidden to fraternize with foreigners."

"Not expressly forbidden, but it does expose both sides to the charge of espionage. Publishing an account of the Leningrad siege might get me expelled, but my wife could be arrested and our children taken away. Loving a Russian isn't for the fainthearted."

She rubbed her shoulder, which had begun to ache again. "I'll remember that."

"So you were at Stalingrad. I heard terrible things."

"Yes, I was in the thick of it for only one day, but it shook me. And a dear friend was killed flying me out. She died because of me. That hurt much more than the shoulder."

He shook his head. "That's the danger of caring about them. Combatants, I mean. You can only lose so many of them before it ruins you. You can't do your job."

She nodded somberly. "On the convoy that brought me here from Iceland, I met a radio operator who said almost the same thing. When you see too much carnage, you die inside and victory doesn't mean anything. When the enemy surrenders, it's over, but you don't get to sail into the sunset."

"He's right. I stopped believing in happy sunsets a long time ago."

With the help of a good constitution and regular meals, Alex slowly regained the use of her right arm. She developed the Stalingrad photographs and ventured out to submit them to the Press Department censors, grateful to be active again. To her surprise, they approved almost all of them. They were long overdue to the magazine, so she hurried to the embassy to have them shipped in the diplomatic pouch. The deputy ambassador welcomed her as always and, impressed by her war injury, allowed her to use the embassy phone to telephone *Century* magazine in New York.

George Mankowitz took the call, and her first words to him were "Sorry to be incommunicado so long. I was injured. Shot, actually."

"What? Where did you do that?"

"At Stalingrad. Well, flying over it, in one of their U-2s and…uh, it's a long story. But I sent off some great photos to you this morning."

"Jesus Christ, Alex! I knew you wouldn't be able to stay out of trouble. We just heard on the news service that the Russians took Stalingrad. Do you want to come home? You've done great work, but you've stayed longer than anyone ever expected."

"No, I'm fine. You could wire me some more money, though. The hotel's a little stingy with the fresh vegetables, and I don't want to get scurvy."

"Sure, kiddo. Anything you want. So, what kind of photos are you sending me?"

"One or two aerial shots of Stalingrad, but they're not wonderful. Better ones of the medics. Incredible what they do there, always under fire, and they're starving."

"Great. I love the human-interest stuff. Men saving lives, men eating from their mess kits, polishing their leather boots."

"It's women, George. The medics are women. And the boots aren't leather. In the winter they wear felt valenki."

"That's what I mean. The public loves those details. Got any women carrying babies?"

"Sure. And kittens, too."

"Okay, don't be a smartass. You know what I mean. By the way, your friend Terry's in town. He called yesterday wondering if I'd heard from you. I told him no."

"Is he planning to come back to Moscow? Good. Call him back and tell him to bring socks. Not nylons. Big, thick wool socks. And four cartons of cigarettes. Seriously. I don't want to smoke them, but the Russians do, and you'd be surprised what you can accomplish with a pack of Lucky Strikes."

"All right, kiddo. I'll take care of things on this end. You keep getting me those great photos, and I'll get you your cash and cigarettes. And socks."

"Great. Say hello to the gang. I'll cable you in a week."

❖

Alex crossed Red Square past the stacks of firewood trained in from the woods outside Moscow. Reports were that the Allies were delivering more coal now, but whatever the case was, people were still lined up with their ration tickets and sleds for a load of kindling.

The early February sky was dark and it was snowing again. She was dressed warmly enough, but her parka was thoroughly stained, frayed at the cuffs, and the dried blood from her old shoulder wound formed a permanent crustiness inside her sleeve. She should have asked George for a coat.

She passed the hotel desk and asked if she had any messages, but the clerk shook his head. Where was Lilya, damn it? If Stalingrad had been taken, she must surely have been reassigned? Why hadn't she written? In spite of her new mobility and the conversation with George, Alex felt depression settling over her.

Back in her room, she stood at the window and watched the snow fall in thick flakes. She'd exaggerated to George about her health, but only a little. Aside from a twinge when she tried to lift something heavy and a tendency to tire easily, she had basically recovered. And she was bored. If only word would come from Lilya.

She stared through the window watching the people pass in front of the Bolshoi, their heads down in the blowing snow. Bundled in coats and ushankas pulled low on their heads, they all looked the same. Even the two women guarding the rarely used anti-aircraft gun on the square seemed miserable as they crouched over a small bonfire near its wheels. She could see some men in uniform on the Square, a few more than usual since Stalingrad had been taken. Perhaps granted a few hours' leave as a reward for surviving when a million men had not.

She paced the room a couple of times, then realized she had a simple, completely banal case of cabin fever. She needed to work again. It was time to check with the Press Department to see where they were granting passes.

A knock at the door startled her. Was the hotel still delivering dinner? She'd cancelled that. Faintly annoyed, she threw open the door.

A frontline soldier in a sheepskin coat stood with his *ushanka* low on his brow. Melting snow still lingered on it and on his shoulders. And then he lifted his head.

"Lilya!" Alex yanked her by the sleeve into the room and embraced her, the melting snow wetting her chin.

"How did you manage to come home? How are you? Why didn't you write?"

Lilya pulled off her coat and hat and dropped them on the floor. She looked utterly adorable in the dress tunic and breeches of an airman. Shiny blue shoulder bars showed she held a new rank.

"You've been promoted!" Alex embraced her again and kissed her, holding her face in her hands. "How long can you stay?" That was the critical question.

"Not long." She sighed. "My leave is for only forty-eight hours, and I went to visit my mother first. While she made me eat borscht, I told her I wanted to see you and that I'd be away for the afternoon. She didn't seem shocked. I think she understands how much you mean to me. But I have to go back to her in a couple of hours and be on the first train at dawn tomorrow."

"Two hours? Then we'll spend them in bed." Alex unbuckled Lilya's belt and dropped it onto her coat.

"I like that idea, but truthfully, I need a bath first. I didn't want to lose time before coming here, and besides, you have a private bathroom, don't you?"

"Yes, I do, and I develop my films there. But fortunately, that's done." She grasped the khaki-colored tunic and tugged it upward. "I wanted to do this every time I saw you walk across the field," Alex said, pulling it over the blond curls disheveled by the fur cap.

"Even the first time?" Lilya laughed, sliding off her boots and unbuttoning her breeches. "What a predator."

"Predator? That from a woman who hunts down German aviators and kills them?"

"All right. Now stop wisecracking and come kiss me."

"Not till you take that nasty underwear off. Come on, I'll run your bath. Lucky you, the hotel still has warm water. But only until five o'clock." She stepped into the bathroom and turned on the tub water. It flowed out in a slender, warm stream.

Lilya followed her in. "Nasty? It's not nasty. I washed it in snow just yesterday." She slipped off the last layers and stood naked with her arms across her chest.

Alex stood up from the gurgling tap and smiled. "How beautiful you are. Those sweet breasts you flashed to me once, you heartless jezebel. The memory stirred my lust for days." She drew her close.

"Mine, too." Lilya pressed against her, kissed her quickly on the lips, and stepped into the tub. She settled in with a sigh and closed her eyes. "Will you bathe with me?"

"There's not enough hot water for two. But I'll *assist* you." She crouched on the tile floor and made little waves on Lilya's legs.

Lilya splashed water on her face and throat with the washcloth. "Yes, I'll need assistance. I can never remember what to wash."

"Well, this part is important." Alex lathered her hand with the tiny bar of hotel soap and rubbed it along the inside of her left thigh, then her right.

Lilya leaned back. "Oh, yes. I always forget about my thighs. Good that you remembered."

Alex slid her soapy hand forward, and Lilya sat up, draping a wet arm over Alex's shoulder and brushing slippery lips over her cheek and ear. Lilya murmured, "Yes, wash that place, too. Wash it a lot. Like you did in the glider."

She rubbed the soap across the crisp pubic hair, making it foam, then massaged it into the soft folds of Lilya's flesh. Gently, she slid fingers along the groove and felt the slick of Lilya's pleasure. Still massaging with her palm, she let two fingers encroach along the curve and slip into the hot interior.

"Yes, just like that. I love that." Lilya moaned into her ear, then covered Alex's mouth, slipping in her tongue so they were both inside each other. Alex thrust, gently and persistently, until Lilya's breath became a pant, and then she withdrew.

"I have something much better in mind, my darling. Come, dry a little and get into the bed with me." She stood up and pulled off her shirt and slacks and stood nude before the slightly bewildered Lilya.

"No, forget about drying," Alex said, and seized her by the hand, drawing her from the bathroom over to the bed. They kissed again, nude wet bodies pressed together, then fell across the bed. Alex took charge, and the pilot who'd hunted down Germans and killed them surrendered in her arms.

Alex pressed hard kisses on her mouth and neck and breasts, grasping the firm young flesh along her sides, alive with desire. Lilya was offering her innocence, a rare and precious gift. Almost roughly, she spread Lilya's legs, thrilled and honored to be the first to give her this pleasure.

Lilya grasped her by the shoulders, trying to pull her back up into an embrace. But Alex was adamant and slid down the slippery damp body, leaving a row of little bites along the belly and pubis. She held Lilya fast around her hips and explored the recesses of her sex, learning it, teaching it, revealing the exquisite joy it could give. She made her tongue dance around the precious place for long torturous minutes until Lilya pleaded for release, and when she'd drawn out the golden thread as long as she dared, she gave the final stroke, bringing climax.

She rested her head for a long while on Lilya's belly, then rose again to lie in her embrace and feel the rising and falling of her chest.

Lilya brushed her lips over Alex's hair and exhaled. "I'm so glad we lived through Stalingrad, if only to experience this."

Alex rose on the elbow of her good arm. "I am too, darling. I just wish Katia could have made it out with us. She deserved to come home to someone's love, too."

"Valeria and Raisa, too. And all of the others we left back there."

"They were cheated of more than love, but I know what you mean. I spent just a few hours on the ground there. It seemed like the end of the world."

"It *looked* like the end of the world, too, when I flew over the city after the surrender. I could make out the streets only by the jagged spikes that used to be walls. Even high in the air, it stank of ash and gunpowder."

Lilya stared at the ceiling, recalling. "I have to admit, I felt a certain bitter satisfaction when I looked down and saw the defeated Germans shuffling along in an endless stream, like insects creeping toward the east. I suppose just like our men did when the Germans captured them."

"It's insane, isn't it?" Alex caressed her cheek. "Captured armies driven in opposite directions, one eastward and one westward. The leaders like mad chess players with all of Europe as their chessboard."

They fell silent again, and Alex gathered Lilya into her arms again. "I don't want you to leave. Do you even know where they're sending you?"

"They've assigned me to the 73rd Guards Regiment at Rostov. Couldn't you apply to come and be our journalist?"

"Impossible. I could follow the night bombers only because Major Bershanskaya invited me. Then Major Kazar had her own strange reasons for letting me join the fighter regiment, but obviously that privilege is withdrawn. And of course I can't follow you personally, much as I'd like to."

Lilya chuckled softly. "It would be like being married, wouldn't it?"

Alex didn't laugh. "I would marry you if I could."

Lilya laughed again. "Would you take my Russian name, or would I have to be Preston?"

"I *had* a Russian name. When I was born, I was Aleksandra Vasil'evna Petrovna."

Lilya repeated it. "What a wonderful name. I'll have to remember it." But already her voice had grown melancholy. She glanced toward the window where the snow now fell against a backdrop of darkness. With an expression of anguish, she withdrew from Alex's embrace and moved to the edge of the bed.

"I'm sorry, my darling, but I promised to return to my mother and give her my last few hours." She stood up and reached for her underclothes.

Alex dressed alongside her, subdued. "I guess it would be ludicrous for me to tell you to be careful. But at least wear my scarf. Do you still have it?"

"Of course I do." Lilya tugged on her breeches and drew it from one of the pockets. "I wear it every time I fly."

"If only I had the power to make it a talisman, to protect you." She knotted it loosely around Lilya's neck, then helped her draw on her tunic and watched gloomily as she became a soldier again. Finally she handed over the military sheepskin coat and fur cap and pulled on her own heavy parka. "I'll walk with you to the street."

Lilya nodded, and they descended the stairs together without speaking until they stood outside on the Theatralny Proezd. The snow was still falling in thick, wet flakes, and several inches had accumulated on the street over the icy layer beneath. Alex was close to tears as she touched Lilya lightly on the face. "Good-bye, my witch of Stalingrad."

Lilya laid a mitten on top of the hand, holding it against her cheek. "Good night, Aleksandra Vasil'evna Petrovna," she said, and disappeared through the curtain of snow.

CHAPTER TWENTY-ONE

February–August 1943

So this is what it's like to be a war wife, Alex thought. In anguish constantly about someone and helpless to protect them. But the antidote to anguish was activity, so she applied again to the Press Department for permission to travel along the front with the other journalists. Within ten days it was granted, and she fell into a rhythm of one- and two-week postings to battle scenes, either during or just after, for the Red Army was growing in confidence and success.

After each assignment, she returned to Moscow to develop her photos and submit them to the censors. She no longer cared if they confiscated two or three, or half her collection. As long as she had something to send George, she could justify remaining.

Life in Moscow was somewhat improved. There were no more air raids, and though the lines were still long for the severely rationed food, the American Lend-Lease had helped, and no one appeared to be starving. Some of the factories had been shipped back from the Urals, and the streets had a bit more activity. Moscow felt like a city again.

On a late winter day, when the snow had turned to slush, she returned from Central Telegraph. As she passed the main desk the clerk called to her. "Miss Preston. You have mail." He held out a brown paper triangle.

Alex's heart quickened. Military post.

She took a seat in the lobby and unfolded it. It was unsealed, of course, since the military censor had carefully scrutinized it, so she knew the message would hold nothing intimate.

Hello, Miss Preston. Thank you for taking so many nice pictures when you were here. We are all proud to have served the Motherland and to present Stalin with the gift of our victories. The days are getting longer, though we still have a lot of snow and appreciate our sheepskin jackets and valenkis. Many greetings from the skies, which we are reclaiming with joy. Yours, Lilya Drachenko.

Alex smiled at the utter blandness of the message. But it did what it was supposed to do, inform her that Lilya was alive. It was all she dared hope for and all, for that matter, that most wives and mothers got from the front.

Emboldened by the field post, she went down the next Saturday morning to the hotel laundry and located Anna Drachenko on duty ironing the hotel's linen. Seeing her, Lilya's mother beamed, seeming indifferent to the stares of the other workers.

"Hello, my dear," she said, but kept on ironing.

"I'm sorry to interrupt you at work, but I wanted to share this with you." She brandished her little paper triangle and offered it.

Anna set down her iron and opened the folded note, a soft smile warming her face. "I see she wrote much the same thing to both of us. The only difference is that she didn't ask you to send mittens. Of course I bought the wool and knitted them in two days."

"That's what mothers are for, aren't they? Well, as long as she's asking for things, then we know she's well." She thought *alive*, but it would have been unkind to say it.

"Thank you for caring about her, dear." Anna laid a callused hand on her forearm. "You're a little like a daughter to me. She told me about your courage at Stalingrad, flying that plane while injured. Have you seen her since? Does she have a gentleman friend?"

Alex took a breath. "No. I've been with the other journalists these last few weeks. As for the other, well, I don't think she socializes with the men. They're all too busy flying. Her best friend is her mechanic, Inna Portnikova, a good soul."

"That's just as well. There's no point in her falling for one of those swaggering heroes. You know what young men are like." She folded the sheet in half and ironed a sharp edge on the fold.

"Yes, I do." Alex thought of Terry and realized she hadn't seen him in a while. What would he think of her new "family"?

"Well, I won't stay longer. I just wanted to share the latest news from Lilya. I'll be going back to the front myself in a while."

Anna set down her iron again. "You must be very careful then. And if you see my daughter, please tell her how much I miss her."

"I promise I will." Alex embraced her quickly, surprised at how comforting it was. With a brief wave of the hand, she turned and ascended the stairs to the main floor.

She was more annoyed than distressed when she entered the lobby and was confronted.

"Ah, my personal NKVD man. I haven't seen you around the hotel lately. Have you been promoted? Or demoted?"

He didn't smile. And she noted that he was looking haggard, no longer the sleek, self-confident government toady who'd warned her months before. She sensed a certain weakness in him and pressed her advantage.

"You never told me your name, Mr…? I mean, you obviously know mine."

He blinked for a moment. "My name is of no importance. I am already taking a risk in talking directly to you."

"All the more reason to tell me your name. Or any name you like. I can't keep referring to you as 'my NKVD man,' can I?"

His mouth twitched and he glanced around as if to see if anyone was watching them. "Call me Victor, then. That's as good a name as any."

"All right, Victor. What can I do for you?"

"You must not be so flippant, Miss Preston. You can do yourself great harm."

"Victor. What do you want from me?"

"I told you before, you should not interfere with the Drachenko family. Associating with foreigners taints them. Especially now."

"'Especially now?' What docs that mean?"

"This." He unfolded the afternoon edition of *Pravda* and handed it to her. The front page held a photograph of Lilya and her commander posing in front of his Yak. The article was a paean to the young aviators, first to the commander and then to Lilya, who had been a member of the Komsomol and now had shown her genius as a fighter for the Motherland. Together and separately they'd downed a significant number of planes, fighters and bombers.

"She'll soon be awarded Hero of the Soviet Union, the highest honor the homeland can bestow," Victor announced. "And there's talk she will marry this young man. But reputation is a fragile thing, and you will ruin everything if you associate with her family."

"I think you have a soft spot for this woman, Victor. That must not stand very well with the NKVD."

"If you mock this advice, you will regret it. Not because I will report you. But others are watching you as well, and they will not give you warnings." He folded the newspaper up again and slid it into the side pocket of his coat. It hung precariously from the pocket edge and added to his overall shabbiness. Nonetheless, she took him seriously.

"I hate the hypocrisy of this government, which calls its people heroes and at the same time treats them like prisoners. But all right, I'll stay away from the Drachenkos."

"Good. Just go and take your pictures and don't cause trouble. Nobody wants trouble." He seemed to sink into his overcoat and strode away, bearing no resemblance whatever to an NKVD agent.

Alex was as good as her word. She stayed in Moscow another few days, and then, as soon as permission came, she returned with the other journalists to the front. The next five months were a blur. She traveled sometimes with Eddy, from the Associated Press; sometimes with Ralph from *The London Times*; and again, near Voronezh, with her favorite, the cynical Henry Shapiro.

She photographed tanks on the attack, then on the retreat, then on the attack again. And she watched the planes overhead—the agile fighters, the bombers, the reconnaissance planes—which she could identify now by name.

Newspapers arrived at the front, and she glossed over them unless she found a reference to air battles. In late April, Lilya's commander crashed and was killed. *Well*, Alex thought bitterly, *at least they'll stop talking about her marrying him*.

And all the while, Lilya's kill count increased. On a trip back to Moscow Alex received a second field post from her, lamenting the loss of her commander, but all Alex cared about was that Lilya lived.

More informative were the occasional articles in *Pravda* and *Red Star*, that told of the success of the aviators, with regular counts of the highest-scoring aviators. Lilya now had two more kills to her name. Alex shivered at every mention of a kill. It seemed a hairsbreadth away from an announcement of being killed.

May came, with its rains and "General Mud" that slowed both the aggressor and the defender, but also the mails. She was with Parker and

Shapiro somewhere between Karkov and Belgorod as the war dragged on in slow motion, and the censor refused all her photos of the mud-splattered jeeps, mud-caked boots, mud-encased motorcycles, mud-covered horses, and mud-paralyzed troops.

At the beginning of June she returned to Moscow but found no field post from Lilya. What did that mean? She forced herself to wait until Saturday, when she would defy Victor's order and search out Anna to find out what she knew.

Every knock at her door gave her a thrill of hope, but when the Soviet Air Force uniform finally reappeared in her doorway, it held the cherubic form of Inna Portnikova.

"Oh, come in! I'm *so* glad to see you." Alex's enthusiasm was genuine.

"Nice to see you again, too. You're looking good. But I'm on the way to catch my train and only have a few minutes. Lilya wanted me to deliver this." She drew a letter from inside her gymnasterka and held it up. "Don't worry, it's sealed. No one has read it, and no one has seen it but me. And I was never here."

They embraced quickly and Inna disappeared down the corridor to the stairwell.

Alex tore open the letter, deliberately unsigned, to protect them both, but she recognized the sweeping handwriting.

My dearest. Forgive my silence, but I dare not send too much field post to you. The censors read everything and it would draw attention to us both. And I could never say that I long for you terribly. I must force you from my mind when I take off in pursuit of the enemy, but always I return thinking only of you. The ground troops cannot move forward for the mud, so our air strikes are all the more important. And since we lost more pilots recently, none of us can take any leave. Stay safe, my dearest, and please wait for me. One day I will come back to you.

Alex kept the letter beside her on the night table while she slept and carried it on her person on her trip back to the front. Soon the low-quality paper began to fray and disintegrate inside her pocket, so she folded it inside another paper to preserve it.

But no more letters came, and no more field posts, and by the end of June, when she again returned to Moscow, her optimism had evaporated.

Weekly messages arrived from George at *Century* magazine, but they became increasingly dreary, and the only relief she had was a cable from Terry Sheridan.

ARRIVING IN MOSCOW WED AFTERNOON STOP STAY AT HOTEL SO WE CAN MEET TERRY END.

Now she at least had something to look forward to, and in the morning, she allowed herself a brisk walk along Red Square and then past the Bolshoi. The great theater was officially closed and its company transferred eastward to safety, but a few brave souls stayed on in a subsidiary company and gave an occasional performance. Now someone had tacked up an announcement of an orchestral concert: Borodin, Prokofiev, and Rimsky-Korsakov.

Checking her watch, she noted it was already noon and so hurried back to the Metropole. The traffic on Theatralny was always sparse, so the car that pulled up caught her attention immediately. She brightened when she saw Terry climb out. The driver, as far as she could see from a distance, was an older woman, but when Alex ran toward him, waving, the car pulled away.

She embraced him cheerfully. "The OSS has old ladies chauffeuring you around?" She laughed.

"Who? What? Oh. That was Elinor, my…uh…secretary." He linked his arm in hers. "I'd have invited her in, but she had to rush off to finish a report." He led her toward the dining room and signaled for coffee as they sat down at a table.

"What brings you to Moscow this time?" she asked.

"Well, for starters…" He pulled a bulky package wrapped in brown paper from his canvas sack. "I knew better than to get nylons and girly things like that, so I settled on the socks and a new set of trousers. They're wrapped around the four cartons of cigarettes you asked for."

She laughed and gave him a peck on the cheek. "Good man. You know how to treat a woman right. Even if she doesn't sleep with you any more."

He made a cartoonish pout. "Is that your final decision?"

"I'm afraid so. Anyhow, you didn't come to Moscow simply to seduce me. What's going on?"

He drew a pack of Chesterfields from his pocket and tapped one out. "It seems we have a troubling issue with the Soviets. Remember all the bodies they found in the Katyn forest?" He lit the cigarette with a handsome Zippo.

"Of course, all those Polish officers the Gestapo killed in 1940."

"That, precisely, is the issue. It's looking more and more like the Russkies did it. Ordered by Stalin, of course." The waiter set down their almost-coffee.

"Isn't that what Goebbels wants the world to believe? That the Russians are savages?" She sipped the hot drink with little enjoyment. It needed more sugar.

"That's the tricky part. Yes, the Germans love it that suspicion is falling on the Russians, and that makes our alliances with them...um... sticky. But more and more evidence is coming to light that it was the NKVD. Churchill seems to think it was, and so does Roosevelt. No proof yet, but there's a stink in the room. Rather than make public accusations against our allies, the War Department has the OSS looking into it."

"How very complicated." She glanced around the dining room. "Speaking of the NKVD, I wonder what happened to Victor."

"Victor? Who's that?"

"One of the NKVD watchers. A rumpled fellow who usually sat over there and who was very bad at tailing me. The last time we met he warned me not to contact the Drachenkos, but he wasn't terribly menacing about it, as if he was losing his taste for the job."

He leaned back in his chair and waved to the waiter for another coffee. "If you don't see him, that's not a good sign. They've almost certainly replaced him with someone who's better at it. And if he warned you not to do something, you'd better not do it."

"I can't follow that advice, Terry. Lilya Drachenko is more than just a good story. She's like a...a sister to me. She's even smuggled letters through me that she couldn't send through field post. I care for her a lot, and her mother thinks of me as a daughter."

"Oh, Alex. Don't fall into that trap. They tell you that because they're all so miserable, they're hoping for a handout. Not to mention that if the NKVD had caught you delivering secret information, they'd have expelled you. It would have been the end of your credentials as a foreign journalist, if you were lucky. You might have also found yourself in jail for a few years. Promise me you won't go near that family again."

"Got it," she said, without actually promising, and finished her coffee. "Listen, I've got nothing to do until my photos dry." Let's go for a walk."

"You mean instead of sex?" The pout appeared again.

"Sorry, old friend. That ship has sailed. Come on and sublimate that horniness in a little exercise. She stood up, then sat down again. "I have an even better idea. The Bolshoi affiliate has a concert today." She looked at her watch. "In just about an hour, in fact. Why don't we go?"

"A concert instead of a roll in the hay?" He sighed. "All right. For old time's sake. Where do we have to go to buy the tickets?" He slid his chair back.

"We don't have to go anywhere. Georgy, the desk clerk, will sell them to you, though I think at this late date, only the most expensive ones will be left."

"This is a loyalty test, isn't it?" He stood up from the table.

"Don't worry, dear. Any man who accepts 'no' for an answer and still agrees to go to a concert passes with high marks. You're going to make some woman a wonderful lover."

CHAPTER TWENTY-TWO

Alex and Terry stood by the side entrance of the Bolshoi while he finished his cigarette. "Nice of you to agree to this," she said. "I've been wanting to see something here since I arrived in Moscow."

"Why didn't you? You were always only twenty yards away."

"Because they weren't here. The portico was bombed, and the main company was evacuated in forty-one to Kuibyshev. Their affiliate gives the occasional concert, but I've been too busy. Until now."

"Uh-hunh." It was obviously more information than he was looking for. "Ah, there's the buzzer." He stubbed out his cigarette butt on the ground and took her by the arm.

Alex glanced around when they arrived at their seat. The theater was in poor condition, the chandeliers removed and the upholstery threadbare, but for all that, the old grandeur of the hall was still evident. They were in the first mezzanine, to the right of the Tsar's Box, and several seats in their row were still vacant. She recognized a few of the other correspondents sitting across from them on the other side of the hall and realized that a good part of the audience was foreign. It made sense. The Russians were all in their factories working fourteen-hour days.

The musicians filed into the pit and tuned their instruments, and a chorus lined up onstage. Then the lights went out.

The concert started with Borodin's *Polovtsian Dances* and she tried to concentrate on the sound, but the war was too much on her mind. She couldn't warm to the idea of dances, and the women's voices in the chorus made her think of the "witches," who were probably taking off just then for another night of bombing.

She shut them out of her mind and tried to let the music affect her, but her flimsy attention was disrupted by the sound of someone entering the hall behind them. She glanced over her shoulder, annoyed.

A soldier stood at the rear of the box, peering into the semi-darkness. A small, slender soldier in an air force uniform broke into a smile.

How did she find them? How did she know? The unanswered questions evaporated, and she rose from her seat. She felt Terry's eyes following her as she stepped to the rear of the box.

Wordlessly, she took Lilya by the hand and led her back to the front row, offering the empty seat next to her. Lilya sat down, the grip of her hand tightening, and Alex almost ached with joy that she'd appeared. If only they could be someplace other than here.

Alex wove her fingers in among Lilya's and held their joined hands on her lap. She caught the whiff of Lilya's skin and hair that smelled of military soap and tried to reconstruct how she'd miraculously appeared. Had she finally been granted leave and stopped first to see Anna again, then gone to the hotel? So many questions and no way to talk.

No matter. In the absence of speech, she had the pressure of Lilya's hand, the smell of her skin, and the delicious music washing over them to make her dizzy with desire.

The music rose to a climax, then fell away again as the first piece ended. The applause began, and they unclasped hands only long enough to join it.

Terry leaned forward to acknowledge Lilya's presence. He nodded a brief greeting, and she smiled timidly back at him. Seated between them, Alex realized that they barely knew of each other's existence. She would have to introduce them formally later.

The orchestra tuned again and began the second piece, Prokofiev's *Romeo and Juliet Suite*. Lilya closed her eyes and slid her foot sideways so their lower legs just touched.

Alex stole a sideward glance at the radiant young face with blond curls that poked out from under her military cap. She slid her glance down to the swell of breasts in the khaki uniform, and a tiny portion of her mind registered the third medal pinned over the left pocket. Another enemy shot down, no doubt. Strange that medals for killing were worn over the heart.

The ballet piece seized her attention momentarily as the staccato melodies danced around her, and she imagined the two of them gamboling in a sunny meadow. The fantasy made her smile; Lilya Drachenko, decorated annihilator of enemy planes, didn't seem the meadow-dancing type.

The piece ended with enthusiastic applause while Alex bent toward Lilya and whispered, "How are you, darling? Are you all right?"

"I'm fine, now that I'm with you," she whispered back, and brushed her lips over Alex's ear.

Another tuning of instruments followed, and Rimsky-Korsakov's *Russian Easter Overture* began with the haunting theme sounding in the distant horns. Flutes answered in bright tremolos, hinting of birdsong and sparkling dew.

The horns called again, nearer, heralding something magnificent, but the other brass instruments followed, darker, almost ominous, as the musical narrative seemed to contradict itself. The rhythmic brass suggested armies, but were they invading or parading in victory? A brief tumultuous storm arrived that gave way to a melody of celebration.

The curious back-and-forth of menace and elation seemed to speak to her. Thrilled by the crescendo of the music, but also gripped by the tension of Lilya's imminent departure, she understood. The passions of the music were their passions, hers and Lilya's, and the magnificent overture seemed to tell their story in a sound painting.

The full orchestra was playing now, the bass instruments pulsing like a great machine that rolled over the landscape. Alex remembered it was a paean to the Resurrection, and the final climax of fanfares was an affirmation of the absolute triumph of good.

When it ended, she didn't wait for the applause but turned to the bewildered Terry and blurted, "We're going to the ladies' room." Then she sprang from her seat and urged Lilya from the box along the corridor and into one of the bathroom stalls.

Deeply grateful for the floor-to-ceiling doors on each cubicle, she drew the slightly giddy Lilya into her arms and covered her mouth in a long, breathless kiss.

Finally she broke off, panting, and whispered, "How did you find us?"

Lilya nibbled at her ear and murmured back. "Twenty-four-hour leave again. Stopped by my mother's house." Another kiss. "Then asked for you at the hotel." She bit her chin. "Clerk recognized me, said you were here, even knew the seats."

Alex threw her head back, amused. Of course, the clerk. He would have melted like wax before Lilya's beauty and told her everything. "How much time do you have left? Can we go back to my room?"

Suddenly somber, Lilya shook her head. "No. Travel takes so long, and returning late is treated as desertion. I'd be arrested. I'm just glad to find you. Especially since it could be weeks…months, before we see each other again."

Alex studied her, trying to memorize the details of the pale-blue eyes, the full muscle around the mouth. "And we wasted a precious hour listening to a concert."

"Not wasted. We were together, and happy."

Alex took Lilya's face in her hands. "Yes, we were. We are. I love you, you wild, reckless woman. I can't bear the thought of losing you to the war again."

"You won't lose me. I'll stay alive for you, and I'll come back, I promise. Wait for me."

"Of course I'll wait for you. How can you doubt it? And when you come back, when it's all over, I want to fly with you. I want to learn how to fly the Yak. Do you think your air force will let me do that?"

"I can ask. It would be fun, wouldn't it? You and me together in the sky. Almost as good as loving you."

"Almost." Alex kissed her again, hard, hungrily, but Lilya tore herself away. "I have to go." She yanked open the cubicle door and left at a run, without looking back.

Alex stood dazed for a moment, then returned to the corridor. Terry waited by the door of their theater box, smoking again. He tapped the ash off his cigarette into a sand urn. "Who's your friend? And what was that all about?"

"That was Lilya Drachenko, on short leave. I told you about her. We've become very close."

"Come on, Alex. I'm not your granddad. I know romance when I see it. I'm not so much shocked by that as I am about your recklessness. What do you suppose the NKVD is going to make of it?"

"Do you think they were watching? Even here at the Bolshoi?"

"Probably not directly, but I'm guessing someone in the hall noted that she was here, and the information will get back to them." He took another puff and blew smoke out of the side of his mouth. "So, you love this woman?"

She hesitated. "Yes, I do. And don't tell me it's insane. I know that already."

"Insane and dangerous. So where are you planning to meet her next?"

"Nowhere. She's leaving for the front tonight. And I'm about to go back with the other journalists."

As they filed out through the side door of the Bolshoi, Terry put his arm around her. "Alex. Please don't get involved with this soldier. You're from different worlds, and she has nothing to offer you. Trust me. It can't end well. There will be no going off into the sunset with this one."

CHAPTER TWENTY-THREE

July 1943

Terry's visit was short and easy to forget, and so was his advice on romance. Not that it made any difference in practical terms since Lilya was out of contact. Alex had only memory and hope to sustain the sense of being "involved." And while she waited, she was still a photojournalist.

Each day she checked in with the other correspondents looking for leads, for openings, for news of what the Press Department would allow. But the Red Army had suffered some defeats, gaining Kursk and then losing it again, and the Kremlin announced a temporary suspension of foreign coverage of the battlefield. Battle reportage would be through Soviet military reporters only, and the news would appear in *Red Star*.

"No matter," Henry Shapiro assured her over their usual breakfast of powdered eggs. "They're letting us cover civilian stories, and I've got permission to report on the new T-34 tank. Want to come along? It involves a long train trip to the Ural Tank Factory in Nizhny Tagil."

"If the alternative is sitting here and rephrasing propaganda from Sovinformburo, then sure. I'll apply this afternoon."

The gargantuan production apparatus of Tank Factory Number 183 was all a photojournalist could ask for. The factory floor, like that of the aircraft plant she'd visited earlier, was hellish but made for spectacular photographs. And as before, the malnourished, mostly female workers who labored in shifts twenty-four hours a day in deafening noise weren't aware of being photogenic. "Hard to believe," Henry shouted over the din. "I bet enough metal passes through this factory complex to build a Midwestern American city."

Alex nodded, trying to breathe in shallow breaths in air that stank of oil, hot steel, and rancid sweat.

While Henry engaged the foreman, she strode along the assembly line capturing the grime-covered women hauling steel. When she'd photographed every aspect of tank construction, she moved outside and got long-distance shots of the thousands of tanks lined up in the field depot awaiting transport. The scenes were powerful, and the self-evident message of the photos would be, "We are strong, we are steel, and we are endless."

On the second day, the factory commissar caught up with her, and when he learned that she spoke Russian, he held forth on the creation and development of the T-34, the patriotism of its workers, and the inspiring productivity of the state factories under Stalin. She expressed her admiration and politely promised to spread the message to the West, along with her photographs.

When she rejoined Harry, he had more good news.

"I've got us a ride to Kursk. The man in charge of transporting the current batch of T-34s invited us to travel on the train carrying them toward the front. I told him we'd be delighted. Should give you a few more great shots."

"Well done, Henry. You're a credit to the profession."

The train left at dawn the next morning, and they took their place in the passenger car with the officers and medical personnel. The summer's day was bright, perfect for photography, and when the train swung around a wide curve, Alex could capture most of the nearly hundred railcars. Each flatbed car bore two new tanks, and each tank carried three men riding, day and night, in the open air across the landscape.

At the Kursk train station, Alex and Henry watched as the tanks rolled off the railcars and rumbled on without pause. "Ugly things, when you really look at them," he remarked while she snapped photos. "Great, lumbering steel beetles. And the whole countryside around Kursk is covered with them, blasting the hell out of each other for a month already."

"A pestilence of panzer," she added, taking the last shot. "Anyhow, I've seen enough. What about you?"

"Agreed. I say we go back with the hospital train to Moscow. I'm ready for a hot bath, a good meal, and the kindness of a woman."

Alex glanced quizzically at him as they crossed the tracks toward the train painted with white crosses.

"I meant my wife. That's what keeps me in Russia, after all, the love of a Russian woman."

That's what keeps me here too, she thought.

They found seats but had to wait for several hours while a seemingly endless line of ambulances arrived and transferred their wounded on board. "And those are the lucky ones," Henry muttered.

They departed in the early evening, and as Alex stared out at the rugged landscape of the Urals, the rattle of the train wheels brought back the memory of her trip from Archangelsk to Moscow. She'd been clean then, devoid of lice and, for that matter, of any idea what the war would be like. How her world had changed since that day.

She'd started to doze when someone came through their car and handed out copies of *Red Star*. The headlines trumpeted the ever-weakening German resolve and the certainty of victory at Kursk. Tired and filthy, with the taste of grease in her mouth, she scanned the first few pages. The number of fatalities wasn't recorded, but the wounded were mentioned as "heroes of the Motherland on their way to our hospitals for care."

The second page held more good news. The air force, which was beginning to gain air superiority, gave several accounts of successful air battles with the tallies for the public's favorite pilots. She scanned the column until she found Drachenko: eleven solo kills and three shared. Was she the only person in the Soviet Union who shuddered at the thought?

❖

After a thorough bath at the Hotel Metropole Alex developed her film. She had a story George would love: the T-34, made by women. The tanks had breathtaking power, but Henry was right; they were ugly machines that crushed and smashed things, and blasted them away. She needed to work on something less hideous now. But what? She'd talk it over with Henry and the others at dinner.

However, when she passed the desk on the way to the dining room, a small brown triangle of field post awaited her. She held it in her pocket, delaying gratification, and went back to her room to read it.

Dear Miss Preston, or dare I call you comrade? I am happy to know you are in Moscow telling the world about our struggle. Here we continue to fight for the Motherland, inspired by the victories at Stalingrad and by the strength of our comrades and our leaders.

It is possible that when my duties here are complete, I may join old friends and fly the planes we both love, so perhaps we will meet again on another airfield. I go happily where I am ordered in our common struggle.

As always, I send my good thoughts to you and my good wishes for your continued stay in Russia.

A simple message of patriotism, that was both exaggerated and sincere and would pass the scrutiny of any censor. She also took note of "the planes that we both love," the irony of which would go unnoticed. Lilya hated the old U-2s and would fight kicking and screaming before she would accept flying in them again.

Alex chuckled, and now she knew what her next project would be. A new article on the Night Witches.

CHAPTER TWENTY-FOUR

Unlike her assignment to Major Kazar's regiment, which General Osipenko had obviously hastened, the request for engagement with the night bombers moved slowly through the hierarchy of authority. Alex checked in first with George Mankowitz, then applied to the Press Department. Then she waited for three more weeks for agreement to filter down from the People's Commissariat of Defense to the Night Bomber Aviation Division, and finally to Major Bershanskaya herself.

By the time she joined the 588th air regiment, it was October, and they had moved forward to Volodarka, in the Ukraine. A series of trains and supply trucks finally carried her out to the air base. When she stepped off the supply truck, a young recruit she didn't know met her and led her to a dugout nearly identical to the one at Stavropol. Apparently, Soviet field bunkers didn't vary much.

"How's the food?" she asked the recruit.

"Pretty good. The old-timers tell me it's much better than before. Less kasha and more spam from America. But the mice get into anything that's not in cans."

"Vishneva, I believe you're on duty now." Eva Bershanskaya stood in the doorway.

"Yes, Comrade Major. I was just on my way." The young woman saluted and slid past the commander at the entrance.

"Nice to see you, Miss Preston. Will you walk with me?" Bershanskaya asked.

"Uh, yes, of course." Alex dropped her kit bag on the nearest free bunk and stepped outside the dugout, where the commander waited. She appeared wearier than before, and her uniform was rumpled.

Alex felt a warm respect for the taciturn commander. Rumors had floated around that she never wanted the command position and had refused it at first, begging to simply be able to fly, but Marina Raskova, the woman who had persuaded Josef Stalin, had also persuaded her. She started off toward the airfield, and Alex fell in step beside her.

"Do you still fly only the U-2s?"

"Unfortunately, yes." They were out on the field now, strolling along the aisle between the planes. Most had their engine cowlings open and mechanics tinkering with their interiors.

"I'm proud of my women," Bershanskaya said. "Already more than a dozen are Heroes of the Soviet Union. They're like sisters to each other. Sometimes more. Very often more. And each death kills a little part of us. We grieve but then return to work the next night. But now tell me the truth. There's nothing new for you to photograph here. Why have you come back?"

Alex thought for a moment. She didn't want to lie to this woman. "I've photographed all over the front and in the factories and railroad stations, but my work was always impersonal. Meanwhile, the women I met and cared about from the 588th have been killed, one by one. Only Lilya Drachenko's left now, and she hinted she might be assigned again to the night bombers. It was where we both started this war, and I suppose, like her, I feel an attachment."

Bershanskaya began strolling again. "So you've come back for Lilya. I'm not surprised. Many people love her, both men and women. But she's close to very few. If she let you in, you're very lucky."

The major's candor put her at ease. "I know I am. And I'm worried. I haven't heard from her in weeks."

Bershanskaya stopped walking and pivoted around to face her directly. "I'm afraid I don't have encouraging news for you. The other women don't know yet, but the commander of the 586th reported yesterday that she disappeared in battle."

Alex's chest turned to stone. "Disappeared? What does that mean? Shot down?"

"It means what it says. Another pilot saw her fly into a cloud, and she never reappeared. She was in borderline territory, so they've sent out a search team to see if she was able to land. If they don't find her or her plane in the next days, they'll report her officially missing and the news will become public."

"And if they never find her plane?"

"She'll be suspected of desertion."

❖

Alex waited in the purgatory of uncertainty.

Weeks passed, and still no news came. The official ruling of suspected desertion sickened her but at the same time gave her hope. As long as Lilya wasn't found, she wasn't dead.

She gathered the women of the 588th around her like sisters waiting for news of a family member. When the night bombers were transferred to the Belorussian Front, she followed them, with only the faintest pretense of being a foreign correspondent. She used only a single camera now, photographing the women's faces, and waited for news after the others had stopped, sensing, or perhaps only hallucinating, that Lilya was alive and near.

She filled the time helping the armorers. The sheer pain of lifting the hundred-kilo bombs from their carts and sliding them into their cradles allowed her to shut down the part of her brain that tormented her. That part whispered the two equally monstrous possibilities: that Lilya was dead or that she was in the hands of the enemy.

Then in November, after the last aircraft had made its final run and Alex staggered off the field at daybreak, Major Bershanskaya summoned them all together on the field.

"I've just received a call from headquarters, and it is my sad duty to tell you that the search parties from the 586th have found Lieutenant Drachenko's plane. It had crashed in what was borderline territory but now is in the hands of the Red Army."

A murmur of disbelief rumbled through the circle of women until someone called out, "What about Lilya?"

The major clutched her hands, schoolmarm-like, over her waist, as if to prevent an escape of emotion. "They found the body of a woman near the plane. It was burnt beyond recognition, but they assume it to be Lieutenant Drachenko."

"No!" someone called out, and a dozen other voices echoed the despair.

"I share your sorrow at the loss of our friend and comrade. We'll keep her in our thoughts, along with comrades Budanova and Beliaeva, and all the others who have fallen, the next time we attack the enemy. That will be all, Comrades. Dismissed."

Alex stood as if riveted, unable to absorb the news, as if it had been delivered in an unintelligible language. Then, numbly, she followed the others off the airfield to the bunkers.

CHAPTER TWENTY-FIVE

Sofija Kovitch shaded her eyes and watched the air battle overhead. The Red Army had pushed the enemy back a few days before, but the Fritzes never lost air superiority and had retaken the woods in front of her. As the daughter of Sydir Kovitch, the leader of a well-armed partisan band, she was confident that the German victory was temporary and that the Soviets would soon drive them out again.

Her father's partisans answered to the Red Army, though their strategies were decided locally. Most wore military uniforms, as she did, and it was a mark of how much they trusted her that they had given her a military pistol as well. She lacked only the boots but would snatch them off the next dead Fritz she came across.

She tilted her head back, watching the six Junkers 88s in battle with a squadron of Yaks. They dove and swooped in their deadly pirouettes until one and then another of the Junkers exploded, and she pounded the air in cheer.

But to her horror, four more Messerschmitts arrived and disabled one of the Yaks. Outnumbered, the remaining Russian craft fled. She watched the damaged Yak descend in a shallow curve and crash in the woods in front of her.

Could she help, or was it too late? She ran toward the smoke and found the crashed Yak in a small clearing, one wing broken and lying on its side. The canopy was open, though, and as she rushed toward it, she could see no pilot. Had he parachuted? Or been thrown? She called out, "Where are you?" It was puzzling, but fire was creeping along the fuselage of the plane so she backed away.

She turned at the sound of voices to see four Germans enter the clearing with rifles raised. Knowing the fate of partisans, she drew her pistol and shot at them, but at the same moment, the rifle bullets ripped into her chest.

Lying helpless in the brush, Lilya heard the woman calling. She struggled to answer, but all that came out was a weak groan. Moments later, she heard the men and then the gunshots.

Her head pounded, and her vision was so distorted she could make out only unfocused patches of green overhead. She felt an excruciating pain in her chest with every breath and couldn't move one of her arms without a jolt of agony.

Through blurred vision, she could just make out the ring of German soldiers gathering around her, their rifles pointed at her head. In the last remnants of her consciousness, she was tortured with regret, and the faces of those she'd failed passed before her: her mother, Katia, Major Raskova, and finally, most cruelly, Alex. Then the darkness closed in again.

Lilya came to in breathtaking pain, rocking back and forth in the back of a horse-drawn wagon. Her eyes still wouldn't focus, but she could make out the form of a man squatting next to her, a rifle laid across his knees. She was captured. Her worst nightmare.

Every rattle and sway of the wagon sent a wave of fire up from her right arm and across her chest, and she was filled with shame. There was no dishonor in being shot down, but pilots who couldn't escape were supposed to have the good grace to die. She, on the other hand, had become a pawn of the enemy.

They'd gone to some trouble to carry her out of the woods, so obviously they planned to interrogate her. She was so weak and in such torment, she was sure she'd say anything to make it stop. Thankfully, she knew little that would be of any use to them.

She moved in and out of consciousness as they rattled along, each time awakening to the same hellish fire and confusion. She couldn't tell how long she'd lain in the wagon, only that she was desperately thirsty. "Water," she begged over and over, but they ignored her.

Finally, when her mouth was like straw and she couldn't move her tongue, she heard someone approach the wagon. Rough hands pulled her by her feet and stood her on the ground, where she collapsed.

Someone snarled at her, and she screamed as they yanked her up under her shoulders from the ground. The two men discussed something between them before dropping her onto a stretcher. They carried her into some kind of truck and laid her on the floor. "Water," she begged again, but they walked away.

She lay, able to do nothing more than breathe. It was perhaps better if she died. At least the Germans couldn't use her. But two men finally came and stood over her.

"He wants to know who you are," one of them said in perfect, accent-free Russian. "Tell us and we'll give you some water."

We? The Russian was on their side? She was barely conscious and wracked with pain and thirst, but she still had room for anger. She knew what questions would come first, and though she was allowed to give name and rank and branch of service, she wouldn't even tell them that.

Lilya Drachenko had been in the newspapers and was a celebrated name in aviation now, as Marina Raskova had been. What a coup it would be for the Germans to have captured someone with so much propaganda value. She had to lie.

"Aleksandra Petrovna," she croaked through cracked lips.

"What regiment do you belong to?"

"Water," she repeated.

Someone kicked her in the hip and shouted in German.

"The 9th Guards." She forced the words out from a raw and burning throat. That, too, was a lie. She had no idea where the 9th Guards were fighting. It would be just one more piece of useless information for them.

Suddenly a cup of water was at her lips. Someone tipped her head so she could reach it, and she drank in desperate gulps.

"Who is your commander?"

"Major Smerdyakov." She lied again, this time a bit more recklessly. Amazing how a drink of water had raised her spirits.

"Smerdyakov? I never heard of him."

"Recently promoted from the ranks." She continued the fantasy. If the fool had ever read Dostoyevsky, he'd have recognized the name.

"That's all for now."

The German left, but the Russian remained. "Stupid woman. Why are you risking your life for Stalin?"

She knew now who this man was. Not by name, of course, but she recognized his argument. She'd seen the pamphlets that his pack of turncoats, the Vlasov Army, had dropped on Soviet soil exhorting people to rise up against Stalin.

She refused to answer him, for it was the wrong question. She was fighting for the Motherland and her struggle had nothing to do with Stalin, even though his brutish face hung in every military office.

"All right, then. Wallow in your pain. You brought it on yourself." He made an about-face and jumped down from the truck.

The tiny spark of hope she'd had hearing Russian flickered out. She'd have to help herself. To start, she had to assess her injuries. Gathering her strength, she used her good left hand to tap her way down her right arm. It seemed like a bone in her forearm was fractured, and the painful swelling in her wrist told her that was damaged, too. Then, at her right shoulder, she discovered the reason for the excruciating pain. Her flight suit was burned away, and the skin held a pattern of blisters and sticky open flesh. Only her leather flight helmet had kept the side of her face from burning.

Why had she collapsed outside? Were her legs damaged? She moved her toes inside her boots and lifted her legs a few centimeters at both knees. No, thank God, no broken legs. It was simply pain and shock.

She patted her abdomen. No pain there, though the lower part of her flight suit was wet. The faint smell of urine was probably her own, though her odor was the least of her worries at the moment. If they tortured her, she was done for. But perhaps it was her turn now, to follow Katia and all the others who had fallen.

Strange, she thought, how absolute helplessness offered a kind of freedom, particularly if you weren't afraid of death. At that moment, she was not. Her only regret was that her mother would mourn. And Alex.

The truck began to move and she fell in and out of a stupor until, hours later, the sound of the rear doors opening again penetrated the gray soup she floated in. A man climbed into the vehicle.

"You're the pilot?"

"Yes, Aleksandra Petrovna." She felt a twinge of pleasure at maintaining the lie.

"Well, Aleksandra Petrovna, I am Pyotr Stepanov. Also a prisoner, but I'm a doctor. The Germans are letting me look after you." He waved over another man and together they slid her stretcher from the truck.

As they bore her along a path to the camp entrance, she looked to the side. The camp seemed to be nothing but an open field surrounded by barbed wire. Within the wire thousands of men sat or lay on the ground.

Dr. Stepanov held the stretcher at her feet and looked down at her. "You're lucky. I can't do much for your injuries, but the Germans have never seen a woman pilot before, so you're a novelty. They're letting me keep you in the medical tent. I have nothing to treat you with, but at least you'll be covered when it rains."

"Uh-hunh." She grunted agreement. Her broken forearm pulsed with pain and she was feverish. The thought of lying in the cooling rain wasn't at all unpleasant.

He was right about the medical tent. It was simply a covered version of the open field. Men lay on the ground next to each other moaning or unconscious and the revolting odor told her some had dysentery.

Stepanov and the other stretcher-bearer carried her to a corner and lifted her off the stretcher. She cried out from the pain of being lifted and then lay panting. "Please, can I have more water?"

"That's another advantage to being here," he said, standing up. "You don't get any extra food, but we have plenty of water."

He returned with a tin cup that he held to her mouth, and the cool water gave her instant relief. While he was still kneeling beside her, a German officer came into the tent, tapped his thigh with a baton, and said something in German. It must have been something witty, because he chortled.

Stepanov translated. "He asked how you lost your plane?"

She didn't think he expected a reply.

The officer continued, still in a jocular tone, and the only word she understood was "Soviet."

"He asks if the Soviet Air Force is so desperate that it uses women."

That, too, seemed like the remark of a man trying to be clever rather than seeking information. What should she say? It would be folly to reply with a wisecrack of her own, yet she couldn't bring herself to be servile.

"Every Russian struggles for the Motherland," she said, and the doctor repeated in German.

The officer made another remark and his expression told her he mocked her. Then, to her horror, he summoned another officer, who aimed a little box camera at her and snapped a photo.

"He says that he's supposed to shoot women in uniform, but you're the only female pilot in the camp, and he wants to show his wife a picture of you," Stepanov explained. "And he wants to know how old you are."

She saw no harm in answering. "Twenty-one."

"Twenty-one," the officer exclaimed. "And already a pilot."

"I was flying at sixteen," she boasted, then regretted it instantly. She was allowing him to engage her and giving more information than she was allowed.

But the officer merely shook his head in disbelief and turned away, taking his cameraman with him.

"Dr. Stepanov." She implored him when they'd left. "What do I look like?"

"If you're worried that you aren't attractive in the photo, I regret to tell you, you're correct. Aside from being rather dirty, your entire face is swollen and both your eyes are ringed in black. I'm sure you're a very pretty girl, but right now, your own mother wouldn't recognize you."

She sighed relief. If the photo somehow made its way back to Russia, at least it wouldn't reveal who she was.

"Now you must let me examine you and wash you. We have only cold water and no soap, but it's better than the men are getting outside in the field."

He helped her to a sitting position but she cried out. "My arm. I think it's broken."

"All right, we'll check all of that. Here, let's take off your flight jacket."

She drew back from his touch.

"Don't worry. I'll respect your modesty. But I have to be able to identify what bones are broken. You mustn't be afraid of a doctor's hands."

"No, it's just..." She never finished the sentence because at that moment he'd opened her jacket and seen the medals on her tunic.

"Oh my. It seems you're not only a pilot, but a very good one." He leaned forward to study them. "Medals for bravery, special aviation, parachuting, and...for the defense of Stalingrad." He sat back, studying her for the first time, then swept his wet rag over her cheeks.

"Blond hair, blue eyes," he murmured. "A fighter at Stalingrad. I know who you are."

She raised her good hand and pushed away the rag. "Please. You can't let them know. They'll make propaganda with me. I can never go back."

"The men who captured you, they didn't find any identification?"

"I don't carry any. If I crash, my comrades will know my plane. But I'd never want the enemy to know who I am."

He nodded. "Yes, I understand. But the medals. We'll have to get rid of them."

"Yes, please." She struggled to help him remove the flight jacket and tunic, though drawing her broken arm through the sleeve was a torment.

Stepanov washed the shoulder burn with cold water. "We should cover it, too, until it heals.

"Can you use my scarf?" She untied the blue polka-dot silk with her good hand.

"Yes. I'll rinse it in water first. It's at least cleaner than your uniform."

When the silk had dried, he used it to wrap the shoulder. He also collected enough rags to wrap her chest, forearm, and wrist, and immobilize the arm. Though it ached terribly, it was a relief to not have to endure the cutting pain that wracked her with every sudden movement.

"I had a daughter about your age. She was a medic assisting me and was killed when I was captured."

"I'm so sorry," she said. "She was lucky to have a father like you."

The stories of Russian prisoners being tortured appeared to be both false and true. Though the camp guards sometimes kicked her or spat at her when they passed, they otherwise ignored her, and her only interrogator was the officer who'd taken her picture.

She cooperated and defied him at the same time. It was easy to create a mix of truth and lies, to narrate a tale that told them little more than they already knew, that the Soviet Air Force was growing daily in strength, that they had air superiority over all of Russia and ever more of the Ukraine. She gave him the coordinates of an air base they'd long abandoned, and since it corresponded with his own reconnaissance reports, he believed her.

"Such a waste of an attractive girl," he said finally. "My daughter is only ten, safe at home and in school. I can't imagine how a man can let his daughter go into battle. But I suppose your father loved Stalin more than his family."

She opened her mouth to speak and then closed it again. How could she explain to this smug Nazi that her father didn't love Stalin, and that opposing him had cost him his life? Duty, patriotism, family loyalty all swam together in her mind, confusing her, and she was relieved when he left.

The fractures in her ribs and forearm, which Stepanov assured her were "clean," seemed to slowly heal, the bones knitting together again by themselves over the weeks. Her main torture was always hunger. All around her she saw men dying, but the novelty of her being a woman pilot gave her enough status that the stronger of the other prisoners brought her scraps of their own scarce bread.

Stepanov was like a guardian angel, particularly in the beginning when she was most helpless. Gentleman that he was, in the first few days, he even helped her to the latrine pit and turned his back while she fumbled with her breeches to take care of her needs.

September came, and, though weak from hunger, she could finally take a deep breath without pain and use both her hands again. In spite of her improvement, she left the bandages around her chest and arms for the warmth they provided in the cooling autumn air.

The interrogating officer returned once or twice, perhaps to satisfy his curiosity about how a woman POW could get along. Each time he clucked in disapproval at her very existence, comparing her with his own well-protected daughter. The two fathers, Stepanov and the camp officer, presented a troubling puzzle. Who was the good father? The one who brought his daughter into battle and lost her, or the one who sheltered her at home while killing the daughters of other men? And what did it say about her own father, who had done neither?

October came, and ever more Soviet planes flew overhead. Surely that meant the Russian line was advancing. Surely it meant liberation.

But instead, early one morning one of the camp officers entered the medical tent. "Everyone on your feet. We're moving the prisoners westward."

With Stepanov's help, she stood up and joined the line shuffling from the tent. What would happen to the patients who were too weak to walk?

The answer came immediately as a guard walked along the rows of helpless men with his pistol drawn. "Get up," he ordered each one, and if the patients were unconscious or too weak to stand, he shot them through the head.

Stepanov was outraged. "You can't do that! They're soldiers just like you." He tried to brush aside the pistol that was pointed at a cringing and already skeletal man. Without a word, the guard swung it around and shot him in the chest, then turned it back to fire a second time into the patient's head.

Lilya tried to go to Stepanov's side, but someone seized her by the upper arm and drew her back. It was the interrogating officer. "Don't fight back if you want to stay alive," he said, and shoved her into the shuffling line.

Outside she heard hundreds of more shots and cringed, knowing each one was an execution. Nonetheless, she stumbled along in the middle of the wide line that curved westward across the scorched Ukrainian landscape.

The padded summer flight jacket she had been captured in was designed for open-air flying, so it gave her an advantage over the men in summer uniforms. She was warm enough for the moment but wasn't prepared for the Russian winter.

They marched in a sluggish column through the day and were allowed to collapse at night, and any who couldn't rise and march again in the morning were shot. She lost count of the days, but when they finally passed through a town, one of the men in the line near her said, "I know this place. It's Vinnytsia."

Just then, it began to snow.

CHAPTER TWENTY-SIX

A week passed after the announcement of Lilya's plane crash, and then another, and Alex herself couldn't have said why she stayed. Perhaps it was inertia, the paralysis of someone whose reason for going on had been snatched away. Perhaps she also sensed a bit of Lilya in the women's regiment that was her family and could not yet tear herself away from it.

In November, the autumn rains turned to snow, and she even considered returning to New York to central heating, good food, and privacy. But she imagined herself in her apartment on 112th Street and found the thought bleak. She didn't even have a cat.

Inna had also transferred back to the night bombers, and they sat sometimes together in their wretched dugout next to the oil-drum stove like bereaved sisters. But during the all-night bombing raids, a camaraderie existed among the women that she loved and that held her, at least until she could gather the strength to start life over.

Then on a blustery December day, when she emerged from the dugout to go for what passed for breakfast, Major Bershanskaya stopped her.

"I hear you know how to fly the U-2," she said.

"Well, I flew one once, over Stalingrad. Not my best day, though. I crashed into a snowdrift."

Bershanskaya wrinkled her nose. "Not a glowing recommendation, is it? But still, we have a job that needs doing, and we're shorthanded."

"What? You want me to go on a bombing mission?" Alex was horrified.

"No, nothing as risky as that. But partisan bands are working behind the enemy lines, more or less under Red Army command. One of them, the Kovitch band, has become our responsibility, and we'll be flying food and ammunition to them. We have the planes and the navigators, and now the supplies, but not enough pilots. All the women are assigned to the bombing raids."

"Deliveries? In enemy territory?"

"Yes, but you'll be far from enemy concentrations. You drop the containers without landing and then fly back. In the dark it's pretty safe. We'll give you a couple of days to practice on the U-2s. What do you think?"

Alex considered the dangers. She'd never flown in the dark and had absolutely no idea how to land without lights. Moreover, as a foreign journalist, flying such a mission would probably also be breaking some kind of international law. It was lunacy.

"Sure, I'll go. You'll have to get me a flight suit, though. The last time I was in the air, I nearly froze to death."

"Come to my quarters after the meal and meet your navigator, Valentina. I'll have a flight suit for you, too."

The sun was just setting over the sparse trees on the horizon when Alex strode out onto the airfield. She flexed her arms and legs, testing her mobility under the thick, padded jacket and breeches. She'd insisted on keeping her own Macy's fur-lined lace-up boots rather than the oilskin boots issued to the Russian pilots. Also unlike them, she wore thick socks instead of footcloths, and her own winter gloves.

In the last light of the winter afternoon, she pulled the flaps of the fur cap over her ears and watched the ground crew finish loading the cylinders into the bomb cradles under the wings. Valentina appeared next to her, and they marched together toward the biplane.

"I presume you know where we're going," Alex said, patting the fuselage as if it were the flank of a horse.

"Sure, I do. I'll show you." Valentina spread out the map of their route on the tail wing of the plane. "We start here." She tapped with her gloved finger on a corner of the map. "Then we fly basically southwest over Volodarka." She traced a line diagonally across the paper. "The drop zone is here, just east of Vinnytsia." She folded the map. "We don't have to land, just come in as low as possible and drop the containers like bombs. Kovitch's men will come onto the field and fetch them."

"You're sure you can get us there in the dark?"

"It's what we navigators do. Besides, I know the zone pretty well. You just fly us there while I read off the map and the compass. We have in-plane radios now, so I'll tell you when to change heading and when we're at the drop site. If we're in the right spot, the partisans will hear our motor and set up signal lights."

"All right. If you say so." Thrilled and terrified in equal measure, Alex climbed into the pilot's cockpit, buckled herself in, and set on her headphones, while behind her Valentina did the same.

The little U-2 fishtailed slightly as it rumbled along the short runway, but soon they were aloft and gaining altitude. She watched the altimeter as they climbed, and the snow-sprinkled ground receded below them.

Valentina's voice came through the earphones. "When we reach 1,000 meters, head west by southwest. That will take us over Volodarka, which is on a bay, on the northwest side. I'll be timing us, but in general, you'll follow the river southwest. It's another hundred or so kilometers to Vinnytsia."

Alex obeyed, concentrating on keeping the plane level and at the right altitude. The night was clear, and it was quite easy to follow the rivers that snaked across the landscape reflecting silver in the moonlight. Where the lines became white ice, she maintained heading and rediscovered them where they widened and became open water again.

"It's pretty calm. Is it because the Germans can't see us, or do they not have any flak left?"

"I wouldn't bank on that. There's still heavy fighting in this part of the Ukraine, flak included. That's why the partisans need our supplies. But we should be at the drop spot now. Go down to 500 meters and circle. As soon as we see the light pattern, we'll know it's them."

Alex circled, as ordered, until Valentina called out, "There it is at four o'clock. You see it? The *L* pattern. Swing around so you can approach down the long arm of the *L* and get to about one hundred meters when we're at the bottom."

"One hundred meters, eh? Why don't you ask for twenty, while you're at it?"

"Twenty meters? Can you do that? That'd be wonderful."

"I was being sarcastic."

Alex aimed for the foot of the *L* below them and watched the altimeter. Two hundred meters, one hundred fifty, one hundred. But they were still some distance from the target. She took a chance, calling out, "Ninety…eighty…seventy…sixty-five. Cargo away!"

With one hand she yanked on the wires that opened the cradles holding the containers, while with the other she pulled back on the control stick. The added speed along with the sudden lightening of their weight caused them to shoot up over the trees at the end of the clearing.

"Well done, Alex. Well done. Now, as soon as you gain altitude, curve back and reverse course. We'll follow the same rivers back."

Alex continued climbing, still heading westward. When she finally leveled out, she peered over the edge of the cockpit. "What's that below? Everything else is in blackout, but something down there's lit up. Aren't they afraid of night bombers?"

"I think it's the concentration camp at Vinnytsia, and the Germans know we won't bomb them. It's filled with our POWs."

"A POW camp, here in the Ukraine? Of course, it makes sense. We have their POWs and they have ours. Do you think it's possible to find out if any of *our* missing pilots are there? I mean, do the Germans keep track of the names?"

"I know what you're thinking. We've all thought it. But she's dead, Alex. Just let it go."

❖

Emotional lethargy had kept Alex there. The hard physical strain and the companionship had sustained her through the grieving, but now she had to leave. With the next delivery of photos, she'd stay in Moscow. Maybe it was also time to go home.

Coming from the mess bunker, she bent forward into the blowing December snow and was heading for her own dugout to sleep when a figure appeared in front of her.

"Major Bershanskaya, good morning."

The major didn't greet her back but merely said, "Please come with me to headquarters. Someone wants to speak with you."

"Uh, yes, of course." The solemnity of the request was ominous, but she followed the commander back to the two-room shed that was both her office and sleeping quarters.

Three officers were waiting. Though they were clothed in heavy sheepskin coats, their maroon and royal-blue caps revealed they were NKVD. Her heart began to pound.

One of them stepped forward. "Alex Preston?"

"Yes?" she answered quietly.

"You will please come with us." The other man grasped her lightly around the upper arm and turned her toward the door.

"Can I fetch my things from the bunker? My clothes and my papers?"

"We have your papers and you will not need the clothes," the officer said, and a moment later, she was outside in the snow again.

A half-dozen women had come forward, and they watched, seemingly as baffled as she was, while the NKVD men pushed her into the rear of their vehicle. A Lend-Lease American jeep, she noted, like the ones she'd seen at Archangelsk.

The men were silent on the long trip to the railroad station, and there was no point in asking why she was being arrested. Unlike Victor, who could be prodded to talk, these agents were like robots.

The train trip, too, was silent, although the two men smoked and spoke occasionally with each other. She sat across the aisle, and though she wasn't handcuffed, it would be futile to attempt escape. No German planes strafed them, and she almost wished they would, though what would she do then? Dash over the snow-covered fields into the woods to die of exposure?

An official car met them at the Moscow station, and when it turned a corner onto a side street called Lukov, she recognized the terrifying building at the end of it.

Lubyanka Prison.

The NKVD headquarters was, in fact, a stately building from an earlier century, but, after the rumors of what went on in its cellars and interrogation rooms, it had an aura of deadly menace. Her chest began to ache.

It was true that the best torture begins with waiting, for in the three days she languished in her basement cell, she went nearly mad. She'd always assumed the powerful men in her life would assist her if necessary, but what if they didn't know she needed them?

She was both relieved and terrified when a guard finally fetched her. Was it to liberty or interrogation? The walk down the corridor to a dark room told her it was the latter. The interrogation room was bare except for a few chairs and an overhead light, and the whole place had the acrid smell of old sweat and cigarette smoke. If she hadn't been weak-kneed with fear, she might have laughed at the movie-set banality.

But the men who filed in after her weren't actors. She recognized all of them. First, the nameless man she'd sometimes seen at the Hotel Metropole. Victor's replacement, obviously. Then Lavrenty Beria, head of the NKVD, who had as much blood on his hands as Stalin himself.

Behind him came Ivan Osipenko and, astonishingly, Tamara Kazar, as slender and rigid as the general was plump and relaxed.

Alex felt like a gazelle encircled by a pride of lions.

Beria was the first to speak. He was small and balding, and squinted through rimless glasses. A trifle schoolmasterish, he also bore an ominous resemblance to photos she'd seen of Heinrich Himmler. He took a step toward her, a sheet of notepaper between his fingers, and she instinctively tried to lean away from him.

"What was the nature of your relationship with the pilot Lilya Drachenko?" he asked.

The question she dreaded most. Forcing calm on herself, she replied, "We became friends of a sort, when she learned I was a pilot too, though I didn't see much of her after she left the night bombers."

"I presume you mean the 588th Bomber Regiment. What were you doing with them?"

"Yes, the 588th. I was photographing them for my magazine." Her voice sounded high and tight. Would they think she was lying? "With the permission of Stalin," she added.

He was unimpressed. "Did Lilya Drachenko provide you with any military information?"

"No, only the basic workings of the U-2 so I could fly it in an emergency. Which is what I had to do at Stalingrad. After the pilot Katia Budanova was shot, I flew us both back to the base." Surely mentioning Stalingrad would help her cause.

Unfazed, he held the notepaper in front of her nose and asked, "Do you recognize this?"

It was on the same kind of paper Lilya had used to write her mother, and as she read it, she became nauseous with fear.

My dear Alex,

I think about our last meeting all the time and am amazed how much everything has changed for me since then. You are so sure of yourself, and you give me courage to see what could be, what is on the other side. I love my Motherland, but I have a vision of life now that goes beyond our governments and our nationalities.

Duty and exhaustion hold me in their grip, but I will get the information that you asked for and that I promised you. There is so much about us you don't know, so much I want to tell you. And I hate that we have to always meet in secret.

When the war is over…

The letter ended abruptly and was clearly unfinished. How excruciating that it was in the filthy hands of the NKVD.

"I've never seen this letter before."

"That's not what I asked you. Do you recognize this letter?" At his signal, a second man, burly and brutish-looking, came and stood beside him.

She saw no point in acting stupid. Wasn't the best lie the one that was nearly true? "It's addressed to me, so I guess it's from Lilya Drachenko, but I never saw it. Where did you get it?"

General Osipenko replied from behind him. "We found it among the things she left behind. What is the secret information to which she refers?"

"I don't know what you're talking about."

Beria nodded and his muscle man slapped her hard, stunning her and causing her ear to ring. In a moment, the warm trickle on her upper lip told her she had a nosebleed.

"You're going to have to do better than that. This letter suggests an exchange of secret information and incitement to treason. Do not toy with us, Miss Preston, and think your nationality will protect you. You would not be the first American to be executed at Lubyanka."

For all her efforts to remain calm, to give them nothing to find suspicious, she trembled. "There is no secret information. I used to be a pilot and I simply asked her to find out how I could learn to fly the Yak. She promised to look into it. Other than that, I'm a photographer. I submitted all my pictures to your censors, and I never incited Lilya Drachenko to anything."

The blow came again, knocking her head to the side and cutting her lip against her teeth. Blood and mucus trickled over her mouth and onto her shirt.

"I can assure you, we have far more disagreeable ways than a simple slap to encourage you to speak." Beria took off his glasses and cleaned them on a handkerchief.

Alex licked the blood from her lips. "I don't know what you want me to tell you. I have no secret information, just an interest in flying. I swear."

A third blow knocked her and her chair over on its side, where she hit her head on the concrete floor. For a moment she was senseless, and when she came to with a throbbing head, she was still in the same place.

"Take her back to her cell. We'll give her the night to think it over," Beria said, and stalked away.

❖

Alex crouched on the floor of her cell. What could she say that would get her out of Lubyanka? Would it save her to admit it was simply a love letter? But she knew of the Kremlin paranoia. The NKVD would find their love, if they bothered to call it that, even stronger evidence of espionage and treason, with a touch of sexual perversion. She almost sobbed with despair.

Cruelly, Terry's warning arose in her memory, taunting her. *It can't end well; there will be no going off into the sunset with this one.* Instead, it was going to end on the floor of a prison cell.

She fell unconscious again; she couldn't tell how long, but her thirst told her a long time had passed when the cell door opened. She flinched and closed her eyes as the harsh overhead light went on.

Squinting, Alex struggled to a sitting position, leaning against the wall as Tamara Kazar entered, lithe yet rigid. Sliding across the floor made her head start pounding again, but at least she wouldn't be lying helpless at Kazar's feet.

"That it should come to this, eh?" Kazar's tone was neutral, not particularly sarcastic. The remark didn't merit a reply.

"A pity really." Kazar stood over her now, her hands clasped, officer-like, behind her back. "I saw immediately what an intelligent woman you were and hoped we might get to know each other. I think you would have been worth the trouble. But you couldn't resist toying with that silly young creature, could you? And look where it's got you."

"That silly young creature was one of your best pilots, and she gave her life in heroic sacrifice." It hurt now to speak through swollen lips.

Kazar shifted her weight onto her good leg and tapped softly with gloved fingers on the other one. "Yes, she *was* a good pilot, but as for heroic sacrifice, you are romanticizing. It appears she didn't give her life at all."

"What are you talking about? They found her body next to her plane. What more do you want?"

Kazar tapped again, perhaps for effect. "They found her airplane, not her. To be sure, the charred body lying near it gave reason to assume it was Drachenko. But…" She bent forward and brought her face close to Alex. She smelled, faintly, of alcohol.

"But what?" Alex hated these cat-and-mouse games.

"She was wearing sandals."

It took a long moment for Alex to grasp the significance, and before she could speak, Kazar elaborated.

"No pilot flies in sandals when she has a perfectly good pair of flight boots. It couldn't have been her."

Alex hardly dared say it. "Then she's alive."

Kazar shrugged. "Perhaps. Though, if she's been captured, she's not much better off."

"You really hated her, didn't you? You hated all of them for questioning your authority."

"For questioning it, and for demeaning me before my superiors. After years of struggle to advance in the military, I was brought down by a handful of spoiled girls."

"Well, you had your revenge, didn't you? You sent them off on 'special duty,' where almost all of them were killed. All but Lilya."

"That was General Osipenko's idea. Not to kill them. He's not that vindictive and neither am I. It was just to put them to work some place where they couldn't undermine the confidence of the regiment. Most of them were happy for the glory it brought them."

"So why do you care about the letter? Do you really think Lilya Drachenko was prepared to commit treason? And that I'm guilty of espionage?"

Alex struggled to her feet and stood woman to woman with the major, refusing to play the supplicant. "You said I seemed an intelligent woman. You seem so, too. I think you know that it's a simple love letter, *not* evidence of conspiracy, and you've had me arrested for personal vengeance." She took a breath. "You're a female officer and surely had to struggle through the ranks. How can you do this to another woman?"

Kazar straightened, if possible, to an even greater rigidity. "What do you know about struggling through ranks, you privileged capitalist brat? I'll tell you a little story."

She paused for effect. "Once there was a daughter of a farmer who owned a little land and sold some of his crop. That made him a kulak, and because he was a kulak, he was executed as an enemy of the people. His land was confiscated and his house destroyed. Now imagine that little girl, living every day with hunger in the ruins of that house with her mother, not even allowed to go to school. And even when her mother curried favor with the party and got her in school, she was shunned as a kulak child, that is, until she gave a report about people spreading anti-Stalinist rumors."

She paused again. "How quickly the doors opened then, to the Komsomol and to the flight school of her dreams, and to the military college, and each advancement cost only a little report, a few names. Then, imagine her delight, twenty years later, to not only receive the Lenin prize, but also to be given command of a regiment expressly approved by Stalin himself." She took a step closer.

"Then, suppose a group of swaggering pilots threatened to destroy that prize. What would you have done?"

Alex was speechless at the tirade that amounted to a confession. "I...I don't know," she answered sincerely. It was a kind of horror story, however you looked at it. "Why are you telling me this?"

"Because I want you to know why you are finishing here in Lubyanka. You're an intelligent woman who chose badly, and you sealed your fate when you joined them."

"Them? The pilots who died at Stalingrad?"

"Yes." Kazar sighed, and her sorrow seemed genuine. "It could have ended differently." She took a step forward and pressed a sudden kiss on Alex's lips.

Then she turned away and marched from the cell, the steel door clanging behind her with a terrifying finality.

Alex estimated that about ten days and nights had passed, though the lack of a window made it impossible to tell. A jailor brought her bread at intervals, but was it once a day or twice?

And all the while she was assailed by fear, dread, guilt, confusion. She feared the NKVD, dreaded the next visitor who might be her torturer, anguished over Lilya's fate in the hands of the Germans, and in her more lucid moments, she brooded over the common tragedy of the two women who hated each other. Both their fathers had been executed, and both had tried to undo the shame with patriotism, but Tamara Kazar had also become a snitch. Alex asked herself what she would have done and had no idea.

Then, when she'd begun to lose hope, the metal door swung open, and in the entryway Terry Sheridan stood like a shining knight.

Two guards marched in, yanked her to her feet, and pulled her past him through the doorway. She glanced back wordlessly at him, ensuring that he followed them down the corridor into a room with a table and papers.

Still without speaking to her, he signed some papers, passed a few packs of cigarettes to her captors, and waited while her manacles were removed. Then he led her down another corridor to the main portal of the building.

"How are you, old girl?" he asked, touching her gently on the back, once they were on the street.

"Been better," she said, and stood impassively as he opened the door to a car, presumably some official OSS vehicle.

Once inside, he turned to her. "Jesus, Alex. How did you let it go so far? How could you have not seen the danger?"

"Could you just get past the 'I told you so' part of the conversation and tell me what you did to spring me? How did you even know where I was?"

"It's our job to know where people are. And besides, the NKVD didn't dare keep a Western journalist hidden for too long. I think the commander of that woman's regiment asked questions, and an inquiry started, and word finally reached the State Department. It's a good thing Harry Hopkins likes you."

"What do you mean?"

"I mean, he's the only one with leverage. When he heard about your arrest, he hinted that the next Lend-Lease shipment of war material might be delayed if the US president knew Stalin was imprisoning American journalists. It was a bluff, but it worked"

"So, my release had nothing to do with my innocence but came down to sheer blackmail."

"It's the way the world works, Alex. And since the powers-that-be will bail you out only once, I suggest you behave yourself for a while."

She fell silent again as they rode through the heartless streets of Moscow, where haggard, war-weary people still dragged their sled-loads of firewood behind them.

"She's alive, Terry. I'm sure she's alive. The body by the plane wasn't hers."

"Alex, for God's sake, you have to get over that woman. This obsession almost ended your life."

She ignored him. "If she's in a POW camp, I can surely find out, right? Through the Red Cross or something?"

"It's not so simple. First of all, neither the Germans nor the Russians give a shit about each other's POWs, and second, it's *winter*. If the Germans have her, she's as good as dead."

"I need to know. One way or another."

"Well, you can forget about looking for her from here. Beria's condition was that you leave Russia. You've got forty-eight hours to get out of Dodge, and you're confined to your hotel until you do."

She exhaled agreement, resignation. "I need to cable George at *Century*. He'll know what to do with me. I sure as hell don't."

"Don't bother. I've already talked to him."

"You contacted my boss? How? Why?"

"How is none of your business. We have our ways. As for why, Harry agreed to spring you from Lubyanka, but we had to have a place to relocate you. The plan was to put you on a plane to New York City, so that's why I called George Mankowitz. He was shocked, but you know George. The magazine's his baby, and you're his best photographer."

"Yeeess? Go on."

"So, he wants to know if you'd like to go to Britain to photograph the buildup for the invasion."

"For God's sake, Terry. I've just been in prison. I'll have to think about it."

"No, you won't. You'll just go. I told him yes, so he got you a place with the US Army Press Corps in London, and we've already got your tickets. Moscow—Teheran—London."

She sat stunned for a moment, but her mind was buzzing. Nothing awaited her in New York. Nothing and no one. No one awaited her in London either, but at least she'd still be a correspondent. Moreover, she had a better chance to monitor the POW camps from London than from New York.

"I see. All right. I need to bathe and pack my cameras."

"Glad you agree. When you're ready, I'll take you to dinner tonight at the embassy. You look like you could use a good meal. Oh, by the way, Happy New Year 1944."

CHAPTER TWENTY-SEVEN

Lilya took stock of her new surroundings. With the exception of a few low buildings on the periphery for administration or to house the guards, the camp was little more than a barbed-wire expanse that kept prisoners in their thousands in the open air. Most had dug holes to crouch in to get away from the wind.

Was it sentimentality toward women? The Wehrmacht wasn't known for that. But for reasons she never discovered, her captors had brought her to a ramshackle wooden structure with a roof but no walls that might have once been a cowshed. Its dirt floor was covered with straw, and some dozen other women were already sitting on it huddled in various approximations of blankets.

Shortly after her arrival, a Wehrmacht officer approached, and she recognized the man who'd interpreted during her interrogation in the previous camp. The Vlasov turncoat. "So, Lieutenant Petrovna," he said, startling her with her new name.

He stood over her now where she crouched on the straw-covered ground. "You know, you don't have to endure this. I'm sure you think you're doing the right thing, but you're suffering for the wrong cause."

"Traitor," she said, and turned away.

But he persisted. "You think so? Ah, but as far as the Kremlin is concerned, you're also a traitor, because you surrendered to the Germans."

"That's not true. I was captured unconscious."

"That will make no difference when your countrymen come to liberate you." She could hear the sarcasm in the word liberate. "Haven't you heard? Stalin has declared, 'There are no Russian POWs, only traitors and cowards.' So once you're over here, there's no going back. If the NKVD doesn't shoot you for desertion, they'll send you to Siberia."

"It's you who they'll execute." She snarled the words. "You and everyone who's gone over to the Fascists. I'm a loyal Communist."

He leaned against one of the posts and crossed his arms. "I was, too. But Stalin isn't. He's just a brute and a tyrant. Don't you know about the purges? Aren't you tired of being afraid of denunciation for the slightest reason? Russian soldiers are crossing over in the hundreds to the Germans. They're tired of having the commissars breathing down their necks and threatening their families, and they know the Red Army's done for."

"Stop it. I don't want to hear that. Leave me alone."

"I can leave you, if that's what you want, but your shoulder bars show you're a lieutenant. A woman who flies planes and reaches the rank of lieutenant so young must be pretty smart. I bet you already have a few medals. Such a woman deserves better than to live in terror of her own government."

"Right now I'm in terror of the Germans. Why aren't you? Who are you, anyhow?"

"Just call me Vovka, The others do. I accept the Germans because they're the lesser evil. Sure, they're brutal on the battlefield. That's just the way war is. It's the peace that they do differently. Stalin has ruined communism, and if the Germans can bring him down, I'll fight with them. In the end, we'll have a better life."

"How can you say that? You actually think that once the Germans seize Russia they'll hand everything back to us and march home again?"

"No, of course I don't think that. But the Germans are a civilized people. They have courts of law." He paused for a moment as if deciding how much to say. "You see, the NKVD executed my father as an enemy of the people. Just like that." He snapped his fingers. "For years I assumed they were right, that all I had to do was prove I was a good Communist and all would be well. But I've seen the light."

She was speechless. That was his reason for defecting? He could have been telling her own story. What did it say about her, that her own father's execution had done just the opposite and made her want to be a hero for the nation?

"I imagine life under the Gestapo would be the same," she said, but the force had gone out of her argument.

"What's left for us to fight for, then?" he asked, though his voice had dropped, as if his argument had lost its strength as well.

"My father…" She stopped and started again. "I don't fight for Stalin, but for the Motherland. For my family and home. The Germans are civilized, you say? We don't even get the same rations as the other POWs, and we're not allowed to get Red Cross packages."

"That's because of Stalin, you stupid girl. He's decreed that captured Soviet soldiers aren't prisoners but traitors, so they're ineligible for aid."

She had no reply, and they both were silent for a few moments. Then he brushed his hands, as if removing dirt from his gloves.

"Well, each person must decide which devil to serve. But you shouldn't let your idealism cause you to starve to death. The commandant's wife needs a house cleaner. No matter how hard she works you, you'll be indoors. Do you want the job or not?"

"What makes you think the commandant will let a Russian into his house?"

"A young, pretty one? Sure he will. So make up your mind soon."

With a dismissive flick of the hand, he turned and marched away, leaving her confused.

"Don't listen to him," someone next to her said.

Lilya turned to see a round face with dark hair and large eyebrows. One of the dozen women clustered together on straw. Close up, she could see it was a face that must have been pretty before the cuts and bruises of capture. A bit like Inna, Lilya thought, and felt immediate warmth. Her padded jacket suggested she'd been among the ground troops. "My name's Olga," the woman added.

"Aleksandra," Lilya said in return. "Do you know that man?"

"Yes, and he's a fool as well as a traitor. He remembers all the little crimes at home and shuts his eyes to the big ones here. You see those hills over there? On the other side of them is a great pit. It's covered over now, but it's full of bodies. Jews and Russians and commissars. That's what they've planned for us."

"But we're soldiers."

"Makes no difference. I was on a detachment outside the camp cleaning sewer ditches, and one of the Ukrainian guards joked that it would be a good pit to execute another batch of Bolsheviks over. His friend laughed and said, 'Let them starve. We tried shooting them in the head and it took all day.'"

Olga drew her knees up to her chin and pulled her jacket tighter around her. "It's just a matter of luck whether you're shot or not."

The other women, who'd withdrawn when Vlasov had entered the cowshed, now edged closer and surrounded them, listening.

"So you think I shouldn't try to get the job?" she asked Olga.

"Oh, you must try. Grab it! Why should you play the martyr? I'd do it in a minute, if he offered it to me. But those bandages that hang out from your cuff? Take them off. They're filthy. It looks like you've been wearing them for weeks."

"A month, actually. I have them around my ribs, too. They keep me warm."

"I'm sure they do, but the commandant won't let you into the house if he thinks you're sick or wounded. Here, let me help you." She helped Lilya slide off her flight jacket and raised her tunic. With deft hands, she unwrapped the bandages from around her ribs. They were oily and discolored, but her ribs had healed well in the meantime, and the bandages were no longer necessary.

"Now the arm." Olga began unrolling the strips of rag that had protected her for a month. Her exposed skin felt cold and vulnerable, and her hand was stiff.

"What did you do to break ribs and an arm? Crash a plane?"

"Well, yes. But I was thrown out before it crashed." She stared into Olga's face, searching for recognition, but saw none.

Once it had seemed all of Russia knew the face of their favorite female ace pilot, but her peroxided hair had grown out during the month of her captivity in the holding camp, and when the Vinnytsia barber had trimmed it short upon her arrival, all that was left was light-brown fuzz.

Lilya looked down at Olga's hands as they massaged life back into her weakened forearm. "Thanks, Olga. You're good at this. Were you a medic?"

"Almost. I trained to be one and was a medical instructor. But in ground training, they discovered what a good shot I was, and they made me a sniper." She lowered her voice to a whisper. "Sixty-three kills. But the Fritzes caught me without my rifle, as I ran out to drag a wounded comrade to safety. I said I was a medic, and I'm sure that's why they didn't shoot me."

"I was a sniper too, and it's a miracle that any one of us made it here," another woman with a Tatar face said. "The Fritzes almost always shoot the women."

"For sure, when I get out of here, I'm going to shoot a few more of *them*," Olga said.

Lilya smiled softly, in spite of hunger, chill, and weakness. Olga had said "when."

❖

As Lilya expected, Commandant Krüger lived outside the grounds of the camp, in a two-story stone house that obviously had belonged to someone important before it was confiscated. A stand of trees protected him from the disagreeable sight of his emaciated and slowly dying prisoners.

The commandant was not at home when Vovka accompanied her to the door, but the commandant's wife received her. Frau Krüger was a hard-faced woman who might have once been attractive, but age had been unkind. Her graying hair was badly tinted, hair dye presumably being currently hard to obtain in the Ukraine, and her eyes drooped on the outside as if she were perpetually about to weep.

Once she was inside, Frau Krüger led her to a door that opened to a cellar. Lilya obeyed the nudge at her elbow and descended the stairs into the darkness.

The light from the corridor upstairs showed a single bulb hanging on a cord from the ceiling, and Frau Krüger tugged on its chain for light. The walls were cement block and the floor concrete. Under the wooden stairs they had just descended, a bin held coal, and Lilya assumed she would be tasked with bringing it up for the kitchen stove. Kitchen. Stove. The very words caused a spasm of hunger.

Frau Krüger plucked at Lilya's jacket sleeve, said something in German, and held her nose. Taking a bar of laundry soap from a shelf, she rubbed it on Lilya's arm, making clear that a personal scrubbing was her first duty.

"*Jawohl, Frau Krüger.*" The weeks of captivity had taught her at least that much German.

Apparently satisfied that her order would be obeyed, the commandant's wife returned to the upper floor and shut the door behind her.

Lilya took off her wool flight jacket, then swept the dank cavern with her glance, searching for a place to wash. A sink stood in the corner, though a turn of the spigot revealed that it gave only cold water. Still, she obeyed and tugged off her uniform, then her rancid underwear, and stood, nude and shivering.

By the dim overhead light, she could barely make out the gray spots of the lice that infested her, but she could feel them crawl across her belly and between her breasts. She sluiced water over her chest and neck and then rubbed the laundry soap over every part of her body she could reach, scratching off the vile insects.

She scrubbed her underwear next and planned to put her soiled uniform on without it while she waited for it to dry. But she heard footsteps behind her and turned.

Frau Krüger stood on the stairs with a man's woolen shirt in her hand. She tossed it across the distance between them and made an about-face.

Lilya drew the shirt gratefully over her damp body and buttoned it closed. It covered her to mid thigh. The concrete floor was intolerably cold, so she drew on her boots again, feeling strange with exposed knees. Then she set about scrubbing her uniform. She would never be able to remove the stains from the weeks lying on the ground, but the smell would be gone, and so would the lice. At least for a while.

Before she was finished, Frau Krüger was behind her again, this time with a wide metal tub of dirty clothing. Her commands in German were unintelligible, but the task was clear. She pointed toward a series of wires stretched between pillars around the cellar, obviously for purposes of drying.

"*Jawohl, Frau Krüger*," Lilya said again. She took the tub and set it at her feet. "*Wasser kalt*," she announced in more of the baby German she'd learned. How was she supposed to do a laundry with cold water?

Seemingly irritated by the remark, Frau Krüger turned abruptly and climbed the stairs. Lilya had filled the sink halfway with cold water when Frau Krüger returned with a large copper kettle that gave off steam from its spout. She spoke again in German, and Lilya presumed it was something like "Don't waste it."

Hot water. It seemed like paradise, and she would have welcomed it for her own scrubbing. On the plank table beside her, she laid out the soiled laundry in order of importance. The commandant's underwear and shirts, then Frau Krüger's clothing, and finally the bed linen and miscellanea. She only hoped the soap—and her arm strength—would last.

Two-and-a-half hours later, her arms ached up to her shoulders and her back was stiff. But all the laundry was clean and hanging on its wires. However, her own uniform was still damp. Would she be allowed to stay until it dried?

No one had come down to check on her, so she climbed to the top of the stairs and poked her head timidly through the door opening.

Frau Krüger stepped from the kitchen at the other end of the corridor with a bucket and rags and pressed them into Lilya's hand. The meaning was obvious.

"Jawohl, Frau Krüger." She scampered back down the stairs and filled the bucket from the basement sink. It was a strain on her barely healed arm to carry it full of water to the upstairs corridor, and she set it down with a thud.

She knelt on the wooden floor and began to scrub with the cold, wet rags. Her arms were so weak that scrubbing was painful, but after half an hour the job was largely done, and she stood back to inspect the floor for any missed dirt. At that moment, the front door opened.

Commandant Krüger stopped in the doorway and smirked at her standing barelegged under his shirt. He slid his glance from her face to her breasts to her bare knees, then strode past her into the kitchen, leaving behind him a trail of wet boot prints.

Helpless to object, she rinsed her rag in the bucket of brown water and dragged it once again back and forth the length of the corridor. As she neared the kitchen, she almost fainted from the smell of frying sausage.

She was hungry every hour of every day, as were all the prisoners, and in the absence of food, hunger became disassociated from the stomach and seemed to grip the entire body. But with food close by, filling the air with the scent of warm fat, hunger became a sharp physical pain as digestive acids arose in her stomach and had nothing to digest.

To escape the odor, she returned to the cellar and emptied the bucket. Her underwear was dry, but her uniform was still slightly damp, and pulling on trousers and tunic made her shiver. Her woolen flight jacket warmed her only slightly.

Not sure whether she had more tasks to do, she marched again up the stairs and called from the doorway. Frau Krüger stepped from the kitchen, bringing the smell of roast pork with her, and inspected the corridor floor. The cleaning seemed to pass muster, for she turned away with a wave of dismissal and returned to the kitchen.

Buttoning her jacket, Lilya left the commandant's house aching and cold, guarded by a Kapo along the short path back to the women's corner. To her relief, she arrived back at the cowshed in time for the thin evening broth they called soup. As usual, it was made from nettles, and she consumed it quickly while it was still warm, picking out the straw that couldn't be digested, no matter how long she chewed it.

While they sat eating, a plane flew overhead, and she heard the clatter of U-2 biplane motors. A few minutes later, in the far distance, she saw an orange glow, then another, and then a third. Her heart leapt. It had to be the biplanes of the 588th on a sortie. The Night Witches tormenting the German troops.

Who had been in the planes? She ran through the names of the pilots who still lived: Nadia, Polina, Ludmila? Perhaps it was Eva Bershanskaya herself. She thought affectionately of the tall, muscular commander.

Comforted, she returned to the cluster of women who were already making up the straw "nest" where they slept in a tight group at night, the stronger women taking turns sleeping on the outside. When she fell asleep, she dreamt again of flying.

The next day was much the same as the one before, though the laundry she'd washed now had to be ironed. She ironed with her left hand, sparing her right arm, but standing for several hours in one place hurt her back and legs. Still, she was indoors, and the electric iron radiated warmth.

The following days of hard physical labor left her bone tired, but she could see that the women who worked outside suffered more. They seemed to waste away, and though she was just as ravenous as they when the soup canister arrived, she was able to stand in line for the weakest of them and take their bowls of nettle broth to them where they lay.

In the second week something wonderful happened. Frau Krüger sprained her wrist and couldn't lift a pot to cook for her husband. Lilya wasn't a believer but uttered a few words of thanks to the sky for the miracle, since now she could prepare the meals. With a bandaged wrist, Frau Krüger led her to the kitchen and pointed to the pots and to the potatoes that needed to be cleaned and the dead chicken that needed to be cut into pieces and roasted.

At the same time, she shook her finger and scowled, and the message was clear. Lilya must not think of putting any of it into her mouth.

"Jawohl, Frau Krüger," Lilya said, and the first day in the kitchen she was meticulous. Though enough food passed through her hands to feed all the women in her cowshed, she made sure every scrap of it was accounted for and that all the table scraps went to the commandant's dog. But when she carried the food to the table and returned to clean the kitchen unsupervised, she ran her fingers along the insides of the cooking pots and sucked them clean before plunging the pots into water. The taste of fat was exquisite, though the tiny particles of it served only to increase her craving. If she hadn't feared someone might see her, she would have licked the pots like a dog.

The next several days passed in much the same way. With rare exception, every morning after roll call she began by scrubbing one or another floor and tending to the linen, which seemed to constantly require washing. At noon she was allowed a slice of bread, of better quality than was distributed in the camp. In the afternoon, she peeled potatoes and cooked whatever meat and vegetables were available. Each time it was dizzying to be around so much food, and only terror kept her from shoving handfuls of it into her mouth.

Finally, in her third week, after an anxious look behind her, she slid some of the potato peels into her uniform pocket. Only a few, so they wouldn't bulge. Plenty of peels remained to mix with the meat scraps for the dog, so no one would notice.

When she was dismissed, under guard as always, she hurried to the shed where the evening soup canister had just arrived. Olga lay on her straw and struggled to rise, but Lilya laid a hand on her shoulder.

"Stay there. I'll bring it to you, with a little surprise."

Lilya took Olga's and her own tin bowl to the woman in charge of the soup. She received the two ladles of warm broth and returned to the shed. "Here's the surprise," she said, and dropped two long strips of potato peel into each tin.

"Oh, bless you, Comrade." Olga took her bowl, and together they consumed the soup, slowly chewing the tough potato skin as if it were a sliver of the finest beef.

November arrived, and cold weather became a deadly threat. Lilya's summer flight jacket was inadequate for winter, and unless she could find something to augment it, the coming months could be fatal. For some of the other women it was worse. On the first morning that Lilya awoke to heavy snowfall, she gathered the straw she'd slept on and woke Olga. "Here, pack some of this inside your uniform like I did. It'll help keep you warm."

Consenting, Olga slid handfuls of dirty hay under her tunic around her midsection and over her back. "It does help but it stinks."

"We all stink anyhow. Stay close to the others and I'll bring you back some potato peels," Lila promised her and began the trek to the commandant's house.

"How do you like your job?" someone asked behind her, and she turned around.

"Vovka. You're looking healthy." She kept on walking while she talked. "So you're my guard today. Still serving your German masters."

"Even as you are." He fell into step beside her. "You know, as long as you're cleaning their house, why don't you offer to fight for them? You'd have regular German meals."

"I'm a coward but not a traitor. There's still a difference." She quickened her pace.

They passed a corner of the men's yard and she saw the other POWs, emaciated and forlorn. Some had shelters, as flimsy as her own, but the majority had none and at night slept huddled in little groups on the ground. The heavy snow was a death sentence for most of them.

"How long do you think you can hold out this way?" he asked, keeping step with her.

"I don't know. If you care so much about me, why don't you bring me some food next time instead of talk? Then, when our troops liberate the camp, I'll tell them not to shoot you." They were near the commandant's house now, and she turned away.

He called after her. "My dear, they're going to shoot us anyhow. All of us."

In December, conditions worsened in the camp, but they improved in the house of the commandant. While Russian POWs died by tens and then by hundreds, Lilya found ever new ways of occupying herself in the kitchen, scrubbing the floor or stove, wiping out the cupboards, cleaning the windows. And she'd grown adept at purloining scraps of food.

The first scrap went into her mouth and down her throat in an instant. But when opportunity presented a second scrap, it went inside her tunic, where it stayed until she returned to the camp in the evening. Then she presented it to Olga along with her soup.

Then providence seemed to take mercy on them. Frau Krüger grew sick with fever and took to her bed. Lilya became responsible for the entire household and had ample opportunity to steal food, as long as the quantities were small. For four days she fed her shed-mates on the heels of loaves, sausage ends, and once, a handful of hazelnuts.

But without his watchful wife, the commandant began to hover around Lilya. He assigned her to clean and iron his uniform, but when she brought it to him in his office, he was waiting in his bathrobe. Before he could disrobe, she draped it over a chair and hurried back to the kitchen.

While she set the kettle on the stove, she glanced around for anything she could smuggle out that evening for the other women. A heel of bread, perhaps. But before she could reach for the loaf, she heard footfall in the corridor.

She turned to see Commandant Krüger, half dressed. His uniform pants were buttoned but his jacket hung open, and under his white undershirt the curvature of his chest muscles was visible, as well as the dark hairs that curled up toward his throat.

"Herr Kommandant." That was all she could say.

He slipped closer and she knew he was going to take hold of her. Her face warmed with a mix of fear and loathing.

He was in front of her now, and she had no place to back away from him. With an expression that was both gentle and lewd, he caressed her face with the back of his fingers.

His hand wandered down her neck and over her breast. She cringed and was glad she hadn't yet slipped any food into her pocket. He squeezed the swelling under his palm.

"Nein." She whimpered, turning her head away from him and trying to make herself small.

He slid an arm behind her and pulled her to him, pressed his pelvis against hers. Timidly, she laid her hands on his chest to urge him away.

"*Du Schwein!*" The high-pitched accusation came from the doorway, and the commandant suddenly backed away from her.

Coughing and clutching her bathrobe across her, Frau Krüger stormed into the kitchen and slapped Lilya across the face. Lilya reeled, holding her cheek.

Muttering, the commandant marched from the kitchen, abandoning Lilya to his wife's rage.

Frau Krüger seized Lilya by the arm and threw her against the wall, slapped her again, and dragged her into the corridor where he stood. Then, in front of him, she unleashed a tirade.

Cowed, or perhaps fed up with the whole scene, the commandant seized Lilya by the arm and dragged her along the corridor to the door. He put his coat on and, mercifully, allowed Lilya to put on her own jacket before pushing her in front of him out the door. Continuing to mutter, he prodded her back toward the camp until they met one of the guards, where he handed her over with an order she didn't understand.

The guard saluted and marched her to a wooden post in front of the women's shed, where he tied her with a cord. It was already evening and the sky was dark. The other women were just coming in from their work details and stared at her, helpless. Immobile and outside the shelter of the cowshed, she began to shiver.

Half an hour passed, and she began to tremble uncontrollably. An hour after that, she could no longer feel her feet. This was the night she would die.

Two dark shapes approached her, and it was only when they were right in front of her that she could see their faces. Olga and another woman.

"We can't untie you, but we can stand by you and keep you warm," Olga said. With a single thin blanket pulled over both their shoulders, they embraced her on two sides. The skin on their faces was cold at first, but slowly the warmth of their bodies radiated into her. They all still shivered, but the trembling of muscles created a little heat, enough heat for them not to die. A guard pacing outside the barbed wire saw them and could have shot them, but a grain of mercy must have niggled his conscience, for he only laughed.

After an hour, two other women came and replaced the first two. Lilya wasn't even sure of all their names, but at that moment, she loved them deeply.

At the third shift, she heard gunfire, and the two women pulled away, exposing her to the icy air. "Someone's attacking," one of them said. The two women fled, and she despaired, but a moment later she saw where they ran.

Toward a cluster of men in Red Army uniforms.

CHAPTER TWENTY-EIGHT

January 1944

Alex landed at Heathrow Airport and checked into the hotel George Mankowitz had booked for her. She'd hoped to enjoy some of the food she'd been craving for two years—sirloin, real coffee, ice cream—but found that Britain, too, was rationing food, and she could have them only rarely in tiny amounts, and at a high price.

George left her in peace for two days, during which she slept a lot, acclimating to the new time zone, and spent one afternoon shopping for new clothes, though the available goods were sparse.

Finally slept out, bathed, shampooed, and wearing new clothes, she met with her boss in the hotel lobby. He looked more British than American in his green tweed and greeted her warmly, shaking her hand with more vigor than she ever recalled.

"It's so good to see you again, Alex. Though you're looking a bit thin." He took her arm and led her into the grand dining room.

"This is the way you look after you've lived in privation for two years, slogged through the mud all over the Eastern Front, been beaten up by the NKVD, and spent ten days in a Soviet prison."

"Yes, Terry told me. What the hell happened?" He pulled out a chair for her and sat down across the table.

"Just a little misunderstanding. I asked someone to find out how I could learn to fly a Yak, and when she wrote me a note saying "I'll get the information for you," the Russians decided that *had* to be espionage. Fortunately, it all went away when Harry Hopkins intervened."

"Yes, Harry's a good man. Sure glad he was in Moscow at the time."

She didn't want to think about how close she'd come to spending weeks or months in Lubyanka and changed the subject. "Look, George, I'm keen to get started again. What have you got for me?"

"Are you sure you don't want to rest up for a few weeks?" He signaled a waiter for two cups of coffee.

"I don't want any more rest anywhere. I want work."

"Well, if that's the case, I've got some, and it's right up your alley. I'm sure you're as aware as anyone that the Allies are planning an invasion soon, and of course, it's going to come from Britain."

"Well, Stalin has been clamoring for a second front for a year now, but just how far along is it?"

"No one knows the exact date, of course. And if anyone does, they're not talking. But it's imminent, and I've arranged for you to meet the planners this morning. They'll tell us what they want us to know, and then we'll talk about what you can do as a photographer."

"You really think they'll want me involved? I mean, they must have their own photographers."

"They do, but they need more. For reconnaissance, for record-keeping, for propaganda. And your credentials are superb. Besides, some big names will be in the press corps for this: Capa, Cronkite, Rooney, Sevareid. You'll be with the best." He looked at his watch. "Come on. I've got a car waiting outside. The meeting starts in twenty minutes."

He left the appropriate change on the table and slid her chair out from behind her as she stood up. The chivalrous gesture was strange to her after life in a war zone where women pulled out their own chairs.

He opened an enormous black umbrella over them both as they hurried through the rain to the waiting car. "Norfolk House, please, driver," he said, and they fell silent for the duration of the drive.

Stepping back out onto the sidewalk with his umbrella again over them, he explained. "The building we're about to enter is the Supreme Headquarters of the Allied Expeditionary Force. SHAEF, for short. This is where all the big planning has been going on since 1942."

At the door of the stately red-brick building, she handed her raincoat to an MP and stepped into the entrance hall. Amid the elegant furnishings of an eighteenth-century mansion, some half dozen military officers were gathered. One of them, a tall, pleasant-looking man with a narrow gray mustache, glanced over as they came in.

"George Mankowitz. How are you, old chap?" He approached them and held out his hand. Haven't seen you for donkey's years."

"Well, you should stop over in New York more often, then, General Morgan. May I present Alex Preston, the photographer I told you about? She's just come back after two years in Russia and is eager to work with you." To Alex he said, "Alex, this is Frederick Morgan, one of the men in charge of Operation Overlord."

He took her hand and shook it with moderate vigor. "Two years. My, my. You must have stories to tell."

"More pictures than stories, General, but yes, I do." She searched for something to say. "Operation Overlord, that does sound menacing."

"We're hoping it *will* be." He smiled, about to add something, but the opening door drew their attention. A portly man had just stepped inside and was handing over a black overcoat and bowler hat. His three-piece pinstriped suit looked slightly rumpled, and his vest was missing a button.

"Ah, Prime Minister. So glad you could come," Morgan said. Winston Churchill slapped him on the shoulder as he passed. "Can I speak to you privately, General?" he asked, drawing him aside.

At the same moment, George touched her lightly on the arm. "Wait here just a moment. I need to fetch our security-clearance badges so we can get inside the conference," he said, also stepping away.

She stood for a moment, nonplussed, studying the elaborate molding around the ceiling. She tried to remember the history of the building but recalled only that it had something to do with a duke.

"Excuse me, but are you the photographer?" a man asked behind her. She turned, about to wisecrack, "Yeah, who's asking?" But the wide Midwestern face and sparse blond hair took her off guard, and instead she stammered. "General Eisenhower. Yes, I am. I…I'm here with George Mankowitz, but he's just stepped away to get our badges." She offered her hand again and received the same sort of soft but firm handshake as General Morgan had given her. Did all generals learn to shake hands that way?

"I understand you took all those wonderful pictures from Russia and the Eastern Front. Congratulations. *Century* magazine is lucky to have you."

"Thank you, General. And those are only the ones that got past the censor. They confiscated the ones that might give a bad impression."

"I'm afraid all militaries do that, for security or for propaganda. Or both. But I saw some awfully good ones of Stalingrad. Did you take those?"

"If they were in *Century* magazine, yes. I was their only Moscow correspondent."

"As I recall, some were aerial photos. Did you get a reconnaissance plane to make a flyover with you?"

"It was a personal favor from Soviet pilot. In an old U-2 biplane, as a matter of fact."

"Brave man. That was taking a risk."

"It was a woman. An ace, in fact, a hero of the Soviet Union. Unfortunately, she was killed while flying me out. Her name was Katia Budanova." Saying the name gave her a pang of guilt.

"I'm sorry to hear it." A bell sounded and the general looked over his shoulder. "Hmm, it looks like the meeting's about to start."

"Oh, dear. I don't have my security badge yet."

He touched her shoulder lightly. "Come on, I'll vouch for you. I'm the supreme commander. I can do that."

❖

"So you can see," Frederick Morgan was concluding his talk, "we need to have a much better understanding of the beaches in question, the obstacles, the gun emplacements, topography, angle of incline, even the quality of the sand to be sure it will support our tanks."

Churchill tapped the ash off his cigar. "Can you give us an anticipated timeline, General? Stalin's breathing down my neck about that."

"I'm afraid I can't, Prime Minister. So much depends on how quickly we can gather the information we need about the landing sites and weather pattern. We'll be using frogmen, night commandos, planes flying at nearly sea level. Our naval photographers will do most of the work, but we'll employ some qualified civilians, including a journalist or two." He nodded toward George Mankowitz.

The discussion continued, but much of the talk was in military language and of little interest to Alex. Most of the time she tried to imagine what kind of plane they would put her in. When it was over, she collected her coat and found herself in another taxi with George.

"You see, Alex? That's how you get the serious jobs. By being at the big meetings and talking to the big men."

"I'll give you that, George. I thought I was coming back to take photos of the buildup, the Yanks invading England, that sort of thing."

"You'll be doing both. While you're out over the channel getting them their shore images, I'll arrange with Morgan for you to snap the bivouacs and the supply depots in ways that will pass the censors. Plenty of GIs drinking tea, too. The readers love that."

"Any chance of going back over? I mean after the invasion."

"An excellent chance, if you're up for it. Ike already likes you, and that's got to be a plus. Come on. I'll take you back to your hotel."

Sitting next to him in the car, she brooded. She was contributing to the war effort, as if the NKVD and Kazar and Lubyanka prison had never happened to her. So why couldn't she shake off her depression? Fingering her collar, she felt the worn parachute silk at her throat and a light went on.

"George, I'm sorry I didn't mention this earlier. Do you know how to begin an inquiry with the Red Cross? I want to find out if Lilya Drachenko is in one of the POW camps in the Ukraine."

"Hmm. Certainly it's possible to file an inquiry, but at this stage, it's extremely unlikely to be productive. The Eastern Front is too unstable, and we're not even sure where all the camps are. Do you know the name of the possible camp?

"Well, the location, at least. Vinnytsia, in the Ukraine. I want to find out if Lilya Drachenko is in any camp in or near there."

He jotted the information in a tiny notebook. "I'll contact someone with the Red Cross, but you mustn't hold out a lot of hope."

She nodded. Hope had shrunk to the tiniest of straws, and she clutched at it.

Scarcely had Alex settled into her London rooming house and gotten used to regular meals, long restful nights, and showers, when General Morgan's secretary telephoned. She was brief and to the point. Alex's clearance had been approved, and SHAEF had an aerial-reconnaissance assignment for her.

And now her Spitfire zoomed in one more time over the beach while she snapped her final ten shots of the cliff side. She marveled at the speed and agility of the reconnaissance plane that allowed them to dart in low and speed away again. *Lilya would love these,* she thought.

After delivering her coastline films to SHAEF, she received permission to photograph the gathering Allied forces and materials, provided she passed her negatives through military censors.

In mid-May she photographed the endless rows of tents and Quonset huts spread out over meadows and fields, the stockpiles of lumber, oil barrels, rubber tires, pontoons, and dried eggs, and the training exercises in the villages of Southwest England. Exactly as the Kremlin had done, the censors of SHAEF allowed her to publish the cheerful close-ups but withheld the larger scenes from publication until after D-day.

She worked with cool professionalism, though one of her film assignments opened the wound that had scarcely closed. On a foggy morning on a wide street in Liverpool, a seemingly endless line of US P-51 fighter planes trucked past her on the way to their air base, their wingtips removed so they could pass through. Airplanes on a city street as far as the eye could see left her awestruck, and as she raised her camera, she felt the ghost of Lilya Drachenko peering at them through her eyes.

Off duty, she didn't know what to do with herself. When she wearied of sitting in her room, she visited the military canteens. The randy GIs left her cold, and the nurses, canteen girls, female ambulance drivers, and Wacs were of only slightly more interest.

But one evening a slender blond woman with Slavic features seemed to sense her interest and sat down next to her. "Hi there. I noticed you were sitting all alone, so I brought you a beer. One of the fellas told me you're just back from Russia. Wow. Musta been cold, huh?"

"In winter, yes, it is." Weather wouldn't have been her first choice of topic, but it would serve. The beer was a nice gesture, too. She took a sip.

The young woman held a cigarette delicately up by her cheek but didn't seem to smoke it. "Can't be much worse than at home in Iowa. Y'know, those Midwestern storms. Days when you just didn't want to go out of the house. So, how'd ya like it?" She sidled closer so that her knee brushed Alex's thigh, ever so lightly.

A bit unsubtle, Alex thought, but she wasn't looking for intellectual discussion. Just solace. The beer was helping.

"There were a lot of days like that, but in a war zone, you can't decide to stay home. The Russians themselves suffered terrible hardships, though they're incredibly tough people."

"I'll bet. The guys must be real animals. So, d'ya have a Russian boyfriend?" She winked.

Alex was taken aback. Obviously they were going to waste no time on small talk. "No. I spent most of my time with the female aviators. Bombardiers and fighter pilots."

"Holy moly! Women fighter pilots." She pressed her cheek with open fingertips that held red lacquered nails. "They must have been brutes, too. I can just imagine them. Big lumpy things that look like men." She tittered. "They'd scare the bejeepers out of me."

Alex thought of gentle Katia, who'd died carrying her out of hell. An inner door that had been slowly opening suddenly slammed shut, and she stood up. "I just remembered I've got to be someplace. Thanks for the beer." She slipped between the dancing couples and left the canteen.

Though the night was warm, she huddled inside her jacket, lonely. Was this the only kind of woman she attracted? Worse, the silly creature with her cartoon notions of Russia could have been Alex herself, two years earlier. She leaned against a light pole, her fists deep in her raincoat as evening mist settled around her, chilling her.

Lilya, my darling, look what you've done to me. Please, please still be alive some place. Loving you has ruined me for anyone else.

CHAPTER TWENTY-NINE

Lilya was hanging limp from the pole when Olga returned with one of the soldiers, who cut her loose. He turned away to fire at the camp guards gathering to repel the intruders, while Olga caught her in her arms and dragged her back to their shed.

"Is it liberation?" Lilya asked through lips that hardly moved.

"I don't think so. It looks like just a small detachment. Olga paused for only a moment.

"Come on, this is our chance." Olga dragged her to her feet again.

She stuffed straw into both their jackets and wrapped their scraps of blankets around their shoulders. "We look like garden scarecrows," she muttered as she snatched Lilya by the hand and led her at a run through the fence hole left by the attacking troops. The other women followed them.

They ran, following the crack of gunfire, trying to catch sight of the retreating intruders. Camp guards pursued them now, shooting down all but four of the fleeing women, but when the Soviet detachment halted and returned fire, the guards withdrew.

Two of the intruders backtracked to where they stood. "What do you think you're doing?"

"We want to join you," Olga had the breath to call out. "Two snipers, a medic, and a pilot. Can you take us someplace where we can get warm? We can fight." Hunched over and wretched, Lilya had to admire Olga's negotiating skills.

He hesitated, but Olga pressed her case. "Why did you attack the camp in the first place if you didn't want to rescue anyone?" Lilya could see now that they weren't in full uniform but were partisans wearing the Red Army tunics over an assortment of trousers.

"We were supposed to do reconnaissance and then hit the administration barracks," the one who seemed to be the leader said. "But we came in from the wrong side, and the guards spotted us."

"Too bad. But you can still help four comrades."

He wrinkled his nose and seemed to consider how much of a liability it would be to return with four women. "All right, but you have to keep up."

Lilya was at the end of her strength, but the thought of freedom invigorated her just enough to muster the will to stagger forward for the next twenty minutes. And finally, when they emerged from a thicket, she saw a troop carrier on a path in front of them.

"Get in," the partisan said, and they clambered in gratefully.

The partisan detachment took them to a shed in the woods that might once have been a hunter's lodge. Firewood was piled up against one wall, and two sentries stood guard. The interior consisted of two rooms, one with a wood stove, table, and kerosene lantern, and the other, as far as she could see through the open door, with crates of munitions and supplies.

As they entered, the commander turned up the wick on the lantern to see them and snapped, "Close the goddam door," at the reporting soldier.

"Yes, Comrade Kovitch," the man said and, waving the other soldiers away, closed the ill-fitting door behind them.

Kovitch himself was unremarkable. Of slight stature, he had an odd diamond-shaped face that seemed to narrow at the top due to a severely receding hairline, and at the bottom by virtue of a mustache and goatee. His uniform that, unlike those of his men, was complete and held decorations, indicated he was a colonel.

"What's this? I ordered you to knock out the camp administration building, and instead you bring me back four women."

"Sorry, sir. But the building was heavily guarded. We were lucky to escape. The women followed us out."

The commander slid his glance over them. "What am I going to do with them?"

Olga was quick to reply. "I was a sniper, Comrade Colonel, and I'm still a sniper, if you give me a rifle."

One of the others chimed in. "I'm also a sniper."

"And you?"

"A medic, Comrade Colonel."

"And you?" He looked at Lilya. It was obvious now that he was toying with them, like a skillful shopper about to make a purchase. But what good was a pilot to partisans?

Olga spoke up again. "She's a fighter pilot, Comrade Colonel. She fought at Stalingrad."

That caught his attention. "Stalingrad, eh? What's your name?"

She hesitated for the briefest second. "Aleksandra Vasil'evna Petrovna, Comrade Colonel."

He peered at her longer than he should have, as if something about her appearance troubled him, and she feared he might have recognized her. But a new sound seized his attention. He stared up at the ceiling of the shed, as if he could see through it, and Lilya recognized the unmistakable clatter of a U-2 motor.

Strange. There were no targets here. What were they doing so close?

"The supplies. Take two of the men and get out there fast with the signal lights," the commander barked.

As the soldier scrambled out to obey the order, Kovitch turned his attention back to the four women. "I've lost several of my best riflemen in the last days. If you are who you say you are, and God help you if you aren't, then I can use you."

He waved over one of the men who'd brought them in. "Take them into the other room and get them appropriate uniforms. They can wait for the supplies to get rifles."

Lilya's head swam. They were saved, but they were going to fight alongside the men instead of being returned to their regiments. Under the circumstances, that was the best she could hope for. Now if they could just get some warm food in their stomachs.

The "appropriate uniforms" they received amounted to padded jackets, and while Lilya's was too large and smelled of machorka smoke and sweat, it was a relief to finally be warm. The soldier also fished out two-finger mittens for them.

Now that their status as comrades was clear, the soldier was less brusque than before and chatted with them as they tried on the jackets. "You're lucky. The delivery just came and we should have extra food tonight. The commander's good about passing it around to the men the first night."

"That's a relief," Olga said, buttoning up the collar of her new jacket. "The Fritzes have been starving us for months. Saves them the cost of bullets."

The soldier looked her over. "You *look* starved. You're going to have to toughen up fast here. We're always on the move and can't carry any dead weight. Good thing you're snipers. We always need those."

He studied Lilya. "We don't need pilots, that's for sure. But he probably kept you because you look like his daughter."

"He has a daughter? There are women in the group?"

"Had. She was killed a few months ago somewhere east of here. We don't usually patrol alone, but she'd just gone out to deliver a message and never came back. We found her body a few days later, near a plane wreck."

A faint memory came to her. A woman's voice in the woods, then soldiers and pain, then nothing. Lilya's hand went unconsciously to her mouth. "Do you know what kind of plane it was?"

"No. Some kind of fighter plane, they said. The patrol came back to report it, but when they returned the next day to bury her, she was gone. Commander Kovitch never got over it." He stepped back and observed that all of them were now adequately dressed. "Come on, help bring in the supplies. No work, no food."

Lilya followed him out, musing over a partisan woman she would never meet and who had died in her place.

By the first week of January she'd gained back most of her weight and had proved herself. She was useless as a sniper, but when it came to trudging through snowy woods on sabotage missions, she was as stalwart as any man. She even inherited a thick ushanka to protect her head and ears when one of the men in the group was killed.

More importantly, the unit supplied her with new temporary papers, thereby confirming her flimsy new identity in the Soviet military machine.

On two more occasions she heard the familiar clattering of a U-2 engine when a plane came in to deliver supplies. None ever landed, and she wondered how close their base was. Could she locate it and return to the night bombers? Major Bershanskaya would surely protect her and not surrender her to the NKVD.

Though the partisans had supplied her with a padded coat, she couldn't strike out alone in winter, uncertain of where she was going and with little food. The other women might also be punished in some way for her desertion. And so she stayed, free and yet a prisoner.

❖

The months passed, and as Lilya had once been a "free hunter" aviator, she was now a "free infantryman." She was assigned to the First Ukrainian Front, but as they fought their way north and west, the detachments around her were thinned by death, and she was rounded up again into the First Belorussian Front.

Regardless of her place in the Red Army, her daily life was the same—crouching under cover alternated with running toward the enemy. At night, life meant shoveling cold food into her mouth and huddling with the other women in whatever shelter was available for a few hours' sleep before the next advance.

And advance they did, kilometer by kilometer, though rain and the spring mud put the whole war into slow motion, like dream paralysis.

In spite of the ferocity of their defenses, the German armies were obviously in full retreat. But as she passed through Ternopol, Proskurov, and Kovel, Lilya saw the wasteland the invaders had left behind them, torching every village and farm, poisoning wells, and slaughtering or driving away the livestock.

If they moved fast enough, they could sometimes put the enemy to flight before he set his fires and could save a village from ruin. In May, they succeeded, and a grateful family of peasants invited her and the other women in for the night. They butchered a chicken, and though the portions divided among six people were miniscule, it was a taste of heaven to have fresh poultry in her mouth instead of bread and a few ounces of horse sausage. Even better, the family offered their bed to them while, for that one night, they slept in their barn.

Lilya and the other women leaned their rifles against the bedroom wall, within quick reach, and removed their boots and heavy jackets. The bed was spacious, for the couple had slept in it with their two children. Still, for four grown women, it was almost as crowded as their nest in the POW camp, and they spent the first half hour giggling.

"Just like the old times at in the camp, eh?" Olga joked, fitting herself onto the outer edge. "If anyone farts, I'm throwing them out of bed, you hear?"

"We smell so bad, we'll never notice," Lilya replied from the other side. In fact, she'd long since ceased to notice odor. The feel of a mattress underneath her was blissful, and she tried to think of the last time she'd slept on one.

It came to her suddenly, and it was her last thought before she slept.

Sandwiched between her fully clothed comrades, she dreamt of lying—clean, nude, and deeply aroused—in Alex's arms.

CHAPTER THIRTY

Alex stood in the pelting rain at a depot at Portsmouth, shielding her camera lens with one hand while she snapped photos of the ongoing troop movements. Thousands of men filed past her into the powerboats to be ferried out to the transport ships.

Drying her lens again, she changed position and got a good shot of another contingent of GIs heading out on powerboats to the ships, their edge-to-edge helmets making them look like a single lumpy carapace on the back of some huge floating beetle.

"He that outlives this day, and comes safe home, will stand a tip-toe when this day is named," someone behind her declaimed.

She knew the quote, which she'd memorized herself in college, and when she turned, she recognized the man as well. Robert Capa, her chief competitor.

"Then will he strip his sleeve and show his scars, and say These wounds I had on Crispin's day," she declaimed back to him, skipping the lines she couldn't remember.

He stood beside her now, facing outward toward the war-ready harbor, and raised an arm theatrically. *"This story shall the good man teach his son and Crispin Crispian shall ne'er go by from this day to the ending of the world, but we in it shall be rememberéd."*

She grinned, remembering the final lines of the speech, and spoke them with him in unison: *"We few, we happy few, we band of brothers!"*

"Henry V," she said. "Almost as good as 'We will fight on the beaches,' isn't it?"

"Well, I suppose people need to hear things like that if they're going to their deaths," Capa said, opening an umbrella over both of their heads.

He was a handsome man, she noted, swarthy and exotic, with thick eyebrows. Though his work was much like hers, she'd always admired it, and now she found she liked him personally.

"What about war correspondents? Do you think we should have something similar? 'We band of camera shutterbugs and paparazzi.' Something like that?"

He laughed a warm, rich chuckle. "I've seen your Eastern Front photos. You're good."

"I hear you are, too," she joked. "Are you going over?"

"Yes, in the second wave."

"Good luck to you. I've been under fire, but in a plane. I wouldn't relish standing hip deep in water with only a camera when it's raining bullets."

"I suppose it's a sort of a 'Henry V Saint Crispin's day' thing. I'm in it for the glory. If I make it, men will speak of me. What about you?"

"I'm going over in a couple of weeks. No glory involved."

He looked at her quizzically, as if wondering what other reason a photographer would have for entering a theater of war. "All right, then. Maybe I'll see you there." He closed his umbrella, leaving her in the rain, and returned to the depot.

She stood for a few moments longer, glad he hadn't asked why she was returning. She couldn't have told him that it was to find a woman she wasn't allowed to love.

❖

On D-day plus three weeks she got her press pass, along with the order to report to the army quartermaster's store to be uniformed as a war correspondent. A group of Wacs assigned to the supreme commander's headquarters would be crossing the channel the next day, and she was scheduled to join them.

The faux officer's uniform provided by the US military to its journalists was almost identical to the one she'd worn when she arrived in Moscow. The jacket of this one, however, had WAR CORRESPONDENT stitched over the left breast pocket and on the left shoulder patch. The army-issue trousers were too wide, though, and she smiled to herself, thinking of the clownish breeches of the night bombers.

Twenty-four hours later, she was on landing craft LCVP 105 along with the Wacs, a dozen crates of communication equipment, and a jeep.

The storm that had made the D-day passage so horrendous had long passed, but the channel waters were still rough, and clambering down a net from a transport ship into the landing craft with three cameras and her rucksack had taken all her agility. But now she was within minutes of landing and without the pleasure of strafing planes or land batteries trying to kill her.

Bracing herself against the wall of the craft, she took a few shots of the harbor, sprung up as if by miracle within two days of the first wave of attack. Then she was in the icy water up to her knees, and holding her rucksack and equipment over her head, she splashed toward the shore.

"Over here!" A GI waved them over to a path to higher ground where a covered truck stood. Alex and the Wacs climbed on and braced themselves on their benches as the truck rocked and bumped over the rutted road.

They passed troops marching eastward on the road, and as soon as the GIs spotted the women, the wolf whistles began. Annoying, of course, but Alex decided that marching into the battlefield entitled them to that degree of misbehavior.

After an hour or so, the truck stopped and an MP helped them onto the ground. "Welcome to the Communication Zone, ladies," he said, and Alex surveyed the field covered with tents, washing facilities, and what seemed to be covered latrines. "You'll be staying here until you're assigned," he added, and led them in batches of six to their respective group tents.

Alex unpacked and laid out her bedroll. She was also relieved to be able to take off her trousers, still wet to the knees, and hang them on the tent pole to dry.

"Swell idea," a handsome, statuesque Wac on the bunk next to her said, and also slid off her wet fatigues. "I was wondering what to do with these." She held up her own trousers and hung them alongside Alex's.

As both stood there in their general-issue cotton underwear, the other woman held out her hand. "Jo Knightly."

Alex smiled and took it. "Alex Preston. I wonder how long we'll be here."

"Don't know about you, but we're waiting to be assigned to Supreme Allied Headquarters. I'm General Eisenhower's secretary and the others are in communication." She reached for a brush and ran it through her short hair, forming it into a modified ducktail.

"Honored to meet you. Where will you be located?"

"We don't know yet, frankly. Those crates that came with us are full of telephone and wireless equipment for his first command post. We're just waiting for orders telling us where to go. What about you?"

"I'm waiting to be attached to the Third Army."

"They've assigned you to Patton? Condolences, hon. Patton's not much of a lady's man."

A woman just across from them laughed. "From what I hear, he's not much of a man's man either. He slapped two shell-shocked GIs in an evacuation hospital and called them cowards."

"Really?" Alex wrapped her blanket around her waist like a sarong and sat on her bunk. "He'd be right at home with Stalin, who has no interest in his men once they're out of battle. Though Stalin doesn't so much slap them as have them shot."

"Where'd you hear that?" Jo asked.

"From Stalin himself, on Moscow radio."

"Gosh, you speak Russian? And you've been in Moscow?" Jo said. "And here I thought I was a big shot for getting to France. What was it like?"

Alex winced. She was always getting the same questions, and they always ended up with the same clichés. She took a breath. "Cold. Dangerous. Desperate."

"Did you see battle?" The question came from a large-eyed woman who couldn't have been more than nineteen.

"Yes, I did." She saw no reason to go into detail.

"Oh, my. Were you in foxholes with the troops? That sort of thing?"

"No. With the Soviet Air Force. A woman's regiment, in fact. Night bombers and fighter pilots." Here we go again, she thought.

A circle of young women had gathered around her now. "Wow. Women in air battles? Incredible."

Jo leaned sideways on her bunk, resting on one elbow. "Did you fly with them? How thrilling, but it must have been kind of humbling, too."

Alex turned and faced her. "Yes, it was. Not just the flying, but the work of the ground crews, who were also women. The duty was grueling. It pushed them really to the limit of their strength, and they never had enough food or warm places to sleep. Even in winter."

"What were they like as people? Like us?" another one asked.

"All different, of course, and in some ways like us, but ferocious fighters." She looked into the middle distance, recalling faces.

"And you could talk to them, too. How wonderful," Jo said with sincere admiration. "Did you have close friends? Someone special?" The question could have meant anything.

"Several of them were special. Marina Raskova, Raisa Beliaeva, Katia Budanova. But they were all killed." Saying their names caused a pang of sorrow but also seemed to honor them. She wanted not to forget them.

"And…Lilya Drachenko," she added. "Shot down in the Ukraine. A prisoner of war, I think. Waiting for someone to liberate her." She fell silent.

"Such wonderful romantic names," the young one chirped.

Jo stared at Alex, and her expression showed she understood all of it. "Is that why you're going back?" she asked softly. "To be the one?"

"Yes," Alex said. "At whatever cost."

Jo nodded and said, almost inaudibly, "It's a precious thing, that kind of love."

"All right, ladies. Lights out!" the officer in charge called from outside their tent.

"Yes, sir!" The woman nearest the lantern switched it off, and everyone took to her bunk.

Jo's voice came from her bunk close by. "A shame we're going in different directions. It would have been swell to pal around with you."

"Appreciate the compliment, Jo. I think you'd be a good comrade, too. But you know, I was on the Eastern Front so long, I think I forgot how to 'pal around' with anyone."

Jo chortled softly. "And you were there so long you started using the word comrade. Anyhow, listen, hon. Anything you need from Allied Headquarters, you let me know."

"Thanks, Jo. I'll keep that in mind." Alex lay back on her cot and closed her eyes, trying, as she did every night, to remember the details of Lilya Drachenko's face.

The Wacs were deployed to temporary Allied headquarters two days later. Suddenly alone, Alex moped a little, snapping the odd photo here and there. And on August 1, she received orders to meet the Third Army at Muneville-le-Bingard, where it was beginning its French campaign. She caught a ride with auxiliary troops south to Rennes, then followed Patton's army as it swept north and eastward.

The battles were hard-fought, but city after city fell. Soon she could see a certain monotony in her photographs: the same ruined buildings and bloated bodies of livestock, the same dead soldiers of both armies. Like in Russia, but without the snow to freeze them and cover the odor.

At the end of August, while she stood with a few GIs overlooking the Seine River at Montereau, news came of the liberation of Paris. She regretted, briefly, that she'd missed the chance to get momentous photos but was certain Robert Capa had gotten them, and she didn't begrudge him the glory.

Buck up, old girl, she thought. *Stay on the program. You still have half of Europe to cross.*

CHAPTER THIRTY-ONE

Summer 1944, Belorussia

Hunkered down in a building outside Minsk, Lilya glanced up as the post courier came in. "Good news, comrade," he said, tossing her a copy of *Red Star*.

She scanned the headline and lead article. "The Anglo armies have landed in France," she said with quiet awe. "Finally we have a second front."

"Took them long enough," the courier said, moving on to the next building.

She had no idea what the beaches of France looked like, but she tried to imagine them covered with Allied soldiers. What a photo opportunity that must have been. Alex would have loved it if she hadn't been so far away in Moscow.

Was she still in Moscow? Lilya realized she had no idea, and the thought that Alex might have left Russia filled her with a deep sorrow.

Just then, a call from their leader brought the detachment to its feet, and she had to quit brooding. A constant regime of battle and marching for weeks at a time without leave—and she was never granted leave—was mind-numbing, but the camaraderie of the battlefield had become her entire world.

The summer months wore on, and while the army still made two steps forward and one step back, Hitler was now retreating on all fronts. Sustained by the constant arrival of good news, she fought patriotically, kilometer after kilometer, loyal to Russia and to her comrades, if not to the Kremlin and the party.

Soon the victories began to pile up. Paris liberated in August, Lithuania fallen in September, and 57,000 German POWs had been paraded through Moscow. Was Alex there, capturing the scene for her magazine?

But in September, as she waited for orders near the Polish border, that loyalty began to weaken. Word filtered back about the uprising against the Germans in Warsaw, and the obvious course of action was to go to their aid. But to her amazement, orders came from the NKVD that the Red Army was to stand down and let the uprising succeed or fail on its own.

She dared to confide only in Olga. "How could they do that? Aren't we both fighting the Germans?"

Olga shrugged. "It's not for us to judge. We don't know what the generals are planning. They're the leaders and we're pledged to follow."

"I suppose you're right, but I thought the Free Polish Army was our ally, and now we're abandoning them. What if our allies in the West did that to us?"

"For God's sake, be quiet!" Olga hissed. "If the commissar heard you, you'd be arrested. Just do your job and keep your doubts to yourself."

Lilya fell silent. Doubts were exactly what plagued her. And when the uprising in Poland was crushed, her youthful faith in the party and the military authorities began to crumble.

She almost feared the days when they were allowed to rest. When she tried to sleep, her mind buzzed with questions. A voice at the back of her mind kept saying that a victory for Russia would be a victory for Stalin and that the very government she feared would be stronger than ever. Was she losing her wits, falling prey to the very thoughts that made her own father an enemy of the people?

She'd grown up thinking "the state" had a complete claim on her. But somehow, being captured and then disavowed, then living among the troops rather than her Komsomol comrades, had given the word "state" a different flavor. A small, hard idea had formed inside of her like a disease, that the state had betrayed her. Now only her comrades, the millions of her brothers and sisters in the Red Army, claimed her fidelity. Men, at least, were good, even if their government was cruel.

Then they arrived in East Prussia and one day, two of the young lads came back from a farmhouse the forward troops had confiscated, both rather full of themselves. They swaggered and smirked at one another, as if they had some amusing secret.

As she attempted to pass them, they warned her to stay away from the farmhouse but wouldn't say why. She ignored them and continued on. Maybe they'd found extra food and were hiding it for themselves. She didn't like being excluded.

Once inside the farmhouse, she heard drunken laughter coming from one of the rooms.

The door was ajar, and when she peered inside, she saw them. A dozen of her comrades formed a circle around something happening at the center on the floor. Only when two of the men lurched sideways, giving her a full view, did she make sense of it.

A woman lay there, moaning and thrashing, though Lilya could see only her bare legs, held apart by two soldiers while a third pumped into her.

One of the onlookers spotted her and slammed the door shut, but now she understood. That is what they were doing when they went off in groups of four and five into the houses of the defeated Germans. Revolted, she fled back to the camp where the first lad stood, rolling machorka tobacco into a scrap of paper.

"Calm down," he said. "She's a German. It's what they did to our women when they invaded. We're just paying them back."

"So, that's how you punish them, by torturing their women for your own pleasure? What if they recapture this sector and do the same to me? You make me sick. All of you. Your mothers would be ashamed."

She stomped away, filled with revulsion. These were men she had called her brothers? The war had turned them into beasts, and the only thing that protected her from the same atrocity was that she traveled with the victors.

At that moment, her last loyalty was destroyed, and she fought on toward Berlin because she had to, in the midst of an army of men she could no longer trust.

What was she going to do on the day of victory?

The question was driving her mad.

CHAPTER THIRTY-TWO

All in all, August had gone well, Alex thought. The Third Army had battled its way back and forth through Brittany and central France, then began its march toward the Rhine. Its commander, George Patton, was used to winning battles, and if photographers were there to document his successes as a tough-guy general, that was just fine.

Alex stayed out of his way, dutifully photographing the victories at Verdun, Nancy, Metz, but in December the retreating Germans suddenly counterattacked, and Patton had to lead his troops back into the Ardennes.

Through snow as thick as any she remembered in Russia, he drove his tanks and marched his infantrymen into Bastogne. The ferocity of the fight took everyone but her by surprise, but by the end of January, the Allies had won.

Finally, in early March, they came to Remagen, where the bridge over the Rhine River had just been lost. Undaunted, the Third Army Engineers transported their men and material, first by raft and ferry, and then by a steel treadway bridge built on pontoons. Alex liked watching the men build things. So much nicer than blasting them apart.

Patton was an enigma. His list of victories was impressive, but Alex couldn't determine whether they were because of, or in spite of, his style. She compared his swagger and snarl with the measured orders of Eva Bershanskaya. Of course, Bershanskaya commanded women, who didn't need to be verbally assailed to obey. But maybe men didn't either.

But whatever the strategies of the Allied armies through the winter of 1944-45, they were winning, and by March it was obvious that the end was in sight. She took her best photograph in March while she rode the back of a Third Army tank rumbling down the autobahn. Asking the driver to halt for a moment, she leapt onto an embankment to gain some height. She directed her camera downward and recorded the thousands of captured Wehrmacht soldiers trudging westward to POW camps on one side of the highway, while on the other, the Allied tanks and jeeps rolled eastward into the heart of the Reich.

Germans this time. On the Eastern Front, it had been Soviets. Masses of people marching together in victory or defeat seemed to be one of the symbols of war.

At sunset, Patton called the march to a halt, and in the spring weather, his men bivouacked on the ground without complaint. Alex, too, was happy to set up her little pup tent for a night's rest. As she was loosening the laces on her boots, the tent flap opened.

"Hey!" She glanced up, annoyed that someone would enter without permission, but her anger evaporated immediately. "Robert Capa, what are you doing slumming with the Third Army? I thought you'd still be on the Champs Elysees."

"Nope. Paris is passé these days. Germany's where the action is. Anyhow, come on, and bring your mess kit. Patton scored a case of wine from one of the villages. He's invited the press for a drink."

"Sure thing." She snatched up her mess tin and followed him to the general's tent.

Patton had his back turned and was just telling some sort of anecdote to a circle of listeners when Alex stepped in. He ended it with "Like I always say, all a girl needs is a good fuck; it shuts them right up," to general male guffaws.

The laughter died back quickly as she came into Patton's sight. He scratched his jaw. "No offense, there. You know how men are."

After weeks of traveling with the blowhard general, she'd had enough. "Yes, I do. They like to talk about fucking, but only around other men. I've always wondered why that is."

The general squinted, as if trying to decide if he'd been insulted, and apparently concluded that he had. "If you're one of those sensitive girls who doesn't like rough talk, you might remember we're on a battlefield."

Somewhere inside her brain, a small voice told her to shut the hell up, but she ignored it. "Oh, I'm quite used to roughness, General. But I'm not 'one of those girls.' I've spent three years on the Eastern Front, have flown a plane under enemy fire at Stalingrad, and was wounded in action. I think I'm a bit beyond the 'sensitive girl' stage."

"Well, aren't *you* the ballbreaker." He snorted. "I don't give a fuck where you flew. You're in *my* camp now, so have some respect. Just who do you think is protecting your ass from the Jerries?"

"Thank you for your service, General, but I've just told you that I've been serving too, and with valor. If I were one of your soldiers, I'd have a Purple Heart." The warning voice in her brain was shocked into silence.

"If you were one of my soldiers, I'd slap you in irons for insubordination," he said.

She was on automatic pilot now. Not a good thing. "Slap in irons? Or just slap me?"

Patton's expression grew hard and he turned to a subordinate. "Sergeant, please escort Miss Preston to her tent. And tomorrow, see to it that she has a ride back to General Bradley's headquarters. I don't need this kind of crap."

He turned back to Alex. "Miss Preston, you are dismissed."

Her face warm with rage and humiliation, she exited the tent but hadn't taken ten steps when she heard, "Miss Preston, wait."

She glanced back over her shoulder. "Do you want to insult me, too?"

The man took a pipe out from between his teeth. "No, not at all. I like seeing people stand up to that old windbag. If he weren't such a damned good soldier, I'd hate him, too."

"And you are…?"

"Lieutenant Colonel John Lynch, Commander of the 3rd Battalion, 69th Infantry." He held out his hand.

She accepted it and liked his handshake. "Alex Preston. Photojournalist and, apparently, ballbreaker. Nice to meet a man who's not afraid of us."

"Quite the opposite. In any case, I was here to plan strategy, and I'm rejoining my battalion in the morning. We're headed toward Leibzig and Mockrehna and, with a little luck, the Elbe River. Care to join us?"

She liked this tall, lanky man who smelled of sweet tobacco. "I believe I would. Can I invite another journalist to come along?"

"Sure, the more the merrier."

❖

The tenacity of the 69th Infantry, together with the little luck they were hoping for, in fact brought the 3rd Battalion to the Elbe River on April 25.

"I gotta hand it to you," Robert Capa said as they stood together on the west bank. "Your instinct about this was good. Here we are at the

Elbe for the meeting of two armies who otherwise can't even talk to each other. A photojournalist's dream."

"*I* can talk to them. And come to think of it, I have a few things I want to ask them, too."

They watched as the forward reconnaissance platoon returned in their inflatable boat. The platoon sergeant climbed up the bank and saluted the colonel. "Everything's in order, sir. The Russian commander suggested that the chosen parties meet officially tomorrow morning on our side of the shore closer to Torgau, in the presence of the press."

Colonel Lynch laughed. "Whaddya know. The Russians like publicity just as much as we do. Well, go back and tell him we'll have our journalists and our best-looking soldiers ready by ten o'clock."

The next day, when the national flags, various IP film cameras, and Alex and Capa were in place, several boatloads of Soviet fighters came across the river. Waving to their hosts, some hundred of them stepped onto the shore along a five-hundred-yard stretch of riverbank.

In spite of the planning, the meetings were rather haphazard. The officers of both sides shook hands, and various soldiers embraced, while at other spots along the bank, men gathered in clusters and exchanged cigarettes and souvenirs. A second lieutenant, who looked like an all-American guy, was chosen to pose next to a sturdy young Slav in front of both national flags. Between them, Alex and Capa snapped several dozen good shots of the event.

Alex acted intermittently as translator, though the banter between soldiers was mostly limited to remarks about each other's boots, weapons, and cigarettes.

It struck her like a slap to the head that the Red troops had just come from the territories she most needed to know about. She chose one of the sergeants and drew him to the side.

"Did you fight in the Ukraine?"

"Of course. I fought everywhere. Why?"

"I need to know. Did you pass through any POW camps? German camps? In Vinnytsia, for example. What happened to them?"

"We liberated a lot of them. Little ones and big ones. In Vinnytsia, too."

"Did you find women?"

"Yes, some. In very poor condition. All our people were, the ones who hadn't starved to death. The ones that were still alive, we sent back home for interrogation."

"Did anyone make a list of the names? I'm looking for someone."

"Everybody's looking for someone. We sent back the tags of the dead ones, the ones we found. Some were buried. The survivors? I don't know. You could contact the Ukrainian Red Cross. Or the NKVD, but I don't think they'll share that information."

"The women. Do you remember any of the women?" She was grasping at straws.

"No. They were skeletons. Nothing you'd want to remember." He took a step back. "Look, I've got to stay with my unit or I'll get in trouble."

"Yes, I understand. Thanks for your time." Beaten, she turned and climbed back up the embankment to where Capa stood.

Colonel Lynch joined them, lighting his newly filled pipe. He sucked in air, and the plug of tobacco glowed briefly. "Interesting to finally see the Russians up close, after all we've heard about them. Look like ordinary soldiers, though their uniforms are pretty ragged." He puffed again and exhaled, spreading the aroma of apple and tobacco. It was the odor of contentment.

"By the way, I got off the field phone with headquarters a little while ago, and this might interest you. Chuikov's army has taken Tempelhof Airport and is already in the southern suburbs of Berlin. Everyone seems convinced Hitler's in the city, in a bunker."

"Really?" Capa had the tilt to his head that she knew signaled intense interest. "What do you think, Alex? Shall we do Berlin?"

She stared across the river, weighing the pros and cons. "Let me chew on it for a while. In the meantime, I need to contact my editor. Colonel, where's the nearest place I can send a telegraph? Have you blown up all the telegraph lines around here so I have to go all the way back to Leipzig?"

Lynch glanced toward the outline of buildings of Torgau, half a mile away. "As you know, we haven't blown up anything here. I'd say you had about as good a chance at Torgau as in Leipzig. If you'd like, I'll send a man to take you both into the center of town."

"Thank you, Colonel. I accept your offer." Alex and Capa packed up their cameras and followed the colonel to a jeep.

"Private, please take our two journalists into town and try to locate the telegraph office. Then bring them back again. We'll be bivouacked just over there near the woods."

Alex and Capa climbed into the jeep, and as the driver pulled away from the bank, Alex heard the crackling of guns in celebration and, faintly, a woman's voice. She glanced back to see one of the female soldiers running after them, waving.

Touched by the gesture, she waved back, took a quick snapshot, and called out in Russian, "Good-bye, my friends," and the jeep drew away from the river.

❖

The telegraph office, when they found it, was closed, but the man guarding it from inside leapt to admit them. Hand gestures and the convenient German word *telegraf* conveyed the idea of what they needed. Obsequious, if not terrified, the young man unlocked the cubicle containing the handset and donned the headphones.

Alex printed out a New York telegraph address and wrote out a brief message, which she knew he could transmit in Morse without understanding.

REPORTING FR TORGAU WHERE US AND SOVIET FORCES JUST MET STOP HAVE PHOTOS STOP WORD IS HITLER IS IN BERLIN STOP WILL GO WHEN FIGHTING DIES DOWN STOP TROOPS HERE REPORT ALL UKRAINE CAMPS LIBERATED STOP CAN YOU CONTACT UKRAINE RED CROSS RE POW NAME DRACHENKO STOP END

She handed the note back to the clerk along with a handful of Reichsmarks, but he brushed the money aside. She didn't blame him. They were all but worthless. Capa was more resourceful and shook several cigarettes from his pack of Lucky Strikes, which he handed over with his own message to transmit. Obviously relieved to have actually gained something instead of being brutalized by either of the conquering armies, the telegrapher was all smiles when he led them to the door.

"Thanks also for paying for my telegram," she said once they were back in the jeep.

Capa lit his own cigarette with a Zippo lighter and blew out a long stream of smoke. "So, what about it?" he asked. "You up for Berlin?"

"You're more into high-risk reporting than I am these days," she answered. "Why don't you go on ahead. I want to wait for an answer from my boss."

"Suit yourself, old girl. Me, I'm tired of photographing handshakes, so I'll be off this afternoon. Maybe I'll see you there." He gave her a hug and a noisy kiss on her ear.

But the next afternoon, when she returned with the same jeep to the same telegraph office, a message awaited her that made her wish he'd waited a day.

George Mankowitz had replied immediately.

GOOD YOURE ALIVE STOP LOOK FORWARD TO PICS STOP OUR MUTUAL FRIEND SENDS URGENT MESSAGE FOR YOU TO GO TO BERLIN DAHLEM FOEHRENWEG EX KEITEL HQ STOP MAJOR JOB FOR YOU STOP END

She stood for a long moment, bewildered. Somebody was offering her a job. But who did George know who might be in Berlin? General Morgan? Eisenhower? Did the Allies still need photographers? Nothing she could think of seemed likely.

Well, it hardly made any difference. She no longer had a war to photograph, so if someone wanted her in Berlin, she was going.

CHAPTER THIRTY-THREE

April 1945

Sprawled on the grassy ground near the river, Lilya chewed what was left of her breakfast. The air was unnervingly still, no sound of bombardment or cannon fire anywhere, and in about an hour, they would be ferried over the Elbe to meet the Americans. Would they be like Alex?

Stretched out near her, Olga wiped out her mess kit "What are you going to do when it's over? Will you go back and be rehabilitated? I'm sure we have a good service record now."

Lilya stared into the distance, tearing off tiny pieces of crust and chewing them almost unconsciously. "I don't see how I can. Bad enough to be captured, but I as much as signed my execution order by working in the commandant's house. That counts as collaboration." She didn't add that she also held a false identity. "What about you?"

Olga picked her teeth with a fingernail. "I'm going back. I know the NKVD will be on my neck, but my father's in the party, and I was in the Komsomol. I fought bravely through this entire war, and the commissar commended me. That's got to count for something."

Lilya shrugged. "Anyhow, it's too soon to worry about it, isn't it? The Germans are still fighting in Berlin, and a bullet or grenade could arrive tomorrow and solve the problem for us."

"Well, it won't happen today, at least. Not while we're here shaking hands with the Americans in front of the press. I'm guessing a lot of liquor and cigarettes will change hands, too."

Someone barking orders ended their conversation, and they packed up their mess kits. Half an hour later, they were in a rowboat drawing up onto the western shore of the Elbe.

The American GIs were interesting. A little taller than the Russians, though a bit soft, like men who ate well every day. As she stood with the other women, random GIs came and stood beside her, though she tried hard not to be photographed. Some of them planted a kiss on her cheek or slid an arm around her back. She didn't care for the casual intimacy with strangers but tolerated it, knowing it was to show how brotherly they all were. In addition, half a dozen photographers snapped pictures of the two armies with large, professional cameras on tripods, while she tried to keep her back turned to them.

One of the men in her unit came toward her smoking an American cigarette. "They're nice, the Americans," he announced between puffs. "One of their journalists even speaks Russian. Strange, though. She asked me about the camps in the Ukraine. If I saw any women there. I told her no."

"She asked you about the Ukraine? Which one was it? What did she look like?"

"I don't know. Dark hair. Nice figure. She was taking pictures."

Lilya rocked back. "A photographer?" She grabbed him by the sleeve. "Where is she? Point her out to me."

"I don't see her now. Go ask one of the guys with the cameras. I'm going to try to get another cigarette." He pulled his arm away and strode back to his group.

Lilya threw herself toward the nearest US army photographer and seized him by the arm. "*Proshu vas!*," she said, breathless, having no idea how to say *please* in English.

"Alex Preston? "*Fotograf.*" She mimicked holding a camera in front of her face. "Alex Preston?" she repeated.

To her astonishment, he raised his eyebrows and nodded.

"*Da, da.*" It seemed to be all the Russian he knew. He pointed toward the road leading into Torgau. She peered in the direction he pointed, and in the distance she could see a woman and two men climbing into a jeep. Incredulous, she hesitated for just a moment, then took off at a run toward the road.

She lurched forward and ran full out, her boots hammering the ground, as the jeep began pulling away. No, no! "Alex, Aleeex!" she called out, waving her arms, but the firing of celebratory guns drowned out her cry.

The two passengers in the jeep seemed to watch her with amusement. The woman—was it Alex?—raised her camera to her face and took a picture, and the jeep drew away from her down the road until it was out of sight.

Lilya stopped, paralyzed, torn between grief and hope. It had to be Alex, and if so, she was in Germany. With the US military. Would it be possible to find her again? A more ominous question arose. After so long a time, would she want to be found? The glamorous aviation hero Alex had fallen in love with was now a grubby little infantryman with sore feet, scars, and greasy brown hair.

She buried her face in her hands.

❖

The distance between Torgau and Berlin cost the Red Army only a short march but a great deal of blood, for they spent the next ten days in constant battle. Though it was clear now to both sides that Nazi Germany was in collapse, the ragtag mix of fragmented regiments, Home Guard, and the wolf packs of Hitlerjugend stood their ground. As the Red Army units had done before Moscow, the Germans fought to the death in Herzber, Luckenwalde, Trebbin, Blankenfelde, and finally in the outskirts of Berlin.

But by the first of May, Lilya was jogging amid a platoon of other infantrymen into the heart of the city. By the second of May, she stood with Olga in front of the Reichstag building gawking up at the enormous Soviet flag that fluttered from its roof.

Berlin had fallen.

Lilya surveyed the mountains of rubble, the ragged hollow husks of buildings, the shell holes on every street, and the countless decomposing bodies. "It's over, Olga. We don't need to fight any more. What do you suppose they'll do with us now?"

"For sure they'll assign us to clear out all the mines and traps the Fritzes have left us, but after that, I don't know. I suppose, keep some of us here for policing and send the rest back."

"Me, if I don't get blown up doing mine clearance, I want to stay in Berlin as long as possible. I'm going to apply for guard duty with General Zhukov. I can stand at attention for a long time. And when I'm off duty, I'm going to look around the big archway. The Brandenburg something."

"What's the point of staying? And why do you want to hang around the Brandenburg?"

"I'll tell you, Olga, because I trust you won't betray me. I'm hoping to find someone, or rather be found by someone, and they'll be more likely to see me if I'm standing near the monuments or the general."

Olga clasped her hands in front of her, "Oh, now I'm intrigued. Who is he? One of the officers? How did you manage to meet him without my noticing?"

Lilya looked away. "I'd rather not say any more. I hope you don't mind."

Exuberant, Olga threw an arm over her shoulder and planted a rough kiss on her cheek. "Well, if you find him, or he finds you, remember who your real friends are."

CHAPTER THIRTY-FOUR

May 1945

Alex was intrigued by the telegram from George Mankowitz, but not enough to enter a city in which house-to-house-fighting was still going on. She'd seen too much of that at Stalingrad. Instead, she waited at the rear of Colonel Lynch's troops while they cleaned up the terrain just north and west of Torgau.

When the announcement came on May 7 of unconditional surrender, she celebrated with some of the troops, then cadged a ride from one of the sergeants to the Berlin suburb of Dahlem.

It had obviously been *the* affluent residential quarter before the war. Even bombed and burnt in places, it still had the signs of a once-green and luxuriant part of the city. They drove along the edge of a now-desolate park and past the Kaiser Wilhelm Institute. Toward the west, the area was heavily wooded, though much had been blasted or cut down for firewood.

"Ah, there it is." Alex pointed with her chin, and the driver swerved.

Foehrenweg proved to be a very small street that shortly curved toward the right and changed its name. They drove along slowly, and she looked for signs of life in any of the handsome houses, largely undamaged by the shelling.

Only a few residences had lights in their windows, and they chose the one that approximated the address they had. Shouldering her camera case and rucksack, she got out of the jeep and knocked on the door. It opened immediately.

"Well, loooky who's here!"

She recoiled, astonished.

Terry Sheridan stepped out and gave her a hug. "So, the maverick returns. You can tell your driver to leave. You're not going anywhere." He waved toward the jeep, and the driver waved back before taking off.

"So what the hell's going on?" she asked.

"Come inside, first. We don't want to attract too much attention with the neighbors here." He guided her to a small, carpeted living room with expensive Biedermeyer-style furniture. Obviously the original owners had good taste. Alex wondered where they were.

A woman with gray hair drawn into a chignon and wearing wireless glasses sat demurely in the corner of a leather sofa. With papers on her lap and at her side, she first hinted at an elderly Marina Raskova, but a second look brought another memory, of a woman standing by a car on 112th Street, New York City, and again, sitting behind the wheel of another car in Red Square.

"Your secretary seems to follow you all over the world. How nice for you."

The woman's expression grew dark. "Secretary? Terry, if you don't stop telling people that, I swear I'll have you assassinated and dismembered."

Alex glanced toward Terry, perplexed. "What's she talking about?"

"Sorry. Alex, this is Elinor Stahl, our station chief. Um…my boss."

"Oh, I do apologize, Miss Stahl. I, of all people, should be ashamed for making that mistake. But Terry did say—"

"Quite all right." The woman warmed only slightly. "Terry can explain himself later. Right now we have other things to discuss, specifically why we requested you be here." She gathered up the papers and set them on an elegant side table.

"Yes, that would be a good place to start." Slightly annoyed by being tricked into insulting another woman, Alex sat down without invitation on the other end of the sofa. Elinor Stahl pivoted around to face her.

"To come right to the point, the Office of Strategic Services itself is in imminent risk of being disbanded."

"Why's that?" The explanation didn't seem to answer the question, but maybe they'd get there.

Stahl removed her glasses and slipped them into a leather case. "You probably know, in principle, that the OSS gathers intelligence. Up until now, it's largely been intelligence about the Nazis that has helped us win the war, with only an occasional foray into Soviet secrecy. But now that we've won, we have to redefine ourselves if we're to survive."

"I see. But what's that got to do with me?"

"As you must have surmised by Terry's appearances in Moscow, he's been keeping an eye on the Russians all along, but always in the context of the war. We know that Stalin is a monster, but until now he's been *our* monster, and we needed him to hold off the Nazis. Since victory, the playing field has changed quickly and radically, and now the Russians threaten to roll over us in the postwar planning. We need to prevent that. To be precise, we need more Russian speakers and people familiar with the culture. You're an obvious candidate."

"Candidate. As in apprentice spy? Terry invited me to spy for you last year and I said no. Why should I change my mind now?"

Terry interrupted. "Because the war is over and the alternative is to go home and photograph fashion shows."

"I *never* photographed fashion shows," she snapped.

"I was speaking figuratively. Look, I know you, Alex. You stayed over here for the same reason I did. The risk, the pace, the drama, it's like a drug."

"You don't know anything at all about my reasons, Terry."

He glanced over to where her spare luggage leaned against the entryway wall and chuckled. "I know that you used to be much more high maintenance. But since you've been in Russia, you've reduced your belongings to a single camera case and backpack. You're a different person. Can you imagine any job back in the States that you'd fit into now?"

Elinor Stahl looked at her watch. "I'm sorry to have to interrupt this conversation. We didn't expect you so soon and were about to leave. We have a meeting with General Zhukov and General Clay, the new military administrator of Berlin. I'm afraid that takes priority right now." She stood up.

"Zhukov *and* Clay? That does sound important."

"It is. For the time being, the room at the end of the hall is our guest room, so please make yourself at home there. When we get back, we can discuss your future, which we hope you'll have with us." She drew a key from her side pocket and tossed it to Terry. "You drive. This time, *you* can be the secretary."

Alex accompanied them to the rear of the house where, to her surprise, a jeep stood in a small garage. A driveway led through alleys away from the house, presumably so that one could arrive and leave unseen by the neighbors in the Foehrenweg. It wasn't exactly secret, but at least discreet.

She watched them drive off, her mind churning. It had been churning a lot recently, she realized, as she returned to the house.

The guest room, with its low wardrobe and miniature chairs, appeared to have been a child's room. The single bed was short and narrow, but it was still an improvement over a canvas military cot. As she'd hoped, the plumbing was intact, though water came in a thin stream and only cold. The toilet flushed. What a luxury.

The gas stove in the kitchen also functioned, so she decided to wash. She heated a pot of water and added it to the cold in the tub, remembering with painful nostalgia the shampoo buckets Inna had made for Lilya and Katia. The thought that both were gone made her feel like weeping.

Mechanically, she washed in the shallow lukewarm bath, then curled up in her underwear on the child-size bed, brooding. Terry was right. She couldn't think of anything she wanted to do back home. And maybe working with OSS in Germany would help her get information about Russian POWs. If Lilya had died, she wanted to know where and how. It was unfinished business. Feeling at once defeated and resolved, she dozed off.

The sound of the jeep returning to the garage woke her, and she hurried to dress before joining Terry and Elinor in the living room. They didn't look especially cheerful.

"How'd it go?"

"Not all that well," Terry said. "The Russians won't give an inch. They want maximum territory in Germany and a huge portion of Berlin. They keep insisting that they suffered the greatest losses of all the Allies."

"Well, that's true." She thought of Stalingrad.

"Of course it's true. And no one is belittling what the Nazis did to them. But they're using their ruined cities as an excuse to control all of Eastern Europe."

Terry retired to the kitchen to make coffee while she and Elinor sat down on the sofa.

Elinor cleaned her wireless glasses and set them on again. "So many issues are on the table: Poland, reparations, war-crimes trials, POW exchanges, refugee movements. These would be enormous tasks even if everyone were acting in good faith, but the Soviets aren't. It's become a game of wits, a vicious one that involves the future of Europe."

Terry returned to the living room with three cups of coffee. Real coffee. She could tell by the smell. "That's why you've got to stay, Alex. If we can show we have expertise right at hand, ready to deploy, so to speak, Truman won't shut us down. Maybe give us another name, but the work has got to be done under some heading or other, and by people like you."

"What sort of work are you talking about, specifically?"

"We need to find out what they're planning for Poland. Who's responsible for the massacre at Katyn. Who's winning the power struggles in the Kremlin. What kind of new weaponry they're working on. We need someone who can read the documents, talk to the people. Someone who knows Moscow."

"Terry, you forget that the NKVD threw me out of Russia. I'm useless to you."

"Not with a different passport and a new hair color. And staying, of course, at a different location."

She finished her coffee and nervously turned the cup in its saucer. "I don't know, Terry. Like I've already told you, that cloak-and-dagger stuff just doesn't sound like me."

"All right, here's my best offer. You sign up with us, and we'll put a priority on investigating Russian POWs in the Ukraine and Belorussia."

"I asked you to do that already, many months ago."

"I know, but we couldn't accomplish much then. We just didn't have anyone on site. But now we can."

"That borders on blackmail, Terry. You know how important that is to me."

Terry lit up a cigarette. "Blackmail's such an ugly word."

"Oh, sorry!" Elinor suddenly exclaimed. "I'd quite forgotten." She slid her hand into her jacket pocket. "Terry was held up talking to General Clay when I went out to the street. As I was standing there alone, one of Zhukov's guards approached me. You could have knocked me over when she asked me in Russian if I knew an Alex Preston."

"What? Zhukov's guard knew my name?" That made no sense at all.

"Apparently so. Anyhow, when I said yes, she asked me to give this to you." Stahl held out a small lump of crumpled material and dropped it onto Alex's palm.

Perplexed, Alex picked it up by one corner and let it unfold. Silk, gray polka dots against a once-blue background, stained with old blood and shredded at the corners. Her hand began to shake.

"What is it?" Terry asked.

"This guard, was she small and blond?"

Elinor shook her head. "Small, yes. Blond, no. You're acquainted with General Zhukov's guards?"

Alex stood and slid the rag into her pocket. "Where are the Soviet headquarters? Can I use the jeep? I've got to go back there."

"What are you intending to do?" Elinor blocked her way. "We've got delicate negotiations going on with Zhukov. I can't let you go crashing in there."

"Please. It's just the guard I have to see. I swear to God I won't go anywhere near Zhukov."

Elinor shook her head. "Holy oaths are useless if we can't trust you to control yourself. This impetuousness, it's not a good quality for our organization."

Stifling the urge to knock Elinor to the floor and seize the keys, Alex took a long breath. "This is not impetuousness, I can assure you," she said somberly. "If you can't trust my discretion on this little mission, then I'm useless to your organization anyhow."

Elinor dropped the key into Alex's hand, but her scowl showed she didn't like it. "The address is Pionierschule 1, in Berlin's Karlshorst district. You'll find a Berlin map in the jeep." She pointed a finger in warning. "Don't screw this up. If you get into trouble in any way, we'll disavow you and leave you hanging in the wind."

"Yes. Right. Sure. Got it. Be back in a couple of hours." Clutching the key, Alex hurried toward the garage and tried not to slam the door behind her.

❖

Even with a map, the trip to Karlshorst took agonizingly long, for the streets were alternately cratered and filled with rubble. Everywhere around her, the *Trümmerfrauen,* old women and young girls, swarmed like ants over the wreckage, collecting bricks and piling them on wagons. The dusty air was filled with the sounds of their coughing and the tapping of their tools as they knocked off loose cement.

The ruins of the inner city gave off the smell of the bodies decomposing beneath them, though Alex registered it all only faintly as she swung around shell holes, hills of brick fragments, and refuse.

It was nearly seven when she came in sight of the Soviet Headquarters and stopped. Guards were posted across its entrance, but from her distance she couldn't make out individual faces. Caution made her park the jeep some several streets away, and she began to walk, heart pounding in anticipation.

She halted suddenly, realizing that her uniform made her conspicuous, the very thing Elinor had warned against. She'd be better off in rags like the Trümmerfrauen. Uncertain of what to do, she watched from a distance, partially concealed behind a broken wall.

Four guards stood before the Soviet headquarters. The nearest one was a short robust woman with a wide Slavic face. Was she the one who'd given the mysterious scarf to Elinor? The next two were men, and the one farthest away, slight of build, was also probably a woman, though it was hard to tell.

Alex withdrew. What now? Distracted, she took a step backward and lost her footing. She stumbled to her knees, cursing. A few yards away, a woman of indeterminate age who bent over a wooden wheelbarrow saw her fall. Standing upright with obvious effort, she climbed to where Alex still knelt and offered her a hand.

"*Danke*," Alex said, getting to her feet, and at that moment she knew what to do.

She pointed to the woman's dress and shawl, then to herself, trying to convey the idea that she wanted to try on the dress. Obviously flabbergasted at the suggestion, the woman backed away.

"*Bitte, bitte*," Alex insisted urgently, and drew a full pack of Chesterfields from her pocket. She held them out tantalizingly, and the woman's tired eyes suddenly were alive with interest.

Again Alex mimed what she wanted. The woman was to hand over the dress for ten minutes. She held up ten fingers and pointed to her wristwatch. She could sit under her shawl until Alex returned and gave the dress back.

The pack of cigarettes was worth a fortune. The bricks might net the woman a ration of bread, but she could exchange twenty American cigarettes for ten times that much. The woman's expression told her the deal was done.

She started toward a depression in the ground, which Alex noted was a cellar, and once inside, the woman held out her hand. The moment she had the cigarettes in possession, she unbuttoned the dress and pulled it over her head. Standing in a soiled under-slip, she pulled her shawl around her bony shoulders.

At the same time, Alex took off her uniform jacket and slacks, and folded them carefully. She had no thought of leaving them, since they would be worth a great deal on the black market, and the woman would certainly disappear with them.

The dress stank of old sweat, but Alex buttoned it up, breathing through her mouth. As an afterthought, she signaled that she wanted the woman's headscarf, too.

Then, gathering up her own clothes, she climbed back up to the wheelbarrow and buried them under a layer of bricks. Before she lost her nerve, she started off down the street toward the Soviet building.

She kept her head down, shoving the heavy wheelbarrow ahead of her, struggling to keep it upright as it hit each brick or shard. Dust rose all around her and she coughed, watching at the edge of her vision as she passed in front of the first, then the second, then the third guard.

As she neared the last one, she slowed and raised her head, trying to focus on the guard's face while everything unfolded in slow motion. Each step she took was a struggle against some invisible force that held her back. Reality stopped flowing, so that all she looked at seemed to lose continuity and instead passed by her in discrete, ever enlarging frames.

The guard swung toward her, peered at her unemotionally, and the unfamiliarity was a blow. It was the wrong uniform, the wrong dark hair around a too-gaunt face. She wanted to sob in disappointment. But familiar blue eyes bored onto hers, and as she came up directly before the guard, she could see something of Lilya Drachenko deep inside her.

The pale-blue eyes widened, then shrank again, uncertain, then closed, and when they opened a second later, they swam in tears. "Alex," she whispered.

"Yes" was all Alex could think to say, her own mouth trembling.

Desperation tinged Lilya's voice. "Get me out. Please. I can't—" Suddenly she jerked her glance to the side and snapped to attention.

Just over her shoulder, Alex saw General Zhukov emerging from his headquarters with another Soviet officer. The two men marched toward the street and stood in animated conversation only a few yards away.

Alex forced herself to pass on, whispering, "Come to the Brandenburg Gate. Midnight," and rolled her wheelbarrow on down the street to the corner. Without glancing back, she pushed on, making a wide circle around the block to approach the cellar from the other direction. She wept now too, silently, joyously, sniffing back mucus that made her laugh at herself. It was the happiest and most confusing moment of her life.

❖

In a state of mind somewhere between serene and jubilant, Alex returned to the house on the Foehrenweg and let herself in.

"I've found her," she announced from the doorway.

"Her? Who?" Terry looked up from his bulletin.

"Lilya Drachenko. The scarf was hers. She's evidently been with the Red Army all this time." She laughed, giddy, as she drifted into the room and tossed the keys onto the side table. "Can you imagine?"

Elinor lifted her glasses off her nose and slid them onto the top of her head. "Drachenko? The pilot you asked Terry to look for through the Red Cross?"

"Your Stalingrad witch?" Terry echoed. "Are you sure it's her? Did you talk to her? What did she say?"

She blinked at the five questions in succession. "Yes, I'm sure. She recognized me and called me by name. But we couldn't talk. Zhukov came out just then, and I had to pass by to stay out of sight. She only said 'Get me out. I can't go back.'"

"She wants to desert?" Terry folded his bulletin, but his tone told her the news didn't thrill him.

Alex dropped down on the far end of the sofa. "Yes, I assumed that's what she meant. So I said I'd meet her at midnight at the Brandenburg Gate."

"Good grief," Terry exclaimed. "That's all you could think of? The Gate's surrounded by ruins and is hardly accessible. It's probably patrolled, too."

"I…I didn't have time to plan anything. The words just came out of my mouth. I passed it coming into Berlin, so I knew it's still standing. Anyhow, it's done and I'm going to meet her, assuming she can get away tonight. If I can, I'll bring her here."

"Here? We're not really equipped to handle Red Army deserters," Terry said, obviously caught off guard.

"Why not? Isn't that what you're always going on about? How the organization specializes in getting people in and out of places? Secretly? Those are almost your exact words."

"She's got you there, Terry." Elinor snickered. "But, Alex, we usually operate with a little more information than you've given us. You don't know her circumstances. Who she reports to. Who's watching her. Where she wants to go. As much as we'd like to help you, we can't rescue someone at the snap of a finger. It's not like in an adventure novel."

Alex stood up and paced, too excited to remain seated. "We'll find out more after I bring her here tonight." She took a few steps in the other direction. "Anyhow, we *have* to help her. That's the condition of my staying on with you."

"Ah, now who's blackmailing whom?" Terry said.

Alex halted and turned toward him. "Blackmail is such an ugly word."

❖

"Jesus! Alex, what were you thinking?" Terry blustered as he halted their jeep before the mound of twisted steel, masonry, and wrecked vehicles. "Unter den Linden ends here. We can't get anywhere near the Brandenburg Gate, not on wheels anyhow."

She climbed from the jeep and eyed the blockage nervously. "You're right. It was a mistake to choose this place. But she took me by surprise. I had only a split second to think of a place we both could find at midnight. Can we climb over that stuff?"

"I suppose you'll have to."

She glanced back at him. "Oh, so you're going to make me go alone?"

"Of course I am. Do you think I'm going to leave a US jeep unattended? All kinds of desperate riffraff are wandering around Berlin. Someone would be here in two minutes to siphon out the petrol and strip off the wheels, if they didn't haul the whole thing away."

"All right, I'll go. Give me the flashlight." She shone the beam onto her watch. "Almost twelve. I've got to start climbing."

"Watch out for rats, though. They're all over the place," Terry said, and she thought she heard a note of sarcasm in his voice.

She struggled on hands and knees over the loose masonry and miscellaneous steel, taking care to shine the flashlight low to the ground to minimize visibility from a distance. Dislodged gravel fell away beneath her, and the squeaks and scurrying away of black spots told her Terry had been serious about the rats. She wondered for a moment what they ate, and then she remembered. That also accounted for the noxious odor.

The mound she climbed revealed itself as part of a ring of rubble, as if it had been deliberately cleared outward from the monument.

At the center, the great columns of the Brandenburg Gate towered overhead, an eerie spectacle. In peacetime they'd probably been illuminated, but now they were black against the night sky. Alex shook her head at the excruciating irony of a triumphal arch in the midst of a gargantuan defeat.

She shone her light on one of the columns, noting that the fluting was chipped and broken by small-arms fire all the way to the top. Every surface that could be inscribed, on wall, column, and base, held slogans and names, incised with a bayonet or knife blade, or scribbled with chalk.

Victory to the Russian people!
Down with Fascism!
Hitler kaputt!
Ivan and Sasha from the 46th Guards stood here.

The foot soldier's share in glorious victory.

"Alex."

She spun around, and her flashlight beam swung with her, lighting a small figure some ten feet away. The raised hand that blocked the light beam obscured her face, but it was Lilya, who ran into her embrace.

Alex held her for a long moment, holding back tears. "I knew you were alive. I just *knew* it," she choked out.

Lilya ran fingers over Alex's face, as if to ensure she was real. "I was so afraid you'd gone, that I'd never find you. It's been so hard."

Alex kissed her breathlessly, clutching at her, gripping her so that she could never be lost again. "I have so much to tell you, to ask you."

"Aleksandra! What are you doing?" A woman's voice, outraged, broke the tender moment. They jerked apart and Alex swept her flashlight toward the speaker. Zhukov's other female guard.

"Olga. Why did you follow me? You shouldn't have," Lilya said.

"So this is your mysterious friend. A woman. I never would have thought." The stranger eyed Alex, though in the dim glow of the flashlight it was impossible to see her expression.

"You shouldn't stay here, Olga. It's dangerous for you. They'll charge you with desertion, too."

"Desertion? Is that what this is? You don't have to do that, you know. We can go back to Moscow together and they won't call us cowards. We'll vouch for each other, tell the truth about what it was like as POWs, how we fought in the Ukraine and at Kursk and Berlin. We were so brave, they'll give us medals. "

Lilya shook her head. "I'm sorry, I can't go back. There's nothing for me now in Moscow. They'll arrest me as a collaborator."

Olga's shoulders dropped. "Please, Aleksandra. Don't leave me. I don't want to go back without you."

Alex flinched, hearing her name spoken by the stranger, but said nothing.

Holding out her hands, Lilya stepped toward her comrade and spoke something into her ear. Whatever it was, Olga took a step back and appeared disconsolate.

"Go back, before they discover you're gone." Lilya urged gently. "Please, I couldn't bear it if you were arrested because of me."

"Aleksandra, please." When Lilya didn't respond, Olga covered her face, then spoke with a voice broken by weeping. "Don't forget me."

"No, my dear. I never will."

Dumbfounded, Alex simply waited until Olga clambered over the mound of rubble and disappeared in the dark. Lilya stepped into her arms again, and this time she also cried, confused tears of both reunion and loss.

Alex held her for only a moment. "Come on," she said, tugging on Lilya's arm. "A jeep's waiting for us."

The jeep bumped over the thousands of ruts and obstacles as Terry rushed them back to the house in Dahlem. In the front next to him, Alex sat sideways, unwilling to tear her eyes from the strange creature in the rear, who was still Lilya. In the dark her face was nearly invisible, but Alex held its outline fixed in her sight, as if to ensure she wouldn't disappear again.

They were silent, for it wasn't the time to talk. Yet the moment itself was precious, when she floated in a sphere of hope and renewal with the person she loved most in the world. They weren't safe yet, but it was as if they'd been held deep underwater and now were swimming toward air.

In an hour, they were back at OSS headquarters. Elinor held the door open, her spectacles on her head. With her commando team safely inside, she set them back on her nose and studied Lilya for a long moment. Lilya herself stood awkwardly in front of her in her infantry uniform and with a sidearm, obviously not knowing what to do with her hands.

"So you're what the fuss has been about," Elinor said in remarkably good Russian.

Lilya glanced at Alex for reassurance, then answered. "I'm sorry about the fuss."

"Are you? In any case, I'm Elinor Stahl. I'm in charge here, and I understand you've asked Aleksandra Preston to help you desert."

"Um, yes. I didn't know that…" she glanced around the room, "that others would be involved."

"Really? You assumed you could just join hands and run away to the West?"

"No, I'm sorry. I just thought—"

"Why are you grilling her like that?" Alex snapped. "You know nothing about her or what she's been through, and already you're insulting her."

Elinor remained aloof. "Insulting? Not at all. But desertion is no small thing, and we're not in that business. We'll need a lot more information before we decide how to proceed."

"Please, everyone, sit down." Terry broke the tension, herding them toward the sofa and chairs. "I'll make us some…I don't know. What do people drink at…" He looked at his watch. "At two in the morning?"

"Anything at all." Lilya looked up at him weakly. "I'm very thirsty."

"How about beer? It's cleaner than the water and won't keep everyone awake." Everyone nodded, and he disappeared into the kitchen while they sat down.

Lilya surveyed the room timidly. "May I ask where I am?"

Elinor leaned back, the monarch of her domain. "You're with us now, and for the moment, the less you know about us the better. Alex tells us that the Russian press reports you as dead. Why do you suppose that is?"

"Well, I crash-landed during an air fight in September 1943. I think it was September, though I'm not sure any more. I suppose the air force found my plane, or at least the wreck of it after the fire. They didn't find *me*, though, and I don't know why they declared me dead. Maybe it makes better propaganda. In fact, I was captured and held in camps in the Ukraine. I didn't want the Germans to make their own propaganda about capturing a famous pilot, so I gave a false name."

"When was the camp liberated?" Elinor's eyes narrowed.

"I was there only for about four months, when partisans attacked. A few of us managed to escape with them. The camp was liberated much later."

Elinor persisted. "But you ended up with the Red Army. How did that happen?"

Terry was back with a tray and four glasses of beer, which he handed around. Lilya downed hers in a single long drink, then wiped her mouth with the back of her hand.

"The partisans often work with the army, even wear their uniforms. Later they handed us over to an official military unit."

"I thought the official line was that there are no POWs, only deserters."

"It was…is. But they needed fighters, so they took me on under the name I gave them."

"And that was Aleksandra Vasil'evna Petrovna," Alex said. "Which explains why that soldier kept using my name." She snorted. "And now I'm listed as a deserter in the Red Army."

Terry set his glass down and crossed his arms, taking his turn at interrogation. "How could you conceal your identity? You were famous. I saw your picture in *Pravda* several times."

"The Germans didn't know me, and when they captured me, I was covered with blood and dirt and isolated with prisoners they expected to die. The Russian doctor who saved me *did* recognize me, but he was shot. And then, when we arrived in Vinnytsia, I'd gotten very thin and my dark hair had grown in." She fingered the hair over her ear. "I guess I still don't look like myself."

Elinor tilted her head, studying her, a hint of sympathy in her expression. "I can imagine that life in a POW camp would undermine the appearance of any attractive woman." She toyed with a strand of her own gray hair. "How did you end up in Berlin?"

"The troops that got us out of the camp were with the First Ukrainian Front, but they moved us around wherever we were needed. At some point they transferred us to the Belorussian front, and we advanced with them. That was first to the Elbe and then to Berlin."

"We? Who were the others?"

"Four of us escaped alive from Vinnytsia, including my friend Olga. Two of the women fell in battle, but Olga helped me stay alive, both in the camp and in the months of fighting."

"The woman who followed you to the Gate, that was Olga?" Alex asked.

Lilya nodded.

Elinor's face darkened. "You mean someone witnessed your being picked up?"

"Yes, but she won't tell, and even if she did, she only knows I deserted to go with a woman who spoke Russian. She didn't even see the jeep."

"I don't think anything will come of it, Elinor," Terry added, suddenly supportive. "Dozens desert every day. It's complete disorder out there."

Lilya shifted her attention back to Alex. "We almost met at Torgau. I chased you, but you drove away too fast. They told me you were a photographer with the Third Army, and I guessed that you'd want to get to Berlin. But even then, I didn't know how to locate you."

"Berlin is a big, chaotic place. How did you manage to track her down?" Elinor's suspicions surfaced again.

"I knew I couldn't. I just tried to be where I thought she might want to be. You know, as a photographer." She glanced again at Alex. "I alternated waiting at the Reichstag building and at the Brandenburg Gate. A lot of photographers came, but none of them was you. I even volunteered for guard duty with Zhukov because he seemed to have journalists around him all the time. I never did see you, but at Zhukov's last meeting, I recognized him." She pointed at Terry.

"But you never spoke to me," he said, clearly puzzled.

"No, I couldn't get close to you. I could only steal a moment to talk to the woman who was with you."

"And lucky for you, I recognized the name," Elinor said. "So, tell me why you refuse to go back home with the Red Army. You were a star aviator and your government will be happy to have you back, even if you were a despised POW."

"Not at all. I gave false information about my identity, but worse than that, I worked as a servant in the house of the commandant at Vinnytsia."

"Plus, she was already a suspicious person," Alex added. "Her father was executed as an enemy of the people."

"I see." Elinor rested her chin in the curve of her thumb. "Well, you've put us in a very delicate situation. The four powers have a major conference soon at Potsdam, and if it were to come out that we'd aided in a desertion, it would damage our negotiations with the Kremlin."

Alex reacted instantly. "Of course the Kremlin won't know. Secrecy is what you do, isn't it?" She softened her tone. "Besides, Elinor, think about what you're getting. You place so much weight on having Soviet specialists and native speakers in the organization. I should think Lilya could be quite useful to you."

Elinor leaned toward Lilya, getting to the heart of the matter. "You're willing to give us information about the Soviet Air Force?"

Lilya hesitated for only a moment. "Why shouldn't I? We're allies, aren't we? We flew your planes, drove your trucks, ate your food. The things I know aren't secret anyhow. Everyone knows how to fly a U-2 or a Yak."

"It *would* be a coup, wouldn't it?" Terry said. "I mean, getting one of their aces. Though we couldn't reveal it while the negotiations are going on, of course."

"You can't reveal it *ever*," Alex said. "If they can't punish her, they'll punish her mother. She told you what happened to her father."

Elinor crossed her arms and leaned back, suggesting she'd made a decision. "Much as we'd like to, we can't get you out of Europe on such short notice."

"But can't you at least hide her?"

"Yes, that we can do, though not in Berlin. The Soviets have too much control here. It would have to be in American-held territory. Wiesbaden, perhaps."

"Good idea." Terry nodded. "Allied headquarters. Traffic going in and out of there all the time. We just have to fly her there."

Elinor shook her head. "Only with permission. The brass might not like getting involved with a runaway pilot, even if she's of high value to us."

"Brass? You mean General Eisenhower?" Alex brightened. "That shouldn't be a problem. We met at a party. I bet he'd approve. Wait. I have an even better idea. If you call Allied Headquarters, you'll probably get Jo Knightly, his secretary. Tell her Alex Preston needs a favor. She offered once, and this is the sort of thing she might be able to pull off."

Elinor chuckled. "That has possibilities. Why bother with a general when you have a general's secretary? I'll contact her and all the other relevant people in the morning." She glanced down at her watch. "That will be in just a few hours." She took a deep breath, signaling the end of the discussion. "So now, I think we've done just about enough for one day and should all get a bit of sleep."

Terry gathered up the beer glasses. "The bathroom's over there, Lilya, if you'd like to wash before going to bed. In the meantime, Alex and I will make up the sofa for you."

At the word sofa Lilya shot a quick glance at Alex, and the question was obvious. Alex shrugged weakly. Against all odds, they'd found each other again, but propriety still kept them apart. Even if Terry knew their relationship, they couldn't flaunt it. It was probably just as well. She needed time to get to know this stranger.

❖

Alex lay on her little bed unable to sleep, every nerve taut. So much had changed so quickly. The war was over. She was safe and Lilya was safe, and they were together. She should have been delirious.

But the ongoing war had normalized her fear and yearning, and when peace and the longed-for reunion came, she'd forgotten how to be happy. In two years, she had idealized the image of the beloved, and the woman lying in the next room no longer matched it. Two years of malnutrition and countless battles seemed to have both hardened her and broken her spirit. The audacious and slightly glamorous pilot now was taciturn and passive.

She recalled their afternoon of brief and explosive passion in the Metropole, which had left her panting. Now, the strongest feeling she had for Lilya was the urge to protect and nurture her. Was the original Lilya still inside this subdued stranger, and could she coax her out again?

She sat upright. They needed to talk.

Drawing on her shirt, she crept past the bedrooms of Terry and Elinor to the living room. She knocked softly on the doorframe, and even in the dark, she could see the shape on the sofa suddenly sit up. "Alex?" it whispered.

"Yes, it's me." Alex hurried to her side and embraced her tightly. "It's all so strange, isn't it? After so much time? For so long, I thought you were dead. The newspapers were full of reports of the crash. For weeks I walked around numb with grief."

Lilya caressed her face and lips with her fingertips. "How did you find out I wasn't dead?"

When the NKVD picked me up and threw me into Lubyanka prison. Believe it or not, it was Major Kazar who told me the body they found at the crash site wasn't you."

Lilya drew back. "Wait. The NKVD arrested you? For what?"

Alex drew her feet up and pulled Lilya's blanket over her legs. "Because they rummaged through your things and found the letter you were writing to me."

"Oh, God. The letter. How stupid of me! And they arrested you for that. Oh, I'm so sorry! Did they hurt you terribly?"

"No, they just slapped me around a little. But then I knew for sure you were alive, though the thought of you being in German hands was just as terrifying."

"Oh, my darling. What a horrible thing to go through, and because of me. How did you finally get out of there?"

"Terry had some influence with people in charge of the Lend-Lease shipments. They threatened to stop them if a prominent American journalist was arrested. It was sheer bluff, of course, but it worked. The NKVD let me go on the condition that I leave Russia immediately. Which I did."

"Back to the US? Every day I wondered where you were. When I thought I could go home, I imagined you waiting for me in Moscow, but after the camp, I didn't know what to hope."

"First I flew to Britain, and then, after the landing at Normandy, I came back with the Third Army. All that time, I assumed you were in a POW camp in the Ukraine. I tried to get a list of names from the Red Cross. Nothing came of it, of course, and nothing could have, with your name change. Why *ever* did you choose Aleksandra?"

She stroked Alex's cheek. "To keep you with me, my darling. Inside of me. Every time someone called to me, I heard your name."

"Hmm. Romantic, in a morbid kind of way." Alex chuckled softly.

Lilya took hold of Alex's hand and pressed it to her cheek. "Now that I've found you, I'm afraid of losing you again. Do you still want to take me to New York?"

"Is that where you want to go? What happened to 'this is my land, my language, my people'?"

"I still feel that way, but Russia has rejected *me*. I managed to close my eyes to the truth for so many years, but now I understand. It wasn't my father who was an enemy of the people. It's Stalin, and the Allied victory is also a victory for him and his secret police. I helped give him that, but I don't want to go back to him. I want to go where you are, and where I don't have to worry about arrest. Or that my mother will be arrested. There's so much I want to tell her."

"Your mother. Yes, you could endanger her."

"Only if I went back. But from what I read in *Red Star*, the Kremlin is carrying on the myth of Lilya Drachenko's heroic death. I guess they've decided to ignore the letter, at least publicly. As the mother of a hero, she's safe. It just breaks my heart that she's alone and thinks she's lost me."

Alex stroked the unfamiliar dark hair, remembering it blond. Well, it would be easy enough to have it blond again. "Only for a while. Once you're safe, I'll contact a journalist friend of mine, Henry Shapiro, who's still there. His wife is Russian, and through her, he can get word to your mother that you're alive. I even know the message we can send that only she will understand. Remember the Pushkin quote? 'Dearer to me than a host of base truths is the illusion that exalts.' She'll know that's from you."

"Yes, she'll know, and it'll make her so happy." She took Alex's face in her hands and kissed her softly, their first tender kiss in two years. Alex felt a wave of excitement and had let her own hand stray to Lilya's breast, when the sound of a door opening jerked them apart.

A light went on in the bathroom. "Night pee," Alex said, resigned. "Whoever it is, it's a warning for me to leave you."

Lilya let her arms slide away from her and sighed. "Peeing in your own private toilet. What a luxury."

"I promise you'll have that in New York. You'll never have to pee on the ground again."

"Oh, I love it when you talk romantic like that."

CHAPTER THIRTY-FIVE

"All right," Elinor announced as Terry poured their coffee. "While you were sleeping, I made some calls."

"Good news, I hope." Alex glanced back and forth between Elinor and Lilya, who crept in from the living room, looking lost. She took a seat at the table and, discovering the sugar, spooned an alarming amount into her coffee.

"First of all, the good news," Elinor said. "I contacted your friend Jo Knightly, who was very helpful. She said she was already drafting a non-specific order calling for 'transport of all nonessential US personnel and property from Soviet-occupied Berlin in preparation for the anticipated sectorization.' She simply brought the date forward to begin today. An hour later she called back to say Eisenhower had signed the order and it would go out this afternoon. She must have hinted to him that we were trying to smuggle someone out, because he remarked, 'Just don't get me in trouble with the Russians.'"

Alex suppressed a smile. Good old Jo. This was even better than being "pals" with her. "So, now we just have to find transportation."

"Way ahead of you," Terry said, joining them with a plate of toast. "Knightly put us on to Lucius Clay, Eisenhower's deputy who handles Berlin affairs, and of course we knew him already. Clay said that Montgomery was about to land this morning for a day of meetings with him and Zhukov."

"How does that affect us?" Alex asked.

"Eat your toast and listen." Elinor covered her own with butter. "He'll be arriving at Tempelhof in a British Mosquito. The pilot's supposed to wait and then ferry him back to Wiesbaden tomorrow morning."

"Yes? Go on."

"The British pilot is a friend of Clay, and while the plane's standing idle, he's willing to fly Lilya to Wiesbaden and then return to Berlin. In Wiesbaden, they can put her up at the base until we work out what to do with her next."

"Is there any *bad* news?" Alex bit into her toast and noticed that the butter was real. Not the margarine she'd gotten used to.

"Only that we have to move quickly. Montgomery shouldn't know about it since it would compromise our negotiations with the Soviets, and he's not happy about sharing his toys anyhow. Of course we also have to get her to Tempelhof and onto the plane. The airport is Soviet territory, at least until the negotiations next month, and in the Soviet view, we're all here at their largesse. Alex got across the city two days ago without being stopped, so they seem to be very lax at night. But they might not be so casual in midday."

"Can we come up with forged papers on such short notice?" Alex asked.

"If we have to," Terry answered. "But they won't be the best."

Elinor watched as Lilya heaped marmalade onto her toast and seemed faintly amused.

"On the good-news side is the fact that it's generally understood that the Soviets will hand over the airport to the Western allies in the coming weeks, so they probably won't be so rigid about keeping us out. They primarily guard the main hall, where the flight traffic passes through."

"Can we get onto the tarmac without using the main hall?" Alex asked.

"We think so. Templehof is built on an ellipse, and one of its wings was a factory where Germans built and serviced Stuka dive-bombers. I'm sure the Soviets are already cannibalizing what's left of the aircraft. If you look like workers, you can probably reach the Tempelhof runway through the factory wing."

"Do you have the materials we'll need to look like workers? Tools, truck, that sort of thing?"

"Yes, we do. Or can adapt them."

"So, assuming we can smuggle her out onto the field, will the plane be waiting for us?"

"That's the plan." Terry spoke up again. "We drive up with our hammers and wrenches, and while we're banging around on the old assembly lines, Lilya will march out to Montgomery's plane, which will be ready for flight at eight thirty. The pilot will have shown his orders to the Tempelhof authorities, the ground crew will have fueled the plane, and everything will look normal. All she has to do is get in and they'll take off."

"Sounds almost too good to be true. But what about me? Can't I fly with her?"

"Sorry, Alex, the Mosquito is a two-seater. Pilot and navigator. We'll arrange for you to join her in a few days."

Alex grumbled assent. It did make sense. She glanced at Lilya, who'd been chewing toast throughout, though they were speaking Russian in order to include her. But she merely glanced back and forth as each person spoke, as if she were a package that had to be smuggled out. Of course she was, but her passivity was troubling.

Elinor took charge again. "Both of you finish your coffee and go down to the basement with Terry. He'll put together what you need for work clothes, tools, and so forth. It goes without saying that if either of you is arrested, the organization will disavow you."

"Yes, ma'am," Alex said, "I'm familiar with that policy." She thought, but didn't say, that it bore significant resemblance to Josef Stalin's policy of "We recognize no POWs."

At eight in the evening they were on the road to Tempelhof Airport. The worst of the shell holes had been filled with broken brick so the road was rocky but serviceable. Terry took the wheel of the truck he'd miraculously procured. That it was an American Lend-Lease Studebaker might explain how he could acquire it, but the Soviet plates and identification stencils were a real coup. She'd have to ask him some day how he managed that.

In the truck rear, Alex perched alongside Lilya on a box of tools. Hunched over in overalls and caps, they might pass for men, but only from a distance. Neither could their travel permit, a quickly executed counterfeit order signed with a scribble, stand up to scrutiny. They bore the stamp of Zhukov's office, but that would only be convincing as long as neither she nor Terry spoke.

Their luck held and they were stopped only once, as they reached the periphery of the airport. Once again, the fluidity and vagueness of the occupation rules allowed cigarettes to work their magic. Without a word, Terry handed over the slightly greasy travel pass to the sentry along with a full pack of American cigarettes. They were so valuable, the sentry was prepared to overlook the anomaly of them being in Russian hands.

A second sentry peered into the back of the truck. But Alex, her face sooty, was enveloped in a cloud of cigarette smoke, and Lilya had an apparent need to blow her nose in a large handkerchief just then. Their identifications, with cloudy photos, could have belonged to anyone, but the pack of Chesterfields that lay on the truck bed within reach was more interesting anyhow.

Without commentary, the guards waved them through and they continued around the curve. At terminal A the three of them leapt out with their toolboxes and tried the first door they reached. It opened to a vast hall that still housed a dozen aircraft frames in various stages of dismantling. The few men who worked at the far end of the hall paid no attention to them as they crossed the manufacturing floor to the side that looked out on the airfield.

Terry took binoculars from the toolbox and surveyed the field. "Ah, I see it. The Mosquito's over there toward the right, and the pilot's just coming from the terminal. He's climbing in now. So far so good. In a few minutes, he'll taxi in this direction, so get ready to make a run for it at my signal."

Even without binoculars, Alex could see the Mosquito and watched as one propeller, then the other, began to whirl. Someone ran out to knock away the chocks from under the wheels, and slowly the plane taxied toward them, skirting the ellipse of terminals. She glanced toward Lilya, dreading to say good-bye, even for a few days. Too many things could still go wrong.

But Alex detected something in Lilya's demeanor she hadn't seen earlier. Her face, which had been pale and impassive at breakfast, seemed to take on color at the sight of the plane. The docility was gone, and a steely intensity, or was it a hunger, was etched on her features. What was she thinking?

"What the hell!"

Terry's outburst yanked her attention back to the field, where two security men had run out onto the tarmac and were signaling the pilot to halt the plane. After a few tense moments, he stopped the propellers and obeyed the order to climb out. He argued with the security men for several minutes, then followed them back to the terminal. Fueled but empty, the plane stood on the tarmac, tantalizing them.

"Goddamn," Terry snarled. "They've pulled the pilot off the plane. The guards didn't draw their guns, so maybe Monty just found out about the plan and nixed it. I wouldn't put it past him." He grimaced. "It looks like a no-go."

"Terry, she *has* to go." Alex said. "We may not get another chance like this."

He lowered his binoculars and dropped them into the toolbox. "Well, she can't go without a pilot."

"I *am* a pilot," Lilya said quietly.

Terry stared at the ceiling, exasperated. "You *were* a pilot. Of a Russian plane. You can't fly a Mosquito."

"I think I can." She was staring out onto the field like a predator at its prey.

"Jesus, Lilya. 'Think so' isn't enough. Besides, you'll still need a navigator to get to Wiesbaden."

"I can navigate," Alex said matter-of-factly. "We both can read an aerial map and a compass, and we know how to use a radio."

Terry rubbed his forehead. "Christ, I'm going to catch hell for this."

"Come on, Terry. You've spent your whole career in high risk. Assuming we don't crash the plane, I think this'll work. And when it's done, you'll have carried off a major coup against the Soviets."

She turned to Lilya. "You're sure you can fly one of those things, right?"

Lilya didn't reply and simply seized her by her upper arm and shoved her out of the terminal onto the field. Once on the tarmac, they began to run for the Mosquito. As they reached the fuselage they heard shouts, in Russian and English. Encouragingly, there were no gunshots.

Ignoring the shouting, Lilya yanked open the hatch on the right side of the fuselage and climbed into the cockpit. Without looking back, Alex scrambled in after her.

Inside, Alex recalled the two-man cockpit of the Grumman, though the dashboard was more complicated, with levers and switches that presumably controlled weaponry. She was frankly at a loss and fervently hoped Lilya wasn't. Their pursuers had reached them now, both the Russian airport security and British soldiers. She snorted at the irony. It was probably the last time the two allies would work together. All five of the men were shouting.

After a moment of groping around the control panel, Lilya found the switch that started the propellers, first one and then the other. The men stood in front of them now, waving their arms, but moved aside when the plane began to roll.

No gunfire yet, Alex thought. So far so—

"Bang! She flinched as a hole appeared in the windshield and a slug lodged in the metal panel over her head. "Crap, now they're shooting at us."

"I know. Don't you hate it when they do that?"

The earphones that hung below the control panel crackled, and Alex slipped them over her head. The voice spoke Russian. "Abort takeoff and exit the plane. This is an order. We will shoot."

"The flight is authorized." Alex spoke into the mouthpiece while Lilya accelerated down the runway. "Repeat, we are *authorized*."

It was both true and not true. Who was to say? Authorized by the OSS and in a general sort of way by the Allied High Command. But not by the Soviets, who occupied the airport. And the whole question of who had authority over what was being hashed out that very day at the highest levels.

She only hoped the confusion would buy them enough time to get off the ground.

Another voice came on, speaking English. "This is Major John Henderson, General Montgomery's aide-de-camp. What the hell are you doing in our airplane? Halt at once or we'll shoot."

"Copy that, Major Henderson. No need to get upset. We repeat, this flight is approved by Allied Headquarters. You may contact General Eisenhower's office for verification. General Montgomery will have his plane back tomorrow, fully fueled and unharmed, except for the hole in the windshield your goons just put there."

The propellers were now a blur and pulling them down the runway at high speed. Then with a sort of chortle, Lilya lifted them off the ground.

The threats continued coming through the radio,

"Who am I speaking to? Who is at the controls? You will be court-martialed."

"My name is Leica," she said, smiling at her inventiveness. "Lieutenant Leica. The pilot is Captain Vedma."

Lilya giggled, certainly recognizing nothing in the English conversation but the Russian word for witch.

Alex continued. "Go ahead and court-martial us, but stop shooting, for God's sake. Your boss is about to start negotiations. Shooting down his plane at this sensitive time would expose him to ridicule and would certainly end your career. Over and out." She broke radio contact and hung the headset back on its hook, where it continued to crackle. "Now let's see if he calls our bluff."

She turned toward Lilya, expecting concern, but the expression she held was nothing less than glee, demonic glee.

"We have the maps?" Lilya asked, without taking her eyes from the control dials.

"Yes, they're right here." Alex pulled a map book from a side panel and found a bookmark already at the aerial map of middle Germany. She studied it for a moment.

"Wiesbaden is southwest at 229 degrees. When we get closer, we can contact them by radio. Terry said they were expecting the plane, so we're fine."

"All *right*, then." Suddenly they shot upward and the map book slid off her lap.

"What are you doing?"

"I'm flying again. Finally!" Lilya sang as they climbed sharply. At some point that suited her whim, the wicked glee returned and she dove, spiraling in the descent.

Alex braced herself on the side of the cockpit "Lilya, please! This is crazy."

"I'm free, Alex. *We're* free. The Luftwaffe couldn't kill us up here, and now nobody can." She nudged the control column, throwing them sideways again, and Alex gripped her seat as they executed another barrel roll.

"All right. I get it. You love to fly. But please, calm down and get us on the right heading. We're trying to escape, remember?"

"I know, Alex. But please give me this. Down there on the ground, with those people, that's your world. But the sky is mine, and being here again after almost two years just makes me want to dance. Let me do one more loop. For Katia."

"It's dancing, huh? Yes, all right. A tribute to Katia." Alex grasped her safety strap. Her brief dizziness as they spun reminded her of what vodka did to her, and she mentally toasted their old comrade, "*Za Katyu.*" Then, as they came out of the loop, she glanced over at Lilya's face, ruddy with excitement. This was the woman she'd fallen in love with, the one who knew friendship and loyalty, but no fear. Lilya was back.

"So, do you have that out of your system now?"

"For the moment. But Alex, darling, please promise me I can fly when we're in America. I want to spend the rest of my life with you, but I also have to fly."

"Why shouldn't you? You don't need a war to fly. I'll introduce you to my pilot friends and help you get a US license. Maybe Terry and Elinor can find a way to use your flying skills, too. Though I think they'll make you promise to not shoot anyone down."

"Uff, you Americans. Always with your stipulations."

Alex snorted and raised a reproachful finger. *"Bad* Lilya! No more killing!"

Lilya snickered and glanced down at the aerial maps on the cockpit floor. "Fair enough, but now you need to go to work. We don't have much daylight left."

"Righto. Navigator checking in." Alex reached between her knees for the aerial map and checked the compass on the instrument panel. "Set a heading, south by southwest at 229 degrees."

Lilya brought them around to the right course and they began to cruise. "Do you remember the first time we flew together?"

"Of course I do. We were chased by a Messerschmitt, and you had to practically drive along the ground to ditch him."

"And the first time we made love in that glider?"

"Never forget it. Deflowering you in a winter flight suit at 25 degrees below zero. When we were almost caught and I left my glove behind, so Major Kazar threw me out of the regiment. All those good times in planes."

"Aleksandra Vasil'evna Petrovna. Are you *always* going to be such a sourpuss?"

Alex laughed. "No, I won't. "And I promise we're going to do a lot of wonderful things outside of planes. But if you want to fly, you have to work hard to learn English so you can get your license. And to cook. Someone has to do the cooking."

"I thought we were both going to be spies. Spies don't cook. They go to elegant restaurants while they're spying."

"Oh, right. I forgot about that. Yes, we'll eat in restaurants." Alex gazed through the canopy at the orange and pink sky of early evening. Off to her right, the blazing sun had just touched the horizon, and the sudden gaudy display of colors above it seemed to celebrate their escape.

She thought, strangely, of Sparks Murdaugh and wondered if he'd survived the arctic convoys. She wished she could send him a message. *Cheers, my friend. The war's over, I'm with my beloved, and against all odds, we're flying into the sunset.*

POSTSCRIPT

The image of the "Night Witches," of young women fighting the German invaders in antiquated open-cockpit biplanes, so dazzled me that I had to tell their story and, wherever possible, use their real names. I have reshaped the facts as little as possible, but, as contrition for the authorial sins I *have* committed, I offer here the historical facts that formed the story's basis.

The Night Witches—(Nachthexen) was a name given by Germans, not Russians, to the women of the 588th Night Bomber Aviation Regiment (later the 46th Guards) who bombed German forward positions on the Eastern Front. I could not determine when or how the Russians became aware of this name, but it has now become part of the regiment's history. While the bombardments probably did not inflict serious damage on the German war machine, they did succeed in harassing the troops nightly and kept them from sleeping, and occasionally, they also managed to blow up an ammunition depot. Of the three female regiments, the 588th was the only one to remain all female and to keep their original commander, Evdokiya Bershanskaya, throughout the war. They were beyond heroic, many of them burning to death in their highly flammable biplanes, which had no parachute or radio. The other female units were the 587th Bomber Aviation Regiment and the 586th Fighter Aviation Regiment, which provided some of the most outstanding female pilots of the war.

Lilya Litviak, the model for Lilya Drachenko, was the most glamorous of the "witches," although, in fact, she spent little time with them before being assigned to the fighter pilots and then to an independent detachment of "free hunters." She had the highest score of shooting down enemy planes of any woman, closely matched by the other ace pilot,

Ekaterina (Katia) Budanova, and both of them were killed in 1943. Her feats described in the novel as well as the shampoo episode are historical. Photos show her as small and blond (apparently chemically assisted), and the general consensus was that she was beautiful. Several accounts state that her father was executed as an enemy of the people, though Wikipedia makes no mention of it. If he was, her admission to flight school was unusual and could only have occurred after her political purification through membership in the Komsomol (Young Communist League.) Accounts of her death vary widely. What is certain is that in August 1943 she was in an aerial battle in the Ukraine when she disappeared over enemy territory. Neither her plane nor her body was found. Her mechanic and friend, Inna Pasportnikova, who survived the war, led a thirty-six-year search for any trace of her. In 1979, they learned of an unidentified woman pilot who had been buried in the village of Dmitrievka. Since no other female pilots had been reported missing in that location, the body (which may or may not have been exhumed) was deemed to be Litviak. In 1990, Soviet President Gorbachev awarded her the highest national honor, Hero of the Soviet Union. Given the flimsy evidence, and even reports of her being seen in captivity, there was room for a novel.

Marina Raskova—The Russian Amelia Earhart, she began flying when commercial air travel was in its infancy in the Soviet Union, and a flight across the entire Soviet Union with two other women made her a folk hero. It was she who had the political clout to convince Stalin to order the formation of the female regiments in 1941. She was adored by her aviators and commanded the 587th dive-bombers until she died unheroically in 1943 by crashing in bad weather.

Tamara Kazarinova (model for Tamara Kazar) was the controversial commander of the 586th Fighter regiment. Some who knew her insisted that she was diligent, dedicated, and merely handicapped by a war wound, while her critics considered her incompetent and claimed her appointment was a reward for denouncing others. Photos of her in uniform show a small woman with a near crew cut, and accounts by those who served under her suggest she was demanding of her pilots and not particularly liked. For reasons unknown, General Osipenko appointed her to the command without the knowledge of Marina Raskova. Her most controversial act was to send her best pilots to fight as free hunters in the Stalingrad campaign in a way that appeared punitive, since most of them were subsequently killed.

Inna Pasportnikova, model for Inna Portnikova, was Lilya Litviak's mechanic, who survived the war and is the source of much of the information available on Litviak.

Regimental Aircraft—Each regiment had its own craft, with the most primitive and vulnerable U-2 wood-and-canvas biplanes assigned to the night bombers. The U-2s had no parachutes or radios and carried lightweight bombs under their wings. The day (dive) bombers flew the three-seater Pe-2, and the fighter planes flew the sturdy Yak 1 and its later variations.

Hotel Metropole. Although foreign correspondents were evacuated from Moscow to Kuibyshev during the German advance, they returned in May 1942, and most resided in the stately old Metropole for the rest of the war. The United Press, Associated Press, Time, CBS, and *The New York Times*, among others, kept permanent offices there and enjoyed a quality of life considerably higher than that of the average Muscovite. Although the nearby Bolshoi sustained damage from German bombardment, the Metropole was spared. Greatly refurbished, the Metropole is still a prestigious hotel in Moscow.

Margaret Bourke-White, the model for Alex Preston, was a photojournalist working for *Life Magazine* in Moscow in 1941. While other correspondents had little access to the Kremlin, she succeeded in getting Stalin himself to pose for a portrait. She was in Moscow when the Germans violated the Non-Aggression Pact and invaded Russia. Like Alex, she wore a military uniform and enjoyed honorary officer's status, though she never met any of the female Soviet pilots.

Henry Shapiro was head of the United Press and a career Moscow journalist. While other correspondents came and went, Shapiro was rooted in Moscow, married to a Russian, and was the first foreign correspondent allowed to visit Stalingrad. Battlefield access was very limited, censorship was strict, and the journalists had to submit all reports to the Russian Press office for approval before telegraphing them, often severely cut, from a single office in another part of Moscow.

Robert Capa (real name André Friedman)—Photojournalist who covered five wars, though WWII only on the Western Front. He landed at Normandy with the second wave of American troops and photographed the men taking fire from the German hillside bunkers. While under fire, he took over a hundred photos, though the London lab developing them lost all but eleven of them in an accident.

Lend-Lease/Convoys—Even before entering the war in Europe, Franklin Roosevelt agreed in March 1941 to supply Great Britain, Free France, China, and the USSR with food, supplies, and munitions. The program, called Lend-Lease and managed by Harry Hopkins and General John York, supplied a vast range of war material by way of merchant convoys with military escort. Delivery was along the long Persian Corridor, the Pacific Route, and (the quickest but most perilous route) through the arctic. Almost four million tons of goods went by the arctic route, though over seven percent was lost. The arctic convoys make up a saga in themselves, with hardships of ice, storms, and enemy attacks that equal the violence of any European battlefield, and the merchant seamen suffered extremely high casualties.

The **Office of Strategic Services (OSS)** was a US wartime intelligence agency formed to coordinate espionage activities behind enemy lines. It was engaged in propaganda, coordinating resistance, and post-war planning. Its Berlin office was led briefly by Alan Dulles (not the charming Elinor Stahl) until it was dissolved in October 1945 and its functions transferred to the State and War Departments.

POW Camps/Russenlager—The Eastern Front was dotted with German POW camps. The camps, identified by their Stalag numbers, rarely had barracks, and for shelter, the prisoners had to dig holes in the earth with their mess kits and hands. Deaths came from disease, exposure, and starvation. One German official noted that, as of February 1942, of almost four million prisoners taken, only one million remained. When the Germans realized there would be no lightning victory, the policy of extermination changed to the use of Soviets as slave labor. As for women prisoners, although Field Marshal von Kluge ordered that "Women in uniform are to be shot," the order was not uniformly carried out. Not only does captured pilot Anna Timofeyeva record being cared for by a Russian doctor in a Polish POW camp until liberation, but I have also seen at least one picture of captured women in Soviet uniforms. POWS were disavowed by Stalin and thus did not receive aid packages like other prisoners. The few who survived until liberation had to prove they had not deserted, and many were sent to work camps upon returning home.

NKVD included the regular police force and the Secret Police of the USSR. It ran the Gulag system of forced labor camps and was responsible for deportations of entire nationalities and rural landowners (called kulaks) to isolated parts of the Soviet Union. It also enforced Stalinist policy by conducting widespread espionage and executions. During and after the war, it changed structure and name several times, separating into various organizations, and one of those evolved into the KGB we all know from Hollywood movies.

Partisans—Unlike the quasi-independent resistance movements in the west, the Soviet partisans were coordinated and controlled by the Soviet government and modeled on the Red Army (and frequently wore its uniforms). Their role was to disrupt the Wehrmacht's rear, in communication, supply, and rail travel. Ignoring the anti-Stalinism of the Ukrainians, the Nazis deported Ukrainians as forced labor and maintained its genocidal programs toward Jews and Slavs. The first Soviet partisan detachments in the Ukraine developed out of groups led by Mykola Popudrenko and Sydir Kovpak (in the novel *Sydir Kovitch*) and became a formidable force in 1943, numbering over 150,000 fighters.

About the Author

After years of academic writing and literary critique, Justine Saracen saw the light and began writing fiction. With eight historical thrillers now under her literary belt, she has moved from Ancient Egyptian theology (*The 100th Generation*) to the Crusades (*Vulture's Kiss*) to the Italian Renaissance. *Sistine Heresy*, which conjures up a thoroughly blasphemic backstory to Michelangelo's Sistine Chapel frescoes, won a 2009 Independent Publisher's Award (IPPY) and was a finalist in the ForeWord Book of the Year Award. The transgendered novel *Sarah, Son of God* followed, taking us through Stonewall-rioting New York, Venice under the Inquisition, and Nero's Rome. The novel won the Rainbow First Prize for Best Transgendered Novel. *Beloved Gomorrah* marked a return to her critique of Bible myths—in this case an LGBT version of Sodom and Gomorrah—though it also involved Red Sea diving and the hazards of falling for a Hollywood actress. Having lived in Germany and taught German history, Justine was well placed to write her three previous World War II novels: *Mephisto Aria*, (EPIC Awards finalist, Two Rainbow awards, 2011 Golden Crown first prize) *Tyger, Tyger, Burning Bright*, which follows the lives of four homosexuals during the Third Reich (2012 Rainbow First Prize), and *Waiting for the Violins*, a tale of the French and Belgian Resistance. (2014 Rainbow Best Historical Novel.) Her work in progress, provisionally titled *Suffer the Children*, tells of two women who take revenge for those who cannot.

An adopted European, Saracen lives on a charming little winding street in Brussels, venturing out only to bookfests in the US and UK, and to scuba adventures in Egypt. When she's home and dry, she listens to opera.

Books Available from Bold Strokes Books

Twice Lucky by Mardi Alexander. For firefighter Mackenzie James and Dr. Sarah Macarthur, there's suddenly a whole lot more in life to understand, to consider, to risk…someone will need to fight for her life. (978-1-62639-325-7)

Shadow Hunt by L.L. Raand. With young to raise and her Pack under attack, Sylvan, Alpha of the wolf Weres, takes on her greatest challenge when she determines to uncover the faceless enemies known as the Shadow Lords. A Midnight Hunters novel. (978-1-62639-326-4)

Heart of the Game by Rachel Spangler. A baseball writer falls for a single mom, but can she ever love anything as much as she loves the game? (978-1-62639-327-1)

Getting Lost by Michelle Grubb. Twenty-eight days, thirteen European countries, a tour manager fighting attraction, and an accused murderer: Stella and Phoebe's journey of a lifetime begins here. (978-1-62639-328-8)

Prayer of the Handmaiden by Merry Shannon. Celibate priestess Kadrian must defend the kingdom of Ithyria from a dangerous enemy and ultimately choose between her duty to the Goddess and the love of her childhood sweetheart, Erinda. (978-1-62639-329-5)

The Witch of Stalingrad by Justine Saracen. A Soviet "night witch" pilot and American journalist meet on the Eastern Front in WWII and struggle through carnage, conflicting politics, and the deadly Russian winter. (978-1-62639-330-1)

Pedal to the Metal by Jesse J. Thoma. When unreformed thief Dubs Williams is released from prison to help Max Winters bust a car theft ring, Max learns that to catch a thief, get in bed with one. (978-1-62639-239-7)

Dragon Horse War by D. Jackson Leigh. A priestess of peace and a fiery warrior must defeat a vicious uprising that entwines their destinies and ultimately their hearts. (978-1-62639-240-3)

For the Love of Cake by Erin Dutton. When everything is on the line, and one taste can break a heart, will pastry chefs Maya and Shannon take a chance on reality? (978-1-62639-241-0)

Betting on Love by Alyssa Linn Palmer. A quiet country-girl-at-heart and a live-life-to-the-fullest biker take a risk at offering each other their hearts. (978-1-62639-242-7)

The Deadening by Yvonne Heidt. The lines between good and evil, right and wrong, have always been blurry for Shade. When Raven's actions force her to choose, which side will she come out on? (978-1-62639-243-4)

Ordinary Mayhem by Victoria A. Brownworth. Faye Blakemore has been taking photographs since she was ten, but those same photographs threaten to destroy everything she knows and everything she loves. (978-1-62639-315-8)

One Last Thing by Kim Baldwin & Xenia Alexiou. Blood is thicker than pride. The final book in the Elite Operative Series brings together foes, family, and friends to start a new order. (978-1-62639-230-4)

Songs Unfinished by Holly Stratimore. Two aspiring rock stars learn that falling in love while pursuing their dreams can be harmonious—if they can only keep their pasts from throwing them out of tune. (978-1-62639-231-1)

Beyond the Ridge by L.T. Marie. Will a contractor and a horse rancher overcome their family differences and find common ground to build a life together? (978-1-62639-232-8)

Swordfish by Andrea Bramhall. Four women battle the demons from their pasts. Will they learn to let go, or will happiness be forever beyond their grasp? (978-1-62639-233-5)

The Fiend Queen by Barbara Ann Wright. Princess Katya and her consort Starbride must turn evil against evil in order to banish Fiendish power from their kingdom, and only love will pull them back from the brink. (978-1-62639-234-2)

Up the Ante by PJ Trebelhorn. When Jordan Stryker and Ashley Noble meet again fifteen years after a short-lived affair, are either of them prepared to gamble on a chance at love? (978-1-62639-237-3)

Speakeasy by MJ Williamz. When mob leader Helen Byrne sets her sights on the girlfriend of Al Capone's right-hand man, passion and tempers flare on the streets of Chicago. (978-1-62639-238-0)

Venus in Love by Tina Michele. Morgan Blake can't afford any distractions and Ainsley Dencourt can't afford to lose control—but the beauty of life and art usually lies in the unpredictable strokes of the artist's brush. (978-1-62639-220-5)

Rules of Revenge by AJ Quinn. When a lethal operative on a collision course with her past agrees to help a CIA analyst on a critical assignment, the encounter proves explosive in ways neither woman anticipated. (978-1-62639-221-2)

The Romance Vote by Ali Vali. Chili Alexander is a sought-after campaign consultant who isn't prepared when her boss's daughter, Samantha Pellegrin, comes to work at the firm and shakes up Chili's life from the first day. (978-1-62639-222-9)

Advance: Exodus Book One by Gun Brooke. Admiral Dael Caydoc's mission to find a new homeworld for the Oconodian people is hazardous, but working with the infuriating Commander Aniwyn "Spinner" Seclan endangers her heart and soul. (978-1-62639-224-3)

UnCatholic Conduct by Stevie Mikayne. Jil Kidd goes undercover to investigate fraud at St. Marguerite's Catholic School, but life gets complicated when her student is killed—and she begins to fall for her prime target. (978-1-62639-304-2)

Season's Meetings by Amy Dunne. Catherine Birch reluctantly ventures on the festive road trip from hell with beautiful stranger Holly Daniels only to discover the road to true love has its own obstacles to maneuver. (978-1-62639-227-4)

Myth and Magic: Queer Fairy Tales edited by Radclyffe and Stacia Seaman. Myth, magic, and monsters—the stuff of childhood dreams (or nightmares) and adult fantasies. (978-1-62639-225-0)

Nine Nights on the Windy Tree by Martha Miller. Recovering drug addict, Bertha Brannon, is an attorney who is trying to stay clean when a murder sends her back to the bad end of town. (978-1-62639-179-6)

Driving Lessons by Annameekee Hesik. Dive into Abbey Brooks's sophomore year as she attempts to figure out the amazing, but sometimes complicated, life of a you-know-who girl at Gila High School. (978-1-62639-228-1)

Asher's Shot by Elizabeth Wheeler. Asher Price's candid photographs capture the truth, but when his success requires exposing an enemy, Asher discovers his only shot at happiness involves revealing secrets of his own. (978-1-62639-229-8)

Courtship by Carsen Taite. Love and justice—a lethal mix or a perfect match? (978-1-62639-210-6)

Against Doctor's Orders by Radclyffe. Corporate financier Presley Worth wants to shut down Argyle Community Hospital, but Dr. Harper Rivers will fight her every step of the way, if she can also fight their growing attraction. (978-1-62639-211-3)

A Spark of Heavenly Fire by Kathleen Knowles. Kerry and Beth are building their life together, but unexpected circumstances could destroy their happiness. (978-1-62639-212-0)

Never Too Late by Julie Blair. When Dr. Jamie Hammond is forced to hire a new office manager, she's shocked to come face to face with Carla Grant and memories from her past. (978-1-62639-213-7)

Widow by Martha Miller. Judge Bertha Brannon must solve the murder of her lover, a policewoman she thought she'd grow old with. As more bodies pile up, the murderer starts coming for her. (978-1-62639-214-4)

Twisted Echoes by Sheri Lewis Wohl. What's a woman to do when she realizes the voices in her head are real? (978-1-62639-215-1)

Criminal Gold by Ann Aptaker. Through a dangerous night in New York in 1949, Cantor Gold, dapper dyke-about-town, smuggler of fine art, is forced by a crime lord to be his instrument of vengeance. (978-1-62639-216-8)

The Melody of Light by M.L. Rice. After surviving abuse and loss, will Riley Gordon be able to navigate her first year of college and accept true love and family? (978-1-62639-219-9)

Because of You by Julie Cannon. What would you do for the woman you were forced to leave behind? (978-1-62639-199-4)

The Job by Jove Belle. Sera always dreamed that she would one day reunite with Tor. She just didn't think it would involve terrorists, firearms, and hostages. (978-1-62639-200-7)

Making Time by C.J. Harte. Two women going in different directions meet after fifteen years and struggle to reconnect in spite of the past that separated them. (978-1-62639-201-4)

Once The Clouds Have Gone by KE Payne. Overwhelmed by the dark clouds of her past, Tag Grainger is lost until the intriguing and spirited Freddie Metcalfe unexpectedly forces her to reevaluate her life. (978-1-62639-202-1)

The Acquittal by Anne Laughlin. Chicago private investigator Josie Harper searches for the real killer of a woman whose lover has been acquitted of the crime. (978-1-62639-203-8)

An American Queer: The Amazon Trail by Lee Lynch. Lee Lynch's heartening and heart-rending history of gay life from the turbulence of the late 1900s to the triumphs of the early 2000s are recorded in this selection of her columns. (978-1-62639-204-5)

Stick McLaughlin: The Prohibition Years by CF Frizzell. Corruption in 1918 cost Stick her lover, her freedom, and her identity, but a very special flapper and the family bond of her own gang could help win them back—even if it means outwitting the Boston Mob. (978-1-62639-205-2)

Edge of Awareness by C.A. Popovich. When Maria, a woman in the middle of her third divorce, meets Dana, an out lesbian, awareness of her feelings brings up reservations about the teachings of her church. (978-1-62639-188-8)

Taken by Storm by Kim Baldwin. Lives depend on two women when a train derails high in the remote Alps, but an unforgiving mountain, avalanches, crevasses, and other perils stand between them and safety. (978-1-62639-189-5)

The Common Thread by Jaime Maddox. Dr. Nicole Coussart's life is falling apart, but fortunately, DEA Attorney Rae Rhodes is there to pick up the pieces and help Nic put them back together. (978-1-62639-190-1)

boldstrokesbooks.com

Bold Strokes Books

Quality and Diversity in LGBTQ Literature

SCI-FI

E-BOOKS

MYSTERY

EROTICA

YOUNG
ADULT

Romance

W·E·B·S·T·O·R·E

PRINT AND EBOOKS